Praise for

C.E. MURPHY

and her books

THE NEGOTIATOR

Hands of Flame

"Fast-paced action and a twisty-turny plot make for a good read...Fans of the series will be sad to leave Margrit's world behind, at least for the time being."
—*RT Book Reviews*

House of Cards

"Violent confrontations add action on top of tense intrigue in this involving, even thrilling, middle book in a divertingly different contemporary fantasy romance series."
—*LOCUS*

"The second title in Murphy's Negotiator series is every bit as interesting and fun as the first. Margrit is a fascinatingly complex heroine who doesn't shy away from making difficult choices."
—*RT Book Reviews*

Heart of Stone

"[An] exciting series opener...Margrit makes for a deeply compelling heroine as she struggles to sort out the sudden upheaval in her professional and romantic lives."
—*Publishers Weekly*

"A fascinating new series...as usual, Murphy delivers interesting worldbuilding and magical systems, believable and sympathetic characters and a compelling story told at a breakneck pace."
—*RT Book Reviews*

THE WALKER PAPERS

Coyote Dreams

"Tightly written and paced, [*Coyote Dreams*] has a compelling, interesting protagonist, whose struggles and successes will captivate new and old readers alike."
—*RT Book Reviews*

Thunderbird Falls

"Thoroughly entertaining from start to finish."
—Award-winning author Charles de Lint

"The breakneck pace keeps things moving... helping make this one of the most involving and entertaining new supernatural mystery series in an increasingly crowded field."
—*LOCUS*

"Fans of Jim Butcher's Dresden Files novels and the works of urban fantasists Charles de Lint and Tanya Huff should enjoy this fantasy/mystery's cosmic elements. A good choice."
—*Library Journal*

Urban Shaman

"A swift pace, a good mystery, a likeable protagonist, magic, danger—*Urban Shaman* has them in spades."
—Jim Butcher, bestselling author of The Dresden Files series

"C.E. Murphy has written a spellbinding and enthralling urban fantasy in the tradition of Tanya Huff and Mercedes Lackey."
—*The Best Reviews*

"Tightly plotted and nicely paced, Murphy's latest has a world in which ancient and modern magic fuse almost seamlessly...Fans of urban fantasy are sure to enjoy this first book in what looks to be an exciting new series."
—*RT Book Reviews,* nominated for Reviewer's Choice Best Modern Fantasy

For Trent

(Although some may call him...*Tim*^H^H^H*Paul*)
I wouldn't have made it through this one
without your help, man.
Thank you.

ACKNOWLEDGMENTS

First off, I would like to say to my editor, Matrice: Did you not *read* the last set of acknowledgments? The ones that said, "Please don't ever make me work this hard again"? But it's a much, much better book for it, so thank you. :)

My LiveJournal friends list came through en masse with New York details, information about the legal system, about high-quality pens, about seventeenth-century London...and every single question they answered got cut in revisions. Regardless, I am extremely grateful to them all. If I were slightly more competent I'd have prepared a list of people who were particularly and especially helpful, but I wasn't that together this time around. Next time, I promise.

Chris McGrath has provided me with another gorgeous cover, and I can't wait to see it wrapped around my words. It's one of the best parts of being a writer.

Trent was my much-belabored usual suspect this time around, while Ted, as usual, patiently offered plot ideas when I got stuck. I also owe a huge debt of thanks to Team Whac-A-Mole (Alison, Anna, Catherine K, Catherine S, Erica and Neal) for whacking spam moles on cemurphy.net. :)

ONE

HUMANS WOULD CALL it a catch-22.

He'd read the book the phrase came from, even sympathized with the protagonist, a man desperate to avoid fighting in a war but with no recourse to do so except claim insanity. The difficulty lay in the military's own desperation for warriors. If he said he was crazy and wanted to fight, all the better; they would take him. If he didn't, that was simply normal, and they'd conscript him regardless.

Gargoyles did not find themselves in such situations.

Alban's shoulders slid down as he passed a hand over his eyes. Gargoyles didn't find themselves in such situations, and yet. And yet.

A woman ran on the pathways below him, finding her stride without fear in the March night. She ran as if Central Park were her demesne and the things that stalked it too slow or thick-witted to capture her. She'd done it before she knew he was there, watching and protecting her. She would have continued long since, had he never revealed himself to her.

But he had, and now she knew. Knew about him and his people, and knew that he soared from treetop to treetop, keeping her safe from monsters worse than him.

Knew that his nature demanded he protect her, once he'd chosen her as his ward.

He'd walked away from their impossible relationship, certain that leaving was the only way to allow her a life with any meaning in her own world. In introducing himself to her—necessary as it had seemed—he'd also introduced an overwhelming element of danger into her human experience. She had accepted that, even embraced it, but he could not. He was a protector, and to protect *her,* he had to leave her behind.

Doing the right thing shouldn't leave such a taste of coal at the back of his throat, burned and ashy. For a span of a few brief hours—days, but in a life as long as his, the hours meant more than the days—he'd flown with her, shared laughter and fear, even known the touch of death and the shaking relief of life in its aftermath. Better to let it go, the memory bright and untarnished, than wait and watch as she inevitably realized she could never fit into the half-life that held him captive.

And she, with the safety her clean, well-lit world offered to her, defiantly began her late-night sprints through the park again. She seemed utterly confident—confident of her own speed, confident of the park's gentle side, confident that he would not abandon her despite his protestations.

To his chagrin, she was right.

A gargoyle should not find himself in such a situation.

Muttering a growl deep in his throat, he flexed his wings, catching the wind and letting it carry him higher into the sky than necessary. He was a pale creature against night's darkness, broad wingspan and powerful form easily visible, but humans rarely looked up. Even if someone did, he would be gone in an instant, a flight of imagination so potent few would dare voice it. Rationality and human experience demanded that he couldn't exist. No one valuing his job or social standing would insist he'd seen a gargoyle circling over Central Park, and should the park's less favorable denizens see him, well, no one would believe them, either.

And Margrit, should she look up from racing insubstantial competitors far below, would never tell.

She still watched the sky as she ran.

She knew better. She knew better for a host of reasons, the most obvious being that if a gargoyle watched her, he would keep out of her line of sight so they could both pretend he wasn't there. Twisting to catch him not only invited injury, but collided thoroughly with the other obvious reason she shouldn't watch the sky: to run safely in the park she had to move like she knew what she was doing. Aggressors wanted victims who wouldn't cause a problem. She'd learned to keep her eyes straight ahead and her chin up, ears sharpened for sounds above those of her own labored breathing. She wore no headset when she ran at night; that was a luxury reserved for daylight hours. Running made its own music in her mind, a cadence she could lose herself to. Words pounded out to her footsteps, broken down into syllables. Law review sometimes, but as often as not a single word caught in her thoughts. *Ir. Ir. Ir-rah-shun-al.*

Irrational.

Alban.

Memories of the gargoyle did more than linger; they waited until she thought she was free of him, then announced themselves again with distressing clarity. Even after weeks of not seeing him, she could bring to mind his strong features and white hair more easily than anyone else's.

Margrit shook her head, trying to chase memories away. The hard motion put a wobble in her run and her foot came down badly, tweaking her knee. She dropped into a walk, swearing under her breath. Her heartbeat ached, less from the run than from wariness that bordered on fear. The park seemed a haven only when she ran through it. Walking off an injury felt like announcing she was too slow and cumbersome to avoid danger.

Worse, though, would be not giving herself the time to recover, and damaging the ligament so badly she couldn't run at all. The idea felt like prison walls closing in. Margrit shivered the thought away, flexing her quads to test her knee. The sharp ache had already faded. She slowed more, then stopped, bending to rub her kneecap. It felt normal, no swelling or stiffness telling her she'd twisted it a moment earlier.

An inconsequential injury, nothing more. Just a twinge to warn her, not something worse that healed itself more rapidly than logic could account for. It'd been the same with nicks from a razor blade, or paper cuts sliced through a fingertip, the last few weeks. The damage had been too slight to justify concern.

Margrit licked her lips as a gag-sweet taste of sugary copper rose in her throat. It carried with it the image of a slight, swarthy man opening his wrist and pressing thick welling blood against her mouth. Only after she'd swallowed convulsively had he looked pleased. Folding his sleeve back down, he'd told her what he'd shared: *one sip for healing.*

Such a gift as a vampire gave.

Margrit shivered, scrubbing her palm over her knee one more time. It'd been a tweak, nothing more. She straightened, chin lifted in defiance of her own disbelief, before she went painfully still, watching a blond, broad-shouldered shadow part from the trees.

Hope crashed as fast as it was born, leaving disappointment in its place. The man was younger than Alban, his hair very short and bleached rather than naturally white. The jacket he wore was leather, not the well-cut suit Alban preferred. Anger and fear curdled Margrit's stomach as she took one cautious step back. The man had the height advantage, but she trusted her own speed. She shifted her weight again, ready to spin and run as she took one more step back.

Body heat warned her an instant too late, hands closing around her arms. Margrit shrieked and flung her head back as hard as she could. She encountered resistance and crunching bone, the hands on her arms loosening in a bellow of pain and outrage. "Fucking bitch!"

Margrit flung herself to the side, powered by adrenaline and instinct, and made herself small as the first man lunged for her. She rolled to her feet just out of his grasp, heart pounding as she danced backward, making enough space to turn and run.

A bright streak fell from the trees, bringing both men to the ground. Membraned wings, so thin that park lights glowed through them, flared alabaster in the dark, then were gone. A man stood within the space they'd encompassed and lifted her attackers by their napes, clocking their skulls together with slapstick ease. One groaned. The other made no sound at all as they slid bonelessly from her rescuer's grip.

He rose, teeth still bared as if in attack. His breath came hard as he looked at Margrit, frustration darkening his eyes. She nearly laughed, able to read all the reasons for his dismay.

He'd blown his cover. She'd forced him to show his hand again, making him reenter her life as a physical presence instead of only a wish. But a gap still lay between them, his nature against her own. He'd chosen to accept that divide, even when she would not have. She had no more idea than he *how* to bridge the distance, but the desire to do so stung her.

He was *beautiful.* Whichever form he took, he was beautiful. Long pale hair was tied back from his face, showing clean lines of jaw and cheekbones that, even in the human shape he wore now, might have been chiseled of stone. Margrit's fingers curled with the impulse to explore that face, to slide her fingers into his hair and loosen it from its tie. Remembered warmth tingled through her hands, as if she did as she imagined. The recalled scent of him was delicious—of cool, moonlit earth. Tightness banded her chest, hungry want born from time apart and feeding on the last vestiges of fear from the attack. Nothing negated danger as exhaustively as passion. For a heady moment she thought she saw the same need rise in Alban and took one rough step toward him.

The gargoyle spread his hands, a singular admission that he had been found out, then closed them in abrupt denial. Gaze torn from Margrit's, he crouched and leapt for the trees again, a smooth motion that left no time for words.

Defeat crashed through hope. Margrit ran forward, fists clenched as she bellowed after him. "Alban! *Alban!* Goddamn it, Alban! Come back here! *Alban!*"

Not so much as a whisper of branches or a flash of light on an outstretched wing came back as an answer. She whipped around, fists still knotted, and nearly kicked one of the supine men in anger. Protocol told her to call the police and make a statement, though no one would believe a story of an unknown hero dropping out of the trees to save her, much less the detailed truth. Maybe she could lay praise for her escape at the half-legendary Grace O'Malley's feet, though the tabloid-styled vigilante was known for saving teens from the street, not adult women from Central Park's violence. Still, the papers would have a field day, and enhancing Grace's reputation might help her cause.

Three minutes later Margrit made an anonymous call to the cops and stalked home, shoe tongues flapping.

"She left them tied to a tree. With her *shoelaces.*" Alban turned on his heel, stalking across the confines of a small room, wings clamped close to his back so his abrupt turns wouldn't knock over piles of precariously stacked books. Candles flickered, their thin flames threatened by Alban's strides. There were no windows, but he hadn't lived in a home with windows in over two centuries, and the lack went unnoticed. A bed, more perfunctory than necessity, was lodged in one corner, its foot flush with a short bookcase.

A blonde woman perched easily atop the shelving unit, arms looped around a drawn-up knee as she watched Alban with open amusement. "It doesn't suit you, love."

"What?" He wheeled again, wings flaring in surprise. The woman curved a broad smile and mimicked walking with her fingers.

"Pacing. Gargoyles are suited to hunching and brooding, not pacing and swearing." She hopped down, leaving the shelves without a wobble. Grace O'Malley was perhaps the most graceful human Alban had ever known, almost as unfettered by bonds of earth as one of the Old Races. She slunk around him, languid humor warming her porcelain skin and curling her full mouth. Another man caught at the center of her prowling might have felt like prey. Alban's stony form, though, stood easily a foot taller than Grace, and her slim body was no match for his in strength.

Not until she'd made a full circle around him did she come to a halt, hands in the pockets of her black leather pants. "Why fight it? Your Margrit's in it up to her neck no matter what you do. She made her own promises to the dragonlord Janx, without part or parcel of you, so there's no escaping the Old Races, not for that one. If you want her, gargoyle, pursue her."

"It is not so simple as that."

"You've said the vampire gave her blood for health. Another sip brings long life, and he's hungry to have a hook in her. You can get what you want, Alban, but not by sulking belowground. I offered you shelter in return for helping to watch over my children. I didn't mean for you to pull the streets over your head and pretend the world wasn't there. Go live. You might find it suits you."

"How do you know what you know, Grace?"

"What?" She launched herself into motion and had her hand on the doorknob before he spoke again.

"How do you know these things about the Old Races?" He had no illusions that the power of his voice might stop her, but he asked regardless. "That two sips of a vampire's blood brings long life, or that I chose

Margrit over one of my own. I've told no one that. You're not one of us, just a human wo—"

"Just." Grace turned her profile to him, pale and sharp. "Now there you might have a problem with your lawyer lass, my friend. Humans don't take kindly to being *just* anything."

Alban gritted his teeth with a sound of stone grinding on stone. "I meant no offense. You are a human woman beneath the streets of New York. Such people aren't expected to be conversant with the Old Races at all, much less possessed of intimate details about us. How do you know so much?"

"Grace has her secrets, love." The answer came back to him coolly. "Living a half-life like this one, trying to give kids shelter and food, and keep them out of the gangs and in the schools, means learning things however you can, and playing what you've got for all it's worth. That's what brought you here." She turned her gaze on him, eyes brown and calm beneath the startling whiteness of her bleached hair. "My knowing about your kind was enough to give you something to trust. That's how we survive down here, gargoyle. I learn things and I keep my mouth shut. It's hours till dawn," she added as she pulled the door open. "Stay in like a sullen child if you will, but a man would find it in himself to step outside and take a stand." The door closed behind her with a resounding clang, leaving Alban to bend his head.

"You forget, Grace," he murmured to the echoing chamber. "As does Margrit." He lifted his head again, straightening to his full height of nearly seven feet, and spread taloned hands to study them in the candlelight. "You forget.

"I am not a man."

* * *

The blankets weighed an inordinate amount, as if they were warm stone pressing Margrit into the bed. Flowing heat tickled her fingers, running over them like water. It contrasted deliciously with cold wind, though the chill was only a memory. She recognized strong arms and the clean scent of stone: the smell of the outdoors and wilderness wrapping her close and safe. Raw, sensual power, housed in such grace it hardly seemed he could be dangerous.

Her heart beat faster as she shifted closer to her captor, desire building even through the confines of sleep. She knew the long hard lines of his body, harder than ordinary humans had words for. She had shied away from exploring those lines more than once, uncertain of how to breach a distance she barely understood. Now, though, she let herself be bold, pressing herself closer to brush her mouth against a stony jaw. Soft skin tasted of fine grit, like the rich flavor of dark earth and iron. He was too tall, even in flight, and she pulled herself up his body, an open act of intent as she hooked a thigh over his hip. His grip changed, holding her in place, and stone encompassed her as city lights spun below her, broad wings spread to keep her aloft with the man—

Not a man, he whispered.

Is this my dream or yours? Margrit demanded. Surprise coursed through her, then a wash of laughter rough as sand in water.

Neither, I think, he replied. *I hadn't meant to think so strongly of you. Memory rides us. Forgive me, Margrit. Goodbye.* A faint hint of wistfulness accompanied his final word: *Again.*

The dream turned to falling, a short sickening plunge.

Margrit jerked awake, covers clenched in her fists, breath cold and harsh. A nearly inaudible click sounded, followed by her radio alarm increasing in volume as she lay on the bed, staring through darkness at the ceiling.

Irrational.

TWO

"MARGRIT?" HER NAME came through the door, hoarse with sleepiness. "Hey, Grit? You awake?"

Margrit bundled herself in a towel, hair dripping in corkscrew curls down her back, and ran to yank the door open. Cameron, the taller of Margrit's housemates, leaned on the frame with the telephone pressed against her pink-robed shoulder. Her eyes, barely open, closed all the way as a huge yawn squeezed tears from their corners. A second yawn overtook her as she thrust the phone at Margrit. "For you."

"It's six-thirty in the morning." Margrit took the phone in astonishment, putting it against her own shoulder to block their conversation from the person on the other end. "Who'd be calling at this hour? What're you doing home?"

"My six o'clock client canceled." Cameron yawned again, this time shoving away from the door to stagger back to the bedroom she shared with her fiancé. "I'm supposed to be sleeping in. G'night." She crashed into the door frame, muttering a complaint as she reoriented herself and made it through the bedroom door on the second try.

Margrit watched Cam go, then brought the phone to her ear. "This is Margrit. Mother?"

"Oh dear," a pleasantly light-voiced man said, his voice infused with mirth. "No, I'm afraid not. I'm sure I could arrange to have her call, if you'd like, but it seems as though it would be rather melodramatic. To do it properly I'd have to kidnap her and make her call, angry and frightened, from the wa—"

"Janx." Margrit closed her bedroom door and slid down it, digging her fingers into her hair to hold her head up. "God forbid anybody should ever subpoena my phone records. Why are you calling the house instead of my cell? How in hell could I explain getting six o'clock phone calls from someone like you?"

She avoided more descriptive terms deliberately, though they danced through her mind. *Crimelord* was the only one she was willing to give voice to, but it didn't scratch the surface of what Janx really was. The handful of times Margrit had been in a room with him, it had been all she could do to keep breathing, his presence burning up the air. As well it should have: she'd gone in knowing he was of the Old Races, but not that she was dealing with a dragon. A red dragon, if ginger hair and flame-green eyes told the truth, though Margrit had no idea if it did, or if it mattered.

"It's six-thirty," Janx said in injured tones. "And I tried calling your cell, but you didn't answer. I thought young people today were connected twenty-four–seven. I'm very disappointed. But I could kidnap your mother," he offered. "If you need the phone records explained, I mean. Or I could—"

"You may not kidnap my mother, Janx." The absurdity of chiding a man of Janx's position—either crimelord or dragonlord—struck Margrit, and she steeled herself to keep a trace of laughter from her voice. "What do you want?"

"Oh, Margrit, you hurt me. Can't an old friend call up to say hello after a few weeks' absence?"

"Old friend?" Margrit kept her voice down with effort. "Pit vipers would be safer friends than you, and old friends don't call at six in the morning unless they're in real trouble. You can't be in any trouble I could possibly help you with. The world's not that capricious." The accusation left aside the middling detail that Margrit, despite her better judgment, rather liked the fiery-haired dragon. "What do you want?"

"Capricious," Janx said with admiration. "Well done, for someone who protests she's just been wakened."

"I'm a lawyer. I'm supposed to be capable of conversing with an augmented vocabulary in order to obfuscate an argument without exerting myself. Besides, I was already awake. What do you *want?*"

"Better than a circus act," Janx said happily. Then his bantering faded, a note of tension replacing it. "I require your services, Margrit. A balance has changed."

Margrit coughed in disbelief. "You called me up at six-thirty in the morning to give me cryptic messages? 'A balance has changed'? What the hell does that mean? A balance changed in January when you had Vanessa Gray killed, Janx. Alban told me that you'd breached protocol by doing that. You're not supposed to go around murdering people's assistants, especially when they've been assisting for over a century. It's not playing fair, or something."

"Margrit, my dear, I would never murder Eliseo Daisani's assistant. That would be an inexcusable act of warfare." Teasing lightened Janx's voice again. Margrit groaned aloud and shook her head against the door.

"Right. You don't kill anybody yourself, right? You just hire people to do it." Janx had all but confessed to arranging Vanessa Gray's assassination, and it had been through his cell phone records that Margrit had helped the police track down the hired killer. The man had never gone to trial. Instead, shortly after his arrest, he'd been found spread in grisly detail across the Rikers Island prison courtyard. Rumor said the inmates were told he'd been arrested for child molestation, and had meted out their own justice. Margrit had no intention of asking whether Daisani had taken matters into his own inhuman hands.

"Don't be silly, Margrit. Of course I kill people." Janx sounded downright cheerful, enough that she pulled the phone away to eye it. Uncomfortable as she was with the thought of the Old Races facing the human justice system, Janx's bald-faced admission was beyond the pale.

"I *am* a lawyer, Janx. You shouldn't go around telling me you kill people."

"You're not recording this conversation, are you?" Thin tension came back into Janx's voice at the question, lifting hairs on Margrit's arms. The dragonlord had rarely been anything but ruthlessly chipper in her experiences with him. She was certain she didn't want to know what was making him cautious, and equally certain she would find out.

"I don't usually record my home phone calls, but if you're going to be calling up regularly to make blanket confessions, I might start. What's going on?"

"We'll discuss it this evening. I'll send a car for you."

"Just as long as Malik's not driving." The djinn, Janx's second in command, had none of the dragonlord's peculiar sense of honor. That Malik coveted power had been obvious in Margrit's first meeting with him, but he was no match in personality or intellect for Janx. A nasty, cruel man, he exercised what power he had over those he considered inferior, and Margrit numbered among them. Janx might play with her, cat and mouse, more interested in the game than domination, but Malik would simply hurt her until she broke or died. She had stood her ground against dragons and vampires, but it was the djinn who frightened her.

Too late, she grimaced at the implied consent in her answer. "Don't bother sending a car. I'll get there myself." Then impulse caught her and she asked, "Tonight?" with as much wide-eyed ingenuity as she could. "You don't think my boss would be okay with me cutting out for a few hours to visit the notorious House of Cards and rub elbows with a gangster?"

"If I'd gotten to him first," Janx said mildly, "I have no doubt it could have been arranged. The situation, I fear, is otherwise, and so I'll see you this evening. Goodbye, Margrit."

"If you'd— What? Dammit!" Margrit glowered at the silent phone, then got to her feet and stomped around the apartment as she finished getting ready for the day.

A Town Car idled on the street, its driver leaning on the hood so he could watch her building's front door. As Margrit exited, he snapped to attention, calling, "Ms. Knight? I'm your transportation."

Margrit looked both ways along the street, as if

someone else might appear and answer to her name. "Are you talking to me?"

"Yes, ma'am." He was a few years her elder, far too young to call her *ma'am.*

Margrit glanced up the street again, a terse smile forming. "I'm sorry. There must be a mistake. Excuse me." She turned and managed a few steps before the driver moved in front of her.

"I'm supposed to give you this if there's a problem, ma'am." He offered a sleek cell phone, so small that his palm dwarfed it. "The number you want is programmed in."

"The number I want," Margrit echoed disbelievingly, and took the phone with dismay curdling her stomach. A glass of orange juice had seemed like a good idea minutes earlier. Now it felt like a bottle of acid had been poured into her belly and left to churn. She pressed the dial button and raised the phone to her ear, wincing preemptively.

"You have a problem, Miss Knight." Eliseo Daisani sounded distressingly pleased to make such an announcement.

Margrit, prediction fulfilled, bit her tongue and waited until her impulse to respond with sarcasm faded. "Good morning, Mr. Daisani. Coming from you, that's an alarming statement." Coming from Eliseo Daisani, almost anything could be alarming. The appalling quickness with which he moved came back to Margrit as forcefully as the taste of his blood had the night before.

"Good morning," he said, undeterred by her stiffness. "I think you'll want to come to my office to discuss your problem, rather than stand there on the street."

"It's a quarter to eight, Mr. Daisani. I'm on my way to work." It was an obligatory line of defense that allowed Daisani to chortle indulgently.

"Of course you are. I've already spoken with Mr. Lomax," he assured her. Margrit bit her tongue again, this time on an exclamation of understanding. Daisani had gotten to her boss first, forcing Janx into the situation he called *otherwise.* "He can spare you for an hour or two," Daisani went on. "Obviously, your ride is there, or we wouldn't be having this conversation."

Clichéd protests leapt to Margrit's lips. *"You can't do this, Mr. Daisani,"* was first and most obvious of them, though it was abundantly clear that he could, in fact, arrange her schedule to his liking. *"I've asked you not to call me at work,"* ran a close second, foiled by Margrit neither being at work yet nor having had the foresight to make that request. She said neither, clenching the phone and staring at the Town Car as people rushed by.

Getting in constituted Daisani winning a round. Margrit ran her thumb over the phone's number pad with a half-formed thought of calling her boss and asking if the business mogul had indeed arranged for her to come in late. She had no doubt, though, that he had, and that Russell would tell her not to be absurd by refusing the vehicle Daisani had sent for her. She'd end up going regardless, and only arrive at Daisani's stunning corporate headquarters breathless from walking. Margrit flipped the phone shut and let the driver open the car door for her.

Minutes later, the security guard at Daisani's headquarters waved her in without asking for identification. Though it told her there was no chance she'd have turned Daisani down, not having to sign in made her feel better. She pushed the elevator button hard enough to hurt her finger, making a face at her own inconsistency.

Polished brass walls inside the lift reflected her sour-faced image back at her. Margrit drew herself up, shaking off the countenance of ill temper. There was no point in facing Daisani already on-edge and sulky. When the doors whisked open, she stepped out with at least a semblance of good nature in place.

On the surface, the front lobby of Daisani's suites hadn't changed since the last time she'd been there. It was opulent, with an enormous curved desk of pale wood dominating the room. No one sat behind the desk, and an embossed brown leather appointment book lay at a careful angle on its otherwise empty surface. The rest of the room was equally ostentatious, all the chairs antiques, many of them covered in rich red velvet that Margrit knew was as soft as it looked. Hardwood floors reflected inset lights from the ceiling, but not harshly; the whole room glowed with a warm, winning ambience.

Because she knew where to look for it, a slightly paler patch on the wood-paneled walls revealed where a portrait had once hung. Margrit walked around the desk and touched the spot gently, unexpected regret rising to clog her throat.

"Miss Knight."

Margrit flinched, yanking her hand away and twisting it behind her back as she faced Eliseo Daisani. "Mr. Daisani. I didn't hear you come in."

The doors behind him, nearly twice the height of normal doors, were open just enough to let him step through. Their size emphasized his: Eliseo Daisani was not a big man, barely taller than Margrit herself. Framed by the doorway, he appeared almost delicate.

"You look well behind that desk, Miss Knight."

Margrit managed a faint smile and stepped out from behind the desk. "You haven't replaced Ms. Gray yet?"

"Ms. Gray was irreplaceable. I believe I've mentioned that." His glance skittered to the pale spot on the wall and he inclined his head slightly. "Perhaps I'm sentimental. The photograph is in my office now."

"I think even a vampire is allowed to be sentimental when somebody who was with him twelve decades dies, Mr. Daisani."

"When someone has been murdered." Daisani's words were gentle, but his expression contorted, barely holding back rage before a fresh facade of good nature rose to replace the darker emotion. "You've become bold since the last time I saw you. You wouldn't have thrown that word around so lightly, before."

"I'm feeling reckless," Margrit admitted. "What do you want from me, Mr. Daisani?"

He came forward, offering both his hands to her, a gesture that could be equally welcoming or condescending. She put one out in return and he clasped it, his touch disconcertingly hot as he all but bowed over her fingers. "The first time we met I offered you a job. I'd like to say that offer still stands, but circumstances have changed."

"Mr. Daisani." Margrit withdrew her fingers from his grasp as politely as she could. "I told you. I'm happy with my job. I'm not interested in coming to work for your law branch."

"No." The word was clipped, Daisani's pleasant front slipping again to reveal anger. "As I said, the circumstances have changed. I find myself in a unique situation, and, to your dismay, you're the person best suited to helping me with it."

Caution chilled Margrit's hands and she forced herself not to take a step back, though Daisani's phrasing brought an unwilling smile to her face. "To my dismay. You're probably right about that. Mr. Daisani, I don't owe you anything. I did what you asked in helping to find Vanessa's murderer. We're even."

"I require a personal assistant." Daisani went on as if she hadn't spoken. "Thus far, a suitable candidate has not yet accepted the position." His eyebrows quirked upward and he confessed, "Nor applied. Miss Knight—Margrit, if I may—you've proven yourself to be delightfully discreet and levelheaded regarding extraordinary matters."

Margrit wished abruptly that she had remained on the far side of Vanessa's desk, so she might use it as a prop and lean on it for emphasis. On the other hand, remaining there, where Daisani wanted her to be, would only enforce his argument. "You mean in the face of learning about the Old Races, and finding out that half the power in this city isn't even human?"

Daisani waggled a finger. "Don't be absurd, Miss Knight. There are only one or two of us who aren't human."

"It's enough. Mr. Daisani." Margrit made his name into hard sounds, stopping him when he would have gone on. "Mr. Daisani," she repeated more quietly. "I owe a dragonlord two favors, and the gargoyle who got me into this mess won't talk to me." Surprise flickered across

Daisani's face and Margrit cursed herself for letting go a piece of information he'd lacked. "I'm not foolish enough to think the Old Races are done with me. Alban thought he could get you and Janx off my back—"

Another hint of surprised interest crossed Daisani's face, and Margrit broke off, setting her front teeth together and pulling her lips back in sheer frustration. Laughter suddenly danced in Daisani's eyes and he clucked his tongue. "Humans are the only species on this planet who have forgotten that baring teeth is a sign of aggression." He stepped forward, raising a hand so quickly she barely saw the movement, only became aware that he'd brushed her jaw when she felt the resulting warmth. Conflicting impulses froze her in place, outrage that he should feel free to touch her, coupled with white fear at how fast he'd moved. "Let me remind you of what I am, Miss Knight. Let me warn you that one of my kind might see such a raw expression as an invitation to courtship."

Her fear dissolved, washed away by a sense of the absurd. Margrit lifted a hand slowly, and put it against the inside of Daisani's wrist. His pulse was desperately fast beneath her fingertips, the beat of a small frightened mammal, not an adult human. But then, he wasn't human. She pushed his hand away with gentle determination, her jaw set. "One of your kind knows better than that how to read human expressions, Mr. Daisani. Don't touch me again."

Astonishment splashed over Daisani's face, brightening it until his smile was wide and genuine, showing flat, human teeth that seemed at odds with every story Margrit had ever read about vampires. "Bravo! Bravo,

Miss Knight! Without a hint of fear! Bravo! How do you do it?"

"That would be telling." The moment of conflict was gone, and Margrit's heart started to accelerate, her body reacting too late to the stance her intellect had taken. She could answer his question—had answered it, when a green-eyed dragon had put it to her, but Janx had taken it as part of a favor owed. Margrit wasn't going to make that bargain again.

"Mr. Daisani, I don't want to work for you. Right now I don't owe you anything, and you're not going to talk me or coerce me into quitting my job. If that's all you had to discuss with me, I think you're wrong. I don't have a problem. You do. It's been very nice to see you again, sir. Good day." She inclined her head and turned toward the elevator.

"Miss Knight."

Margrit stopped with her hand over the button, waiting.

"Alban Korund has made no effort at all to get me off your back, as you so eloquently put it. You may wish to reconsider where you place your faith, young lady. Unlikely as it may seem, there are worse choices than Eliseo Daisani."

She nodded noncommittally, pressing the elevator call button. A moment later the door chimed and opened and she stepped in, not yet willing to draw a breath of relief.

A breeze stirred the elevator's still air, and Daisani stood beside her, smiling. "By the way, Margrit, do give your mother my regards. A remarkable woman. Remarkable, indeed."

Then he was gone and the door closed, leaving Margrit to stare, wide-eyed and silent, at her reflection in the polished brass.

THREE

MORE THAN ONE speculating glance followed her when she arrived at the Legal Aid offices. Whispered conversations broke off until she'd passed, leaving little doubt that Daisani's arrangement with Russell Lomax had slipped out. Knowing any response would be protesting too much, Margrit nodded greetings and made her way to her desk. She had a trial to prepare for, defense for a rapist who claimed his innocence with sneering mockery. Evidence, to her private relief, was on the prosecution's side, but her job was to defend, not judge.

She flipped the case file open, skimming through material she'd long since memorized in search of any errors she might've made that could lead to appeal. There were none; she knew it as well as she knew her own reflection. It was habit, the ritual she went through the day before a trial.

"Ms. Knight?"

"Grit." Margrit looked up to find a youthful receptionist leaning over the edge of her cubicle. "You can call me Grit. Or Margrit," she added, at the look of bewilderment on the young man's face. "If Grit's too weird. What's your name?"

"Sam." He stepped around the cubicle, an envelope in one hand and the other extended for Margrit to shake. "I never heard *Grit* as a nickname for *Margrit.* You really know Eliseo Daisani?"

Margrit sighed and closed her case file as they shook hands. "We've met several times, yes."

"What's he like?"

"Short, and accustomed to getting his own way."

Sam grinned. "You don't think much of him, huh?"

"I'd never be impolitic enough to say that."

"There's a betting pool on how long it'll take you to go to work for him."

Margrit laughed. "Really? What's the buy-in?"

"Ten bucks. A couple people've got you pegged for handing in your resignation as soon as the Newcomb trial is over."

Margrit reached for her purse. "Come on, I'm made of sterner stuff than that. I give me at least four months. Just don't tell anybody else I'm betting on me."

"Four months?" Sam looked dismayed. "And I'd already signed in for five." He took the ten she handed him anyway, stuffing the cash in his pocket. "Oh! This is yours. A courier brought it by before you came in." He offered the envelope, marked with an NYPD stamp across the seal. "They say you're going places. That you've got a lot of friends in the police department, and that the mayor knows your name, too."

"'They'? What am I, notorious?" Her cell phone rang and she dug it out of her purse, lifting her chin to dismiss Sam, though she added, "Four months. Don't forget," as he waved and disappeared down the corridor. Margrit smiled, tilting her phone up to check the incoming call.

A knot of tension she didn't know she'd been carrying came undone at the name on the screen and she answered with a smile. "Tony. Thank God. Somebody I want to talk to." Wanting to talk to the police detective was a good sign, though a flash of guilt sizzled through her. Tony Pulcella represented the ordinary world, separate from the one she'd been immersed in since Alban's reappearance the night before. For a moment she wasn't certain if it was Tony she was glad to hear from, or if it was simply a reminder of reality that was calming.

"It's only twenty after nine, Grit. It's that bad already?"

"You wouldn't believe me if I told you." She slid down in her chair, head against the padded rest. "It's good to hear your voice, but aren't you supposed to be out catching bad guys? Is something wrong? Are we off for dinner tonight?"

"I'm sorry," he replied, answer enough. Margrit's smile fell away. She had no name for what their relationship had become over the last months: more than friends, but no longer lovers, with a weighty question mark hanging over whether they would be again. Innumerable things had changed the shape of their romance, most of all the pale-haired gargoyle who'd haunted Margrit's dreams the night before.

Alban's image lingered in her mind as she brought her attention back to the phone call. "I'm sorry. What did you just say? I wasn't listening."

An edge of concern came into Tony's voice. "You okay, Grit?"

"I'm fine." She straightened in her seat, deliberately shaking off the gloom that had settled over her. "Say that again. Something about a party?"

"Yeah. You ever heard of Kaimana Kaaiai?"

"Nope. Should I have?"

She could almost hear Tony shake his head. "Me either. He's some philanthropist out of Hawaii, one of those kinds of guys who rents his mansions to homeless people for almost nothing, because he can't live in all seven of them at once, anyway."

Margrit's eyebrows shot up. "I'd be willing to try being homeless in Hawaii…."

"You and me both. Anyway, apparently he's got this thing about early-twentieth-century architecture, and he's in town for a week to do some glad-handing and donate some funding for that speakeasy down in the sewers."

"The subways, not the sewers," Margrit said pedantically. "Cam never would've gone with me to look at it if it'd been in the sewers. Besides, sewage probably would have ruined those amazing stained-glass windows." They were more astonishing than anybody knew. Although abstract at first glance, if the three windows were layered over one another, they showed representations of the five remaining Old Races in glorious, rich color.

"Right. Well, I guess the city needs money to put in a seriously high-class security system down there, and they've been negotiating with this Kaaiai guy over it."

"Okay. What's that got to do with dinner tonight?"

"The guy's got a security detail, but one of the things he does is always get a few locals to work on it. He feels like he gets a better sense of the city that way, and besides, locals recognize the real trouble."

"And he wants you?" Margrit laughed at the incredulity in her own voice. "I'm sorry. I didn't mean to sound so surprised. I'm sure you can do it. It's just—"

"Just that I'm a homicide cop without any high-reaching connections," Tony finished. "Six brothers and sisters and none of them are in anything like this league for casual socializing. I have no idea how he came across my name."

"Have you asked?"

"I haven't met him yet. He comes in this afternoon."

"Aha. So we're off for tonight. Well, damn."

"I can make it up to you."

Margrit tilted back in her chair, an eyebrow arched. "How?"

"The lieutenant says she's heard Kaaiai is generous to the people who work for him, and I guess he is. He's issued a package of invitations for the events he'll be attending while he's in the city. Theater, dinners, lunches, concerts—the guy's booked. Looks boring as hell to me, but the point is I can bring a date." Wryness crept into his voice. "Anybody who passes the security clearance and doesn't mind her date working all night and not paying attention to her."

Margrit laughed. "You know anybody like that, Detective?"

"I had a girl in mind," he said good-naturedly. "She works for Legal Aid, but I think this is probably her kind of thing. She's gotten kind of high-profile lately."

"Really?" Margrit's laughter left a broad smile stretched across her face. "What's she done?"

"Got the governor to pass clemency on a murd—"

"Self-defense."

Tony hitched a moment before agreeing. "Self-defense case."

Margrit leaned forward in her chair again to put an elbow against her desk and press her fingers into the inner corners of her eyes. Long before the Old Races had interfered in her life, her job had been the major crack in her relationship with Tony. Coming, as they did, from different angles on the same side of a flawed legal system, the topic incited them to breakups as often as passion got them back together.

The case she had on the table was the sort they could never discuss. The very necessity of building a decent defense for a rapist was offensive to the cop in Tony. Margrit sympathized, even wondered sometimes if he was right, but her ability to abhor the crime and still do her job effectively was a dichotomy Tony could barely fathom. Arguing that anything less than her best would create an opportunity for appeal or mistrial fell on deaf ears.

Curiosity tickled her, making her wonder if Alban would have the same difficulties. The world he came from might be so different from Margrit's own that no evident double standard in human behavior could distress him. Margrit curled her lip, trying to push the thought away as she listened to Tony's amused litany.

"Then she took on the richest guy on the East Coast over a squatters' building, and he backed down. I think she's got some high-minded ambitions. Hanging out with this kind of crowd might be good for her career."

"She sounds like somebody you wouldn't want to mess with."

"I dunno, I kind of like messing with her. Whaddaya say?"

Margrit laughed. "I think it sounds fantastic, but isn't offering tickets to exclusive events very much like bribing an officer of the law?"

"I'm not getting any personal gain out of it." A thin

note of strain sounded in the words, as if Tony was censoring himself on the topic of how he might be rewarded. Margrit pinched the bridge of her nose harder. Weeks ago, he'd used her to set a trap for a killer, and she'd lied to him consistently about Alban, leaving them both regretful but not repentant. Their relationship had been rocky since then, as they tried to work out with words what they'd always solved before by going back to bed together. But too much had changed this time for such an easy resolution, and while Tony had agreed, she thought he'd expected a quicker return to the intimacy they'd once shared.

She put on a smile and deliberately lightened her voice, forcing pleasantry back into the conversation before it soured too much. "It's a date, then. Or not, as the case may be."

Tony hesitated a barely noticeable moment before responding in kind. "Great. I sent a courier over with the invitation—"

"I got it a few minutes ago. Hadn't opened it yet."

"Good. I'll see you tonight, okay?"

"I look forward to it," Margrit said, and hung up the phone with a silent chastisement. There were things Alban could never offer her, just as Tony couldn't spread wings and fly with her above the city. Tony was solid and reliable, and when something came through from him, it was tangible: evenings out, time spent together, and in this case, a deliberate attempt to help her career. That was selfless, especially considering the ease with which they argued over her job. There were things to be said for the ordinary. It would stand her well to remember that.

The memory of a kiss, stolen in the midst of flight,

heated her skin and made Margrit knot her fingers around her phone. Alban's body playing under hers as muscle bunched and stretched, bringing them in leaps from danger into safety. The sting of air imploding against her skin as he shifted from one form to another, becoming more and less than a man within the compass of her arms. There was nothing ordinary in those memories, and the ache of desire they brought didn't belong in the workplace. Margrit caught her breath and spat out a "Dammit!" that did nothing to relieve the pulse of need that had caught her off guard.

"Margrit?" A coworker's concerned face appeared over the edge of her cubicle.

Margrit put on a smile. "Sorry. I'm fine."

"It's okay. Hey, have you finished the paperwork on the Carley case?" He tapped his finger nervously on the cubicle's metal frame and Margrit started, shaking her head at the reminder.

"Sorry, no." She dug the files she needed from below a stack of papers. "I'll have it to you by five."

"Thanks." He beat the flat of his fingers against the cubicle edge twice, then scurried off. Margrit tucked an errant curl behind her ear and moved the files again, hunting for the courier package and the evening's agenda. A moment's search told her the soiree was at eight. Plenty of time to go home after work, get a snack and find something appropriate to wear to a high-society function.

She puffed her cheeks out and exhaled noisily. Plenty of time. The only problem was squeezing in a dragonlord who wouldn't take no for an answer.

Janx was not going to kill her. Margrit smoothed a hand over her stomach, the nubbly silken fabric there sending a wave of chills up her arm. Janx was not going to kill her for the same reason Daisani wouldn't: she was useful to him. Especially to Janx, because she owed him two favors of incalculable size. At worst, he would be irritated.

At worst. Margrit's stomach flip-flopped, another shiver washing over her. At worst, a man whose presence could eat up all the air in a room would be irritated with her. At worst she'd annoyed someone who considered her life to be an amusing trinket to play with.

She hadn't left work on time, research for the Carley case turning out to be more time-consuming than she'd expected. Then she'd found a deep stain on the dress she'd intended to wear, wine discoloring creamy velvet. Margrit had stood over the dress for long moments, too frustrated to move on. Finally she'd called, "Cameron?"

Her housemate, clad in a T-shirt and workout shorts that showed long legs and a dramatically scarred shin to great advantage, appeared at the bedroom door. "What's up?"

"Do you have anything I could wear to a posh reception at the Sherry-Netherland?" Margrit expected the laughing response. The other woman was eight inches taller and had a fashion model's slender build, in contrast to Margrit's hourglass curves. "I need a dress by eight."

"Nobody expects you to be on time," Cameron said airily. "Get shoes, put your hair up and we'll hit Prada."

"You've got a lot of faith in my credit line."

"Well, you can't go to the Sherry in something less," Cam said pragmatically. "Fear not. I'm the world's most efficient shopper. We'll be out of there in twenty minutes. Get your shoes."

Margrit got her shoes and Cam proclaimed them capable of going with anything, then hauled her across town to a boutique fashion shop. In the space of three minutes, she dismissed everything Margrit's eye landed on, instead settling on a white, knee-length raw silk dress. The saleswoman, whose expression on their arrival had indicated it was too close to quitting time to have to deal with customers, looked startled, then approving. Margrit fingered the dress gingerly, its long, off-the-shoulder sleeves and straight neckline unexciting to her eye. "Are you sure it's dressy enough?"

"I'm certain. Trust me on this, Grit. You're going to be overwhelmingly understated. Put it on and see if I'm right."

And she had been. The dress snugged against Margrit's curves as if it'd been made for her, a six-inch kick pleat behind the knee allowing her room to walk despite the hip-and-thigh-hugging fit. Margrit pinned her hair up before leaving the dressing room, letting a few corkscrew curls fall down her back, and came out with a guilty smile. "You were right."

"I'm a genius," Cameron said with satisfaction.

Margrit ran her fingers over the raw silk, tempted but still hesitant. "You sure I shouldn't just go for basic black?"

"You should never wear black." Cam put a fingertip against Margrit's bare shoulder, leaving a white mark against cafe-latte skin when she released the pressure. "Not with skin tones like that. You've got drama inherent in your coloring. Crimson and cream, that's what you should wear."

"I have a lot of those in my wardrobe," Margrit admitted. "I always thought of them as being battle colors, though, not playing up my skin."

"Really." Cameron's eyebrows quirked, a smile darting into place. "You have a lot of wars to fight, Margrit?"

"Against the man, every day, sistah." Margrit made a fist and thrust it toward the sky. Cameron laughed then Cam caught Margit's hand to study the slight point the dress's long sleeve came to over Margrit's wrist.

"You need a ring. How much time do we have?" She looked for a clock, then clucked her tongue. "I know a great costume jewelry place a couple blocks from here. Let's pay for this and go."

"I like how you say that like we're both paying for it. It's seven-thirty," Margrit said in despair. "I'll be late."

"Nobody expects you to be on time," Cameron repeated. "And we *are* both paying for it. See?" She ushered Margrit to the saleswoman and handed over Margrit's credit card as if it were her own. "You'll show up at eight-thirty and make an entrance. It's what all the stars would do."

And it was what she had done. The evening had passed in an exhausting, exciting blur. Margrit proved a terrible New Yorker, blushing and stuttering at coming face-to-face with a handful of genuine celebrities. Tony caught her once, his wink making her blush harder.

He could have been a celebrity himself, wearing a tuxedo that made his shoulders a dark block of strength, as if he'd stepped out of a Bond film. Genuine delight had lit his eyes when Governor Stanton, arriving without his wife, had squired Margrit around the room for half an hour, making introductions.

She liked the tall, unhandsome politician, their camaraderie genuine. They'd greeted Mayor Leighton together, Margrit focusing hard not to wipe her hand on her dress after she extracted her fingers from his clammy grip. Stanton had pursed his mouth curiously at her expression, but said nothing, his silence conveying a subtle sense of agreement with her feelings toward the mayor.

He introduced her to Kaimana Kaaiai before excusing himself. The philanthropist struck her as Daisani's nearly perfect opposite: a big man with very dark eyes who spoke with an easy Pacific Islands lilt, he seemed almost embarrassed by the attention his money brought. Margrit felt an unexpected rush of sympathy for him, and, as if he sensed that, he gave her a rueful smile before turning to the newest group to be introduced. Margrit slipped away, finally at ease, and spent hours chatting with people, until she realized the reception room was beginning to clear out. Only then, noticing how badly her feet hurt, did she retreat to a corner to remove her shoes. Even accustomed as she was to both running daily and wearing heels, stilettos still made her feet ache. "I should've brought tennies to wear home," she mumbled to them. "I've already lost all my cool points by taking my shoes off at the Sherry."

"On the contrary. Think of it as a…humanizing factor." Eliseo Daisani's Italian leather shoes came into Margrit's line of sight and she ducked her head.

"Something you know a lot about, Mr. Daisani?"

"You might be surprised. I'm impressed, Miss Knight. I believe you've conquered a good portion of the city's elite tonight. Was that your intention?"

"Saying so either way would be imprudent, don't

you think?" Margrit looked up as she slipped her shoes back on. In her heels, she was a little taller than Daisani, and the idea of letting him catch her literally flat-footed made her uncomfortable. "You didn't come say hello to the governor. You must be the only person here who didn't."

"Jonathan and I greeted one another."

"You made eye contact. I saw that. What's the story there, Mr. Daisani?" She stood, hardly expecting an explanation.

"Perhaps you'll learn the answer to that someday. I don't suppose you've reconsidered my offer since this morning."

"I don't suppose I have," Margrit agreed. "I know you're richer than God, Mr. Daisani, but I went to a fair amount of trouble to earn my law degree. I don't want to use all that education being your personal assistant. Besides, I'm finding out you're a terrible nag. Who'd want to work for a nag?"

Surprise creased Daisani's forehead and he gave a quick dry huff of laughter. "I see. Well. Having been put thoroughly in my place, I think I'd better bid you good evening and retreat to reconsider my strategy. No nagging." He bowed from the waist, never breaking the eye contact that let Margrit see his amusement. "Until later, Miss Knight."

Goose bumps lifted on Margrit's arms as she watched him walk away, not daring to breathe, "Not if I see you coming," until she was confident the noise in the hall would drown her words. Only then did she let her shoulders relax, and lift her gaze to look over the people left at the reception.

Out of dozens present, two watched her with clear

and open curiosity. Governor Stanton might have been expected, as he'd attended to her for a good portion of the evening. The second, though, made a stillness come over Margrit when she met his dark, liquid gaze. After a moment the Hawaiian philanthropist smiled and looked away.

Her breath caught as if she'd been released from a hold imposed upon her. Janx had done something similar, his use of her name weighing her down so thoroughly she had been unable to walk away from it, or him.

Janx. Margrit's fingers curled in recollection and she looked at her aching feet apologetically. "Sorry, guys. The night's not over yet."

FOUR

"MARGRIT KNIGHT." JANX rolled her name in his mouth as he always did, as if it were a morsel to be savored. His gaze took her in precisely the same way, inch by inch, judging and admiring what he saw. "I am not a man to be kept waiting, my dear, but I think in your case I will make a rare exception. For me?" He opened his hands to encompass her silk dress and upswept hair, then brought them back in, folding them over his heart. "Such beauty is well worth waiting for. Do let me take your coat, so I can admire you properly." He stepped around the cafeteria table that served as his desk, leaving thin wisps of blue smoke behind, and slipped Margrit's coat from her shoulders. "Exquisite." The word was murmured above her shoulder like the promise of seduction. "The color is lovely. So few women can wear white convincingly."

Margrit groaned and walked away to move paperwork and sit on the table, facing Janx as she loosened the straps of her heels and dropped them on the floor. Hard metal folding chairs were the only seating in the room. She hooked her toes under the nearest and pulled it closer, then planted her bare feet on its cold seat with another quiet groan. For a moment she just sat there, reveling in the chill that soothed the ache in her soles. "What do you want, Janx?"

The dragonlord murmured, "Ah," with such disappointment it might have been a child's *aww.* "It is to be strictly business tonight? How unfair, to arrive so late and so lovely, and then to deny me my little pleasures."

Margrit propped her elbows on her knees, rubbing her face delicately and watching Janx through her fingers. His dark red hair had grown since she'd seen him last, falling across his cheeks in slashes that played up the green of his eyes, even in the smoky room. He wore a priest-collared shirt and slacks, both hanging well and making her realize he was broader of shoulder than she remembered. His hands were in his pockets, his stance casual and beguiling, and the pout playing his mouth was neutralized by the laughter in his eyes. Margrit had yet to see something erase that perpetual amusement for more than a moment, and hoped she wouldn't. She'd managed once to make Eliseo Daisani laugh in the midst of a crisis, but even that had ended in a threat against her life. Repeating the experience with Janx wasn't a risk she wanted to take. So long as he found her entertaining, she was safe.

Which gave her the courage to drop her hands and say, dryly, "I'm so sorry, Janx. What was I thinking? Maybe we should do a waltz or two around your office before we get to the nasty matter of business. I'd hate for you to think I don't adore you."

He wasn't as fast as Daisani. Margrit saw him move, quick long strides that somehow suggested a larger creature transferring its attention from one spot to another. His approach was consummate grace, fire flowing across an open space like a living thing. Then he was beside her, making the air crackle with dry heat.

"I prefer a tango. Tell me, do you dance?" His pupils dilated as her heart cramped and missed a beat for the second time that day. Eyes half-lidded, like a snake's, he stepped back with a smile that revealed curving eyeteeth, and offered her a hand. "Dance with me, Margrit Knight."

She straightened her spine by slow degrees, the threat of imminent danger making her light-headed. The taste of reckless abandonment was always tempting. She'd spent the evening smiling and greeting people who might help her career, people who could keep her climbing the narrow hard road of success. Few of them, she thought, would have to fight the impulse to dance with the devil. The urge that pushed her toward agreeing was the same one that kept her running in the park at night. A life as focused as hers was made worth living by the risks she took outside the structure.

She slid the chair away and dropped her feet to the floor. The burnished steel wall of the room showed her dull reflection as she stood and took one step forward, her hand poised above Janx's. His smile curved wider, surprise and delight in it. Margrit tilted her head, and asked, very softly, "Is this your second request, dragonlord?"

For one astonished moment the glee drained out of Janx's face, leaving his eyes brimming with jade outrage. Then his lip curled, and in a voice unlike any Margrit had ever heard from him, he said, "Oh, you're good. You're very good."

It was not a compliment. Margrit let the corners of her mouth flicker in acknowledgment, and kept her hand in the air above Janx's. His nostrils flared and he dipped his other hand into a pocket, coming out with a cigarette that he lit with a scrape of his thumbnail against his forefinger. The breath he exhaled an instant later sent streams of thin blue smoke swirling around him, and then a smile as thin as the smoke played over his mouth. He took her hand, bowing over it. "To business, then, my dear lady. To business."

Not until he had walked around her, returning to his place at the table, did Margrit allow herself to draw a careful breath and lower her hand. Facing him was an exercise in small movements.

His usual amusement had returned in full by the time she'd done so. "You are so terribly brave, Margrit Knight. Is it truly honor among thieves that makes you so?"

"I don't see any thieves around here, Janx. In fact, I don't see anybody at all. Where is everybody?" Margrit glanced at the windows overlooking the empty, darkened casino on the warehouse's bottom floor, then brushed the question off as she sat down again. "We've been through this. I trust you to keep your word, which doesn't mean I don't appreciate that you're dangerous. You were also annoyingly cryptic on the phone. What's going on?"

"How much do you know about us?" The question, put forth bluntly and with none of Janx's typical humor, made Margrit's shoulder blades pinch. She felt as if she'd been called on by a law professor whose expectations outstripped her knowledge of the subject.

"You mean the Old Races?" She hid an irritated moue, knowing she was stalling in order to come up with an adequate answer. Janx nodded, gesturing for her to continue with a fluid motion that sent smoke swirling around his head.

"There are five of you. Five left, anyway. Dragons and djinn, selkies and gargoyles, and the vampires." She listed them the way she'd first heard them named, with dragons and djinn woven together, wonderful to pronounce. "There used to be others. Mermaids, anyway, and Bigfoot."

Janx's mouth flattened with vague insult and resigned acceptance. "Siryns and yeti."

"Siryns and yeti. Sorry. Anyway, I know the dragons came from some volcanic area and spread out because they don't like company. I got the idea it was the Pacific ring of fire, but I don't know why." She wrinkled her eyebrows curiously, but Janx passed a hand across his chest, refusing the question.

Margrit shrugged disappointment, but went on. "Djinn are from the deserts and selkies are from the sea, if there are more than one or two left. Gargoyles came from the mountains." She hesitated, remembering Cara's reluctance to say more.

"You've left one out," Janx said lightly. "The vampires. What do you know about the vampires?"

Margrit smiled uncomfortably and shook her head. "That they say they don't come from this world at all."

"And what do you believe?"

"I wouldn't even know where to start, Janx. I've seen a selkie change skins and a gargoyle transform in my arms." Color suffused her cheeks as heat ran through her body at the sudden, shocking memory. More than just in her arms. Alban had transformed as she'd clung to him, arms around his neck, legs around his waist. The implosion of power had been an erotic charge lancing through the core of her, enough to make her blush even now.

Curiosity lit Janx's eyes to pale green, and Margrit forged on before he could speak. "Malik turned me into fog and hauled me through the city, and I've seen Daisani move so fast he looked like he was in two places at once. What I believe is you people aren't human. Anything beyond that I just don't know. Why?" she added warily. "Is there a vampire army congregating in the Hellmouth?"

"Not," Janx said, smiling, "as far as I know. Do you know how many of us there are?"

"A countable number. In the thousands, maybe, not even tens or hundreds of thousands." She wet her lips, studying the red-haired man across from her. "I got the idea there were maybe only dozens of dragons left, but I don't know why. Fewer than anybody but the selkies, though. Maybe it just seems like dragons would be hard to hide."

"The dark ages were not easy on my people," Janx admitted in short tones. "Your Saint George, to give an example."

"If there really was a Saint George and a dragon, or dragons, why don't we have bones and fossils?" Margrit leaned forward, eager for the answer.

Humor came back into Janx's gaze. "You've been waiting to ask that, haven't you? We know when one of ours has died, Margrit Knight. We come and take his body to the boiling earth he was born of. There's nothing left for your scientists and tabloid reporters to find."

"Tabloids," Margrit echoed. "So some of you have died recently. I'm sorry."

"Are you."

"Yeah. Yes, actually, I am." She lifted her chin. "This world of yours, the world the Old Races belong to. A few months ago, I didn't know it existed, but now that I do, despite everything, I wouldn't go back to not knowing. You…make things possible, Janx." Margrit heard the note of longing in her voice and cleared her throat, trying to modulate it. "I used to read stories about the Loch Ness monster. I never believed them, but I wanted to. I wanted there to be something incredible in the lake. It just wasn't rational." A smile curved her mouth until her eyes crinkled, honest delight flooding through her. "I've seen six impossible things before breakfast, now. I can believe in the Loch Ness monster if I want to. You—all of you, Alban and Daisani and even Malik—gave me that. You might see me as a pawn to be played in some enormous game I don't understand, but you've made it possible for me to believe in magic. I regret the passing of anything that takes the magic out of the world, even if it'd bite my head off as soon as look at me."

Blue smoke sailed from Janx's nostrils, paling his eyes to granite-green, making them unreadable. "I think I begin to understand you, Margrit Knight. Stoneheart was wiser than he knew, breaking centuries of silence with you."

"Why do you call him that? You call me by my full name and you give Alban nicknames. Why do you do that?"

Janx smiled, revealing curved eyeteeth again. "Who's to stop me? What you don't know, or understand, about the Old Races is this," he said abruptly. Ice skimmed over Margrit's skin, reminding her that easy banter and Janx's playful manner were not the reasons she'd come to an East Harlem warehouse at two in the morning. "We keep ourselves in line through a series of checks and balances. Everyone owes someone something. It keeps us honest, for the most part."

"God," Margrit said involuntarily. "I'd hate to see you with free rein."

Something nasty happened to Janx's smile, a reptilian coldness coming into it. "Yes," he agreed. "You would. It begins to look something like this."

He stood with startling abruptness, scooping up the paperwork she'd shifted earlier. He flipped open a folder, dealing mug shots out of it as if they were cards from a deck. Each photograph landed with astonishing precision along the edge of the table before her. She touched the second one, frowning at it. "That's…I know him. He's the man you were going to have drive me home in January."

"Patrick. He's dead."

Margrit jerked her hand back, her gaze skittering to Janx, then to the other two photographs he'd dealt. "They're all dead," he confirmed. "Patrick, to whom you showed so little trust—how shall I put it? He oversaw the day-to-day aspects of financial fecundity."

"He shook people down for the money they owed you," Margrit translated.

Janx exhaled, a sound laced with acid humor. "He oversaw that arm of my organization, yes. You ought to have trusted him," he added petulantly. "Patrick never looked for trouble. He only hurt people when it was strictly necessary, and I can't imagine you'd have made it so."

"How reassuring. What happened to him? Them," Margrit corrected. The faces of the other two men were unfamiliar. One was extraordinarily good-looking, charismatic even in the unflattering light of a mug shot. "And who were they?"

"I assume you're more interested in their positions than their names. The handsome one ran one of my larger substance rings, and the third—"

"I really shouldn't have asked. I swear, Janx, all I need to do is wander in here with a tape recorder sometime and you'd talk yourself right into a jail cell."

"Electronic devices tend to come to a short end around here, Margrit. You know that. Besides, you wouldn't really put me in jail, would you?" Janx's eyes widened, a protestation of hurt innocence that belied any care for the dead men whose photographs lay on the desk.

Margrit worked her mouth, trying not to let herself laugh, then avoided the question by tapping Patrick's picture. "So what happened to them?"

"Margrit." Janx sounded both disappointed and annoyed. "Eliseo Daisani happened to them, obviously."

Her eyebrows rose. "Are you sure?"

"Am I—Margrit," he repeated. "Aside from the fact that no one else would dare, do you really think Daisani would allow Vanessa's death to go unpunished? It's tit for tat, nothing more. My lieutenants for his woman. I might even call it a fair trade." His voice, usually oiled with humor, betrayed the faintest scratch of discord.

"I take it they're all human, then." Margrit spoke through her teeth, anger rising on behalf of the men Janx dismissed with only a hint of regret. "God, you people are bastards. These men probably had families, Janx, people who cared about them."

"They did. But then, I like to imagine their loved

ones knew what kind of men they were. Drug dealers and thugs are expected to come to a bad end, Margrit. Who could really be surprised? This is very much the natural order of things in the world, my dear. People die and ambitious new men replace them. Frequently their deaths are thanks to their replacements."

"So how do you know that isn't happening now?"

"Because there's a pattern to these things, Margrit. I control my people. I watch for the ambitious ones, and when they're strong enough, I present an opportunity for advancement. One does not replace three men in five days, when doing this. I need to be sure each new piece fits in with the whole before I'm ready to change another aspect of my organization's leadership. This is not ambition. This is revenge."

"And a fair trade," Margrit said sharply. "So what do you want from me?"

"You have no idea how much I would like to burn that second favor on something as delightful as a dance."

"I don't need poetry, Janx. Just tell me what you want."

"Humans," Janx said without distress. "So demanding, so shortsighted. You want everything so quickly. You must learn patience, my dear. It would stand you well in dealing with the Old Races."

"Janx, you've got a hundred of my lifetimes to look forward to. I've got threescore years and ten. Maybe that's why I don't want to waste time with you flirting around the subject."

"Margrit." Janx turned the corners of his mouth down, a picture of injured feelings. "I'm not flirting." Charm and lightheartedness slid from his eyes, cooling their color. "I'm trying to soften the blow."

She braced, as if what happened next might be a physical attack. Jade glinted through Janx's eyes again, a smile playing over thin lips. "I do like that about you, Margrit Knight. You transform fear into defiance so quickly. Does it cost you?" He dismissed the question as easily as he asked it, brushing it away with long fingers. "Vanessa Gray was Daisani's right hand for over a century, but she was only human. Forgive me," he said with an upward dance of his eyebrows, "but from our perspective you are—"

"Pawns," Margrit said flatly. "Easily played and easily discarded, just like your lieutenants. I get it, Janx. What do you want from me?"

"Malik is my right-hand man."

Margrit stared at the dragonlord without comprehension, then came to her feet, shoulders rising with tension. "Malik's one of you. Djinn. Daisani can't do anything to him. It's against your laws. The price of killing one of the Old Races is exile. Nobody'd deal with Daisani anymore."

"Eliseo Daisani will hardly fail to avenge his lover of thirteen decades over something as desperately irrelevant as race or exile. I have no proof that he's behind these murders, and he's hardly going to provide it. Nor will he be so clumsy as to leave a trail back to him in Malik's case."

"If he was going to, why wait? It's been months."

"I believe a tool for revenge has only recently arrived." Janx's voice went quieter yet, a song in its softness. "The djinn are a desert race, Margrit Knight. Amongst the surviving Old Races they have only one natural and true enemy."

Margrit spread her hands, then slowly closed them,

grasping understanding. "The selkies. Water creatures." Surety filled the guess, and Janx's brief smile confirmed it. "I thought there weren't any left."

"Margrit. Don't be disingenuous with me."

"Well, that's what everybody keeps telling me. I met one, but she disappeared. I didn't think there were enough left worth mentioning. I thought that was the whole thing about them. They crossbred with humans and died out. What's that got to do with Malik? What's it got to do with me?"

"You don't know." Amusement washed through Janx's expression as he approached her, leaning against the table and folding his arms over his chest. "That's lovely. Margrit, my dear, all I care about is that I believe Malik's assassination is in the making. I expect you to stop it."

FIVE

MARGRIT'S LAUGHTER SHOT high, hurting her throat. "Me? I'd just as soon stick a needle in my eye, Janx. Or better yet, in his."

"I know." Janx beamed. "That's what makes it a favor. Isn't it wonderful?" Delight leached out of his mercurial voice, leaving it heavy. "I could make this a demand, Margrit, not a favor. Be grateful I'm inclined to play fairly."

"Is that a dragonly trait?" Margrit asked tightly. "Does your hoard only shine properly if it's gotten through fair trade?"

"Not at all. But jewels, once obtained, must be treated with care so their gloss remains unmarred."

Another laugh broke free, horror mixed with shock. "Am I a jewel in your hoard?"

"Be grateful that you are not gold, my dear. Gold is soft, and easily distorted." Before the threat settled in her bones, Janx went on, voice light and casual, though the words carried weight. "Jewels crack under pressure, but retain their heart until shattered. I've made Malik's life your responsibility, and you can't refuse me."

"How exactly do you expect me to keep him alive?"

His beatific smile darted back into place, lighting his eyes. "That's not my problem, is it? Consider yourself fortunate. As a human, you have no constraints on what you might or must do to ensure his survival. Not, at least, in regards to the Old Races, and our lives are lived enough in shadow that I think human justice will never see any transgressions you may be forced to commit in my service."

"What—" Margrit's voice broke and she swallowed, clearing disbelief and fear away. Her blood raced until she itched with it. Aching feet or not, the impulse to bolt into action, to run as far and fast as she could, was barely held in check. "What do you expect me to *do?*"

"Whatever is necessary, my dear. Whatever is necessary. Malik will be your constant companion—"

"Like hell." Margrit stood, painfully aware the heaviness of the action was nothing like Janx's fluid movements. "Like hell. Absolutely not. I will not have him following me around. For one thing, I can't do my job with a minor gang lord hovering over me. It'd ruin my career. For another, Malik hates me."

"You had the nerve to put him in his place, Margrit."

"And I'd do it again. That's not the point. I'm not exposing myself to his presence. You might order him to leave me alone, but if he disobeys—"

"It might be hard on him, but it'll be infinitely worse for you. I believe you've used that argument in the past. Refusing me may be just as bad for you as Malik's company."

"I can live with that." Margrit set her teeth together, then beat Janx to the punch: "Or not. I'll..." Her hands cramped and she looked down to see them fisted so tightly that, unfolded, they showed nail marks in her palms. She watched the half-moons change from white to red, using the changes as a timer with which to gauge her own temper. Only when they'd returned to her natural color did she trust that her thoughts were under control again, rational thinking overcoming blunt panic. She raised her eyes to find Janx with his feet kicked up on the table, fingers steepled in front of his mouth as if to hide the smirk that shaped his lips.

"Two things," she grated. "First, forget the whole favor-owed thing for a minute. I will not have somebody like Malik following me around. If you want me under a death sentence, carry it out yourself, Janx. Do me that much honor, at least." Her pulse slowed in her throat as she met Janx's gaze, fatalism outweighing fear.

He folded his fingers down until only one remained pressed against his pursed lips as if he'd whisper, "Shh." After a moment his eyes lidded, catlike, so slowly Margrit couldn't be sure if she saw a subtle nod accompanying the action. He curved his finger down over his chin, then *did* nod, another small motion. "If it comes to that, perhaps I will. But how do you propose to keep Malik safe if he isn't at your side?"

"How do you think I propose to keep him safe even if he is?" Margrit asked incredulously. "The second thing is I don't know what the hell you know that I don't, but you'd better fill me in, starting at the beginning. Even if there were any selkies left, it's just as much against your rules for them to kill Malik as it is for any of the other Old Races. Why—"

"What few of them may be left are already exiled. The selkies, as a people, have nothing to lose. Imagine you're one of the very last of a dying race, Margrit. Imagine you're a young mother with a child, and what you might do to protect that child. And imagine what incentives a man like Eliseo Daisani might be able to offer you to shatter one last taboo."

"You can't possibly think Daisani's going to send Cara Delaney after Malik. Cara's—" Margrit broke off, remembering the fragile selkie girl's huge dark eyes and shivering fear. That was the impression that haunted her when she thought of Cara, but the girl had shown an unexpected strength, too, the last time they'd spoken. "If Daisani'd gotten his hands on her, he wouldn't have given me back her selkie skin," she said, trying the argument out on herself.

Janx quirked an eyebrow, his thoughts clearly following hers. Margrit bared her teeth and glanced away, nodding. "Unless they'd agreed to hand it over to me as a red herring. It breaks up any link between them that a lawyer—well, I—might find. I don't believe it," she added more sharply.

The dragonlord spread his hands, neither agreement nor disagreement. "But let us say Cara's appearance sparked the idea that it was possible. If she lives, then others do, and Daisani's a resourceful man. We call in favors from afar, when circumstances warrant it."

Margrit shivered, unsubtly reminded of the assassin Janx had hired to murder Vanessa Gray. "And you think there's another selkie in New York now. A selkie methodically whacking your lieutenants as he works his way up to the top. Why not start with Malik and be done with it?"

"If it were my hit, I'd use a series of unrelated killers assigned to specific, select targets. I wouldn't waste Biali on the mundane task of taking out a pimp, for example. The point is not to deftly remove one man, but to cause chaos in my organization and fear amongst my people."

Margrit held her breath so long her heartbeat echoed in her ears with increasingly urgent thuds as she stared at Janx. The sudden inhalation that followed made her lungs ache. "I really do not want to know what you *would* waste Biali on, but it's killing me not to ask." She held her breath again for another moment, then shook off temptation as best she could. "So I'm supposed to find this selkie and dissuade him? Just for the record, what happens if I fail?"

"You don't want that to happen," Janx murmured.

Margrit snorted a laugh and nodded. "Any idea where I should start?"

"You've a tendency to be refreshingly direct, Margrit. You could simply go to the source."

"Go accuse Daisani of plotting murder? You've had better ideas." She stood, shaking her head. "Why don't you just keep Malik under wraps for a while and see who comes looking?"

Janx's mouth twitched with rueful humor. "If you have any suggestions as to how to keep a djinn in a bottle, I'm willing to listen. No one likes to be caged, but short of putting him in a box made of salt water, I don't think a djinn *can* be. Stop this unraveling from happening," he said more quietly. "Too many more losses, Malik or not, and my House will not stand. I need assistance, Margrit Knight, and you have a soft spot for the Old Races. Help me."

She sighed explosively. "You know I'll try."

Janx's smile lit up again and he stood, bowing gracefully in farewell. "I have every confidence that you'll succeed."

* * *

That was more confidence than Margrit had. Janx's words echoed in her dreams and followed her into the office the next morning, after far too little sleep. She'd had more than one half-formed plan since leaving the House of Cards, ranging from taking Janx's suggestion and arriving on Daisani's doorstep to demand to know if he was behind Janx's lieutenants' deaths, to a somewhat more pragmatic visit to Chelsea Huo's bookshop to ask the little proprietor if she had any information about selkies, to standing on a rooftop bellowing for Alban. Instead, she'd gone home in the cab Janx called for her and collapsed, falling asleep so quickly that when morning came she was surprised to discover she'd undressed the night before. Now she sat at her desk, cheek propped on her hand and her eyes not even halfway open, tired mind humming with the same possibilities that she'd considered the previous evening.

A new stack of papers, topped with a note claiming "Urgent!" had arrived on her desk since she left work yesterday. The note was now half-hidden beneath a cup of coffee, the rare indulgence her only chance of making it through the morning.

"Russell wants to see you."

"What?" Margrit flinched upright, rubbing her face and clutching her coffee. Sam offered a sunny, morning-person smile over the edge of her cubicle.

"Russell wants to see you in his office. Morning, Margrit." His grin got broader. "Late night, huh?"

"Way too late." She stared at her coffee a moment, then lifted the cup with focused determination, taking a large swallow before bumbling down to Russell's office to lean in the doorway. He invited her to come in with the same gesture that told her to wait a moment for him to get off the phone. She sank down in a chair, fingers wrapped around the cardboard coffee cup, and watched the man in silence.

His curling hair had been clipped short recently, a Caesar cut that emphasized the gray. It succeeded in making him look distinguished, that enviable stage aging men seemed to reach more easily than women. His linen shirt was still crisp this early in the day, and the suit jacket that hung over the back of his chair had threads of silk in it, details that reminded Margrit that her boss dressed better than a public employee was assumed to be capable of affording.

He hung up the phone, nodding at her coffee cup. "You've had a lot of those lately. Thought you didn't drink caffeine."

Margrit squinted. "I don't think I've had a cup of coffee since January." Not since a series of late nights tangling with the Old Races had worn her out. It was her fault the meeting with Janx had been set so late, but blaming the dragonlord was more appealing than admitting her own culpability. "You've got a mind like a steel trap, Russell."

"Well, someone's got to remember the details. They seem to think I'm the best man for the job." His eyebrows rose. "Good party last night?"

Margrit's own eyebrows drew down. "It was, but how did you know…?"

Russell slid a section of newspaper across his desk, rotating it to face her. Margrit, on the governor's arm, was in the forefront of a color photograph, reaching out to shake Kaimana Kaàiai's hand. The caption beneath it proclaimed: **"Legal Aid counselor Margrit Knight,**

escorted by Governor Jonathan Stanton, makes an impression at a private reception for philanthropist Kaimana Kaaiai. Kaaiai is in New York for ten days to meet with city officials regarding a donation for the recently discovered 'subway speakeasy.'"

Margrit huffed and looked up with a smile. "At least it isn't lurid." Russell's return smile was perfunctory and left his eyes judging. Margrit set her coffee cup aside, eyebrows wrinkling again. "What's wrong, Russell?"

"You've had a good few months, Margrit. The Johnson clemency case, then the scene with Eliseo Daisani. It's made you high-profile."

"You put me on the Daisani case, Russell. That was your decision, because the clemency case had gone so well. If I'm high-profile it's in part because of choices you've made."

"It's an observation, Margrit, not an accusation. But I'm curious. Everyone here knows Mr. Daisani's been wooing you toward his corporation, and this—" he tapped the society page of the paper "—is professional-level glad-handing. You're too young to be bucking for my job. I'd like to know where you see yourself going over the next few months and years."

"I've been thinking about a vacation to Bermuda." Margrit held up a hand to ward off Russell's displeasure. "You sound like Mr. Daisani, Russell. He thought I'd get one or two particularly attractive cases under my belt and bail for something with better pay and an office with a view. I'm not planning on leaving Legal Aid anytime soon, but don't get me wrong." She sat forward to plant a fingertip against the photograph. "I like this kind of exposure. I didn't go to the party last night to hang out with the governor, but I'm not going to look a gift horse in the mouth. I had a great evening with a powerful man, and if something positive comes out of it, I'm not going to reject the possibility out of hand." She sat back again, putting on a smile she didn't entirely feel. "Do all your employees get this kind of hands-on career counseling?"

"Only when they appear to be on the verge of becoming a shooting star. Why did you go, Margrit?"

She leaned forward again, glancing over the photograph until she found the man she was looking for, his face mostly obscured by someone standing in front of him. "That's Tony, Russell. He's on Kaaiai's security detail, and he got me an invitation to the reception. That's all."

"Really." The fine skin around Russell's eyes tightened. "That's all?"

"Scout's honor." Margrit held up three fingers in a pledge as she sat back again.

Russell nodded slowly. "Then would you like to tell me why Mr. Kaaiai has specifically requested a meeting with you this morning?"

Margrit laughed out loud, hoping surprise was more attractive in laughter than in jaw-dropped gaping. Russell's expression tightened again, Margrit's burst of humor unexpected and clearly unwelcome. "I'm sorry," she said, genuinely meaning it. "I have absolutely no idea why he wants to see me. Are you sure?"

"His secretary called my private line a few minutes before you got in. Margrit, far be it from me to stand in the way of your ambitions, but—"

"I'm not leading you on, Russell." Margrit heard her voice go flat. "I know it's hard to find good people for

Legal Aid, and you want to hold on to me. I think if I intended to leave I'd have the courtesy to tell you early enough to allow you time to find a replacement. But I honestly have no plans to leave, and I really have no idea what Kaaiai wants to talk to me about. If he makes me an offer I can't refuse, you'll be the first to know, all right?"

Russell's mouth pursed before he sighed and nodded. "All right. He'd like you to meet him at ten-thirty."

"Where?"

"He's staying at the Sherry. Suite 1909."

Margrit twisted her mouth. "His hotel. Maybe there's a perfectly disgusting animal reason he wants to meet with me."

"Business meetings at reputable hotels, Margrit, are not—"

"That was a joke," she said. "A joke, Russell. Sorry. I won't make one again." She collected her coffee cup as she stood, glancing down at herself. Taupe skirt with a matching jacket, white blouse. Flats instead of heels; her feet still hadn't forgiven her. "Will I do?"

Russell looked her over critically, then nodded. "Go on, Counselor. You've got worlds to conquer."

Margrit took a gilded elevator to the nineteenth floor, trying not to laugh at herself as she all but tiptoed down the silent hall. She felt like an intruder into a private world as she tapped on the door to Kaaiai's suite.

A plain woman with rich brown hair opened the door, stepping out of the way to invite Margrit in. Margrit smiled her thanks and absorbed the room at a glance—two sets of doorways leading to other rooms; overstuffed couches; a bar of beautiful glossed wood—before

Kaimana Kaaiai was on his feet, striding across the lush carpet to clasp Margrit's hand in his. The woman who'd opened the door became part of the background, ready to be called on without being obtrusive.

"Ms. Knight. Thanks for coming on so little notice." Kaaiai sounded genuinely glad to see her.

"It's my pleasure, Mr. Kaaiai. I didn't imagine I'd get another chance to speak with you."

"I bet you didn't." Despite his easygoing lilt, he seemed to select his words with care, as if trying to leave an impression of being one of the boys. He carried his weight as if it were comforting, tailored suit adding to his imposing size without making him seem fat. "Tea or coffee? I only have half an hour to give you right now, but there's no point at all if we can't sit down and have a drink." He motioned her to one of the couches, settling down on its far end with a grace that belied his size. His assistant went to the bar unbidden.

"Just water would be fine, please. Even tap water. I'm a native. I can take it." Margrit offered a smile to the woman, who opened the bar refrigerator and took out a bottle of water without changing expression.

"She doesn't smile," Kaimana confided. "I try to break her resolve, but it only works on bank holidays and leap years."

Margrit laughed. "We don't have bank holidays, Mr. Kaaiai. Or has Hawaii adopted them without telling the rest of us?"

"Sadly, no, so you see my problem. Thank you, Marese." He accepted a cup of coffee from his assistant, who nodded gravely as she offered Margrit a glass of water and the half-empty bottle.

Margrit murmured thanks as well, then brought her

attention back to Kaaiai, who regarded her steadily over the edge of his cup.

"I saw you speaking with Eliseo Daisani last night, Ms. Knight. You're friends with him?"

Margrit blinked, reaching for the coffee table to set her water aside. "I'm acquainted with him. The idea of being friends with Mr. Daisani is alarming."

"How closely acquainted?"

Caution held Margrit's tongue as she studied the man who questioned her. Thick black hair, sun-browned skin and dark liquid eyes made a reassuring package. "We've spoken in private a handful of times," she said carefully. "Why do you want to know?"

"Someone suggested you might know more about him than he'd want made public," Kaaiai said easily. "That might be useful if it's true."

Margrit's thigh muscles bunched, announcing their readiness to run. She relaxed them deliberately, as much because she was on the nineteenth story of a hotel with nowhere to go as the sheer impracticality of running in slip-on flats. "Who told you that?" She kept her voice light and curious, noncommittal.

"A girl named Cara Delaney."

"Cara! Do you—you know—do you know where she *is?* I've got her— I need to see her immediately, if you know where she is." Margrit came to her feet, hands clenched with passion. "Please, she disappeared weeks ago and I've been trying to find her. She was a—" She broke off, searching for the right descriptor.

"A friend?"

"A client. A confidante, maybe. Please, if you know where she and Deirdre are, it's imperative I see them.

At the very least I have a delivery for Cara, something of hers I've been waiting to give back."

"How well acquainted with Mr. Daisani are you, Ms. Knight?"

"I'm—" Understanding caught Margrit unawares, a weight bouncing inside her chest where her heart ought to be. Janx's mild chastisement, *don't be disingenuous with me,* rang in her ears as she wondered if he'd known. She discarded the idea almost instantly; his theory as to Daisani's incentives wouldn't appeal to a rich man, and the dragonlord would have gained nothing by leaving Margrit to find out on her own. Janx was looking for Cara's equivalent, not Kaimana Kaaiai.

"Does it not show up on television?" she asked distantly. "The way you move? Because I know you've been on TV." And it seemed impossible that Janx wouldn't have watched footage of the man funding security for the speakeasy, which had once been his and Daisani's meeting place. Margrit found herself looking at Kaaiai as if she could see through him, as if answers lay beyond him somewhere. "Your eyes are like Cara's. So dark they're all pupil. I don't know the password, Mr. Kaaiai. I don't know if I should assume everyone here is on the same page."

Kaaiai glanced toward Marese, then back at Margrit. "You can make that assumption, Ms. Knight. Marese is discreet."

"So was Vanessa Gray." Margrit folded her fingers into fists again, then released them. "If I were to say 'dragons and djinn,' or that it's all wrong that Eliseo Daisani doesn't go bump in the night, or that outcasts seem to be my specialty, would that tell you I'm part of your secret club?" She sat down again, one leg folded under her, and her hands clenching the couch cushions. "You're one of them, aren't you? You're like Cara. A selkie. I thought you were all Irish."

"We have a legend among our people." Kaimana's expression gentled, aging and growing distant, as if he looked back through time and memory. "That once we all came from the same place in the sea, but over thousands of years we spread around the planet. Some of us went north and across the frozen oceans, living on the edges of the world. Even now the Inuit tell stories of seal skin-changers, as much a part of their legends as the selkies are of Irish lore." He sighed, passing a hand over his eyes with a gesture born to water, its fluidity beyond human measure. "Only the gargoyles know for certain, but we believe that even if we're not all born in the same part of the world, we still belong to the same culture."

Silence followed his story, until Kaaiai brought his focus back to Margrit and smiled suddenly, grounding himself in something closer to her world. "That will do, as a password. And, no, it doesn't translate well on television. We're all equal in the camera's eye, it seems. Why?"

Adrenaline burned out, leaving Margrit sinking under a wave of exhaustion. "Nothing important." Even if Janx didn't know about Kaaiai's heritage, it seemed impossible that the selkie would trouble himself with a crimelord's people.

Unknotting that tangle would wait. Margrit drew in a deep breath and still couldn't raise her voice above a scratchy whisper. "Mr. Kaaiai, I have Cara's sealskin. If you know where she is, I've got to return it to her. I promised. I know she said she could survive without it, but that must be like being a bird with clipped flight feathers. Surviving isn't flying. Do you know where I can find her?"

Pleasure emanated from the selkie. "You're not curious as to why I think your acquaintance with Daisani might be useful? Just Cara? She's your only concern?"

"She told me Deirdre would die without her sealskin. Maybe Cara's not that vulnerable, but I made her a promise and I haven't been able to keep it. So, yes, right now all that really matters to me is being able to return it." Embarrassing sentiment stung Margrit's nose and she looked away. Nerves prickled along her back as she heard one of the suite doors open.

"I told you," Cara Delaney said in a soft voice. "I told you she was one of the good ones."

SIX

"CARA!" MARGRIT JOLTED to her feet for the second time, this time rounding the end of the couch to skid across the carpet toward the petite selkie girl. She seized Cara's shoulders to hug her, then, appalled at her own rudeness, released her grip. Cara laughed, stepping forward for a gingerly embrace.

"I'm sorry," Margrit blurted. "I didn't mean to manhandle you. But I was afraid you were dead, with your neighbors tearing your apartment apart and then you disappearing. Where did you go?" She released the other woman, giving her a scowl disrupted by delight.

"It's all right." Cara's dark eyes were full of pleasure. "I don't think anyone's ever been this glad to see me. A few of the others came just after you left, and took us away. I'm sorry if you were worried, but once we had Deirdre's skin we thought it was safer for us to disappear, so Daisani couldn't get to it again. You won the fight against him." Admiration lit her irises to amber. "Even without me you kept fighting for the building. Thank you, Margrit."

"The building wasn't about you at all." Margrit pulled her into another impulsive hug, surprised to find herself trembling with relief. "Daisani just got lucky with his workmen finding your skins, Cara. He was having a temper tantrum," she said, only considering how ill-advised the words were after she'd spoken. Damage done, she shrugged, glancing toward Kaaiai. "It turned out it was actually over the speakeasy down in the subways that you're offering security financing for. It used to belong to Daisani, and he was pissed off at Grace for giving it up to the public. She—"

"Grace," Kaaiai interrupted. "Grace O'Malley? They told me about her in the grant for financing. I can't understand why anyone would let themselves be saddled with a name like that. The real Grace O'Malley was a brigand and a murderer, not a hero."

Margrit crooked a smile. "Humans do that, Mr. Kaaiai. We make romantic heroes out of violent, awful people. Billy the Kid. Bonnie and Clyde. Captain Jack Sparrow," she added with a wink. "Anyway, the modern Grace is a sort of vigilante. Maybe she's trying to redeem the name."

"*Vigilante* implies violence," Kaaiai said with a note of disapproval. "I was given to understand she eschewed violence."

"I've met her. She says she doesn't kill people." Margrit shuddered and brushed her fingertips over her forehead, where Grace had once pressed the barrel of a gun. "I don't think she does. I think she just scares them. She's been trying to get kids off the streets for years, from the bottom up, literally. She's got areas staked out in the storm drains and tunnels under the city. One of them was under your building," she said to Cara. "Daisani was after it, not you."

"All of this," Cara murmured. "All of this because of a mistake?" She glanced toward Kaaiai, apology written in her eyes. "Maybe—"

"No," he said with gentle certainty. "No, Cara, you were right to come to me, and right to suggest what you have. I apologize, Ms. Knight, go ahead. I didn't mean to interrupt."

Margrit glanced between the selkies, curious, then offered a smile to the girl who'd been her client. "I don't have it with me, Cara, but your sealskin is safe at my apartment. Daisani gave it to me. I earned it," she corrected, watching Cara's eyes darken further. "I remember what you said about owing him, and I took the warning to heart, but I think it's too late for me."

"Not necessarily." Kaaiai stood, inserting himself back into the conversation physically as well as vocally. "If you're on our side, Ms. Knight—"

"Your side?" She shook her head, stepping away from Cara to face the broad selkie male. "I don't even know what sides there are. I'm not on anyone's side."

A memory of alabaster skin seared her, carved angles of a wide, beautiful face whose blue-tinged shadows would never know sunlight. Desire flared at the remembrance of a scent like sun-warmed stone and strands of heavy white hair flowing over her fingers. A tremor had caught them both as she'd brushed fingertips over the soft membrane of wings, a sensual, silken touch. She'd made her choice to stand beside Alban as his advocate, first when he'd asked for her help, and later when he'd rejected it. If there were sides to consider, Margrit already knew where she stood. "I'm not on anyone's side," she repeated without conviction.

"Cara tells me you've spoken with Janx. I know for myself you talk to Daisani. My official job here in New York has nothing to do with the Old Races, Ms. Knight, but having an attaché like yourself who can move between the two of them freely would allow me to accomplish some other business while I'm here. Unless you have a specific loyalty to one of them that could compromise your position as a negotiator?"

"A neg— Mr. Kaaiai." Margrit put all the firmness she could into his name. "I think you're overestimating my ability to influence anything in your world. I owe Janx two open-ended favors. Eliseo Daisani gave me a drink of his blood because I caught a bad guy for him, and he's trying to get me to work for him. At best I'm walking a high wire between those two. You want me to start running back and forth on it playing messenger?"

"What if I could turn that high wire into a platform?"

"Can you?" Margrit's voice was dubious. "I don't know what it would take, but I don't think a handful of selkies are going to be able to pull off that kind of trick. I've already had one misguided gargoyle try to rescue me, and all it's done is drag me deeper into the hole."

"Alban Korund." Kaaiai said the name thoughtfully. "I've got more experience at this sort of thing than he does, which probably doesn't reassure you."

"Not really. What?" Margrit asked, with a glance toward Cara. "You don't curl your lip and call him 'the outcast'?"

Kaaiai gave Cara a brief smile. "Young people are staunch in their prejudices."

"I've noticed old people are, too," Margrit said dryly. "It just seems a little weird to me that a people who've chosen exile for their whole race would call Alban's kettle black. I don't even get the idea that he broke one of your laws, just that he walled himself off from his people."

"To a gargoyle, there's not much worse. I think none of us can understand." Kaaiai indicated not only himself and Cara, but Margrit, with a small circular gesture. "None of us share the intimacy gargoyles do, with their ability to exchange memories and thoughts. Deliberately exiling ourselves from the Old Races was a choice we made as a community. It didn't leave us *alone* in the fashion that Alban Korund keeps himself. I think it would be like cutting away your hand, or your heart, to do what he's done."

"And it's unforgivable?"

"It's incomprehensible. There aren't many of us as a whole, much less within the individual races. The idea of turning our backs on our people..." Kaaiai shook his head. "Whether it's forgivable is for the gargoyles to say, not me."

"What would you say, if it were up to you?"

Kaaiai lifted a big shoulder and let it fall. "I would welcome any of my people back with open arms, but we've lived apart from the rest of the Old Races for a long time. We may no longer think as they do. Which brings me to the point of asking you here, Ms. Knight."

Caution spilled through Margrit in cool waves. Janx's theory sat badly with her, but Kaaiai's easy admission that the selkies had changed gave it weight. She glanced toward Cara, whose eyes shone with enthusiasm as she looked from Kaaiai to Margrit and back again. The desperation that had once marked the young woman was gone, girlish hope replacing it. Even when fear had driven her, though, she'd advised Margrit against bargaining with Daisani. Cara's conviction had seemed unalterable, and all appearances suggested her situation had only improved since then. If she, desperate and afraid, refused to work with Daisani, then it seemed unlikely a man like Kaaiai, clearly a leader, would condone or participate in the murder of Janx's lieutenants.

"I'm listening." Margrit focused on Kaaiai, putting thoughts of Janx away. There would be time, and if Janx's fears were right, the more information Margrit got now, the stronger her hand would be later. "What do you think I can do?"

"We've spent generations hiding ourselves in our fight for survival. It's time to challenge the order that has held the Old Races in place for millennia, and decide how we can best approach a new world. We need an advocate, Ms. Knight, and you're the obvious choice."

Margrit left Kaaiai's suite with her thoughts in chaos and closed the door gently, as if doing so would hide the way she grasped the knob and sagged against it. The security guard posted in the hall slid her a sideways glance, impersonally curious. Margrit arranged her face in the semblance of a smile, then gave it up and exhaled heavily, still leaning on the door.

Alban's sharp-cut features played in her mind's eye. Of the Old Races' three worst offenses, the gargoyle had broken two of them for her: he'd told her about their existence, and then he'd killed one of his own to protect her. The laws, Margrit had argued, were antiquated, but he'd insisted on enforcing his own exile. And now a selkie presented her with a chance to face those laws and do her best to knock them down.

Intellect warred with ambition. She had no birthright to so blatantly and deliberately challenge their traditions. But she *wanted* to, and a better opportunity would never be offered. Laws were meant to be tested and changed as time passed. The ability to help shape a future for the Old Races was as much a brass ring as anything she coveted in her ordinary life.

Her own arrogance was breathtaking. Margrit tilted a smile at the ceiling. Perhaps that was one of the reasons behind the Old Races' law of not telling humans they existed. The almost assured destruction of their peoples, should humanity learn of the monsters that lived with them, was the obvious reason for secrecy. But the belief that humanity's path was the better one was as much a danger to the fabric of the Old Races' society as outright exposure. Margrit might well be doing none of them any favors by taking the stand that Kaaiai had offered.

None of them save one, and there was no indication he would appreciate it.

The elevator dinged, music muffled by the carpets. Margrit shook off the stillness that held her and managed a step or two away from the suite doors just as Tony Pulcella emerged from the elevators. They stared at each other, equally startled, before Margrit laughed. "Tony!"

The big Italian cop grinned and came down the hall with long strides, pulling her into a hug. "What're you doing here?"

"I was about to ask you the same thing." Margrit smiled up at him, dusting imaginary motes off his shoulders. He wore a suit without a tie, looking well-pressed and handsome. "I forgot you were on security detail."

"Still don't know how I got the job." Tony gave a good-natured shrug.

Margrit's smile died abruptly, leaving her mouth

curved but empty of emotion. She shot a glance over her shoulder at the closed suite doors, anger bringing color to her cheeks. It was almost impossible Kaaiai had asked for Tony by chance, without knowing his erstwhile girlfriend had had dealings with both Janx and Daisani.

"Gotta say it's less stressful than homicide, though. Maybe I oughta take a turn at doing this for a living. The hours are still crazy, and it's boring as hell, but private security's not as rough as being a cop. Might make it easier for us. What would you think? Hello?" he added after a few seconds, waving his hand in front of her face when she didn't reply. "You with me, Grit?"

Margrit nodded, bringing herself back to the conversation. Outrage on Tony's behalf was useless. Confessing to him she suspected he'd been placed on security detail so Kaaiai could have a discreet method of getting to Margrit sounded insulting to his skills, even if she could explain the extraordinary world that Kaaiai belonged to. But it gave her a little more measure of the man who'd made her an on-the-surface irresistible offer. Like Janx and Daisani, Kaaiai seemed to have no compunction against using humans to obtain his ends.

"I'm here. Sorry. I was thinking." Her eyebrows furrowed as she pulled Tony's suggestion back to mind. "Wouldn't you hate it? You just said it's boring, and you've only been doing it twelve hours."

"For what I hear some private security pays, I could stand being bored. Might even help you pay off those student loans you're always complaining about, if you're nice," he added with a wink.

"You know that's posturing." Her parents had paid for her schooling, an extravagance Margrit often felt embarrassed by, surrounded as she was by coworkers who had tens of thousands in loan bills.

"So maybe I could take you on some nice vacations." Tony's expression turned serious. "We've had this problem with our schedules all along, Grit. I know I said I'd look at business school if you really wanted me home by six every evening, but maybe something like this would work out for us. It'd kinda let me keep one foot in the game and you wouldn't have to worry."

"It's worth thinking about." Even as she spoke, guilt pounded through her veins in cold splashes. The offer that Kaaiai had laid out entwined her ever-more thoroughly in a world Tony didn't belong to, and it was an offer Margrit doubted she'd resist. The breach they had worked so hard to close over the last weeks suddenly loomed again, widening with every moment. "But this probably isn't the best time to talk about it. Shouldn't you be at work?"

Tony glanced over her head toward Kaaiai's suite. "Yeah, I— Hey, shouldn't *you* be? What *are* you doing here, Margrit?"

"Mr. Kaaiai asked to see me." Truth was the only answer she could come up with, feeble in its honesty. "It turned out he was a friend of Cara Delaney's, the girl who asked me for help with the Daisani building, remember?"

"I remember." Tony's gaze darkened. "Was?"

"Oh. Oh! No, is. Is. She's okay, Tony." Relief brightened Margrit's voice. "I just talked to her, in fact. Some of their friends packed her up and moved her out of the apartment that afternoon. They were afraid to get in touch with me in case Eliseo Daisani was trying to find her. She and Deirdre are okay."

Answering relief turned Tony's frown into a quick smile. "Maybe that's how I ended up with this job. Your client rubbing elbows with the rich and famous. I gotta say, Grit, I could get used to you working with the high and mighty."

Another stab of guilt assailed her. Margrit tried to push it off with a smile. "A young squatter and her baby don't exactly qualify as high and mighty, Tony. Maybe it is how you got the job, though. Kaaiai could've looked me up and found out we were dating. Good for both of us, huh?" It was a less ugly interpretation than she'd imagined.

"Great for both of us. Look, I'm on till eleven tonight, or later if the function runs late, so—"

"So no dinner date. That's okay. He's only in town for ten days. We can handle a week and a half's worth of disruption."

"I'm glad." Tony's voice lowered. "Wasn't that long ago that ten days meant we weren't seeing each other anymore."

"Things change." For a moment the words sounded full of alarming portents. Margrit shivered and stood on her toes to steal a kiss. "I should get back to work. I'll see you when we can, okay?"

Margrit smiled and Tony released her, waiting until she'd reached the elevator to call, "Hey." When she looked back, he lowered his voice to say, "Love you."

"Yeah." Margrit dropped her gaze, trying to hold Tony's image in her mind, then looked up with another smile. "You, too, babe. I'll see you later."

SEVEN

OPENING ARGUMENTS WERE brief and direct, but absorbed Margrit's attention to a degree she was grateful for. A single day of interaction with the Old Races had thrown her world into chaos, and the opportunity to focus on something as ordinary as her job was almost liberating in its mundanity. Afternoon sunshine slipped across the courtroom through skylights, counting away minutes and hours of debate that she heard herself pursue with a passion she didn't feel. Her client was guilty of rape, the evidence against him conclusive, but he'd insisted on a plea of not guilty and had forced a trial.

She'd faced the prosecuting attorney before, and approved of him in a clinical way. In a case like this one he focused heavily on the facts, leaving circus-ring tactics aside. He was still a showman, as most good lawyers were, but with the weight of evidence on his side he made only modest efforts to appeal to the jury's emotions. They didn't need to be led by the nose: it was enough to imagine the unspeakable crime being perpetrated against their mothers, their sisters, their daughters, themselves.

Nor did her client make a good defendant, even

when not expected to speak for himself. She had discussed with him his posture, his expression, his body language more times than she could count. He still sat with open, sneering arrogance, as if his own sense of invulnerability would keep the jury from condemning him. Margrit had defended men like him in the past. They were always furious and astounded when they were found guilty.

The afternoon start to the trial meant it was unlikely to be concluded before the following morning, and even that would be quick, by Margrit's estimation. Her shoulders unknotted a degree when the judge's gavel came down for the final time that day, and the prosecuting attorney stepped across the aisle as her client was led away. "This is his last chance for a plea bargain, Counselor."

Margrit shook her head as she shuffled papers into order. "A fact I'll try to impress upon him, but he doesn't believe he's going to be found guilty."

"Margrit, he was damn near caught in the act."

She breathed a laugh, glancing up at her counterpart. Jacob Mills was a good ten years older than her, with gray starting to run through short-cropped, tight curls at his temples. He was exactly the kind of man her mother approved of, although the age difference would probably make Rebecca Knight raise an eyebrow. Margrit briefly entertained the idea of marrying another lawyer and dismissed it immediately: she had enough arguments with Tony, never mind someone trained in debate as she was. "I know, Jake. I'd just as soon we could all go home now, too, but I don't think he's going to take a plea."

"You know my offer. It hasn't changed."

Margrit straightened, paperwork back in place.

"That's generous. I'll give you a call tonight if he goes for it. Otherwise..."

They shook hands, exchanging resigned smiles as Jacob finished her sentiment: "Otherwise, I'll see you in the morning."

Despite the hour—it was well after five when she finished a fruitless discussion with her client—urgent voice mail brought her back to the office. She told herself that was the price of haring off to talk with selkies all morning, and kicked her shoes beneath her desk as she sat down to a pile of case files that hadn't been there earlier.

A draft of cool air disturbed her studies some time later. Margrit glanced at her computer screen before twisting to see who else was working late. "Maybe we should get some di—"

A slim goateed man holding a glass-headed cane and wearing a dark suit stood a few feet away. "How generous. Do you always propose dinner to your wards, Margrit Knight?"

Margrit slumped, heartbeat rattling hard enough to kill any appetite she might have had. "Malik. How'd you— Never mind. You didn't screw up anybody's computer, did you?" Her cell phone had dissolved into a mess of useless electronic pixels after it had been treated to Malik's ethereal manner of travel. Janx gleefully confessed that any electronics touched by a djinn met the same fate. It was impossible to put a bug on the dragonlord, so long as he employed Malik al-Massrī.

Irritation filmed Malik's sharp features. "No. I'm not here for petty vandalism. I understand you're to be my..." His thin nostrils flared, as if the words were so distasteful as to produce a foul odor. "My protector."

"Trust me, I'm not any happier about it than you are. I don't suppose you'd be happy to just sit tight in the middle of the House of Cards, with four big burly guys keeping an eye on you, huh? It'd make life a lot easier for both of us." Margrit bit her tongue on continuing. It was safe enough, comparitively, to respond to Malik's arrogance with her own when they were at the House of Cards, under Janx's watchful eye. Now there was no greater power on hand to control the djinn, and she didn't want to offend him any more than she already had.

That led directly into her second reaction, which was gut-cold fear. Margrit had sized Malik up as dangerous in the first moments she'd met him, his ambitions and sense of self larger than he was. He was easy to offend, and she'd already done it more than once.

"On the contrary." Malik took a few gliding steps toward her, his limp faint but noticeable. She came to her feet in nervous anticipation, as if there was somewhere to run. "I believe I'm a great deal less happy about it than you are. I do not require a human keeper, no more than sunlight requires that the shifting sand attend it."

"You people have such gorgeous phrases." Margrit startled him into silence, which helped her to regain her equilibrium. "People—humans—don't talk the way you do. Not unless they're making speeches. Look, I don't even pretend that I could keep you safe if somebody wanted to take you out. You, you go…" Margrit fluttered her fingers in the air, not wanting to actually say "go poof," though that was what the djinn more or less did. "I don't even know how you injure somebody who turns incorporeal. It must be possible." She focused briefly on the cane she'd never seen him without, then brought her eyes back to his, finding anger darkening there. "Oh, come on. I'm not making fun of you. You'd know if I was. I'm just saying it's possible, right?"

Malik hissed, "Obviously."

Margrit lifted her hands in supplication. "So Janx thinks somebody who knows how to hurt a djinn is out there, and he brought in somebody outside of his usual chain of command, outside of your people's rules, to keep an eye on things. Shouldn't you be flattered he's that concerned about you, instead of pissed off?"

"Flattered. When the best 'protection' he'll afford me is a weak human woman who admits her own uselessness as a guardian. Would you be flattered?"

"No." A smile ghosted over Margrit's mouth. "You're not supposed to be making a counterargument here, Malik. I'm trying to sway the jury. Play along."

"This is not a trial or a courtroom, *sharmuta*." The last word's sentiment was clear, and a sting of color came to Margrit's cheeks. Malik took a final step forward, curling a hand over—*into*—Margrit's throat. Air turned to unbreathable fog, clogging her throat and sending her heartbeat into terrorized spikes. She staggered back, trying to escape the djinn's touch, but he flowed with her, fingers wrapped in her throat, almost palpable. Margrit swallowed convulsively, feeling a foreign body invading her throat like the thickness of a bad cough, swollen nodes closing off the possibility of breathing. Her chest ached, too little air caught there. Her chair caught her in the knees and she sat down again, a violent, awkward motion that Malik moved with easily. He leaned into her, fingers tightening around her windpipe, until his face was inches from hers.

"If I see you near me, if I discover you following me,

if there is a hint of your presence, I will turn on you and kill you. I can rip your throat out like this, tear your heart from your body. I could make you a sacrifice to the wind, a better fate than you deserve. I will not be watched by one such as you. Do you understand me?"

Hot tears born of fear and rage spilled down her cheeks as Margrit nodded. Malik smiled, triumphant and vicious. "Goodbye, Margrit Knight."

Then he hissed, jerking his hand back so quickly Margrit coughed and clutched her own throat, hardly believing she still breathed. Water made two bright marks on Malik's wrist, shimmering, almost steaming, before he swiped his sleeve across them and smeared the tears away, leaving red spots behind. Margrit laughed, rasping her throat. "Just like the Wicked Witch, huh? All I have to do is throw a pail of water on you? Get out." She pushed to her feet, drawing from a reserve of anger that went deeper than pain or fear. "Get out of here, you son of a bitch, and don't you dare ever threaten me again. I know how to hurt you now."

Malik curled a lip derisively, then faded in a swirl of fog, leaving Margrit standing alone with the crashing of her heart. Her chest still hurt, though she was unsure if it was from lack of oxygen or newborn relief. Only after long seconds of silence did she collapse back into her chair, fingertips pressed against her eyes as she tried to steady herself. Her stomach was a knot of churning sickness, sending tremors through her body. Tears would solve nothing, but they clung to her eyelashes and made her fingertips wet. She could fling them at Malik if he came back, tiny droplets made into a weapon. The thought gave her something to hang a rough laugh on. She dropped her hand, dragging in a deep breath as she stretched her chin toward the ceiling.

"Margrit?"

Margrit screamed loudly enough to echo and leapt out of her chair. It fell over in a clatter of metal and plastic, crashing against the desk. She found herself with a fist drawn back, ready to hit anything that approached.

Her boss stood in her cubicle door, a hand clutched over his heart. "Good God, Margrit, are you all right? You scared the hell out of me!"

Margrit croaked, "Russell. You scared me."

"No kidding!" He let go of his heart to hang on to the edge of her cubicle and stare at her. Margrit planted both palms on her desk and dropped her head as she tried to calm herself. "Are you okay, Margrit? I thought I heard you talking to someone."

"I'm... Yeah, I'm okay. I didn't know you were here." She chuckled weakly. "Obviously. I was...on the phone."

"It's nearly eight. What are you still doing here?"

"Is it that late?" Margrit turned away, picking her chair up. It was heavy and awkward, made worse by her hands still trembling. Russell came in to help, his eyebrows drawn with concern.

"It is. I know you're hopelessly dedicated to the job, but you should have gone home after the trial." He trailed off, frowning at her. "Everything go all right?"

"It's fine. I'm losing spectacularly and Martinez won't take a plea, but that's his problem, not mine. We're back on in the morning. Might even be out of there by noon. I can't see the jury hanging around arguing about this one." Margrit pressed her hands into the fabric of her chair, watching her knuckles whiten.

"I came back to follow up on some paperwork, and I guess I lost track of time. What are *you* doing here?" She glanced up at her dapper boss with a smile that felt fragile. "Even the head man gets to go home sometime, right? You look like you're going out," she added, realizing he wasn't in the suit he'd worn earlier that day. The one he wore now wasn't quite a tux, but its sharp clean lines looked as expensive.

"I am. Dinner with my wife. It's her birthday, and I forgot her gift at the office." He slipped a hand into his pocket and came up with a jewelry box that he balanced on his fingertips, eyebrows elevated in invitation. Margrit opened it to reveal a gold ring set with diamonds and pink alexandrite. "It's her fifty-fifth. Think this'll help her forget that?"

"It's gorgeous." Margrit smiled and closed the box again as she returned it. "I think she'll love it."

"I hope so," Russell said dryly. "It cost a month's salary. You don't have to mention that to anybody."

Margrit laughed. "Russell, you dress so well I can't help thinking a month's salary goes a long way."

He brushed a mote off his suit and shook his head, smiling. "You would, wouldn't you? No, back in the days of the dinosaurs I made some money in stocks. I shop out of that budget. Come on." He tilted his head toward the door. "You need to get out of here. I'll walk you down."

Margrit cast a glance at the paperwork on her desk. "But—"

"Boss's orders. Besides, you haven't yet told me what our rich Hawaiian friend wanted." Russell picked Margrit's coat up off the floor where it'd fallen with the chair and put it around her shoulders. "Will you be abandoning us to pull in a corporate paycheck with a philanthropist's agenda?"

"Well, now that I know I'll never match your wardrobe on what I make at Legal Aid, I'm considering it. No, he saw me talking to Eliseo Daisani at the party last night and wanted to know what I knew about him." Margrit sat down long enough to retrieve her shoes and put them on, then turned off her light and fell into step beside her boss. Malik was probably long gone, but she felt safer in Russell's company.

"I'd think he could find out anything he needed to through more usual avenues. What'd he want to know?" Russell held the door for her, and Margrit, left to lead, headed for the stairs instead of the elevator. Russell muttered, "I forgot you took the stairs," but caught up easily.

"I always take the stairs. That way I can eat as much Ben & Jerry's as I want." Margrit trailed her hand along the railing. "I'm sure he's got people who do nothing but research other people for him, but I get the idea he likes to pretend he's a man of the people. Could I have used 'people' any more times in that sentence?"

"I don't think so." Russell flashed a grin at her, then glanced toward the parking garage.

"Can I give you a lift anywhere?"

Margrit smiled and shook her head. "No, thanks. I'll take the subway home. Probably faster, anyway. Tell Joyce happy birthday."

"I will, thanks. See you in the morning, Margrit."

"'Night, Russell." Margrit tightened her coat around herself with a sigh, then hurried for the subway station.

* * *

Halfway home from the subway Margrit took a detour, impulse driving her to the park in the skirt suit she'd worn to work, rather than changing into running gear before going there. The sky had lost its last hints of twilight, and she hoped wearing daytime clothes might signal a change of intent to her gargoyle protector. Curiosity would impel most humans to investigate. Gargoyles might be made of harder stuff, but she hoped not.

She slid her fingertips over the sleeve of her jacket, imagining briefly what Alban's expression might be had she worn the white silk dress of the night before. He was, if anything, an element of earth, so perhaps the close-fitting dress wouldn't bring fire to his eyes, as it had with Janx. But it might have brought a subtle shifting to the forefront, the rooted approval of stone. A glimmer of Alban's admiration meant more, even in her imagination, than Janx's easy flattery ever could.

The temperature dropped further and her determination to face Alban girded as a lawyer instead of in exercise gear seemed increasingly foolish. She might have kept warm by running, and the gargoyle would watch from above no matter what she wore.

A few runners, familiar strangers to her, nodded greetings or flashed smiles, though they'd never exchanged names. One, a tall raw woman with dreadlocks pulled into a thick ponytail, spun as she passed, running backward and cocking a curious eyebrow at Margrit's outfit.

"Meeting someone," Margrit called in explanation, and the woman's expression cleared into a smile. She turned away again with a wave, stretching her stride out until night rendered her invisible.

"So much for New Yorkers' legendary indifference." A hint of an Eastern European accent flavored the statement, as did a heavy sense of the inevitable. Hope and relief prickled Margrit's skin, then sank inward, filling an emptiness inside her with warmth. It seemed absurd to tremble as she turned, but her steps were unsteady as she did so, searching for the speaker.

Alban stood almost swallowed by shadows at the edge of the fountain's circle of light, suit jacket flipped open to allow his hands to ride in his pockets. His stance was broader than usual, feet planted shoulder width apart as if he expected to take a hit. Even his posture was more human than she'd seen it before, shoulders rounded and weight rolled forward through his hips. His head was ducked, so that when she met his eyes it was through fine strands of white-blond hair falling loose from their ponytail and into his face.

"Did Grace teach you to stand like that? Like a fashion model," Margrit said as Alban's gaze came up writ with confusion. "Aggressively sexy for the camera. She stands that way." A flash of the two of them together, both pale, Grace in her unrelenting black leather and Alban a studied contrast in his business suit, made Margrit curl a hand in a fist, then loosen it again. In the intervening weeks, Alban might have shared considerably more than a new way to stand with the under-street vigilante, but that was the path he'd chosen. Just as Margrit had chosen a sunlit world, and a boyfriend whose work demanded much, but didn't steal away every hour from dawn to dusk.

No. Alban had chosen that particular path for her.

Margrit's hand curled a second time, as if she picked a fight with herself. She'd chosen her daylight life as much as Alban had, by opting not to pursue him until the Old Races sought her out again. Laying blame at the gargoyle's feet was cheating, and she didn't like the impulse.

"I need your help." She spoke too abruptly and the words were all wrong, nothing of what she wanted to say in them. Alban's expression remained impassive. "Staying away from me to try to protect me doesn't work. I'm in over my head with your people again, and I really could use your help." Still the wrong words. Margrit set her teeth together. "Alban, I… Come on." She gave an unhappy laugh. "Give me something here, will you?"

But for a breath of wind stirring his hair, he might have been carved of stone. Like talking to a brick wall, though Margrit couldn't conjure up any humor at the thought. After a few seconds she pulled her lower lip between her teeth.

"Yeah. Yeah, all right, fine. Have it your way." Hands knotted into fists once more, she nodded, then turned and walked away. Disappointment churned in her stomach and she told it to go away, trying to build a slow anger from it instead. The gargoyle had gotten her into the Old Races' world, and if he didn't want to help her now that she was ensconced, then to hell with him. A petulant impulse to *show him,* like a child would, latched onto growing anger and helped it flare.

"Margrit." Alban's voice cut through the darkness, soft and weary. "Margrit, wait."

EIGHT

FRUSTRATED HUMOR LANCED through burgeoning anger as Margrit recalled the first time she'd walked away from the gargoyle. He hadn't called her back and she'd been oddly dismayed, as though he'd failed to fulfill his role as required by the script. The mysterious stranger was supposed to call the principled woman's name, and she was supposed to falter, then turn back to face the love she'd been denying.

Now, finding her steps slowing and coming to a stop, Margrit discovered it was just as frustrating to play the part as it was to have it stymied. A woman of her age, from her era, wasn't *really* supposed to be so easily swayed, not by something as simple as her name being called across a dark pathway. That was for the movies, not her life.

Margrit turned around slowly, ironically aware of her own fickle nature. Alban had moved closer, coming into the light. He looked as she felt: conflicted, hopeful, wary, helpless. "I didn't think you'd stop."

"I'm not sure I would have, if my intellect were in charge. I guess it isn't, because now it's killing me not to run toward you in slow motion. The only thing that's stopping me is I'm waiting for the music to swell."

A smile etched itself into one corner of Alban's mouth. "Next time I'll try to arrange for an orchestra. Margrit—" He broke off, then spread his hands. "What's happened? Your life seemed…settled."

"How can anything be settled when I've got a gargoyle watching over me?" Margrit tried to keep accusation from her tone, making the question a genuine one. "Thank you, by the way. For jumping those guys the other night. You know that's the first time anyone's ever actually come at me? The news said mugging attempts in the park are up since January."

"You mean, since Ausra murdered four women." Alban shifted his shoulders as if he might move wings. "I've noticed more police recently. I'm sorry. I know you view the park as your haven. To have it violated must be distressing."

"It'd be more distressing if you hadn't fallen out of the sky to save me last night. Alban…" It was Margrit's turn to trail off, staring across the distance the gargoyle kept between them. Amber streetlights took what little color he had and distorted it, yellowing the silver of his suit jacket and turning his shirt sallow. Margrit glanced at her own clothes, cream bleached to a sickly white and tan deadened into neutrality. Her skin was as unhealthy a shade as Alban's shirt.

"Can we go somewhere else?" For the second time she surprised herself with abruptness. "Out to dinner, something, I don't care. Just somewhere inside, somewhere real." She looked up to see Alban abandon the wide stance he'd taken and come to his full human height, more than a foot taller than her.

"Real?"

"Indoors," Margrit repeated. "So the light doesn't screw up the colors. So I can see you properly. Please."

"Margrit." Her name came heavily, a sound of defeat. "It's better for you to remain apart from my world. Dining with me only…prolongs the inevitable."

"Which inevitable is that, Alban?" She stepped toward him, watching him tense and glance toward the trees, as if seeking escape. "Are we talking about inevitable heartbreak? An inevitable clash of your world and mine? Inevitable ending to whatever this thing between us is? Or are we talking about the fact that I'm inevitably stuck in your world already, because that's the inevitable *I'm* facing." She kept her voice low as she approached him, trying not to let irritation flare. "I've been accosted by a dragon, a djinn, a vampire and a selkie in the last twenty-four hours, and nothing you do is going to change that. I'm part of your world. If there's an inevitable here, it's that we're involved with each other. Did you really think I'd be allowed to stay out of it once I knew the Old Races existed?"

"Accosted?"

Margrit let her head fall back, blowing out an exasperated sigh. "Well, at least something got your attention. Nobody seriously hurt me, but your world's not going to leave me alone." She took a breath and held it, touching her fingers against his sleeve. "Can we please go somewhere else and talk? You might not feel the cold, but I do, and I really am hungry. I came here from work and I haven't eaten."

"I'm unaccustomed to dining in public."

"I'm unaccustomed to having to ask a guy three times to get a dinner date out of him. We're both going to have to adjust. Will you *please* come out to dinner with me?"

Alban hesitated a moment longer, then retreated one step into shadow. "No. Margrit, I am sorry for involving you in my world, and I should have acted sooner, before the inevitable did draw you back in. I'll do what I can to loosen the chains that bind you. I swore to protect you—"

"So *help* me, Alban! Skulking around in the sky isn't protecting me, not when Janx wants me to keep Malik alive, and Malik'd rather kill me than let that happen!"

Alban flinched, his expression incredulous as he searched her gaze for truth. For a moment a thread of hope tightened in Margrit's heart. A relieved smile curved her mouth and she moved forward, but Alban retreated again, deliberate and intricate as a dance. "I'll deal with Janx," he growled. "Forgive me, Margrit. I shouldn't have let this go on so long." He set his jaw, resolution coming into his eyes. "I will not watch for you again at night. I will not be here to protect you. Fondness kept me lingering too long as it is, and has done neither of us any favors."

Cold clenched Margrit's stomach, dismay born from belief. "I don't believe you. You're a gargoyle. You protect. That's what you do, what you are."

"And the best way to protect you is to leave you very much alone. My mistakes are to your detriment. I will always be sorry for that." Alban pulled in a deep breath, broadening his chest. "Be well, Margrit Knight. Goodbye."

He turned and sprang into the shadows, into the sky, a pale blur of winged imagination before treetops and distance took him away. Margrit shouted his name, running a few steps forward before stopping again in openmouthed fury as the gargoyle disappeared from sight for the second time in three nights.

* * *

Regret and rage wound through him like snakes, conspiring to take away his breath. He ought to have known better; he *did* know better. It wasn't only Margrit who might look for him in the night sky, and of those who were likely to, she was the least troublesome. He ought to have kept his word to himself, his promise to the beautiful lawyer, and stayed away. Instead he'd let sentiment rule him—he, a gargoyle, bending to the whim of emotion—and now Margrit paid the price.

Well, if irrationality was to govern him, he would ride it as far as it took him.

He folded his wings and dove, flight from the park having carried him high and to the north. He back-winged only a matter of yards above the rooftop he sought, wings aching with the strain of pulling out of the dive. Then again, it wasn't a soft landing he intended. Stony weight smashed down, Alban landing in a three-point crouch that shook the roof, and, he trusted, echoed deep into the warehouse establishment below him. Caution made him transform to his human shape, heavy taloned fingers turning to a clenched mortal fist before his gaze.

Seconds later the rooftop door flew open and half a dozen armed men spilled through it. Alban lifted his gaze by degrees, knowing full well the picture he made: a solitary, pale man splashed against the black rooftop, a place with no easy access. The wind lifted his hair and opened his suit coat, making a flare like wings as he came to his feet with slow deliberation. The men who surrounded him—tough-looking, as if they'd seen their share of battle—exchanged wary glances, unsure of how to respond to his fearless stance.

One raised a gun as Alban stepped forward, daring to block the gargoyle's path to the door. "You can't go in th—"

"Stand down, Ricardo." It wasn't the voice Alban wanted to hear, but it would do; Malik appeared in the doorway, his cane held by its throat as he swung it. "Korund. What a surprise."

Alban walked forward until he stood inches from the djinn, staring more than eight inches down at him. "I am already an exile. If any harm comes to Margrit Knight, I have nothing to lose by avenging her. You would do well to remember that." He felt surprising freedom in voicing the threat, as though it broke shackles he'd been unaware of wearing. "I will see Janx, and I will see him now."

"Janx doesn—*nnk!*" Fury lit Malik's eyes as Alban planted a hand against his collarbones and shoved him against the door frame. It proved that Alban's decision to transform to a human shape had been wise: had the armed men now behind him known that Malik was other than human, Alban would never have been able to put a hand on the djinn. The distinctive sound of weapons cocking followed hard on Malik's outraged protest. Alban ignored them and stalked down concrete stairs toward Janx's office. Malik's voice sounded, ordering a stand-down for the second time. The door above banged shut, no heavy mortal footsteps following him. An instant later Malik coalesced in front of Alban, rage contorting his features.

Alban ignored him, startled to discover how little he had to say to the djinn. Malik vaporized again rather than be trampled, and a hint of small-minded glee bubbled at the back of Alban's mind. He and the djinn could, at best, stymie one another. Malik might be capable of taking the breath from Alban's body, but could do nothing to the gargoyle's stone form, and gargoyles, as a people, were far more patient than the djinn. A gargoyle could remain in his stone shape until his djinn tormentors grew bored and left.

It would hardly come to that on Janx's threshold, though. Malik didn't reappear a second time, no doubt gone to warn his master of Alban's arrival. That was unnecessary; short of human methods of destruction, only a gargoyle could manage the building-shaking landing Alban had made a minute earlier, and the only other gargoyle in New York was in Janx's employ.

Concrete steps turned to iron grating, creaking beneath Alban's weight. As the casino below came into view, he paused, fully aware of the windowed alcove to his right that overlooked the same broad room he studied. This was Janx's House of Cards, the center of more criminal activities than Alban could easily name. The police, he understood, often managed to arrest minor players in Janx's empire, but Janx himself went unscathed. Whether that was because he owned enough of the city to keep himself safe or because the authorities feared what might rise in his place, Alban didn't know.

Below him, the desperate and weary played poker and roulette, hoping for a life-changing break of luck. The air tasted of despair, neon lights turning smoke to off-colored swirls as dull as the hope in the room. No one looked up: so human of them. Alban might well have walked through the warehouse's upper reaches in his natural form and gone unnoticed. The temptation to risk it by shifting flared and died again. Anger had carried him this far, but a gargoyle's temperament didn't lend itself to impetuousness. Alban came down the stairs, following a hallway to Janx's office, disconcerted by its familiarity. It was not a place he would consider himself comfortable in. Perhaps the ire that drove him burned away minor uneasiness.

Janx waited at the window within his alcove, a cigarette held loosely in his fingers as he watched the casino below. Neon light colored his skin to red and made his smile bloody as Alban entered the room. "I can't wait to hear this."

"How much credit do you deserve, Janx?" Alban kept his voice to a low rumble, undermining the dragonlord's light tenor and amusement. "How much of my arrival here did you orchestrate?"

Janx turned from the window, cigarette moved to his lips so he could spread long-fingered hands in a protestation of innocence. "I can only hope I'm clever enough to have arranged this. Tell me your suspicions and I'll tell you if I'm that deucedly maniacal."

"Margrit Knight was attacked in the park two nights ago. Did you send the muggers to force my hand? To create a situation in which she was inexorably drawn back into our world?"

Hard-edged regret followed astonishment in Janx's jade gaze, answer enough, before a lazy smile slid into place and masked his true emotions. He drew breath to speak, and Alban made a short gesture, cutting him off. Janx's lashes lowered and he pursed his lips, echoing Alban's gesture more languidly. "I would have," he said, rather than lay claim to the devious behavior. "Weeks ago, if I'd thought of it. My compliments to you, Stoneheart. Who would have imagined you to have such a suspicious mind?"

"It seems I've been keeping bad company of late. Call off your favor, Janx. You know Margrit can't keep someone like Malik safe. Whatever game you're playing at has nothing to do with his life."

A corner of Janx's mouth turned up in slow wonder. "*Au contraire,* my old friend, it certainly does. Though you're right about Margrit being doomed to fail. It's a test."

"For Eliseo. To see how much she's worth. Call it off."

Janx brought his palms together in a lazy clap. "You've become sly, Alban. Whatever is the world coming to?"

"Janx."

"Do you want to bargain, Stoneheart?" Janx stepped away from his window to drag a folding chair from the table, whipping it around to sit on it backward. Alban watched Janx's theatrics without changing expression, and remained standing, knowing he loomed, even in his human form.

The dragonlord thrust out his lower lip. "Margrit is much more obliging than you are, Alban. She plays along."

"Margrit is human." Alban's voice dropped another register, scraping the bottom of a mortal vocal range. "I am less fragile than that."

"If you want to bargain, Stoneheart, let's be about it. What do I gain for releasing Margrit from the favor she owes me?"

"How long has it been, Janx?" The depth left Alban's voice, replaced by softness. "How many years?"

Jade eyes darkened and muscle tightened in Janx's jaw. "You know the answer."

"I want to hear you say it."

"Three hundred. Three hundred years and forty-two, since London burned and you swore an oath to men not of your race."

"Not men."

"We have no other word for ourselves. It's lost to time and human influence, if we ever had one. We have always been 'the people,' among our languages. Do not," the dragon said impatiently, "play word games with me, Alban. Your bargain. I would hear it."

Alban stepped forward, leaning on the laminate table. It creaked beneath his weight, as if he wore his gargoyle form. "My bargain was made three and a half centuries ago. Let. Her. Go."

Janx surged over the table, landing a hand's-breadth from Alban. Though more slender in build, the dragon-lord stood nearly of a height with Alban in his human form. For all that he moved gracefully, his breath came harsh and loud. "You would not." Green flame brightened and danced in his eyes, disbelief warring with outrage. "You cannot."

"Bad company, Janx. Perhaps I've learned something in all my years of exile, after all."

"Or in the last weeks, the world rejoined and rediscovered. You would not *dare.*" Uncertainty began to give way to fury, the color in Janx's eyes shifting from green to the shade of low-burning embers.

"All these centuries of exile, Janx. All for the sake of a promise made. I have nothing left to lose. Don't," he added abruptly, granite hardening his voice. "Don't try to hold Margrit over my head now, like a trinket whose life commands mine. If any harm comes to her, I have no more stomach for you or Eliseo or your ages-old games. I hold your secrets, Janx. If you want them kept, make Margrit's safety your priority."

Janx rolled his jaw, eyes dark with anger. "The favor's been asked and agreed to, Stoneheart. If I call it back, I've burned it up. Your little lawyer's too good a negotiator to let that go. And another of my men died tonight. I will not let Malik go unattended."

"Keep him from foolishness in the day and I'll keep him safe at night."

Janx pursed his lips. "How? I gave Margrit an impossible task. It's no easier for a gargoyle to watch over a djinn."

Alban shrugged. "So long as he carries his cane, I can track him, and I've never seen him without it."

"His *cane?* Do you have a deep sensitivity to baubles, Alban? I thought that was a dragonly trait."

"Avarice for baubles is a dragonly trait. Sensitivity to stone is a gargoyle's gift." Faint humor rolled through Alban when Janx's expression remained confounded. "The head's not glass, Janx. It's corundum. White sapphire. The easiest of any stone for my family to track."

A ripple of disbelief crossed Janx's face, heightening Alban's humor. He kept it contained, amused enough by the dragon's disconcertment to draw the moment out. "You thought it was glass. I never knew the dragonly trait for sensing wealth was nothing more than human legend. Malik must enjoy that."

"Admiring wealth is not the same as sensing its presence." Janx's voice was hoarse. "That stone is as large as his fist. Where did he get it?"

"I can't imagine. And if you want me to be able to track him, you won't ask, or he'll put it aside. Do we have an accord, Janx?"

Another spasm of avarice crossed the dragonlord's face before Janx visibly set aside his interest in the stone. "Split the favor. Margrit's duty in sunlight, yours by the stars. I have other reasons to keep that game in play." At Alban's slow nod, Janx fell back a step, a scowl fitting over his lively features. "Who taught you to fight, Alban? I don't remember this in you."

"You should." Alban's voice roughened again. "My brothers would never have trusted their most precious confidences to anyone weaker than themselves. Time's dulled your memory, dragonlord." He smiled faintly. "You should ask a gargoyle to remember for you."

Sudden greed flashed in Janx's eyes. "Oh, I intend to. I intend to, Alban. Like it or not, after all this time, you've chosen a side. You came to me, not to Eliseo." Greed faded into a sharp smile as he spread his hands. "Welcome home, Stoneheart. After so long, let me welcome you to the House of Cards."

NINE

HURRYING HOME THROUGH the park without the confidence of having her inhuman defender watching from above was more nerve-rattling than Margrit would have imagined. Bad enough to be without his protection; worse still to be dressed in work clothes, unable to run reliably. She unlocked the front door to her apartment building and stepped inside, a rope of tension released from within her shoulders, as if the door closing behind her made the world a safer place.

It wasn't cold enough outside to make her feel as numb as she did. Margrit climbed the flights of stairs to her apartment heavily, legs aching with the effort. It simply hadn't occurred to her that Alban might flat-out reject her request for help. That he might disappear into the night like a ghost, leaving behind nothing more than the certainty that this time he meant it: he would not return to watch over her. Without Alban she had no support amongst the Old Races, no one she trusted.

"Grit? Is that you?" The question sailed out of the kitchen almost before Margrit had the key in the lock, Cole's baritone carrying concern.

"Yeah. Sorry I'm late. I was at the office." Margrit

followed her housemate's voice to the kitchen and sat down on the stool next to the telephone.

Cole turned away from doing dishes, an eyebrow lifted dubiously, then both rising in surprise. "You really were. I figured you'd be running in the park."

"No." Margrit looked at her hands. "Not tonight."

"Maybe you should. Not that I want to encourage you to do stupid things, but you sound like the dog died." Cole picked up a dish towel, drying his hands, then folded his arms across his chest. "What's wrong?"

"I'm thinking about taking another job." The idea formulated as she spoke.

Disbelief shot Cole's voice into a higher register. "You're kidding. What, did a position open up in the D.A.'s office? I thought you and Legal Aid were bound in holy matrimony."

"Not with public services at all. I saw Eliseo Daisani yesterday, and he offered me a job again." Margrit's temples throbbed badly enough that she touched one, expecting to feel the vein popped beneath her skin.

"Elis—*the* Eliseo Daisani?" Cole asked, as though there were several possibilities, and as though he'd never said it before. Margrit smiled faintly, which did nothing to alleviate her headache. A headache was a malady, the sort of thing Daisani's blood should wipe away. Maybe it didn't work when the aches and pains were born of tension.

"That one, yeah. The very, very rich one."

"The very rich one who used to date your mother?"

Margrit winced. "If that's what they did, yeah, I guess so. I try not to think about why my mother knows him, Cole. You're not helping."

"Just wanted to make sure I had the right Daisani,

Grit." Cole crossed the kitchen to crouch in front of her, taking her hands in his. "Why in the hell would you do that?"

For a fleeting moment Margrit considered telling the truth: *I'm about to have a dragon pissed off at me for failing to protect his liegeman djinn, and the gargoyle I thought would help me has walked away. The vampire's all I've got left.* Daisani was the only person who could protect her if she failed to keep Malik alive. Moreover, if Daisani was behind Janx's lieutenants' deaths, maybe she could use herself as a bargaining chip to protect Malik. And Kaimana Kaaiai wanted her to be his courier between Janx and Daisani, anyway. Working for Daisani would only make that easier.

Margrit pulled her hands from Cole's and pressed them to her face. "I'm defending this guy," she said into her palms. "He's a complete bastard, a total son of a bitch. A rapist. The good news is I'm going to lose. Evidence is completely on the prosecutor's side, and my guy's too fucking dumb to take a plea. But I'm in there doing my best to get him off, because that's my job, and Jesus, Cole, what kind of job is that?" She looked up through her fingers, finding his worried eyes studying her. "I don't know. Maybe it's just finally getting to me."

The worst of it was that the argument sounded plausible to her own ears, and from the sympathy tempering Cole's expression, it resonated with him, as well. Margrit sighed. "Compared to that, a posh office with a park-side view and a big fat paycheck's starting to sound pretty good."

"Ah, c'mon, Grit," Cole said gently. "Daisani's building doesn't even overlook the park."

Margrit exhaled a soft burst of laughter, winning a smile from her housemate before he asked, "You eaten recently?"

"Um..." She tipped her head back, stretching her throat. "Not since lunch, I guess. I don't even remember if I ate lunch."

"Then you probably didn't. You never forget a meal." Cole pushed himself upright and went to the fridge. "Cam'll be home in a few minutes. You can have some dinner and we can talk about it. This is kind of out of nowhere, Grit, and you shouldn't be making decisions with low blood sugar." He left the fridge door open as he pulled leftovers out, taking a newly washed plate from the dish rack to pile scalloped potatoes and ham onto it. Margrit watched silently, trying to push down an overwhelming rise of emotion that made her nose sting and her chest feel full.

"I could do that myself, you know," she said thickly. "I'm a hundred-percent capable of using a microwave."

"You're fine where you are. Have you talked to Tony about this job change idea, Grit? Your parents? Russell?"

"Nobody. Just you." Margrit got up to close the fridge and leaned on its broad orange surface.

Cole glanced over his shoulder at her. "So you're trying the idea on for size."

"I guess." She folded an arm around her ribs and bent the other up, pressing her knuckles against her mouth. "Did you always want to be a pastry chef?"

Cole chuckled. "We're not making this about me, Grit. But yeah, I guess. I used to get under Mom's feet in the kitchen. By the time I was fourteen I did most of the baking at home."

Margrit dropped her knuckles enough to grin. "That must've gone over well with the guys."

"Remember I grew up in San Francisco. Everybody just assumed I was gay." Cole grinned back. "Actually, nobody cared if I was queer as long as I fed them, so it went over fine with the guys." His smile broadened. "It went over even better with the girls. Anyway, people were always telling me I should be a chef, but I wanted to bake, not cook, and it took forever to get the idea there were jobs specifically for bakers."

"Hence the dust-gathering business degree?"

"Pretty much. I thought it'd be good to finish that up in case baking didn't pay the bills. But yeah, it's what I've always liked doing. No mid-career crisis." The microwave dinged and Cole took a plate of steaming food out and slid it toward Margrit. "Your dinner, *madame.*"

"It's a little early for me to have a midcareer crisis. Thank you." She took a fork from the clean dishes and broke up the scalloped potatoes, leaning in to inhale the steam. Her stomach rumbled and she pressed a hand against it, laughing weakly. "Guess I'm hungry."

"You're always hungry. I've seen you eat a five-course meal and look for a snack twenty minutes later. I don't know why you don't weigh three hundred pounds."

"Because I run in the park every night," Margrit said reasonably. Cole made a face, then looked pleased as she took a bite of potato and sighed contentedly. "S'ferry good," she promised around the mouthful.

"Of course it is. Okay, Grit. Tell me something." Cole elevated an eyebrow in challenge and Margrit nodded agreement around another mouthful. "How much of this job change idea is about Tony?"

The bite or two she'd taken turned heavy in her stomach. Margrit straightened up, feeling heat come to her cheeks and doubting she could blame the warm meal. "Tony?"

"Yeah, Tony. The guy who called here four times this evening trying to invite you to dinner."

"He— Crap. I thought he was working. I thought— Why didn't he call my cell?"

"He did. You didn't answer."

"Crap." Margrit closed her eyes and pushed the food away. "I turned the ringer off while I was in court. I didn't see any messages from him when I checked earlier."

"It was hours ago now. So come on, 'fess up. How much of this has to do with him? I know you two've been trying to stabilize things."

"And my job's a sore point." Margrit looked back at the potatoes, unable to find an answer. The easiest one was to let Cole believe he was right. It rankled, though, in a way that pretending the morality of defending criminals bothered her didn't. *If* she'd been pretending. For a disconcerting moment, Margrit was unsure whether she had been or not. "I really hate the idea of giving up my job for a guy," she finally said.

"You would." Wryness colored Cole's response. "It's archaic. Nobody's going to give you a hard time, Grit, you know that, right?"

"Yeah." Margrit wet her lips and tried for a smile as she looked at her dark-haired housemate. Guilt stabbed her, though, and she dropped her eyes again. She hadn't lied, but she'd given Cole a neutral statement that could easily—obviously—be interpreted as an agreement to his hypothesis. It was a wonderful trick to pull off in a court. Using it against a friend made her feel tired.

And yet it was better than the truth. "Cole, don't say anything to Tony, okay? I need to talk to him myself."

"You mistake me for a busybody. That's Cameron." Cole jerked his chin toward the meal she'd abandoned. "Eat your dinner. Talk to your parents and Russell and Tony and get things figured out. And if you decide to go work for the richest man on the East Coast, when you get the Upper East Side penthouse apartment Cam and I are *totally* moving in with you."

Margrit laughed, surprise washing away some of her gloom. "But no pressure, right?"

"Absolutely none at all." Cole winked and turned back to the dishes, leaving Margrit to finish her dinner with thoughts of surviving the Old Races swirling in her mind.

"What do the gargoyles know of the selkies, Stoneheart?"

Janx asked the question without preamble, dancing a cigarette through long fingers and watching the casino below through the windows. Malik had appeared in the shadows, a smear against burnished walls. His glower and the throttlehold he had on his cane were more damning than words could be, making it clear that he resented Alban's presence. Alban, no happier about it, doubted the djinn would appreciate their solidarity.

He shifted his shoulders, making the hem of his coat swing. "I know as little as you do. They bred themselves out, disappeared into humanity. If there are full-blooded selkies left they're well-hidden and deeply secretive. Cara Delaney is the only one I've seen or heard of in decades." Though Margrit had mentioned a selkie, Alban recalled with a jolt. He hadn't thought to ask if it had been Cara, though using the phrase "accosted by" in reference to the slight girl seemed overblown.

"I didn't ask what you knew." Janx came to his feet and stalked to the windows, his impatience drawing Alban away from his thoughts. "I asked what the gargoyles know. Lore keepers, living memory, history-makers."

"Recorders," Alban objected. "Not makers. Even when I last joined the memory, the selkies were a dying race. You know that, Janx."

"I know that's what we believe. But that selkie girl came into my territory—"

"Yours?"

Janx shifted his attention from the casino to Alban, the weight of his gaze enough to give even a gargoyle pause as the air went still and hot around him. "Mine," Janx said in a low, even voice. "Do you contest my ownership, Stoneheart?"

"I only thought Eliseo might object," Alban said mildly, not intending it for an apology. Jade glittered bright in Janx's eyes before his lashes tangled, shuttering emotion. When he looked up again it was with the long-toothed smile that so often graced his face, and the heavy pressure in the room lightened.

"That's a topic for Eliseo and myself, and none of your concern, kind as you are to show it. Now, if I may continue without further interruption?" His eyebrows, half-hidden by falling locks of hair, arched, and he smiled another serpent's smile when Alban inclined his head. "I'm grateful. That selkie girl came here and now I sense a change in the currents. I would know how many of them are left. Ask the histories."

"Janx." Alban's gaze flickered to Malik, then back to the dragonlord. Janx fluttered a hand in a swirl of smoke, and Malik curled his lip before dissipating. Neither gargoyle nor dragon moved for several seconds, waiting for the djinn's scent to fade, proof that he was truly gone, before Alban said, "It is not my secret I protect by remaining outside of the gestalt."

"Gestalt." Janx laughed, bringing his cigarette to his lips. "What a very human word, Alban. After so little time, she's corrupted you so thoroughly. First in your loyalties, now in your language. Where will it end?"

Alban rumbled, deep sound bordering on a growl even from the lesser breadth of his human chest. Janx's eyes narrowed and he gestured with the cigarette again, following the swirl of smoke with obvious pleasure. "I've learned what I can about the gargoyles' memory-mind. You can enter and extract memories without leaving any of your own. Our old secrets will be safe."

"You've been misinformed." Alban turned away, watching the frantic casino below. "Entering the histories is never a process of only taking. The mental bonds that link gargoyles are fluid. Surface memories, the most recent or the most recently brought up, can be read and made part of the—" He broke off, then repeated, "Gestalt," with a note of defiance. "Willpower alone defines how much is read, and I am badly out of practice. An active seeker might pull more from me than I want shared."

"Are you claiming your will is weak, Stoneheart?" Janx's voice floated on the air, mocking and light. "After your earlier arguments? Do you now say a gargoyle who has held himself deliberately apart from the memories and minds of his people for three centuries is weak-minded? I would think such discipline would take extraordinary willpower, when done by choice instead of force."

"In time, it ceases to matter. I've become unwelcome in our memories, and without a clear show of repentance, an offering of my experiences will likely be driven out. I believe that's why Biali stays in New York," Alban added, more to himself than the dragon. "To enforce an exile I put on myself. He has reason enough to resent me."

"How delightful." Genuine good humor brightened Janx's voice for a moment. "The only two gargoyles on the planet holding a grudge match, and they're both in my employ. I do so love life, don't you? You work for me now, Stoneheart." Humor dropped, leaving heat without anger. "You'll pursue my request, and keep secrets safe at whatever cost. I want to know how many selkies are left, and if possible, what they're doing here. Find out, and tell me."

"Ask properly." Alban lifted his eyebrows in cool challenge as Janx's eyes popped with surprise. "There are rituals, Janx."

"And if I refuse?"

"Then I may also refuse." He hadn't required that Margrit follow the rituals when she'd sent him into memory to see what he could learn about his life mate's death. But Margrit was human, and the laws that governed the Old Races didn't apply to her.

All the more reason to keep away from her, and do what he could to make sure she remained as uninvolved as possible at this late hour. Alban waited on Janx, keeping his expression neutral. Those two things, at least, a gargoyle was good at.

After an exasperated moment Janx blew out a breath and muttered, "I come to the moonlit memory of our people to seek what we've forgotten beneath the burning sun. I come from fire born of earth and wind born of sky. My name is Janx, and I ask that you share history with me, your brother. Happy now?"

An ache clawed its way through Alban as Janx followed the form, then burst in an unexpected bubble of humor at the dragon's petulant ending. "Yes. Thank you."

Janx huffed another sulky breath and Alban dropped his gaze, half to hide a smile and half in acknowledgment of the loneliness the ritual had awakened. It had been centuries since he'd heard the phrases Janx had spoken. They'd left a hollow place inside him, so empty he hadn't recognized it until it was filled again. The promises he'd made so many years earlier weighed heavily, borne down now by a taste of regret he thought he'd long ago left behind. "I'll return when I have what answers I can bring you."

Wisdom, if it dictated anything, dictated that he retreat to Grace's hideaway and try from there to do as Janx… Alban hesitated over the next word, torn between *asked* and *demanded.* Duty and desire warred in him again: duty bound by his word, desire to reject that contract and disregard the dragon's wishes. Duty won, as it must; that was his nature, as profound a part of him as the wings that let him fly unfettered above city lights. Caution, the other god that ruled him, warned again against the poor wisdom of searching the memories beneath the open sky.

But a memory haunted him, the bleakness of mountain peaks and deep valleys that represented the overmind that belonged to all the gargoyle race. It had once been vivacious, a place of life and ever-growing knowledge, but too many had died. Terribly few of the peaks grew now, blunted by time and aging memory. Foothills, the memories of children, were few and far between: all signs of a dying people. Reluctance to enter that dour realm again drove Alban high through the city towers, as if remembering under the stars might help bring life back to what had once been a great repository of memory and legend.

All the history of the Old Races. Not just the remaining five, but innumerable other peoples whose light had faded as humans swept the planet. Exploration and settling was their nature, as much as solitude and contemplation was a gargoyle's. Humans had not meant, in the first many thousand years, to encroach upon habitat used by different peoples than themselves.

It had been far more recently that mankind began to hunt the legends: dragons and sea serpents, closely related but diametrically different. Wild men in the mountains, always few thanks to the harsh climate in which they existed, were hunted to the brink of extinction and beyond, until only tales of Bigfoot remained. Harpies, winged and bitter even before their female-heavy tribes were decimated, and the siryns whose songs were so haunting that sailors spoke of them even still. Vampires, hungry for the very blood that gave humanity life, were feared even more than dragons. Men who destroyed vampires were heroes among mortals.

All of their stories and more lay in the gargoyles' memories, in the minds of the one race bound so tightly to stone that daylight took life from them and left nothing but the protective state that could shield memory against even the ravages of time. That was the purpose of Alban's race, beyond all else: to preserve history.

His people had once gone amongst the others, listening to stories and opening themselves to their memories so histories might be fully recorded. They might be hidden from the world but they would never be forgotten, even as the unadaptable died and were lost to time.

Only the remaining handful had learned the precarious balance between pretending humanity and remaining true to their own natures. Of those, whole tribes of djinn remained in the deserts, riding sandstorms and acting out their hate against humanity in brutal raids that left reporters bewildered and humanitarians horrified. They were the most united, possibly the most populous, of the Old Races, but their ambitions were reined in by desert boundaries, more by choice than necessity. Humans were too many, and the Old Races, even together, far too few.

Gargoyles, after the djinn, still held the most numbers, but even those were countable: fewer than fifteen hundred when Alban had last known. The others diminished far more rapidly, with dragons counting in the tens or dozens, and the selkies thought to be all but gone. The memories carried more sorrow than joy now, their price heavy in emotion and heavier still in cost of daylight hours unshared with the rest of the world.

Alban settled on a building top, reluctance weighing his wings until he could fly no longer. Duty and desire tangled together, becoming more difficult to discern: the last price paid for bearing the memory of the Old Races. A plea for information carried in the gestalt was not to be refused.

He closed his eyes and let memory ride him.

TEN

SALT TAINTED THE air. Salt and the scent of fish, bound to the incessant roll of water against the shore. Such unfamiliar sounds and tastes verged on unpleasant to a creature born of inland mountains. The craggy peaks Alban was familiar with lay to the east, blue with distance created in his own mind. The landscape of memory could juxtapose unrelated features and moments in time without difficulty, but to navigate them required structure. It had been a relief to leave behind remembrances of the gargoyles themselves, the worn mountain range too much a shadow of what it had once been.

No barrier had risen up to bar his way this time. No challenge from Biali, the gargoyle set to watch over the exile. No dispute over whether Alban had a right to histories. Perhaps it was because he sought memory for another race, rather than for himself. Perhaps it was a sign of forgiveness, though Alban doubted it. Stone did not forgive easily.

He wheeled in the sky, watching a black echo of his own form flash over the village below. Young children ran back and forth at the water's edge, dragging sealskins with them and popping up water-sleek heads when the surf surged. A handful of indulgent older children, not grown enough yet to fish the waters and provide for the village, watched over them without worry; drownings happened, but rarely, amongst a people born to both ocean and earth.

This was their existence for centuries immemorial, a life of hard work and idyllic play. Time passed in a blur, children growing up, hunters lost to the seas mourned, the selkies' numbers increasing slowly, but more consistently than other Old Races had. Increasing enough that some of the more daring left their native shores to explore the world beyond.

Memory skittered, pulling Alban far away from the village below, until in the distance of his mind it seemed he hovered above a world pinpointed with water-blue light. Along coastlines where the children of selkie explorers had settled, bright spots gleamed then faded away, legend in the making. Within the bodies of continents another series of sparks lit up, earthier brown, and faded more rapidly.

Then bloodred tinged the whole of the world and Alban's focus was drawn down to a single representative village again. The waters turned brown with pollution, waste from human settlements. Human towns and villages encroached on selkie territory, driving them farther into the sea, farther from fishing areas, farther from sustainable life, until the soul of what they'd once been was diminished to little more than stories carried on the waves. Sorrow colored the telling of memory, one death after another, until a single old man stood alone on a windswept beach. Alban alighted beside him, settling into the comfortable crouch that was a gargoyle's hallmark, and waited.

"Thank you for coming. I know it's been a long journey, and now I have so little time before dawn." He gestured toward the east, where the sky already brightened with the first promise of sunrise.

"You've aged." The voice was not Alban's, the scrape of granite on granite, but something smoother: stone so hot it flowed, warmth emanating from every deep word. Confusion laced that comforting warmth now. "We do not age, my friend. The Old Races do not age."

"My mother was human, Eldred." The old man turned from watching the horizon and encroaching dawn to smile unhappily at the expression of shocked revulsion Alban felt shape his face. "I have stayed behind to tell you this. We are dying." He looked eastward again, shaking his head. "All of us are, we Old Races, but perhaps we selkies fastest of all. Is it so terrible?" He put his hands out, studying lines of age and thickened veins. "Is it so terrible to do what is necessary to ensure survival?"

"Humans." Disapproval roiled in Eldred's liquid voice. "Humans weaken what we are."

"And yet you never suspected." Glendyr lifted a still-strong chin, gentle defiance in the action. "Centuries of friendship and you've never imagined me to be anything less than one of our peoples. I prefer to let history judge us, rather than the passion of new knowledge. We're dying," he repeated. "With sunrise I go into the sea to join my family. We will not return. The selkies will live or die apart from the other Old Races, so that we might honor our living and our dead without censure from all. But history should know. Remember us, Eldred. Remember my people."

Glendyr bowed, fluid movement of a creature born

to water's weightless environment. His smile, as he straightened, was a thing of regret and love. Alban lowered his gaze, undone by the selkie man's grace, and Glendyr put a hand on his shoulder, a brief, easy touch. "Goodbye, Eldred."

He stepped back, scooping a seal fur from the sand and swirling it around his shoulders as he strode into the sea. Gray predawn gave him soft shadows as water drank his calves, his thighs, and then he dived forward into the small waves. A seal's head popped up in the first colored rays of morning, never looking back as Alban curled a hand against his thigh, a last motion before sunrise swept over him. His words lingered on the gold-drenched sea, and he hoped that Glendyr heard him before the waters closed over his head forever.

"Goodbye, my friend."

With the whisper, memory shifted again. In the two centuries hence no gargoyle had more than glimpsed a half-blood selkie, nor did any other of the Old Races come bearing tales of selkie survivors. Their desperate, hateful attempt to save themselves had wiped them out as surely as straightforward slaughter. Better to have died cleanly, lay the undercurrent of thought within the memories. Better to have gone the way they all would, with pride of people if not, in the end, the length of years.

Alban exhaled, eyes closed heavily as memory sloughed away. Dawn was dangerously close, the excursion into the whole of a race's history more time-consuming and draining than he'd feared. Too late by far to return to Janx; the story of selkie ruin could wait until evening. Even Grace's hideaway was too far to reach safely before sunrise took him.

Twice. Twice in a quarter year he'd been caught outside at daybreak, when for centuries past he'd hidden away safe from discovery during daylight hours. There was no blaming Margrit this time, but Alban lifted his eyes to the horizon with a smile regardless. The human woman was a bad influence, driving him to impetuosity that was wholly against his nature. He must relearn caution, or pay its price. And he would.

Later.

Stone took him.

Discussing the possibility of a job change with anyone, even Russell, was premature until she'd made sure the offer still stood. Margrit hadn't slept well, most of the night spent staring at the ceiling in the darkness, looking for a way around allying herself with Eliseo Daisani. Morning had come with only one other answer: Kaimana Kaaiai.

That thought still nagged at her as she pressed the button for the elevator she'd always taken up to Daisani's offices. It chimed pleasantly, but the doors didn't open. Margrit made a fist and thudded it against the seam with great care, as if she might discover an inhuman strength within herself if she let go of caution.

The fact that she stood in Daisani's building and not Kaaiai's hotel told her she'd made her choice even if her thoughts still ran in circles. Kaaiai had offered her more freedom within the context of her position amongst the Old Races than anyone else, but he'd also drawn Tony into their world, even if only superficially. Margrit had no doubt that Daisani would use her friends to manipulate her if he found it necessary, but so far he'd played a more honest hand than that.

The regards he'd passed on to her mother more than once suddenly struck her. He'd made no attempt to use that connection to encourage Margrit to work for him. She bounced her palm off the elevator doors more forcefully, then pulled her phone out of her purse to dial the vampire's number. "Your elevator won't let me in," she said irritably when he answered. A surprised silence follwed by, "Do forgive me. I'll have security override the lock," greeted her.

A moment later the doors opened and Margrit took the lift up to Daisani's offices, where he met her with an expression of restrained interest. "Miss Knight."

"Mr. Daisani. I never needed a security override before."

"I've expected you in the past, or have had an assistant between myself and the public. May I take your coat?" Daisani slipped it onto a hanger, settling it in a discreet closet before turning to examine her. "You look nearly as fine as you did at the reception. For me?"

"I'm in court forty minutes from now."

"Really," he said, clearly surprised. "I thought under the circumstances you might not be prepared for court."

Margrit glanced down at herself, taking in the trumpet skirt whose slender lines helped lend the illusion of height and femininity, and the cream silk blouse that played up her cafe-latte skin tones. Dangling earrings swung at the corners of her vision, though no corkscrew curls came loose from the low chignon she wore. "Circumstances? If you mean my clothes..." She sighed. "You're right. I'll be changing into something more formidable. Yes, for you."

Daisani's eyes lit with curiosity and he crossed to lean against his desk, arms folded across his chest as he studied her without speaking. Uncomfortable, Margrit returned the regard, then examined his office. Morning sunlight colored the sky behind him, glowing through floor-to-ceiling windows that ran the length of the room. Heavy red velvet curtains, fully open, hung from automated tracks at each end. Daisani's desk sat off center, making room—as if the enormous office might be cluttered otherwise—for a set of soft and comfortable couches facing the windows. Bookcases lay just beyond the seating area, arranged with hundreds of volumes and a handful of extraordinary knickknacks. Margrit's gaze slid to where a pair of selkie skins had been briefly pinned, glad to see an empty spot there. A bronze-cast bronco rider on the shelves caught her attention before she looked back at Daisani. "You've replaced the Rodin."

"Vanessa had chosen it. I have enough reminders, day to day, of her absence. You didn't come here to discuss the artistic decisions for my office, Miss Knight. I'm frankly bewildered as to why you *are* here, this morning of all mornings."

Margrit curled her water glass toward herself. "I need to know something that you're probably not going to tell me."

"A good lawyer should know better than to lead her witness that way, Margrit. Or are you hoping I'll succumb to a fit of contrariness?" Wariness encountered Daisani's tone, a caution Margrit was unaccustomed to hearing from him.

"Something like that. We're off the record, Mr. Daisani. You know Janx is losing his seconds-in-command left and right."

"Careless of him," the vampire murmured, his eyes

shuttering before he peeked up to judge Margrit's reaction to his teasing. Then his mouth twisted at the unamused expression she felt on her own features, an apology. "Not a morning for humor. Of course not. Forgive me. Yes, I'm aware."

"Off the record," Margrit repeated. "Is it you?"

Daisani stepped back, pure surprise turning him briefly vulnerable. "You came here today to ask me *that?* Oh," he added instantly. "Yes. Of course. I see why you would, under the circumstances. No, Miss Knight, it's not me. I can't say that I'm in the slightest bit dismayed—I may offer a reward to those persons responsible—but it's not me."

Margrit's fingers tightened around her water glass as she absorbed his response. After a moment she heard herself say, "Fuck," with quiet, precise clarity before she turned away from the vampire to find a seat. "Fuck. I believe you. I didn't think I would."

"Then why did you come here?"

Margrit breathed a laugh as she sat down. "So when you lied to me I would have a degree of moral high ground to stand on when I offered up a trade."

Daisani came to sit beside her, deliberately moving with human slowness. "A trade, Miss Knight?"

"Sure." She stared out at city rooftops. "It was going to be a very good trade. You were going to lie to me about being behind Janx's murders and I was going to accept your job offer in exchange for you sparing Malik's life."

From the corner of her eye she saw Daisani's jaw actually fall open a few centimeters. She glanced toward him as he pulled himself together, his spine straightening. "You've surprised me, Miss Knight," he said after a few long seconds. “I would never have imagined you to be so opportunistic, especially with the body still cooling. I’m caught between utter admiration and being completely appalled.”

Margrit’s stomach lurched and she came to her feet, cold sweat standing out all over. “Body? What— Malik can’t be dead.” Her heartbeat was suddenly loud and fragile in her ears. If the djinn was dead, those beats were numbered, and she had a frantic desire to count them, acknowledging each last one.

“Malik? No. My God. You don’t know.” Daisani stood as well, reaching for her elbow. “No, as far as I know, Malik is alive and well. It’s Russell Lomax, Margrit. He was found dead this morning at the Legal Aid offices, less than an hour ago.”

ELEVEN

MARGRIT LOST HER case, and lost it badly. The judge asked twice if she was interested in the proceedings, and Jacob Mills gave her more than one concerned glance across the aisle. She rallied a little for the closing arguments, but Jacob's obliterated hers. As she watched her client being led away, she only hoped she hadn't done so badly as to earn an appeal.

Tony met her just outside the courtroom doors. She stopped dead, taking in his drawn expression and the lack of color in his usually ruddy skin. "So they're investigating it as a homicide."

Dread washed out of Tony's features, replaced by dismayed relief. Margrit squeezed her eyes shut, unable to blame him for not wanting to be the one bearing bad news, and equally sympathetic to his sorrow that she'd already learned what he'd come to tell her. "*Are* they investigating it as a homicide? Or are you just here because I need you?"

"Both." Tony's voice cracked on the word and Margrit moved forward, walking blindly into him. He caught her and she knotted her arms around his ribs, trembling with the effort of holding on. People brushed by them, reporters and lawyers, witnesses and victims.

A camera flashed and the weight of Tony's arms lessened as he reached out. Margrit caught a glimpse of him putting his hand over the lens. The photographer swore, but backed off, and Tony tugged Margrit a step or two away. "C'mon. Let's get somewhere more private."

She nodded, letting him lead her from the bustle. Her heels clacked and echoed as they stepped out of the main hall into a quieter passageway. Tony turned to her then, expression still serious. "We don't know anything yet. We've been reviewing security tapes, but we haven't seen anyone unusual entering or exiting the building, at least not this morning. It happened early enough that we're pretty sure we've already talked to everyone who did enter the building through normal channels. We've started going through last night's tapes, and we've got somebody working on his case files."

"Is there anything I can do to help?" Margrit's voice sounded thick to her own ears.

Tony put his hands on her shoulders in gentle concern. "Probably not. Most of your office has taken the day off, Grit. Maybe you should, too. We just have to do our job."

"I could—" She swallowed. "I'd feel better if I could do something, even if it's trivial. Maybe I could…help go through case files."

"Margrit." Tony squeezed her shoulders carefully. "It's our job, not yours. I'll keep you as informed as I can, okay?"

"Yeah." She closed her eyes, then opened them again hastily, the tiny weakness too clearly a prelude to tears. "Thank you."

"No problem." He frowned until it looked like it hurt. Margrit reached up to run a thumb over his forehead, smoothing wrinkles, and his scowl turned to a weak, concerned smile. "You okay?"

"No." Margrit smiled just as weakly. "No, I'm really not, but I can't fall apart yet. Not here."

Regret spasmed over Tony's face. "I wish I could bring you home and take care of you for a while."

"It's okay." She summoned a better smile into place and squeezed his arm. "I'll be all right, really. I'll take a cab home and go to pieces on Cameron or Cole."

"Yeah. It's just, you know. I'd kinda like to be the one you go to pieces on."

"I know." Margrit stepped into his arms to hold on to him again for a long moment. "I know. But you've got to go to work and find out what son of a bitch did this. Be careful, Tony, okay? For me?"

"I'm always careful." Tony stole a kiss, then brushed his fingers over her cheek. "You be careful, too, okay? I'll let you know everything I can, as soon as I can. Walk you out?"

"Yeah." Margrit held still, though, making Tony turn back to her. "How did he— How…?" She took a breath as reluctance darkened Tony's eyes. "It's going to be in the papers anyway. I'd rather you told me."

"Yeah." Tony thinned his lips, then sighed. "He was suffocated. They don't even know with what yet."

Margrit lifted a hand to her throat, coloring with the recollection of struggling for air, and shuddered. "Okay. Thank you."

Tony frowned again, taking her hand and pulling her into another hug. "We'll get him, Grit. Whoever it is, we'll get him. C'mon. Let's get you in a cab to go home. I'll come by tonight if I can, all right?"

"That'd be good." Weary emotion knocked at Margrit's

heart, a brief wish that it might be Alban who'd see her that evening, but the gargoyle had made it more than clear that she was no longer his concern. Living in both worlds was impossible.

That, unexpectedly, broke her. A sob caught in her throat as Tony led her down the courthouse steps and hailed a taxi. "You'll be okay," he promised as he helped her into the vehicle. "Just hang in there, Grit. I'll see you tonight."

Margrit nodded, not trusting her voice. Tony gave the cabbie her address, then closed the door and stepped onto the curb to watch her go. She waved goodbye and slid down in the seat, keeping her eyes closed throughout the drive. A litany of disbelief ran through her now that the court case was no longer a distraction: "No, oh no," whispered over and over again. She tilted her head back, trying to stretch tightness out of her throat, and swallowed against the sting there, to no avail. The cabbie's voice telling her they'd arrived startled her, and she handed over a twenty and climbed out without waiting for the change. Reaching her apartment seemed like the only important thing to do; in its refuge she could let go of control for a few minutes and give in to grief and shock. For once she took the elevator, exhausted by the idea of five flights of stairs.

She let herself in quietly, as if the sound of the lock turning might send her flying apart. Closing the door just as silently took concentration, and when she had, she put both hands on the knob and rested her forehead against the door.

A high-pitched giggle broke the silence. Margrit's mouth turned up at the corner and she tipped her head toward her housemates' bedroom, glad she'd come in quietly. They'd get drawn into her misery soon enough. It would've been a shame to interrupt their time together by storming in. Margrit took a step back from the door, inhaling deeply.

Their bedroom door flew open. Cameron leapt out with a shriek that rang octaves above Cole's bellow from the kitchen end of the hall. Water sprayed everywhere to the whir of machine guns, with Margrit caught in the cross fire. She gasped, too startled to scream as Cameron's and Cole's shouts turned from glee to surprise. The machine-gun sounds ceased, as did the rain of water, and Margrit, dripping, looked back and forth from one to the other.

Cole wore boxers and nothing else, his black hair slicked with water and dropping into curls around his ears. He stood in a puddle on the kitchen floor and clutched a brilliant green water gun awkwardly, as if it might disappear if he held it still enough. Cameron, at the other end of the hall, wore a sports bra and boy shorts, her long blond hair plastered to her skin. Her machine gun was orange and she held it aloft, water running down her elbow toward the floor. Her eyes bulged with surprise, and her cheeks were flushed with laughter and embarrassment.

Margrit drew herself up and faced Cam, who stood only a few feet away. She put her hand out imperiously and Cameron, turning ever-pinker with guilt, handed the gun over. Margrit turned on her heel and stalked to Cole, her other hand extended. Cameron followed behind her, footsteps squishing in the damp carpet. Cole, looking mortified, gave Margrit his gun. She stepped past him into the kitchen, gun muzzles lowered, then looked back at her sheepish housemates.

"It's two in the afternoon," Cole mumbled. "What're you doing home, Grit?"

"That's, um, not a dry-clean-only outfit, is it, Grit? I'm sorry," Cameron said just as diffidently. "We didn't expect you to come home."

"It's not dry-clean," Margrit assured her, then lifted the guns and smiled at Cole. "I'm slaughtering you both, that's what I'm doing."

The guns whirred and shot bolts of water as Cameron and Cole split, both shrieking like children. Cole slid across the kitchen floor, crashing into the balcony windows with a shout, and Cameron disappeared down the hallway, returning seconds later with a much smaller water pistol, the trigger of which she pulled repeatedly as she waded forward against Margrit's onslaught. Cole sat down, howling with laughter and kicking his feet against the slick linoleum and Cameron wrested one of the machine guns from Margrit. The two women stood three feet apart, shooting water and laughing until the tubs were empty. Margrit threw hers away, cheeks and stomach aching, then passed a wet hand over her face. Hot tears warmed her fingers, high emotion shattering the defenses she'd gotten through the morning with.

"Margrit?" Cameron's hilarity fell away as Margrit's face crumpled, and Cole scrambled to his feet.

"Grit, what's wrong?"

Margrit took a shaking breath, trying to control herself. "I'm home early because Russell was murdered this morning."

Cameron's arms closed around her, and Margrit began to cry.

"What I really want to know," Margrit said a while later, still sniffling, "is where you got the water guns."

Cole, who'd pulled a T-shirt on and brought Cameron

a robe, ducked his head and smiled. "Chef brought them in this morning. His oldest turned twelve yesterday and they had a blowout water fight birthday party. Everybody was supposed to go home with one, but some of the parents wouldn't let them, so he brought the spares in to work."

"Bet getting rid of them was his wife's idea, not his." Margrit rubbed her wrist under her nose. The couch sucked her in, even with Cameron's arm around her shoulders.

"Yeah," Cole said. "Women. They're no fun." Cameron flicked a finger in Cole's direction and he smiled again. "Valkyries don't count."

"It's good to be on a pedestal." Cam hugged Margrit. "You okay, hon?"

"No. I'm exhausted. I want to go to bed and sleep for about three days. I completely blew the case this morning." Margrit shook her head. "And I've got to…I don't know. I should find out what's going on with work. See how people are doing."

"They're probably doing about like you are, Grit. Russell was a good guy. Even when he pissed you off." Cole looked rueful. "Which he did a lot."

"Yeah, I keep thinking about that. The stunt he pulled with the Daisani building up in Harlem, you know? The whole public perception thing. Pretty black girl makes good, gives back to her community by defending a squatters' building. Never mind that I grew up in Flushing with a zillion dollars. What mattered was selling the image. I was so angry. 'Course, I learned to play that card, too. Cara Delaney would've made such a great witness. She looked so fragile. Everybody would've loved her and hated Daisani."

Cameron hugged Margrit's shoulders. "Well, that's what a good lawyer does."

"What, plays the hypocrite?" Margrit laughed, perilously close to tears again. "I know. He was a good teacher. Yesterday he was getting all over my case about my career path. I can't believe he's dead." She put her hands over her mouth, her fingers icy. "I thought he'd be around forever." A miserable smile moved her fingers. "Or at least until I took his job."

"Ah, c'mon, Grit. You have bigger plans than Legal Aid, don't you?"

Kaimana Kaaiai's broad face flashed in Margrit's mind, bringing a cascade of images, all the men and women of the Old Races she'd met. She curled a lip, their thoughts unwelcome in the face of loss. Unwelcome, but pointed; Kaaiai's request lent her an opportunity for *bigger things* on a scale Margrit could barely find an equivalent to in the human world. "I guess so."

"Thought so." Cole got off the couch, scrubbing his fingers through his hair and creating a poof of loose curls. "Why don't you take a nap and I'll make something fantastic for dinner and we can all go out afterward and get shit-faced?"

"You know," Margrit said after a moment, "I can't think of a single reason why that wouldn't be a good idea. Cam?"

"Aside from being a teetotaler, nope. I'll bloat myself with ginger ale." Cameron nudged Margrit off the couch. "Go rest. I'll wake you up if Tony or anyone calls."

"Thank you." Margrit got up and headed for her bedroom, peeling half-dried clothes off as she went.

* * *

"Margrit?" Cam scratched on the door and pushed it open, voice quiet and apologetic. Margrit rose up in bed with a sharp breath, sleepily confused as to where she was. "Hey," Cameron said softly. "Sorry. You've got a phone call."

"Tony?" Margrit scrubbed her hands over her face and swung her legs off the bed, trying to wake up.

"No, he says his name's Kaimana Kaaiai. Isn't he—"

"Yeah. The guy I met at the reception the other night. What time is it?" Margrit squinted toward her clock. "God, I've been asleep two hours? Feels like about three minutes." She got to her feet, and thrust her hand out for the phone imperiously.

Cam handed it over. "Yeah. I'm sorry, but I thought you might want to talk to him."

"No, it's okay. I was expecting a call."

Cameron nodded and waved goodbye as Margrit brought the phone to her ear, wishing she sounded more awake as she said, "This is Margrit."

"Margrit, hello, Kaimana Kaaiai here. I'm sorry to call at such a bad time."

"No." Margrit shook her head and reached for a pair of jeans, trying to wake herself up through action. "It's okay. Nothing you can do about it." She'd traded sounding tired for brusqueness, and couldn't decide if it was an improvement.

"Still, please accept my condolences."

"Thank you. Mr. Kaaiai, if you have a little time this afternoon—"

"Please call me Kaimana."

Margrit took a deep breath and held it a moment, trying to work civilization back into her tone. "Kaimana.

Thank you. If you've got time this afternoon, or if I can meet up with Cara, that'd be great. I forgot to set up a time to do that yesterday." For a moment the impulse to crawl back into bed and pull the covers over her head assailed her. It seemed impossible that it had only been yesterday that she'd remet Cara.

"Just what I was going to suggest. Marese has cleared my schedule. You could come over, or I could drop by."

"Here?" Margrit coughed in horror. "I live in a shoebox apartment with two friends, Kaimana. It's great for us, but it's a little underwhelming for you."

Kaimana chuckled. "I wasn't always rich, Margrit. But if you'd be uncomfortable with me visiting, come to the hotel. We'll have an early dinner."

Margrit looked at the jeans she'd pulled on and swallowed a sigh. As if he'd heard, Kaimana added, "In the room, if you like. No need to dress up."

"That would be great. Something light," Margrit said, mindful of Cole's offer to cook for her. "I'll be over as soon as I let my housemates know, and catch a cab."

"I look forward to it." Kaimana hung up and Margrit put the phone down, staring mindlessly across the room for a few seconds. Then she shook herself and got a box out of the closet, unfolding tissue paper to check the state of the sealskin she'd been keeping safe. The fur was never as soft as she expected it to be, though it looked rich and comforting. Satisfied with its condition, she closed the box and pulled a fitted T-shirt on before leaving her room for the kitchen, where the scent of a red sauce was starting to fill the air.

"Hey, look who's awake. You get any rest?" Cole

turned away from the stove to smile at her. Margrit wobbled a hand.

"A little. I've got to run an errand. I might be late for dinner, but if there are leftovers I'll be grateful, okay?"

"We can wait, if you want."

"Nah." Margrit managed a small smile of her own. "You know how Cam gets if she doesn't eat regularly. *Moody,*" she intoned.

"In the same way grizzlies are moody."

"I *heard* that!"

They both laughed, Cole calling, "I looove you," toward the living room. Cameron snorted and Margrit went to find shoes, her heart lighter than it had been all day.

Had she chosen another pair, she reflected as the city crawled by, she might have walked to the Sherry faster than she'd arrive in a cab. There was no rush hour in New York, only brief spates when the crush lessened. Six in the evening was not one of those times. Margrit frowned at the low backless heels she'd put on as if it was their fault she'd chosen them. Concentrating on them gave her something less debilitating to think about than the day's events, but she was grateful when the cab pulled up to the hotel and she could put off emotional warfare with social niceties. Marese let her into Kaimana's suites with the same deadpan expression as before, and Kaimana himself turned from a small table by the balcony.

"I went ahead and ordered some appetizers. If there's nothing you like I can always call for more."

"It'll be fine. Thanks." Margrit smiled and shook the selkie's hand. "Is Cara here?"

"I'm afraid not. She's attending to some other business for me." Kaimana nodded toward the box Margrit carried. "If you'd like to put that aside, I'll be delighted to deliver it to her."

Reluctance clutched Margrit's heart and she hugged the box, then wrinkled her nose and balanced it on the couch corner. It didn't matter who gave it to Cara, as long as the selkie girl got it back. "I hope I'll get a chance to see her again. Is she part of your entourage now?"

Kaimana gestured to the table, then held Margrit's chair for her. "My entourage. What an idea. But I suppose so, in a way." He took the seat across from her, eyebrows arched as he lifted a bottle of white wine. Margrit made a moue and nodded, and Kaimana poured two glasses as he spoke. "I'm sure you'll see her again. In fact, that's something I wanted to discuss with you, in a roundabout way."

"Cara?" Margrit lifted the glass and took a small sip of wine, then did a double take. "That's very nice."

"It should be. I think it's older than you are." Kaimana smiled at the startled expression Margrit felt cross her face, then brought the conversation back on topic. "Less Cara than the others, but you'll certainly see her again. I'd like you to arrange a meeting with Janx and Daisani. Somewhere public."

Margrit set her wineglass aside with a sound of disbelief. "Janx and Daisani don't meet in public, Kaimana."

"I have confidence in your resourcefulness."

"*Why?*" Margrit cut his answer off before he spoke. "Not why do you have confidence, although I'd like to know that, too, but why in public? You're not as rich as

Daisani, but it can't be good for your image to be hanging around with people like Janx."

"If I were concerned with my human image, you'd be right, but this isn't about my mundane existence. It does have to be public, somewhere easily accessible, and ideally somewhere that crowds gather. I'd prefer not to tell you the details, for your own sake."

"There's no way not knowing is going to make me safer."

Kaimana narrowed his eyes in thought. "In this case, I think it might. It allows you to plead ignorance, which might be the wiser course."

"You want me to *lie* to Eliseo Daisani and Janx—" Margrit broke off in turn, realizing she'd never heard the dragonlord referred to by a second name. "And Janx? Are you nuts? They'd kill me. Both of them. They'd take turns."

"Not lie. Misdirect. And I think I can guarantee they won't be interested in you once we've met. They'll have other things on their minds."

"It's the 'I think' part that makes me nervous." Margrit picked up an appetizer and bit into it without looking to see what it was. Heat flooded her mouth, bringing tears to her eyes, and Kaimana nudged a wineglass toward her. She took a swallow that did no justice to the vintage and wiped her eyes as alcohol cut through the hot oils. "Why would I agree to this, without knowing what your plan is?"

"Because I believe the end result will rattle the sea floor and change will ride on the tide, and you think we must change or die." Kaimana waited a moment, watching her, then nodded as Margrit felt reluctant agreement settle over her. "Tomorrow, if it's possible, Margrit. Set the meeting for tomorrow night."

* * *

Margrit climbed the steps to her apartment and let herself in, rubbing the back of her neck as she did so. The lingering scent of sauce and grilled meat made her stomach rumble, reminding her she'd eaten only a bite or two at the hotel. "Anybody home?"

Voices fell silent in the living room, then picked up again with, "There she is," and, "In here, Grit." She kicked her shoes off and walked barefoot through the kitchen.

"I could use another eight hours of sle— Mom?" Margrit blinked in surprise as her mother stood up from the easy chair Cole normally claimed. Cole scrambled to his feet as well, old-fashioned manners coming through as they always did when Rebecca Knight visited. Margrit had never been able to decide if she was relieved or distressed that other people found her mother as intimidating as she did.

Rebecca looked out of place in the mismatched apartment, her elegant fragility more suited to museum halls as a sculptor's masterpiece. Her fine-boned, narrow figure lent her an illusion of height, and while Margrit had learned her dress sense from her mother, Rebecca's tailored suits always hung better and enhanced her cafe-latte skin's warmth better than anything Margrit ever wore. A few dark freckles across her nose were her most humanizing factor. When she blended those away with makeup and took her hair down for an evening out, Rebecca Knight became the equivalent of a screen goddess to her daughter's eyes. Margrit had always had the half-formed idea that Rebecca's refinement came from her outward form, and that her own lusher curves made her hopelessly earthy in comparison to her polished mother. Wearing jeans and a T-shirt, even a dressy one, while

Rebecca wore a fitted suit, made the idea stand out in relief in Margrit's mind as she hurried to give her a hug. "Mom, what're you doing here?"

"I was in the city today and heard about Russell on the afternoon news. I thought I would come over and see if you were all right. Why didn't you call me?" Rebecca put her hands on Margrit's shoulders and looked her over.

"I had a court case this morning," Margrit said inanely. "I just didn't think of calling. I'm sorry. Thank you for coming."

"You're welcome. Are you all right?"

"I'm okay, all things considered. Still really tired." She pressed a hand against her forehead. "I lost my court case."

"You wanted to lose it, didn't you?" Rebecca asked.

"Yeah, but I wanted to lose it because evidence was on the prosecutor's side, not because my boss wa—" Margrit cut herself off, not trusting emotion to remain steady. "Did you let Daddy know?"

"I did. We thought maybe you could come out to the house this weekend and get away from the city for a little while."

"Maybe next weekend. I don't know anything yet, but I imagine Russell's—" Margrit swallowed to strengthen her voice. "Russell's service will be this weekend. I'd like to come out," she added more quietly. "I could go to church with you and Daddy. I'd like that."

"All right." Rebecca kissed her cheek, looking pleased. "Now, would you like me to stay? I'm in the city again tomorrow anyway."

Margrit smiled a little. "No, it's okay. I think Cameron

and Cole have got me covered. I'm going to eat something and maybe we'll go out for a while and…" Her smile faltered. "And have a drink to absent friends."

"All right. Bring Tony along next weekend, if you like." Rebecca smiled toward Cameron and Cole before Margrit walked her to the door. The moment it closed behind her, Cam appeared in the kitchen doorway.

"'Bring Tony along,' eh? Is that a parental capitulation I hear there? I thought she didn't like Tony."

"I don't know what it was. She must feel really bad for me." Margrit shook her head. "She doesn't dislike Tony. How could she, really? He's a great guy. She just wishes her daughter would date a black man instead of a golden-brown one. My mother the activist. Even romance is a political statement. I mean, I understand where she's coming from. She grew up in the sixties and she was one of the first black women stockbrokers at her firm. But what'm I supposed to do, dump Tony because his family's from a few hundred miles farther north than ours?"

"Nah," Cole said from the kitchen. "You two find plenty of other good reasons to dump each other regularly without getting political. Besides, his family's been on this continent as long as yours has. You can get married and have cute little melting-pot American kids, instead of African-Italian-American kids. All those hyphens would send them to tears."

"Besides, the acronym sounds like a scream. AIA!" Cam flung her hands up dramatically, earning a quick laugh from her housemates. Cole looked around the doorjamb over Cam's shoulder. "You want me to heat up your dinner, Grit?"

Margrit hesitated. "I was thinking I might go for a run."

"It's seven-thirty! It's dark out!"

"I know. I'll bring my pepper spray and my phone, and I'll call if I'm not going to be back in an hour." Margrit pulled her shoes on, glancing apologetically at her friends. "I really need to run, guys. I'll be careful, I promise."

"You better be, or I'm going to tie you to a bungee cord so you can't get past the door." Cameron raised a fist threateningly and Margrit smiled.

"Good to know you care. Back in an hour, I swear."

TWELVE

MARGRIT TOOK THE stairs down to the street two at a time and swung around the door frame on the way out of the building, trying not to think. The jog up 110th brought her to the park already warmed up, and she stretched out into a run as she reached the paths. Habit born of safety measures kept her gaze ahead of her and glancing around, something she'd abandoned for watching the sky when she knew Alban was there. The gargoyle's absence, Russell's death, Janx's ultimatum: everything felt off-kilter and reluctant to be buried in physical movement.

An exhausted laugh burst free from Margrit's lungs. She hadn't thought of Janx or his second-in-command since Daisani's bombshell, and she hadn't gotten what she'd hoped to out of the vampire. Without some kind of support from the Old Races, she couldn't imagine how she might hope to protect Malik. She couldn't even protect ordinary people.

Her hands knotted into fists, throwing her stride off. Russell's death wasn't her fault. Where that guilt came from, she didn't know; even if she'd gone to work early to talk to him, she'd have been more likely to get herself killed than to have saved him. Daisani's bloody gift helped her heal quickly, but didn't give her a vampire's speed or a gargoyle's strength. She was hardly a match for most assailants. Her guilt came from an irrational assignation of culpability, but even teasing herself with what Cole called "fancy lawyer talk" didn't lessen the regret tightening her heart.

Barely past the playground, a thick stump of a man crouched by the pathway, his position so natural it seemed as if he belonged there, more decorative than a living person. His white hair, cropped short, glowed beneath the park lights, wind stirring it in the only indication that he was more than a statue. Glad to be distracted from her own thoughts, Margrit swung wide, as if a few feet might make the critical difference should he spring from his crouch. She stretched her stride out, putting on speed before her name came after her through the night. "Hey, lawyer. Knight. Margrit Knight."

She turned to run backward a few steps, then stopped at the edge of the path, yards away from the man who'd called her name. He remained where he was, shoulders hunched and head lifted to meet her gaze. Distance and darkness smoothed the ravages of a scar on the left side of his face, but memory told Margrit that his eye there was nothing more than a closed pit. Disbelief laced her voice. "Biali?"

The squat man pushed out of his crouch, muscles in his arms playing like an aging prizefighter's. "Yeah."

She crossed the path, coming to stand within a few feet of the blunt man. He was taller than her, though not nearly as tall as Alban. "What are you doing here?"

"Running errands for Janx. He wants to see you. C'mon."

"Where's Alban?" Margrit bit her tongue too late, angry at herself for asking. Alban had made his choice clear enough: he wouldn't be looking for Margrit on anyone's whim.

Impatience and dislike creased Biali's scarred face, reminding Margrit that it had been Alban who'd left that mark on the other gargoyle. "Why should I know? Come on."

"I haven't gone for a run in two days," Margrit protested. "You're here. Wait for me. I'll be half an hour."

"Wait for you. While you run around in Central Park. Are you trying to get yourself killed?"

"You can keep an eye on me." She pointed upward, winked and started running without waiting for the outraged exclamation that followed her.

Flying with Biali was *not* like flying with Alban.

Neither of them were happy about it. Biali kept his head turned away, as if an unpleasant odor lingered. Margrit, not trusting his grip on her waist, deadlocked her wrists around his neck, her own teeth bared out of determination rather than delight. There was none of Alban's gentle surety in cornering or catching drafts, no warning in the way Biali held her that they were about to climb or fall through the sky. Flight with Alban had been an exercise in freedom, joy undiluted by the hammering of her feet against the earth as it was when she ran. Flying in Biali's arms was a study in refusing to scream.

It had been his idea. Margrit had stared disbelievingly, just as he had when she'd announced her intention to run in the park. It was faster, he'd argued, and more to the point, didn't force him to use human means of transportation. His mocking, "You're not afraid, are you, lawyer?" had driven her to agree.

Not afraid, but very glad to have her feet touch down on the roof of the House of Cards and for Biali to release her. He did so with a peculiar expression, before nodding his head slightly, as much of a gesture of respect as she'd ever seen from the scarred gargoyle. Margrit gathered her voice enough to say, "Thanks for the lift," before looking for an escort inside.

"I'm all you rate." Biali stumped ahead, yanking open the steel roof door with casual ease and not bothering to see if Margrit followed him. He transformed before the second door, an implosion of space shivering the air, and it was a stocky man in jeans and tight a T-shirt who led Margrit through the building to Janx's alcove.

Janx sat just as he had the first time Margrit met him, leaning back in a metal folding chair with his long legs propped on the table and crossed at the ankle. His hair, falling in dark red lines across his cheeks, played up smoldering anger in eyes gone darker green than she'd seen them before. There was no languid grace in the way he moved his hands or head, though thin smoke whirled after those motions in its usual slow dance. Heated air burned Margrit's lungs, and her throat convulsed with the struggle not to cough.

"You have a strange way of showing your loyalty, my dear." The customary warmth was gone from Janx's voice, leaving controlled rage to replace it.

Nerves hollowed her belly again, sickness that was beginning to feel familiar. "Malik's not dead, is he?"

"Not at all. In fact, I was sent a dispatch this afternoon that informed me Malik was under the express protection of Eliseo Daisani, and that any injury that came to him would be considered an act of war. I understand you're also to be congratulated on your new employment, but under the circumstances I feel strangely reticent."

Margrit laughed, a shrill sound of shock, then forced herself to move forward as if the air didn't want to hold her back. Difficult, but not impossible; job training had taught her not to show fear if it was at all possible to hide it. Then again, it'd taught her not to show surprise, either, and she'd given that game away. There'd be hell to pay later, when she dealt again with Daisani, but for the moment she seized on the opportunity he'd created for her. "Really? It was practically your idea."

Janx kicked his feet off the table as she spoke, leaning forward with his hands clamped together until the knuckles whitened with passion. "I'm fascinated to hear how you came to that conclusion."

Margrit smiled and dragged a chair from the table, swinging it around on one leg so she could straddle it, and draped her arms over its back, a deliberate echo of how he had sat two nights before. "You gave me a Herculean task, Janx."

Something indecipherable slid through his expression, and cockiness grabbed hold of Margrit. "That means impossible," she explained, nearly laughing at her own audacity. Adrenaline made her dizzy, pulsing in her veins the way it hadn't even during her run. Russell's death was easier to put aside when she was suffused with the thrill of fencing with a dangerous opponent. Buoyed, she kept her helpful smile in place as insult and anger darkened Janx's pale golden skin to ruddy. Even the smoke lingering around him seemed to thicken, disturbed by his deliberately slow inhalation.

"My people know better than yours what *Herculean* means, my dear, and let me warn that you tread on lava shells."

Curiosity bumped cockiness out of the way. "I get the idea, but lava shells?"

"The thin surface of magma exposed to air and hardened into a crust. It appears trustworthy, but cannot be walked upon, Margrit. Humans might survive a fall through thin ice into a frigid lake, but you will not survive a plunge into lava."

"Right." Some of her invulnerable edge fell away and she reached for it again, keeping her voice clear and direct. "You said to protect Malik through any means necessary. I don't have the capability, physically, to do that. So I went to the source of the threat as you defined it, and negotiated. *Et voilà.*"

She spread her hands, mimicking one of Janx's own gestures, and hoping she masked her own perplexity. Daisani hadn't agreed to the proposal she'd barely made, but she doubted his offer to protect Malik was altruistic. "You didn't give me a how-to manual, Janx. You just said to do it. But I want to know something."

"Another favor, Margrit?"

"No. I just want to know why you didn't tell me Kaimana Kaaiai was a selkie. Did you know—" She gave a thin laugh as Janx's eyes lost their animation, going flat and dark as a snake's. "You didn't know. I thought you must not. If you'd known and hadn't told me, I'd…"

A hint of life returned to his face. "You'd what? I wonder. Scold me fiercely?"

"Something about that effective, probably. It seemed childish, knowing and not telling me. I think more highly of you than that."

Janx's eyebrows flicked up. "I have no idea why."

Fully aware the dragon would hear her, she muttered, "Neither do I," then spoke in a more normal tone. "Kaaiai doesn't seem like the type to be skulking around killing your men. Why risk his status?" A knot of horror bound itself below her breastbone. It hadn't occurred to her that Kaimana might want Janx and Daisani in the same place so he could easily rid himself of them.

No. Long gone from the others or not, selkies were of the Old Races, whose law prohibited killing their own kind. Even if the selkies ignored that law—they were already exiles—Kaimana wouldn't have requested a public setting if he had murder on his mind.

"And yet knowing this, that I believe selkies are the tool used to eliminate my men, knowing that there was a selkie in our midst, you chose to bargain with Eliseo, and not Kaaiai."

"I had something Daisani wanted." Half a dozen other explanations came to her lips as well, but Margrit held them back, trusting the simplest statement to be the most effective. "And you have something Kaaiai wants."

"I do?" Dangerous curiosity piqued in Janx's gaze. "A roster of those most important to me, perhaps, so he or his people need not work to determine it themselves?"

Margrit smirked. "I don't think so. I don't actually know what. He just asked me to have you meet him tomorrow night at the Rockefeller Center at eight o'clock."

"And why would I do that?"

"So you can find out what's going on. You're the one who said a balance had changed, Janx. You're the one who changed it. Maybe you're going to have to reap what you sowed."

Admiration curled the corner of Janx's mouth, while his eyes remained a hard jade. "My dear Miss Knight, was that a threat?"

Tension sluiced out of Margrit in a quick laugh. "Oh, God, I hope so. I love the idea of threatening you boldfaced. Me. L'il ol' human me."

Janx watched her, unblinking, until her own eyes started to water. It took effort to not turn her head as she let her eyelashes shutter for a moment. In that brief instant, Janx's expression changed, so when she met his gaze again he was smiling. Margrit lengthened her neck uncertainly. "What?"

"How delightful. You so brave, and making so many meetings and manipulations on your own. So much effort on his part, all for nothing." Janx sat back, picking up a cigarette and waving it in the air with lazy contentment.

"On whose part? What are you talking about?"

"Alban, obviously."

Margrit tilted her head, uncomprehending. "Alban dumped me, Janx. Whatever he's done, it's got nothing to do with me."

"On the contrary, my dear. It has everything to do with you. You must understand the scale of time we are discussing, Margrit." Janx's voice softened, as if he spoke to a child. "Your country was not yet founded when Alban chose to stand apart from his people's collective memory, and less than thirty years old when he folded himself in grief and turned his back on all the Old Races. We're speaking of an era when the fastest method of communication was handwritten letters sent on sailing ships from one continent to another. A time when wars were fought with erratic muskets and horse cavalry. Slavery was still a way of life."

"Slavery is still a way of life all over the world, Janx." Margrit refused to look down and mark the color of her own skin, keeping her gaze forthright on the red-haired man's. "What's your point?"

Janx set his cigarette aside and leaned forward, hands clasped together on the table in front of him. "I only want you to understand how extraordinary it is, then, that your true and brave Stoneheart has come to me and offered his services, all in the name of releasing you from your favors to me."

At some juncture, the ability to feel shock had to burn out and leave her unable to reel with another hit. At some point, but not yet. Margrit swayed with the impact of Janx's words, hearing herself ask, "Did it work?"

"Yes and no. A gargoyle is useless at daylight security, but the nights, at least, you need not worry about Malik."

"Not that I'm ungrateful, but why?" The back of her head felt slightly detached, as if surprise had taken up residence there and was having a look around on its own. She laced her fingers against her skull, trying to hold herself together. It was an obvious tell, the kind of thing she'd never allow herself to do in court.

Janx's chair creaked as he leaned back, folding his own hands behind his head in a much different display of body language. "Isn't it romantic?" he asked happily. "The lonely gargoyle, sacrificing his principles to render services to an enemy over the love of a mortal woman. His condition—free her from the favors she owes me, and he will be my slave." The last words turned into a purr. Janx kicked back in his chair, and smoke dipped and swirled around him, coloring the air. Margrit stared unseeing at the whorls as Janx offered her a broad, delighted smile. "It's the stuff of fairy tales, don't you think, my dear?"

"Yes, but *why?*"

Janx kicked forward again, beaming openly. "To tell the truth, he only negotiated the one favor away. Malik's safety, and that at night. But you, clever girl, have taken care of the daytime details, haven't you, and built a multitude of other conniving schemes on top of that. I'm afraid the third favor is still your burden, though. Stoneheart's strengths do not lie in making bargains. So I still hold your mark, and now have Alban at my beck and call. Why *not,* my dear? Why ever not? And the very best part is that now you know he brought me the rope to hang him with because of you. Because in knowing, you'll find your loyalties drawn to me, in order to protect the good and noble Stoneheart."

"My loyalties?" Margrit broke into skeptical laughter. "You think blackmail begets loyalty?"

"Not from the heart." Janx's smile went wide again. "I don't care if you curse me every night for the rest of your mortal life, Margrit. I hardly expect to win your love. But I will have your cooperation, and that, my dear, is enough. Especially with your new job. I'm reconsidering. I think that congratulations are in order, after all. My dear lady, you could hardly have made this easier for me. Eliseo," he said happily, "is going to spit."

"Do vampires do that a lot?" Her voice cracked again and Margrit swallowed hard, wishing for a glass of water. "It seems more like a dragon thing to me. Spitting fire and all that."

"That's because you don't know as much as you think you do." Janx was on his feet, coming around the table and offering his hands. Margrit took them without thinking, and he drew her up. His fingers were cool, but hers were icy, from panic warring with relief in her veins. Janx lifted them to his mouth, more to smile over them than brush a kiss against cold skin. Her hands went colder still, until Janx's felt hot. The smile he offered said he'd noticed both the permission granted and the chill that had overtaken her.

"You'll be my eyes and ears inside Daisani's corporation, Margrit Knight. How positively wonderful. You'll report back anything you think might be of the slightest interest to me, and I assure you, nearly everything Eliseo Daisani does is of interest to me."

"I just bet it is." Margrit took her hands from Janx's and turned away to rest her fingertips on the doorknob before she looked back. "Is there anything else?" She was vividly aware of having not been dismissed. Aware that she was making a play to change the power balance between them. Not to dominate it; that was beyond her scope. Just to change it, to press her advantage where she could, was enough.

Acknowledgment glittered in Janx's eyes as he recognized what she was doing. "You are so very brave, Margrit Knight. So very brave indeed. I believe that will be all, at least for the moment. Do remember the task I've set you to."

"Malik's safe, Janx. Daisani's my employer. If you want me to spy on him, I will, but that's your third favor. You might want to think hard about whether that's how you want to spend it." Margrit executed a short bow and exited the alcove with her heart throbbing in her throat.

THIRTEEN

"MARGRIT." ALBAN STOOD a mere handful of steps beyond the office door, his white hair colored to neon-blue and surprise clear in his voice. For a moment Margrit saw him as an outsider might: in his human form, his broad shoulders and alabaster skin were as discreet as they could be within the casino's walls. Even so, he looked dangerous in the manner of a big man—dangerous because anyone so well dressed and well coiffed in Janx's House of Cards was an employee. Mortals not privy to Janx's true nature still knew him for what he was in the human world: a crimelord, able to buy and sell people and their dreams as easily as others might buy and discard a newspaper. A man of Alban's physical stature and quiet grace was the sort who would be sent after bad debts and old loans. Even his coloring was a beacon of warning to the human mind, for no one so pale could be entirely natural. Human nature dictated two options when presented with something new and potentially alarming: retreat or explore.

Margrit reared back as if she'd retreat, then scowled at the door behind her. Janx's office provided nothing like a safe haven, and returning would lose her what little autonomy she'd just earned. Jaw set, she looked back at Alban, whose expression hadn't yet cleared. "Margrit, why are you here?"

"What does it matter?" Abrasiveness did nothing to keep emotion away. She wanted to dart forward and crash into the solidness of Alban's body, to find shelter in his arms, and wanting that angered her. "I got involved in your world, Alban. I can't get away from it now just because you make a couple of sweeping statements." She twisted to the side as she passed the gargoyle, trying not to brush his clothes.

"Margrit." Alban's voice arrested her. "It matters because Janx should have released you from your vow to protect Malik."

"Know what?" Margrit turned to face him, hands knotted at her sides. "Believe it or not, I got that covered, Alban. I dealt with it, so you went and broke your vaunted neutrality for absolutely nothing. Now, if you'll excuse me, I've had an incredibly bad day, and I need Biali to take me home before my friends start to worry."

"Biali?"

An unkind pulse of gladness swept her at Alban's tone. Out of everyone she might have admitted to relying on, Biali would cut the deepest, and Margrit knew it. She'd shared memories with Alban, giving her a sense of the female gargoyle both he and Biali had loved, and over whom they'd fought. It was petty to lash out with Biali's name as a weapon, but Margrit had a greater sense of injury than justice.

"I'm here, lawyer." The other gargoyle appeared at the end of the hall, arms folded against his thick chest as he leaned against the wall. Alban's eyes darkened and a nasty mix of smugness and guilt sizzled through

Margrit, the latter suddenly turning to a kind of hopeful desperation.

"What do you want from me, Alban?" She lowered her voice. "My life got turned upside down when I met you. Straightening it out is killing me, because I don't really want it to go back to the way it was. I don't want you to walk away from me. If I haven't made that clear, maybe it's because I don't know how the hell to make this work, either. What do you want me to do?"

"Carry on." Alban's gravelly voice scraped along her spine. "You seem to be doing well enough on your own." He stalked into Janx's office, the door crashing shut behind him. Margrit, fists clenched and eyes downcast, admitted she'd deserved that.

"Come on, lawyer." The acid usually present in Biali's voice was gone, replaced with a sympathetic note he seemed uncomfortable with. "He's not worth it."

Instead of saying *Hajnal thought he was,* Margrit held her tongue and let Biali take her home.

Janx turned with raised eyebrows and an expression of bemusement as the door slammed behind Alban. "Stoneheart."

"What's she doing here, Janx?" Alban made no pretense at calm, knowing himself for a bad liar at the best of times. "We had a bargain."

"Which I'm keeping. So, in fact, is she. Your word on Malik's safety in the darkness, hers in the daylight, and I'm impressed, if dismayed, at the hand she's played. Alban, my old friend, I do believe you're in a temper. I didn't even know you had one." Janx put a finger over his lips in an exaggerated gesture. "No, wait, of course you do. It was you who shattered Biali's face, wasn't it. How careless of me to forget."

Alban curled a fist against an invasive image of Margrit's dark warmth clasped in Biali's thick arms. Of all the things he'd imagined when he'd turned away from her, that she might go to his rival had never occurred to him. Biali didn't like the human lawyer, and Alban had thought the feeling mutual. To find himself wrong seemed to turn the blood in his veins to slurry, making each heartbeat thick and painful. "I want her out of this, Janx."

"You should have thought of that before you revealed yourself to her. You know as well as I do that there's no easy turning back once they're part of our world." Janx flicked a careless hand. "Oh, perhaps if she gathered her wits about her and ran far and long, but I don't think Margrit's the sort. Be done with her, Alban, and tell me what I want to know. We have," he added pointedly, "a bargain."

"I'm not your creature, Janx. Don't test me." Despite that warning, Alban drew a deep breath, then inclined his head. Janx had satisfied the rituals of asking that the memories be searched, and to do so and refuse an answer was outside of Alban's scope, outside his comprehension. "The selkies are gone. I have no other answer for you."

A shadow contorted Janx's features. "That's not possible."

"The last memory we gargoyles have of the selkies is their retreat into the sea, centuries ago. If you don't believe me, ask Biali."

"I have." Janx spat the admission, his face twisting when he saw Alban's surprise. "I know what I said. I didn't want to taint your answers. You're the less likely to amend your responses to thwart a rival, but I had to be sure. It's possible memories have been kept apart. Kept private."

Alban's broad shoulders moved in a dismissive shrug. "It is our custom to preserve specific personal memories from the whole, when asked. You know that better than most. But this last memory is one the selkies clearly intended to share. What's driving this, Janx? Not Margrit's selkie girl."

"She's only a harbinger." Janx stalked to his table and flung a folder across it. Alban stopped it with a fingertip and regarded the dragonlord for a long steady moment. Janx glanced away, as much apology for or admission of rudeness as he was likely to offer, and Alban opened the file.

Photo after photo showed human bodies lying in graphic displays of gruesome death, shredded and torn as though they'd been flailed. He turned the photographs over one at a time, studying each briefly before going on to the next. Four men, none of them familiar to him, but linked together by the manner of their deaths, if nothing else. Memory rose unbidden, whispering to him that one people among the Old Races used this method of killing. And yet it wasn't that race Alban put a name to, asking instead, "Eliseo?"

"You *have* grown suspicious, Stoneheart. How admirable. And yes, obviously, using the selkie girl's appearance as a cover." Janx leaned over the table and planted a finger on the pile of photos. "But why then would he agree to Margrit's terms?"

"Margrit's terms," Alban repeated heavily, certain

he didn't want to hear what they were, yet just as sure he should.

Janx looked up from the photographs of his men. "Oh, of course. Sleeping Beauty knows nothing of what passes while she slumbers. Margrit's gone to work for Daisani, Alban. How nicely your court is divided—thee for me, and she for he."

Stone's unyielding aspect rolled the words over his skin, refusing to absorb them. Alban had warned her more than once against accepting gifts from Daisani, against making bargains with Janx. It struck him that Margrit, too, could harden like stone, and let all the wisdom in the world slough off her. His eventual answer was half a question, and all weary regret: "For Malik's safety."

Janx flashed a smile. "As you say. It was clever on her part, annoyingly clever. And Daisani's agreed to her little plot, so I put it to you again. Why would he, if he were doing this?" He gestured at the photos.

Alban didn't spare them another glance, still working to comprehend the magnitude of Margrit's choice. He couldn't: what it meant for her to work with Daisani was beyond his ability to fathom, except that no matter what he did, she would never be free of the Old Races.

Complex emotion rose in him, cracking stone and leaving the flavor of rock dust in his mind. Relief. Dismay. Chagrin and admiration. He might have called her an enigma, but for the fact she wore her heart on her sleeve and revealed her intentions so clearly.

It occurred to Alban with slow clarity that he was, perhaps, a fool. A fool for pushing her away, and all the more of one for succumbing so swiftly to the most profound of those emotions climbing in him: hope. He shouldn't allow himself hope when it was he who'd broken off with her so deliberately, and yet. And yet.

He barely knew his own voice as he made an answer to Janx's question. "Revenge is said to be a dish best served cold. Perhaps having Margrit in his court—out of yours—is worth more to him than Malik's timely demise."

Janx darted a lizard-quick look at him. "Not a statement I would expect from you, Korund. Has she changed your worldview so dramatically, so quickly? I thought stone did not alter when it alteration found."

"'Nor bend with the remover to remove,'" Alban murmured. There was too much appropriate to the sonnet just then, and he closed his throat on more, saying instead, "You remember. Somehow that surprises me."

"We all remember," Janx said sharply, before his voice returned to its usual teasing lilt. "You fail to finish the stanza, my friend. Why is that?"

"My worth is not unknown, Janx, nor has it been for three and a half centuries." Interaction with humans changed everything. That was the reason for staying apart; it was how and why those Old Races who survived kept their identities, both individually and racially. Alban had clung to that belief for two hundred years, holding himself apart, uncorrupted, untouched by the human world.

And all around him, the Old Races had adapted, leaving him behind as a relic of a long-gone way of survival. A life outside the shadows had seemed an impossibility for someone such as himself, and he had been content to live in the darkness. This wanting, this desiring something more—gargoyles did not find themselves in such a position. Alban sighed, turning his attention back to Janx. "She said she met a selkie a few nights ago."

"Kaimana Kaaiai. A philanthropist," Janx said distastefully. "He's helping the city turn our speakeasy into a tourist showcase. Too rich to be tempted by much Eliseo could offer, and presumably not stupid enough to start hunting my men in traditional selkie fashion. It's not impossible, but I'd consider it improbable. And his visit's been planned for weeks. Daisani's had time to set it up."

"You've proven it only takes a few hours to set a trap, if the stakes are high enough." Alban moved to the windows, watching the casino below.

Janx's chuckle followed him. "When opportunity knocks it shouldn't go unanswered. If it's Daisani, why wouldn't Kaaiai put a stop to it? Is he willing to risk making an enemy of me?"

"Maybe you're less alarming than Eliseo." Alban heard Janx's huff of indignation and smiled. "Maybe he doesn't know. Do the news stories say, 'The victim was employed by the notorious House of Cards, an illegal gambling establishment run by a man known only as Janx'? Is the method of murder being reported in the papers?"

"Stoneheart." Janx's tone turned sour. "Of course not. I wouldn't allow the one, and the police wouldn't allow the other. They don't want copycats."

"So it's sheer arrogance on your part to assume that Kaaiai has even the slightest idea your men are dying." Alban put a hand against the glass, idly testing its strength. It flexed slightly, enough to tell him how little effort it would take for him to shatter it. "You forget, Janx, that not all of us are caught up in the game you and Eliseo play."

"You say that as though you aren't."

"No." Alban curved his fingers against the glass, nails slicking over it where talons would scrape, then turned back to Janx. "No, I think that's a mistake I'll never make again. Where is Malik, dragonlord? I have a duty to render."

"You don't trust Eliseo's word?"

"I won't risk Margrit's life on it. Solve this riddle, Janx. Loosen us all from these ties that bind us."

"It's a Gordian knot, old friend. One loop loosened draws another one in." Janx fell silent, leaving his last thoughts unvoiced and still ringing too clearly in Alban's ears: that Margrit Knight was the thing drawn inexorably closer, no matter how he might try to free her.

Malik curled a lip and dissipated when Alban approached, highlighting the difficulty of both protecting and damaging a djinn. Setting watch over any of the Old Races seemed an exercise in futility; part of the reason they'd survived despite small populations was they were simply not easy to kill.

Still, the djinn hadn't gone far, the white corundum he carried a flare in Alban's mind if he chose to follow it. Only one other stone within the city was as easy to locate, but the egg-shaped star sapphire he'd once gifted Hajnal with lay belowground, safe with his own belongings in Grace's hideaway. Other pieces of corundum, less significant, itched at him when he put effort into sensing Malik's stone, but none of them had the same pull. Alban crouched on the warehouse roof, waiting patiently for Malik to move far enough away from the casino to be worthy of concern. It was a far cry from the vigilance Alban showed in watching over Margrit, but her speed, strength and size were only human.

Her wit, however, was beyond him. Alban made a fist and pressed his knuckles against the rooftop, balancing himself on three points. Had he imagined she might turn to Eliseo Daisani when he refused to involve himself more deeply in her life, he might have chosen differently. Bad enough for her to have bargained with Janx. Adding a debt of any sort to Eliseo on top of that made her safe exit from his world virtually impossible.

Which had been her point all along. Alban sighed, half-tempted to shift into his gargoyle form so he could wrap his wings about himself, a proper shroud of frustrated dismay. All his centuries of standing apart had taught him how difficult it was to remain uninvolved. Margrit could never leave the Old Races behind without leaving the city. Even then, word would spread through the network that kept them all connected. In time, no matter where she went, if any of the Old Races lived there and needed human help, they would come to her.

And he'd known that when he'd approached her two months earlier. Known it and let himself break habit and caution and speak to her anyway, with far more appalling consequences than he could have dreamed. As a youth he'd fought one of his own kind, and stayed his hand less from mercy or fear of exile—he'd been too young then to appreciate what that meant—than from an unalterable belief that no crime was as great as taking the life of one of his own people.

Biali had thought little of his choice, for all that it was his life Alban had spared. Hajnal had thought better of it, though she'd held the opinion that fighting over women was for humans, and she'd scolded Alban with a disgusted silence for a full six months before relenting. Neither of them would have thought that Alban could rise up in a protective rage and save the life of a human woman by taking a gargoyle's.

He flinched, the memory still raw and unacceptable. Ausra had been insane, driven mad at birth when her dying mother's memories had cascaded into an unformed mind, but reason had had very little to do with Alban's choice that night. He had moved instinctively and placed Margrit's life above Ausra's, even knowing there was a slim chance the latter was his own daughter. Time and examination of her memories had told him she was not; she had been a daywalker, Hajnal's near-impossible child by a human captor. Hajnal's daughter, Alban's last link to his onetime life mate, and he had taken her life.

His fist tightened against the concrete, knuckles bearing down as though to leave an impression there. Not quite his last link; memories passed from one gargoyle to another upon a death, so nothing was ever completely lost to them. The mental link they all shared made intimacy easy and deception difficult; it was why he'd stood apart as thoroughly as he could. Hajnal's memories had passed through Ausra, shattering her infant mind and leaving her with a bewildering, meaningless array of information that she had never found a way to cope with. Alban had received them on Ausra's death, and through painstaking meditation had sorted madness from truth, trying to fully understand the sequence of events that had led Ausra to her demise at his hands.

He blanched again, a tiny physical reaction that struck him each time he faced that truth. Emotion ran deeper than guilt, ringing closer to bafflement. Ausra's death was a memory he kept in a box, barely able to look at, much less comprehend how it had come to be. Intellectually, he could follow the steps, but it became a disaster of rage and fear and protective impulses when he struggled to sort out his feelings. For one moment in the conflict the question had been Ausra's life or his own, and he'd been willing to choose her over himself. It was only when Margrit's life was endangered that he'd acted against what he believed to be his every impulse. Even that he thought he might in time come to terms with.

What made the memory unbearable was the fear that he would make the same choice again.

"You think too loud, Korund."

Alban opened his eyes, not allowing himself the luxury of another flinch. Biali stood a few feet away in his blunt human form, taking no notice of the rooftop wind that cut through his T-shirt. Never handsome, his scarred features were contorted with anger so deep it seemed to come from the bone. He held himself so still Alban could see muscle trembling with the effort, and that was unnatural for a gargoyle. "How long have you been there, Biali?"

"Long enough."

Dread and relief released themselves as a wave of exhaustion. Bad enough to be caught with a criminal's secret, but for a gargoyle—for him—it might be worse still to go undiscovered. "Where's Margrit?"

A smirk came into Biali's whole being, changing his stance and the cant of his head. "Thought she'd be a screamer, but no, silent as sunrise."

Fury flashed through Alban, searing weariness away.

He didn't realize he'd moved until he was already stretched through the air in a lion's leap better suited to his natural form. Biali laughed and stepped aside, letting Alban hit the rooftop in a roll that made his pale suit filthy and brought him to his feet yards away from the stumpy gargoyle. "There's the man I used to know. Willing to fight when something mattered. Pity you didn't fight for her, Korund. She might not have flown in my arms tonight." His smirk contorted into a sneer and he jerked his chin toward the perch Alban had abandoned. "Go back to playing watchdog, 'Stoneheart.' It suits you better than meddling with the world."

FOURTEEN

"HE'S EXPECTING YOU this morning." The security guard gave Margrit a brief smile and nodded toward the elevators.

"Yeah." She returned the smile tiredly as she passed by. "I bet he is." After Biali left her on her rooftop, she'd turned down Cameron and Cole's invitation to go out, opting for sleep instead. Emotional exhaustion had left her without memorable dreams, though she'd awakened once with the sensation of flying. The alarm clock had been incomprehensible and unwelcome, only making sense after several minutes of progressively noisier beeping. It still seemed very early as she took the elevator up to Daisani's offices.

The front room—Vanessa's massive office—was abandoned, but the oversize double doors leading into Daisani's were ajar. Certain he would've heard the elevator chime and her heels against the hardwood floor, Margrit rapped twice before stepping inside.

Daisani, a finger lifted in warning, turned from overlooking the city, then tapped his earpiece with the same finger. Margrit nodded and helped herself to one of the couches at the far end of his office, too worn-out to stand on ceremony. A crystal jug and glasses sat on the coffee table, suggesting Daisani had indeed anticipated her early-morning arrival. Margrit leaned forward, eyes half-closed as she poured herself a glass of water. After a moment Daisani said his goodbyes and lifted his voice. "Forgive me, Margrit. I didn't expect you quite this early. Working on tomorrow's business already, I'm afraid. If you'd like to be very rich by next weekend, I'd consider buying up some stock in the—"

"Mr. Daisani," Margrit said, half in despair. "I'm a lawyer. Just stop right there."

"You and your mother," Daisani said cheerfully as he came to sit across from her. "How is Rebecca, by the way?"

"She's going to be very surprised to hear I'm working for you." The necessity of being alert enough to banter finally warmed Margrit's blood, pushing off some of her weariness. "Maybe even more surprised than I was, although I'm not sure that's possible."

"Was that not the purpose of your visit yesterday?" Daisani poured himself a glass of water, his smile as sparkling as the crystal. "Did I not do as you asked?"

"It was, and you did, but—"

"Wonderful. The corporation is hosting a gala tomorrow night in the ballroom downstairs. A thank-you to our good friend Mr. Kaaiai, for the generosity he's showing the city in funding security and restoration of the subway speakeasy." Nothing obvious changed in Daisani's smile or delivery, but hairs rose on Margrit's arms as an undercurrent of alarm swept through her. "I'd like you to attend," he asked. "It can be your coming-out party, as it were. Your first public appearance as the new face of Daisani Incorporated."

"My—as the—*what?*" She blinked in astonishment. "Mr. Daisani—"

"Not that there's anything wrong with the old face," Daisani said modestly. "But you're fresh, young, beautiful—"

"And you have a burning desire to have your company represented by a sellout? Mr. Daisani, I—"

"Eliseo," he said, as magnanimous as he'd been modest. "We're going to be very close, after all."

Margrit tried not to grind her teeth. "Eliseo. I can't come work for you under these circumstances. For one thing, I'd be a laughingstock, and that's the nicest word I can think of for it. *Opportunistic bitch* is closer, and even that's being kind. I've got a career at Legal Aid, and I need to be there for my friends and coworkers. Quitting now would be ugly."

"Don't be silly. A murder occurred in your offices. No one would blame you for walking away. Besides, it was your idea."

"I didn't know Russell had been murdered when I made that proposition!"

"You're a lawyer, Miss Knight. You should know the folly of making a bargain without having all the information in hand."

She sat back, feeling the color drain from her face. "That's a low blow."

"Yes." He spoke without the slightest hint of repentance. "Yes, it is, but the circumstances aren't extenuating. You came here to make a cold-blooded deal to save your own skin, my dear, and nothing has altered that situation."

"So you get everything you want for free, and I can't

back out? You said you weren't behind killing Janx's men."

"I don't think you fully understand." Daisani got up with the inhuman smoothness Margrit was becoming accustomed to. "It's true I haven't put hits out on Janx's people, but I've taken on Malik's safety as my full responsibility regardless, and I've done so at your behest. If anyone, human or otherwise, should be so foolish as to assassinate him, I *will* use the full force of my resources to eliminate that person or persons. In more time than you can imagine, I have never offered such protection to one of my rival's people. If I withdraw it now, Janx will see it as an act of cowardice, and strike against me, or he will see it as an act of mockery, and will strike against me. Either way, Margrit Knight, it will begin a war."

"I thought the Old Races didn't fight wars among themselves." Alban had told her that, historically, they hadn't, their numbers always too small to risk all-out battle.

"The Old Races don't make this sort of alliance, either. You seem to have more of an ability to rock our foundations than even I anticipated."

"So why'd you say yes?" Margrit shook her head. "If agreeing to my terms shifts the status quo that much, why play along? I can't be that important. Other humans know about you. There's Chelsea Huo. There's..." She fell silent, uncertain of who else might share their secrets.

Daisani shot her a look of complex amusement. "Chelsea. Yes. Chelsea's tongue is too sharp for my tastes, Margrit. I have no desire to be under its lash day in and day out, even if I could draw her away from her books."

"I guess that tells me how to get out of this."

He chuckled. "It wouldn't be that simple. Vanessa had her edges, as well. You by yourself aren't important, perhaps, but you've upset a balance that Janx and I have held between us for centuries. You've involved Alban in the world again, and anyone capable of drawing him from the granite shell he's been wrapped in is worth noting. I would prefer having him in my grasp, truth be told, but he would make a terrible personal assistant. I'd have to shift all my meetings to nighttime, and despite my people's reputation, I rather enjoy a stroll in the sunlight."

"Why does he matter? You and Janx are both obsessed with him." Margrit stilled the impulse to put her water glass aside and get up to pace, suddenly afraid that movement would turn Daisani's predatory eye on her, as if she were a rabbit beneath a circling eagle.

He smiled. "I'd suggest asking him, but he wouldn't tell you. Which, in its cryptic way, answers the question. The details aren't important, Margrit. What is is whether or not you intend to keep your word."

"My word." She laughed sharply. "I didn't *give* you my word. I barely even touched on my plan before you dropped a bombshell on me. I sure as hell didn't come here this morning to tell you I was taking the job."

"No? Did you come to tell me you weren't?"

Embarrassment and guilt seized her, making her drop her gaze. Daisani chuckled again and returned to his seat. "One never enjoys being caught posturing, does one?"

"I'm not posturing." Her throat constricted further, turning the words to a whispered protest. "I made—Dammit." She looked up, jaw set with frustrated resolution. "When I came here yesterday to make that bargain it was in good faith. Yes, it was in good faith because I'm in between a rock and a hard place, and couldn't see another way out, but I'm doing the best I can. And you're right. Russell's death doesn't change the mess I'm in with the Old Races." She got to her feet after all and paced toward the windows. "But I feel like I have different obligations to my real life now."

"Your real life." She could hear the curiosity in the vampire's modulated tones. "What is this, then? A figment of your truly remarkable imagination?"

Margrit turned back, arms folded under her breasts. "This is the life I can't talk about to anyone. It's the world I got myself involved in without really appreciating how hard it would be to protect someone who wasn't human *from* humans. Everything I do with any of you happens behind this huge facade. I could almost justify taking a job with you before Russell died. Now…Jesus, I don't know. On the one hand, you've got a good point about someone being murdered in the office, and me wanting to get out of there. On the other, anyone who knows me is going to have a hard time believing I decided to run away instead of investigating and trying to make sense of what happened. They won't believe I'm willing to abandon Legal Aid, my principles, my work, my *life,* after my mentor's death. I'm not sure I'd believe it."

"Then investigate." Daisani spread his hands at her astonished double take. "If it's an image of consistency that's distressing you, Margrit, then by all means, investigate. Help your fellow lawyers put themselves back together and mourn Mr. Lomax properly. Discover the truth. But don't fool yourself into thinking you'll earn Lomax's job as your reward. You're far too young and pretty. If you were fifteen years older and your beauty had matured as well as your mother's has, you might seize that brass ring, but not now."

The insult sent heat rising in her cheeks. "You think I only want to find out what happened to further my career?"

"Of course not. I'm sure you're genuinely determined to see Lomax's murderer be found and brought to justice. And if you remained in public service, that dedication might pay off, a decade or two down the road. But you did come here to make a bargain, Miss Knight, and I've accepted it. I would think a week or two of transition time would be appropriate even if Russell hadn't died, so I'm willing to take that as writ now. Pursue that case to your satisfaction. But attend Saturday's party, and do so as a member of my corporation."

Margrit stared at the dapper vampire a few seconds, then rolled her jaw and nodded as she recognized a window of opportunity. "All right. Okay, you win. My turn. You've got an appointment tonight."

Daisani's eyebrows rose. "And who has arranged this?"

"Your new personal assistant. Kaimana Kaaiai would like to meet with you at the Rockefeller Center at eight o'clock. I said you'd be there." Perspiration made her hands clammy, but Margrit kept her gaze steady.

"Did you. And what does Kaaiai wish to discuss with me?"

"I don't really know. Something important about all of you." Margrit circled a finger in the air, indicating the Old Races. "You're not going to make a liar of me, are you?"

Daisani pursed his mouth, watching her warily. "I suppose not, Miss Knight, but I'll expect you to come with me. This is just the sort of social engagement Vanessa used to attend with me. It puts a polite veneer on things."

Margrit nodded stiffly. "I'll meet you there."

Daisani chuckled. "That wasn't intended as a negotiation."

"I'm a lawyer, Mr. Daisani. Everything's a negotiation." She took a deep breath and drew herself up. "My boss was just murdered. I told my housemates I was thinking about coming to work for you. My life has been totally disrupted. I need to go home after work and be normal for a little while. I'm neck deep in your world, but I've also still got to live in mine. To *live* in it, not just drift through every once in a while. I'm having a hard enough time balancing all of this. Don't take the life I used to have away from me. Isolated animals get sick and die of broken hearts."

"Falling ill is not an issue that should concern you any longer, Margrit."

"I'm betting even a vampire's blood doesn't keep hearts from breaking. I need my friends. I need my life. Maybe Vanessa learned to do without those things, but I'm not her."

"No," Daisani said after a moment. "No, you certainly are not. Very well, Miss Knight. You may return to your family." Mocking came into his eyes and he produced a flourish, an elegant bend and dip of his hands so elaborate Margrit half expected a prize to be pulled from his sleeve. Instead he held his thumb and forefinger a delicate fraction of an inch apart and extended his hand. "Take this rose, and return to me before the last petal falls. If you do not—"

Margrit reached out and plucked the intangible rose from his fingertips, so sure and swift it felt as though there was no make-believe in the gesture at all. "Then when I do return the castle will have fallen and the

Beast will have perished. Thank you for my freedom, my lord." She ducked her head over the illusory flower and inhaled.

The scent of roses lingered in the back of her throat as she left the building.

Work was quiet chaos. Margrit moved from one task to another with mindless efficiency, accomplishing more than usual in order to prevent herself from thinking about the yellow police tape cordoning off Russell's office. An entire section of the department was closed down to make room for police work. Tony, back on duty, gave her a grim nod when she came in, as if promising to come talk to her when he could.

Her coworkers—those who were there; a noticeable number were out—seemed to be caught in the same web of necessity Margrit was, silently focusing on work for extended periods. Caseloads were shifted around, no one objecting when they might have normally. The quiet was interrupted in waves, sudden bursts of conversation that faded away into new flurries of activity. Once someone laughed, then cut it off in a gasp of guilt. Margrit got up after that, abandoning paperwork to hurry downstairs and out to the street, where city sounds drowned out the uncomfortable pall of the office.

A woeful Sam leaned against the building, studying the sky. Margrit went over to lean next to him. "Couldn't take it anymore, either, huh?"

"This wasn't how the first week of work was supposed to go. I couldn't take watching people make a break for the door when *they* couldn't take it anymore. I'm right there at the front. Everybody had to go by me and nobody's looking at anybody today."

Margrit nodded. "I didn't make it to the office yesterday. Was it bad?"

"Yeah." Sam knuckled his fingers over his mouth. "A lot of people went home. Pretty much anybody who didn't have a court case to argue or something major to prepare for. Cops were all over the place, interviewing everybody. How'd your case go?"

"I lost. I just hope he doesn't get an appeal based on my incompetence."

"I'm sure he won't." Sam gave her a wan smile, then tilted his head at the street. "I'm going to get a cup of coffee. Want to join me?"

"No, thanks. I just needed a minute outside. I'm going to head back in."

"Okay." He pushed off from the wall and disappeared into sidewalk traffic. Margrit took a deep breath, straightened away from the wall and turned, to nearly collide with Tony.

"Whoa." He caught her shoulders, then pulled her into a hug. "Sorry. You okay?"

"Better now." Margrit held for on a moment, breathing in his scent. "How's it going?"

"Different degrees of crap. You got a couple minutes? I can tell you what I know. Well, you know what I mean."

"You can tell me what you're allowed to." Margrit crooked a smile at the tall cop, feeling a sudden surge of confusion. Their jobs both precluded telling each other everything and always had. Her inability to talk about the Old Races seemed abruptly normal, as though it were simply another obvious part of the constraints of their jobs, and she found herself wondering how it had created the schism it had between them. As she'd told Cameron, it was almost impossible not to like Tony, and it seemed as though she was remembering that for the first time in months. "I love you, you know that?"

Surprised pleasure lit Tony's face. "Haven't heard it for a while. What brought that on?"

"I don't know. Finding my feet on the ground all of a sudden, maybe." There was no pang of regret at the idea. The months she'd spent disbelieving Alban's absence had kept her untethered. Now that he'd distanced himself from her so sharply, it seemed she might be able to get on with her life. She could find a way to manage both worlds, if she thought of the Old Races as a client whose confidentiality couldn't be breached. "I've got a few minutes. What do you know?"

"More than I ever wanted to about Russell." Tony sighed and tugged Margrit up the building's outside stairs, sitting down with her and lacing his fingers through hers. "Did you know he used to be a stockbroker?"

"He said something about making money in stocks the night before he died." Margrit shook her head at the awkward construction of her sentence. "I mean, not that he made money the night…you know what I mean. I was giving him a hard time about how well he dresses. Dressed."

"Yeah." Tony squeezed her hand and smiled. "Anyway, yeah, he worked for Global Brokers Incorporated way back when and made a killing. There was some talk about insider trading, but nothing ever got proved. I guess we're going to have to look into it if we don't find anything closer to home."

Margrit straightened, surprised. "GBI, that's my mother's company. I wonder— No, she couldn't have known him. She never mentioned it. Small world, though."

"I swear, if you get me singing that song..." Tony bared his teeth threateningly. "Anyway, he went to law school after striking it rich. We've had people working on his case histories and comparing them to recent parolees." He hesitated so long that Margrit frowned.

"You found a link, didn't you."

"Not... No. Not like you're thinking. Nobody handy who just got out of jail and came to repay the piper. But you wouldn't—I'm not telling you this, Grit, you know that, right?"

"Telling me what?" She made a moue of innocence.

Tony nodded. "Okay. I know cases get overturned on appeal all the time."

"Yeah...?"

"Yeah. So you wouldn't believe the number of overturned cases where Russell was the first line of defense for somebody who worked for Janx. He lost so many cases it can't be coincidence, Grit. Something like ninety percent of them got overturned on appeal."

Cold ran down Margrit's spine and chilled her hands until Tony's felt like a furnace. "Janx?"

"There's no way I'd be telling you this if..." Tony exhaled. "If you hadn't met him in January. If I hadn't gotten you into that. But I did and you did, and I'm kinda freaked out seeing a connection between your boss and a pretty major crimelord. I don't know what enemy of Janx's Russell was working for, but man, that's what it looks like to me, Grit. So I gotta ask. Do you know anything that could help us out?"

Every heartbeat sent a new wave of ice splashing over Margrit's skin. Two minutes earlier she'd thought she could manage the split between her ordinary world and the Old Races. Now the two crashed over her again, leaving her with no way to answer Tony without potentially betraying an entire people. She pulled her hand from his and hid her face, hearing a laugh that bordered on a sob break from her throat. "Are you sure? How do you know these guys worked for Janx?"

"Some of them have turned up dead recently," Tony said grimly. "People we've seen associating with him. But more of them— Grit, I've been working the Janx angle for years. I know that guy's organization better than he does. I know all the arrests that've been made in conjunction with him. There's probably only three guys on the force who would see a pattern here, but I'm seeing it. It's one of those detail things that's more gut instinct than logic."

"Russell used to say somebody had to keep track of the details, and he was the best man for the job. Somebody else said that to me, too.... Oh." Margrit raised sightless eyes to stare over the street, a host of trivial moments cascading together and forming a picture.

Eliseo Daisani had used the same phrase the first time she'd met him, infusing it with humor and self-deprecation. One point didn't make a line, but there had been peculiar notes in Daisani's conversation the morning before. Shock and grief had wiped it from her mind, but he had said, "You came here to ask me that?" when she'd asked if he'd known about the murders, and then said, "Yes. Of course. I see why you would, under the circumstances." It had been meaningless to her then, but thrown against the context of Russell losing court cases for Janx's people, it now stood out.

"I know that look, Grit. What're you thinking?"

She pressed her lips together until they ached. "What I'm thinking could be a huge embarrassment to the police department if I'm wrong. Can I…can you give me an hour or two to follow up on it, Tony?"

"Shit, Margrit." He stood and she followed suit, the two of them eyeing each other without pleasure. "You'll tell me if it pans out? We need anything we can get." He pushed his hand through his hair and glanced toward the Legal Aid building. "That's why I'm even *here.* I'm supposed to be on Kaaiai all week and instead I'm pulling double duty because a couple of those names brought up red flags on our Janx file."

"Oh, God, I forgot. When have you been sleeping?"

"Caught a nap at the station this morning. Grit, are you going to give me what you've got?" Tony turned his attention back to her, wary expectation in his gaze. A sizzle of guilt shot through Margrit as she recognized the same pattern of withholding information she'd displayed in January reemerging.

"If it turns out to be anything, I will, Tony, I swear. But believe me, you don't want to shake the tree I'm thinking of if you don't have an ironclad reason to. I don't even want to put ideas in your head."

"All right." Tony nodded, as if he knew that Margrit wouldn't offer up her thoughts until she was ready to. She caught his hand and held it a moment in apology, irrationally stung when he gently pulled away. "You do your thing, Grit. Tell me if you can."

"I will. I will, Tony, I promise." The words had too much familiar deception. Margrit ducked her head again and hurried down the steps. When she looked back a moment later, Tony was gazing after her, unhappy resignation creasing his features.

FIFTEEN

MARGRIT STOPPED IN the coffee shop to tell Sam she'd be out for a while, promising she had her cell phone if anything came up. Then she took the subway across town, neither her shoes nor her time frame allowing her to bolt across the city on foot as she wanted to. Tony's expression haunted her through the short journey. He deserved better, but she'd told the truth: if she was wrong about a connection between Russell and Daisani, it was better for Tony not to have that worm in his ear. He was a good cop, not likely to be led by unfounded suggestion, but once a pervasive idea took hold it could easily blind someone to things he should be seeing.

And if she was right…

Margrit left the subway still uncertain as to what to do if she was right. Miring Daisani in Russell's murder investigation seemed absurd, even if the links were there. Tony, if he heard Margrit say that, would see it as truth falling before financial power, and she'd be hard-pressed to argue. She had no other way of explaining the reasons for her reluctance.

Alban's image rose in her mind, blotting out Tony's. Margrit made a frustrated noise and ducked into her mother's building.

Rebecca Knight met her in the elevator lobby, alerted to her arrival by a phone call from the first floor. Surprise and worry etched unusually deep lines around her mouth.

"Margrit, what's going on?" Her mom pulled her into a hug, then leaned back, gaze searching. "Come on, sweetheart. Let's go to my office."

Margrit held on a moment, then nodded. "That'd be good."

They greeted a few people as Rebecca led her down a maze of broad hallways, before ushering her into an office that could have been deliberately designed as the opposite of Eliseo Daisani's. Where Daisani used rich deep colors, she had pale ones: cream carpets and birchwood accessories with overtones of gold and orange were played up by sunlight diffused through blinds over the tall windows. The soft light youthened Rebecca and created an almost literal aura of competency about her when she was backlit. It was extraordinary advertising, giving the subtle impression that a client's money was very nearly in the hands of God, and therefore unimpeachably safe. A tiny smile curved Margrit's mouth. No wonder Rebecca intimidated people.

Her mother offered her a seat. Margrit took it, then stood again almost immediately, earning more concern. "Margrit, what on earth is going on? Is it Russell?"

"Yes. Mom, I—" Margrit's pulse accelerated as though she stood in front of a jury. "Mom, I need to ask you a couple of questions and I need you to tell me the truth. I know we're not..." She sat down again, rubbing the knuckles of one hand into the other palm. "We argue over a lot of things," she said. "And I know you try to protect me and guide me even when I don't tell you everything. Nobody tells each other everything." Nervous energy drove her to her feet yet again. "Right now I need you to."

"Well." Rebecca lifted her eyebrows slowly. "In the beginning, there were the dinosaurs…."

Margrit laughed out loud, taken completely aback. Rebecca leaned into the couch, a hint of smugness sparkling in her eyes. Margrit came over to hug her, and Rebecca returned the hug, still radiating contained amusement. "Sweetheart, I have absolutely no idea what's wrong, but I don't think I've seen you this nervous since you took the bar."

"I know. I just don't think this is something you'll want to talk about. Mom, did you know Russell when he worked for GBI? Thirty years ago?"

Surprise tightened the skin around Rebecca's eyes, and for a moment Margrit could see her drawing herself into a shell that hid natural feelings. Her heart skipped a beat as she recognized the defense mechanism: for the first time, it struck her as similar to what she did when courtroom nerves were starting to get the better of her. It was her game face, intended to be impenetrable. "We're more alike than I think, aren't we?"

Fresh surprise softened Rebecca's gaze again, a careful smile curving her lips. "I'm afraid so, sweetheart." She took a breath and held it a moment, then released it. "I did."

Margrit found herself echoing that breathing pattern, and coughed. "And you never mentioned it because…?"

Rebecca gave her a shrewd look, her lips pursed. "Wouldn't it be more efficient to just ask what you want to know, Margrit?"

"I'm trying to be a good lawyer, Mom. Trying not to lead my witness." Daisani's chiding from the day before had left an impression deeper than she had realized. "I've got a lot of puzzle pieces floating around and I've made a picture from them, but I want to hear your perspective to see if it's the right one."

"And is this under the lawyer-client confidentiality clause?" Rebecca's light teasing carried an undercurrent of discomfort. She stood as if to shake it off, taking a few quick steps to her desk and then turning to lean against it. "I never mentioned that I knew him because I didn't particularly like him, and I didn't want to prejudice you against your employer. Until you went to work for Legal Aid, Russell and I hadn't spoken to each other in nearly thirty years. There was no reason to. We had nothing in common."

"Except whatever it was that made Russell rich and makes Mr. Daisani say that you're a remarkable woman," Margrit said carefully.

Rebecca's shoulders drew back. "He said that?"

"The first time I met him. He said you were remarkable, and if you were a little less ethical, you'd have been rich beyond the dreams of avarice." Rebecca exhaled and turned her head to the side. Margrit swallowed and went on, still choosing her words cautiously. "Tony said there was some question about Russell leaving GBI back then. Some hint of insider trading, but nobody ever proved anything."

"I thought you weren't leading your witness, Margrit."

"Mom," Margrit said, very quietly.

Rebecca wet her lips and nodded, still looking away. "I'm sorry. You're right. This isn't something I want to talk about." She fell silent a moment or two, then lifted her chin and looked back at Margrit. "Russell and I were both handling some of Eliseo's smaller businesses, under the supervision of one of the full partners. It was a test, to see how well we worked on high-stakes, high-pressure operations. Eliseo oversaw a significant amount of what we did personally, partly to add to the pressure."

"And partly…?"

"In retrospect, it seems clear it was also partly to see if we could be bought. During lunch one day he gave us papers detailing a sale going through on one of his information technology companies." Rebecca lifted a hand to touch her hair, then let it fall again with a sigh. "I don't believe it actually occurred to me to act on the tip, but Russell went to bed still in debt from student loans and awakened a millionaire."

"What'd you do?"

"Confronted him, of course. Whether or not he acted illegally, it was certainly unethical, and he didn't want to determine legality in a court of law. He'd either be found guilty or he'd have the question haunting him for the rest of his career. I told him to leave the company or I'd push it to court."

Margrit's eyebrows crinkled with confusion. "Why not bust the whole operation? You had the goods on Russell and Daisani both."

Rebecca hesitated a long moment. "Because Eliseo Daisani isn't the kind of man you imprison, and there was no way to accomplish the one without some risk of the other."

A bolt of sympathy hit Margrit powerfully enough to steal her breath. She started to stand, but was arrested by her mother's voice: "I suppose that's very difficult for you to understand. As a lawyer, I imagine you see prison as an egalitarian accomplishment. Guilt deserves punishment."

"You'd be surprised. Mom, why do you—" She cleared her throat, trying to rid herself of an ache there. "Why do you say that? That he's not the kind of man you send to jail?"

Rebecca focused on Margrit as if she'd forgotten she'd been speaking aloud. "It's hard to send someone with that much money to prison, sweetheart. You know that."

Margrit opened her mouth and closed it again, an unexpected wave of defeat crashing over her. "Yeah." She sank back into the couch, deliberately keeping herself from dropping her face in her hands. A moment of connection had passed, and she had no idea how to bring it back without potentially betraying Daisani's secrets. For a moment she wished vividly that she had a gargoyle's ability to join with another being on a profound mental level, leaving no secrets unshared. The burden of knowing about the Old Races would seem far less heavy if she knew even one ordinary person who could understand. "Yeah, I do know. So do you think he stayed in Daisani's pocket after that?"

Rebecca hesitated again. "It's hard to do business in this city without some kind of interaction with Eliseo or his companies. I avoid working with him directly, but we manage a dozen of his holdings out of these offices alone." She tapped a finger against her desktop, clearly uncomfortable. It was another moment before she spoke, resolve hardening her tone. "I didn't trust Russell Lomax, Margrit. I suppose I don't forgive easily, but he breached my trust and the company's trust by playing on inside information. It's because I mistrusted him that I say I wouldn't assume his law career went untouched by Eliseo Daisani, but I imagine there's only one person who could really answer that question for you, now that Russell is dead."

"I guess I'm going to have to ask him." Margrit turned the idea over in her mind, wondering if there was a way to use the connection between her former boss and her new one to wriggle free of the employment agreement she'd entered. The idea of blackmailing Eliseo Daisani made her huff a tiny laugh.

Rebecca returned to the couch to take one of Margrit's hands. "You're better off staying away from Eliseo if you can. I don't mean to suggest you can't run your own life—"

"Yes, you do." Margrit nudged her mother's shoulder. "You always think you know best."

"That's because mothers do," Rebecca said with a prim sniff. "It's easy to get caught up in his world, is all I'm saying, Margrit. Wealth carries its own kind of glamour."

"Mom, I didn't exactly come from the sticks. You and Daddy make a lot of money."

"We're paupers compared to Eliseo's financial empire. Trust me." Rebecca's voice turned wry. "I know how much he's worth. It's no secret I want you to do well financially, but once you're part of Eliseo's world you never really break free of it again." Her voice held an odd note, sending curiosity surging through Margrit.

"What do you mean? You haven't dealt with him since then, have you?"

"Not personally, no, but I can never forget, either."

Margrit swallowed the confession of her impending employment, and felt another shock of guilt. It was too large a change, too close to Russell's death, for her to seriously contemplate, much less share. Daisani had promised her a little time; she'd take it before admitting to her friends and family the new direction her life was heading. There was still some small chance she might find a way out of the commitment, though that, too, made her uncomfortable. Daisani was right, and the circumstances under which she'd suggested working for him hadn't changed. Only everything around them had. "I'm still going to have to talk to him. Tony's found some information in Russell's case files that…well, it's what made me come here to ask you about Russell's ties to Mr. Daisani."

"Really. And I thought it was just a social call." Rebecca's smile faded, leaving concern in her brown eyes. "I want you to be careful, Margrit. It's easy to agree to things you'll later regret when talking with Eliseo."

Margrit laughed. "I've noticed that. I'll be careful, Mom, I promise. Thanks for looking out for me."

"It's what mothers do." Rebecca stood, glancing toward a clock. "I don't mean to send you away, sweetheart, but I have a meeting in a few minutes."

"It's okay. Thanks for seeing me." Margrit climbed to her feet and gave her mother another hug, then excused herself with a wave.

A twenty-minute cab ride brought her back to Daisani's corporate headquarters. Margrit nodded to the security guards on her way in, and one waved her over. She cast a glance at her watch before crossing to him.

He slid a key across the security desk. "Mr. Daisani

sent this down for you after you left this morning. Said you'd be needing it. It's for the elevator bank," he explained.

Margrit felt her expression clear, then cloud again. "Must be nice to be that confident. Thank you." She palmed the key and nodded toward the other guard, then went to examine the elevators. A moment of fiddling opened the doors of one with a chime, and she stepped inside with a resigned sense of inevitability. Her reflection in the polished brass walls showed just that, and Margrit shook herself, putting on a better game face. When the doors slid open again, the mirrors showed a well-dressed, confident young woman stepping out of the elevator. Vanessa's office was abandoned, though voices came from a room at the opposite end of the floor from Daisani's office. Mouth pursed, she walked in without knocking, and Daisani stood up from a boardroom table with a smile. Half a dozen other men stood as well, less friendly than curious.

"Margrit. Excellent, we were just about to get started. Gentlemen, this is my new assistant, Margrit Knight. She's a top-notch lawyer, so don't bother getting clever with your contract language. Margrit?" Daisani smiled again and gestured to a seat to his right, an obvious place of honor at the head of the table.

Bemused, Margrit nodded, said, "Gentlemen," and sat down to riffle through the stack of file folders at her seat.

Within seconds she wished her mother was there. Thirty years of experience in dealing with finances would have been helpful in understanding the fine details of the paperwork she'd been presented with. Margrit stuck a pen in the corner of her mouth, chewing it as she studied the contracts. Part of her wanted to giggle, more from relief than real humor. She felt as though she'd walked into a theatre performance and was expected to know her lines and stage directions without knowing the story. Knowing that Daisani was manipulating her with the situation brought a gurgle of irritation that was mostly buried by the sensation of playacting.

Unexpectedly, her first priority was getting through the meeting without embarrassing herself or her employer: she could deal with the rest of it later. Discussion went on around her, Daisani and the others flipping through papers and arguing over points she only half listened to as she perused the files with as much concentration as she could muster.

Down the table, one of the businessmen watched her surreptitiously, his hand palm-down on the table and held studiously still. Margrit finished skimming through a contract, seeing nothing that sent up a mental warning, and turned to the next file, whose front page was dominated by a brightly colored pie graph that made her think of board games. A muscle in her watcher's hand jumped and he stretched his fingers again, then broke into laughter with the rest of the businessmen, the result of a half-heard self-deprecating joke Daisani made. Margrit drew out some scratch paper and tapped her pen against the pad, smiling absently when he glanced her way, then returning to the files. Eventually she heard him say her name, and looked up with a blink.

"You've ignored us entirely for nearly two hours, Margrit," he repeated. "Would you care to join us now for a celebratory lunch? I think we've broken out the details to a sufficient degree by now."

"I don't think you have." Margrit shifted her papers into a different order, digging up the pie-graph file and two others, then rapping her pen on the scratch pad, where she'd left a pageful of arrows and notes. "They're written to obscure it, and they do a good job, but these three reports and the contract riders are all moving to buy options on the same company. Different branches, which is why it's hard to see, but this is the risky one, a media development project for a new cable station. Lot of capital needed there, and it's shaky, which is why it looks like a good sale. But it's got a couple of widely diversified backers, one in the corporation's oil industry and the other in clothes manufacturing. They sweeten the pot to take on the risk of a failure with the cable station, but if I've got these figures right they leave the corporation with holdings that are just shy of majority numbers. It's slick, but the legal department should have caught it. You might want to check and be sure everybody's still on your payroll." Margrit squeezed the back of her neck. "I'd say celebrating is premature."

Daisani curled a slow smile and stood. Everyone, including Margrit, followed suit, and Daisani opened his hands in mock apology. "Forgive me, gentlemen, but it appears there'll be no deal today. I'll be back in touch after a new legal team's examined everything." Insufferably polite handshakes went around, more than one of the businessmen giving Margrit a sour look as they left the room. Daisani turned to her, eyebrows elevated. "Well?"

She sat down again, rolling her head to loosen her

neck. "The tall one down the table from me was watching everything I did. He twitched and tensed up when a couple of those reports were discussed, so I started looking for the smoking gun. You could've lost a lot of money."

"Unlikely. I was aware of the contract problems, but since you arrived so precipitously I thought I would see where you took things, given your head." Daisani poured her water over a plant and brought her a new glass, ice ringing against the crystal. "These meetings are, in part, tests."

"For me?" Margrit's voice shot up, offense coloring it.

"For the men I'm working with. Once in a great while someone's honesty overtakes his avarice, or the other way around, and that tells me things I wasn't formerly aware of. I couldn't have made this a test for you. I didn't know you'd be here. But it worked out nicely, didn't it? That was very well done, Margrit, and that's exactly why I need you. The human perspective is indispensable to me. It's unlikely I'd have noticed the body language that tipped you off."

"That's flattering, but it's hard to believe. You must pay attention to that sort of thing." Margrit's temper settled at the realization that Daisani couldn't have known she'd come back during his meeting.

Delight shaped Daisani's thin features to a sort of good looks, his smile going further to create an illusion of handsomeness. "My first impulse is to listen for the heartbeat, the taste of fear, the bodily reactions that give someone away. These men are very good at hiding those things. I know human emotion well. I've studied it for centuries. But even after so long, my sense for the subtler hints of high emotion is drowned beneath the sound of a beating heart. As a lawyer, you're trained in body language as much as legalese. And you've just proven that you're willing to step up to the plate, whether you want to or not. You could have turned around and walked out of here."

"What, and lose face?" Margrit picked up her water glass and drained it, wishing the action wasn't so obviously a distraction. "Besides, I needed to talk to you."

"I'm at your disposal." Daisani sat down, hands folded in front of him, the picture of attentive interest. Margrit set her glass aside and studied him for a few seconds, then sighed.

"Why didn't you just tell me Russell was in your pocket?"

SIXTEEN

DAISANI WENT STILL the way it seemed only the Old Races could, all life in him stopped. A heartbeat later his eyelashes flickered, a tiny motion that in Alban would have gone unbetrayed. Fair enough; Alban couldn't move as obscenely fast as the vampire could. They all had their strengths.

Then Daisani was in action again, standing to pour another glass of water. The frozen moment was so thoroughly vanquished Margrit half wondered if she'd imagined it. "What an astounding conclusion," Daisani said. "Tell me how you came to it."

"Oh, for—" Margrit let out an exasperated breath. "Russell got rich off insider trading from one of your companies. He had too many cases overturned on appeal when he'd been defending Janx's men. You both use the same phrase—that somebody's got to keep track of the details, and you're the best man for the job."

"It's hardly an uncommon phrase."

"Eliseo." Margrit recognized the same impatient tone she'd used with her mother a few hours earlier. Daisani tucked his chin in and lifted an eyebrow in surprise. "You also thought there was an obvious reason for me to come to you about Russell's death, in wake of Janx's peoples' deaths. You just said human intuition was indispensable to you. This is my intuition at work."

He wet his lips, reminding Margrit unnervingly of how she'd licked her own lips, to get the vampire's sugary, sticky blood off them. A shudder ran through her, lifting hairs on her scalp. To her relief, Daisani ignored her reaction. "Who else have you told about this connection of dots? You've obviously spoken to your mother." He was at the window, leaving Margrit to blink and try to convince herself she'd actually seen him move.

"I didn't tell her about the Janx link. Does she know about you, Mr. Daisani?" Desperate hope drove Margrit to her feet. "Does she know you're a—"

"She knows I am extraordinary." Daisani spoke to the windows, his voice reverberating softly off the glass. "She was younger than you are now when we knew each other. There was an accident. Construction, one of those rare moments when something goes wrong. A cable snapped. I believe it was determined to be sabotage, in fact. I bought the offending company for an embarrassingly low price and sold it seven years ago at a two hundred forty-four percent profit."

He fell silent and Margrit stepped forward slightly, afraid to interrupt. "We were to meet for lunch that day, she and Russell and I," he said eventually. "She was on the opposite side of the street from me, perhaps halfway up the block. I'd just gotten out of my car and she saw me and waved. I think I saw the shadow rather than the girder itself, or perhaps my subconscious comprehended faster than my thoughts could. I pulled her to safety, though I'm afraid I bruised her ribs quite badly. My strength isn't remarkable, but the cessation of momentum…"

He turned to offer Margrit a half smile. "I recall it quite vividly. She's taller than I am, you know, and she wore heels, as you usually do. I remember it very clearly, the way she looked down at me. Humans so typically refuse to believe what they see. Logic dictates that I simply must have been closer than she thought, because no one can move that fast. On the rare, rare occasions when one of us is exposed in that fashion, it's what people force themselves to think.

"Your mother did not for one moment disbelieve her eyes. The sidewalk and steel were still ringing from the impact, and I doubted anything I said would be heard, anyway. I put my finger over my lips—" and he did, a light careful motion "—and Rebecca didn't so much as nod. She simply looked at me for what may have been the longest moments of my life, then turned away to see if anyone had been injured in the accident. No one was," he added more brightly. "The newspapers called it a miracle."

"But why?" Margrit blurted. "Why'd you risk it?"

Daisani arched an eyebrow. "I wanted lunch."

An incredulous laugh slipped out. "Of course. I should've guessed." Margrit flattened her hands against her mouth, then sighed. "I haven't told anyone about the link. I'm not even sure I could prove it if I did. I don't imagine you've got any obvious connections to Janx." Relief mingled with regret over having not told Tony more than she had. His suspicion that she was withholding information from him would only make things more difficult between them, but she couldn't see arguing the tenuous connection in a legal case. The two rivals were linked by an ancient feud, not modern associations. A flare of irritation arose in her and she added, "Even if you did have him get Malik to run me down."

Daisani flashed a smile. "But not through a traceable meeting, I'm afraid. I'm glad you haven't mentioned this to your police officer friend. It would only complicate things."

"Do you have any idea how much it complicates *my* life to not tell him? What do I get out of keeping my mouth shut? Do I get to walk away from here free and clear?"

"Is that what you want? You acquitted yourself very well earlier. I dare say you were even enjoying it."

Margrit admitted, "I was," grudgingly. "But I still feel like Russell's death changes everything. How many more people are going to die because of this fight you two have going on?"

She saw a hint of amusement in Daisani's eyes and knew she'd lost the bid to change the subject gracefully, but he responded, "I told you. I'm not responsible for Janx's losses."

"And you're just going to sit back and let Russell get killed?" A needle of doubt slid into Margrit's certainty and she forced it out again. Daisani had all but admitted her theory was correct.

"My talents are many, but bringing people back from the dead isn't among them. Would you have me escalate this dangerous business even further?"

She bit back an irrational *yes!* as defeat sluiced through her. "No. That wouldn't help. I'd rather have justice than revenge, but if it's not you, who is it? Who do I go after?"

"I believe I've agreed to give you the time to discover

that before you begin working here full-time, Margrit." Another glint of amusement passed through Daisani's eyes. "Am I being unreasonable?"

"Only in so far as you're not letting me have my own way. Things in my world have changed. It seems like things in yours ought to change, too, to accommodate me." She lifted a hand, stopping anything he might say. "And I guess you have, giving me time to follow up on this. It's just…"

"I do understand," Daisani said mildly. "But you don't get to be in my position by being accommodating, I'm afraid. You offered a deal. I accepted it. You've cited being a turncoat to Legal Aid as your reason to welsh on our agreement now, but I suspect the real problem is that having given your word, you're reluctant to go back on it even if you have good reasons."

"That and there's an actual possibility you'll bite my head off if I refuse. That's less of a problem in the real world."

"You're afraid of disappointing me."

"Literally afraid. Not nervous or worried, but afraid. Because I don't know which way you'll jump." Margrit scowled at the vampire. Admitting fear seemed like a bad idea, but frustration with the situation overrode her caution, pushing her to the truth. "If you were human, I'd expect you to make it hard, maybe impossible, for me to find another job if I wanted to leave Legal Aid. But you're not, and I don't know what the hell you do when people disappoint you. I have a pretty good idea of what *Janx* does, in a mob boss kind of way, and I don't want to risk that, either."

"The obvious solution is to not disappoint me."

Margrit's scowl deepened. "Well, it doesn't look like

I'm going to, does it? Some kind of overdeveloped sense of responsibility made me step up to the plate when I walked in here today. The rest of it is just me making noise." She sighed and dropped her chin to her chest, both grumpy and relieved at the admission. "Can I ask you something?"

"Certainly. Whether I respond or not…"

"Yeah." Margrit looked up. "Why didn't Janx stop shunting people to Legal Aid and hire a lawyer of his own instead? He must've known Russell was doing your evil bidding."

Daisani straightened, clearly caught between offense and amusement. "My evil bidding?"

"Come on, you were manipulating the legal system to your own ends, and I'm a lawyer. What else would I call it?"

"Capitalism at its finest, perhaps. You'd have to ask Janx, Margrit. He rarely pays out for his men when they get into trouble. It keeps the connections between them more tenuous. I suppose he may have found a degree of pleasure in keeping one of my people running laps around several of his, as well, but I'm the wrong person to ask."

Margrit sighed. "I guess so. I'm just tired of chasing all over hell's half acre for answers." She groaned as she looked at the time. "And it's almost four. I've blown most of the day. Again. When I come to work for you I want a twenty-hour-a-week schedule if I'm going to be dealing with your esoteric factions all the time. Otherwise I'll feel guilty at never being in the office."

"I think I can assure you that any time spent out of the office dealing with esoteric factions will not be held against you with an eye toward a completion of more mundane tasks. You'll be my personal assistant. We can always hire another one for you."

"Oh, well, hell." Margrit raised her hands in acquiescence. "If I'm going to be somebody's boss, I want my salary doubled. I'll see you at Rockefeller Center tonight, Mr. Daisani. I'm going to go home and try to be normal for a while."

"Cam?" Cole's greeting came from the kitchen over the sound of food sizzling. "You're early."

Margrit took a deep breath of the rich peppery scent and collapsed against the door with a contented sigh. "No, it's the other woman in your life. The dusky-skinned beauty, remember? Whatever you're cooking smells delicious."

"Garlic, onions and butter. A healthy evening meal." Cole appeared in the kitchen doorway, grinning. "The only dusky beauty I ever dated turned out to be just-friends material. Dating was a disaster. Like dating my sister."

"Cole Grierson, are you telling me you've dated your sister?" Margrit threw her coat over a hook and toed her shoes off, padding to her bedroom. "Because I think that's illegal even in Louisiana, and you're from San Francisco."

"My disgusting childhood secrets are out," Cole called, then sobered as he asked, "How was work?"

Margrit tugged running pants on under her skirt and lifted her voice to answer, "It sucked. A lot of people were out and everybody who wasn't was walking on eggshells. I was actually out about half the day." She'd returned to work to find it moribund, no one speaking any more than necessary, and she'd felt no guilt at leaving as quickly as she could. She finished changing clothes and pulled running shoes on before heading for the kitchen. "I spent a lot of time talking to Eliseo Daisani today."

Cole turned to look at her, poorly restrained curiosity in his expression. Margrit managed a weak smile. "I think I'm going to take the job."

"Whoo." Cole turned the burner off and folded his arms across his chest. "You sure about this? I don't want to rain on your parade, but they say not to make big decisions right after something awful's happened. Have you talked to your parents? Or Tony?"

"Not really. Not about the job. And you're right." Margrit rubbed her hands over her face. "About big decisions, I mean. I still think I could do a lot of good in the public sector, but there are things going on with his corporation that I can make a real difference in." She offered a tentative smile. "Bleeding heart liberal in charge of their charitable resource funds, you know?" The grain of truth there made it bearable to say, but explaining the aspect of Daisani's world that Margrit thought she might really make a difference in was impossible. "It could give me the groundwork and connections to do something else in five years. Maybe stop trying to fix the legal system from the inside, and focus on save-the-world organizations instead. I think it's…" She swallowed, trying to taste the veracity of her own words. "I think it's the right choice."

Cole puffed out his cheeks, then stepped forward to offer her a hug. "In that case, congrats. When're we moving to Park Avenue?"

Margrit tilted her nose in the air. "Oh, I don't know. I may have to audition other people to be my chef. I might find someone better, you know. Agh!" She laughed and stumbled as Cole pretended to shove her. "If I promise to be back at the house by six-fifteen will you make me some of whatever that wonderful-smelling stuff is going to be?"

"Not if you're going to be threatening my station as house chef, I won't. Oh, all right, no fair with the puppy-dog eyes. In honor of your new job, yes. But if you're going to be home at decent hours, I'm going to make you start doing your share of the cooking." Cole lifted an eyebrow in warning and Margrit cowered, then put on her best stern lawyer face.

"You don't tell Cam she has to cook."

"Cam's culinary skills are limited to hard-boiling eggs and peeling potatoes. I know this from bitter experience. You, however, claim to just be too lazy to cook."

"It's true. Tell you what, I'll make dinner next week. If I do a bad enough job, I'm permanently off kitchen duty, right?"

"You're a perfectionist," Cole said serenely. "If you cook dinner I don't think your work code will let you do badly if you're capable of doing well."

"Eliseo said that to me, too. Do I have it tattooed on my forehead, or something?"

"Ooo-ooo-ooh. Eliseo, she calls him. Eliseo, like—"

"Cole."

"—he's a pal, not the richest guy on the East Coast. Eli—"

"Cole!"

"—seo, boss with benefi—"

"Cole!"

He grinned at her so widely it looked as though his

cheeks must ache. "Dinner's at six-thirty. Have a nice run."

And that, Margrit reminded herself on the way out the door, was the normal life she wanted to get back to.

"Ooh, the ice rink! We'll go with you!" Cameron's enthusiasm left Margrit spluttering, her protest that she was meeting Daisani proving no deterrent. Cam only demanded, "How many chances are we going to have to meet Eliseo Daisani?" and went charging off to find the ice skates with a child's enthusiasm.

"Probably quite a few, now that I'm working for him." Margrit's grumble fell on deaf ears.

Cole took in her wrinkled forehead and lowered his voice to ask, "Is this a bad idea, Grit?"

"Eliseo's not the only one I'm meeting."

"You've got a date?"

"Not the way you're thinking. No, come along. Just don't be mad if I kind of disappear some, okay? There's going to be a lot going on." The answer seemed weak, but telling her housemates they couldn't join her because it might be dangerous bordered on absurd. That it was true only made it more difficult to say.

"I can talk Cam out of it. Romantic evening home alone, all that," Cole offered just before Cameron bounded out of their bedroom, two pairs of skates brandished triumphantly.

"We haven't been skating in ages. Last time we went was when you proposed, Cole. You can buy me another big mug of hot chocolate."

Margrit cracked a smile. "I don't think an evening in is going to compare to a reenactment of your engagement night. It'll be okay. Just don't get too attached to hanging out with me." Cam, rooting through the coat closet, kept up a cheerful litany of things Cole could buy for her, and Margrit's smile turned to a laugh. "Somehow that doesn't seem like it's going to be a problem."

Cole murmured, "All right," and squeezed Margrit's shoulder, then lifted his voice to repeat, "All right," to Cameron. "But I'm not buying you another diamond ring, okay? I just want to make that clear right now."

"How about earrings? Or a tennis bracelet?"

"You don't play tennis."

"I could take it up!"

The trio took a taxi to the Center, Margrit watching the sky fade from gold to black as Cameron and Cole continued their banter. Cam eventually leaned over to nudge her, curiosity making her eyes bright even in the fading light. "You forgot your skates."

Margrit pulled a smile into place. "You two get to have fun for me. I'm working. Can you imagine Eliseo Daisani ice skating?" He would be impossibly graceful, though she had no idea if his tremendous speed would be achievable on skates.

"I can hardly imagine him at all. I can't believe you're going to work for him, Grit." Cameron sat back again, eyes wide with good humor. "You happy about the new job?"

"I'll let you know," Margrit promised. "Tell you what," she added as the cab neared their destination. "You two go ahead and hit the rink. I've got to find Eliseo. I'll make sure to introduce you before he leaves, okay?"

"You'd better. My clients will all be very excited that you're working for the rich and famous now. I'll have to give them full reports."

"Cameron, how do you get any weight lifting done if you're so busy gossiping?"

"I talk," Cam said. "They grunt and listen while they work." Cole broke into a whistling tune that dissolved into laughter as Cam's elbow caught him in the ribs. "Listen! *Listen!*"

"Listen to what? Help! Help! I'm being abused!" He opened the door and stumbled out of the cab, with Cameron batting ineffectually at him. Margrit paid the driver and climbed out, then pulled them both into hugs.

"Thanks for coming, guys, even if I'm leaving you to entertain yourselves most of the evening. I needed some nice ordinary human interaction."

"As opposed to inhuman interaction." Cole lurched into a zombie walk, arms out and eyes rolled back. "Grr, argh."

"I'd have brought my *other* boyfriend if I'd known you wanted ordinary human interaction," Cameron said in an aside, then hugged Margrit a second time and chased after Cole, both leaving dignity far behind.

"I love you guys!" Margrit shouted after them, then swallowed a yelp when a deep voice behind her said, "I can see why."

She spun around, raising a hand defensively, and relaxed again to see Alban standing a few feet away. "What are you doing here?" She glanced toward the horizon, where scraps of color still lingered.

"Watching Malik." Alban looked around with a sigh. "Or not, as it may be." He returned his gaze to her, his voice and manner growing more formal. "I'm to tell you hello."

"From *Malik?*"

"From Grace. I believe she's here tonight, as well.

She said she wanted to witness Eliseo and Janx's first public meeting in a century."

An image of Alban's tall alabaster form beside Grace's earthier milk-and-bleach colors flashed so strongly through Margrit's mind that she blushed with the memory of it. It was a few long seconds before she trusted herself to say, ungraciously, "Oh. That's nice."

Alban ghosted a smile. "That was the least convincing thing I've ever heard you say. Would you like to try again?"

"No." Margrit frowned at her hands, then spoke quietly. "I'm envious of her, Alban. She's beautiful, and she's had you in her clutches for weeks while I've been up here trying not to watch the sky. How am I supposed to compete with that?"

Alban drew a breath to answer, then stilled, looking beyond Margrit. Cold drained down her insides, leaving her heartbeat slow and painful in her chest. She turned, every muscle stiff and protesting the movement, to find Tony standing a few feet behind her, his expression betrayed.

"At least you knew you had competition."

SEVENTEEN

"TONY." MARGRIT STARED at him, numbness radiating out from the trickle of cold at her core. "Tony, what are you doing here?" She cringed as she spoke, recognizing the question as the worst thing she could have said.

"Kaaiai sent me." His answer came from miles away, cool and hard. "He knew you were uncomfortable with whatever's going on tonight and he thought it might make you feel better to have me around. What are you doing with him, Margrit?"

"I'm not *with* him. I didn't even know he'd be here." She threw a frustrated look at Alban, who stood still and silent as the stone he could wrap himself in. There was no help in his expression, no offer of explanation, only a neutrality as terrible as Tony's own.

"Has this been going on since January? Anthony Pulcella," Tony said, directing the introduction beyond Margrit, his voice tight with anger and hurt. "We haven't met formally."

"Nothing's been going on, Tony. I just remet Alban a few days ago."

"Alban Korund." The gargoyle nodded a greeting, never breaking his gaze from Tony's. "We haven't, and

I regret the circumstances by which you know me informally. Had there been a way to come forward and clear my name, I promise you I would have taken it. Margrit spoke highly of you as a good man."

"Just not good enough." Tony transferred the weight of his hurt to Margrit. "Not good enough to tell when I'm being cheated on."

"Tony, there's been nothing to tell!" Margrit felt Alban shift minutely beside her, as if he detected the scent of her half-truth, and shame heated her face. She clenched her hands, tears of frustration stinging her eyes, though she wouldn't let them fall. "I'm sorry. I should've told you I was—that I'd— Shit! Goddammit, I'm not seeing him!"

"He's why you've been running so cold. Not just the last few days, but since January. What's he got that I don't, Margrit? Money? Good WASP breeding? Your mom's going to love it when you bring him home. Can I sit in on that one?"

"He lets me fly." Margrit barely heard her own whisper, but Alban relaxed again at her side. Tony saw it and stepped forward with a snarl.

"You know, maybe good breeding means I oughta step back and let the lady make her choice, but I'm from Brooklyn. I believe in fighting for what I want."

"Tony, don't you dare. Tony, don't you—!" Margrit surged forward, putting herself directly in front of the police detective. "Don't you *dare* start a fight over me. How many times do I have to tell you this isn't a John Wayne movie? It's my life, *our* lives—"

"Our?" Tony stared down at her, then cast a nasty look at Alban. "Funny, Grit, but *our* lives look a lot more crowded than they used to."

"Margrit." Alban touched her shoulder. "You're going to be furious with both of us either way. Perhaps you ought to allow us to settle at least some of this as men prefer to." The faintest strain lay on the antepenultimate word, startling Margrit into looking at the tall blond man.

"Alban, what—" Turning moved her just far enough from the way. Tony threw a punch she saw from the corner of her eye. "Tony!"

Knuckles smashed into meaty flesh as Alban brought his hand up, catching the hit in his palm with such immense grace it seemed slow and elegant. Astonished rage lit Tony's eyes as Alban held the detective without strain. "I will not fight you, Detective Pulcella," he said quietly. "I am stronger than you, and faster, and it would solve nothing. Women are not trinkets to be battled over. I have learned that the hard way, by nearly losing a wife over just such foolishness, and I will not do it again. Margrit will make her choices and we will respect them by treating one another as gentlemen might, not roughhousing schoolboys. Do we have an agreement?"

Lazy clapping, sharp staccato sounds, shattered the impasse. Tony stopped struggling against Alban's hold, staggering back a step or two when the resistance was broken. The gargoyle caught the detective's wrist to make certain his rival didn't suffer the indignity of falling, then released him almost as quickly.

"Oh, bravo, bravo, well done indeed." Janx's delighted tenor sailed over the trio. "Such chivalry, Stoneheart. Perhaps that heart isn't so stony, after all. Margrit, my dear." The redheaded dragonlord insinuated himself between Alban and Tony, taking her hand and bowing over it. "I had no idea you'd be arranging such a performance for me this evening. It makes leaving home worth the journey. And Detective Pulcella." Janx turned from Margrit, holding her fingertips with his own a moment longer than necessary. She shivered, withdrawing her hand and glancing toward the ice rink. Cameron and Cole were at the head of a short chain of skaters playing crack the whip, weaving in and out of the crowd. "How delightful to see you in a social context. This will go over well with your superiors, don't you think?"

"Margrit?" Tony's voice cracked with outrage, and she bit back the curse she wanted to lay at Kaaiai for sending the detective to her side. "Margrit, what've you gotten yourself into?"

"Margrit." Janx clasped a hand over his heart, turning to her with injured eyes. "You haven't told him about us? I'm wounded. I thought we'd agreed the time for secrecy had ended."

A bubble of absurdity broke inside Margrit, thawing cold dismay and anger. "I'm afraid Janx is right. So are you. I've been keeping secrets, Tony. The truth is, you can't put a successful bug on Janx to bring him down because Malik can disrupt electronics by phasing them into air molecules and back again. Where *is* Malik, Janx? He must be around here somewhere." She glanced around, finding Malik only a dozen feet away, unobtrusive but close enough to overhear the conversation. He glowered as she waggled her fingers in greeting, the fine line she trod making her heady. "That's what happened to my phone back in January. Janx is actually a dragon, and that gargoyle costume Alban hid in at the Blue Room is really his natural form."

Tony's countenance darkened with insult and injury

as Margrit rattled blithely on, while Janx kept light amusement on his features as he watched her. Alban, behind her, radiated disapproval, though Margrit was certain if she turned to look at him she'd see none of it on his face. She was glad Janx had released her fingers, or his reptile-cool skin might have shattered her composure. She held on to what nerve she had left, finishing, "I'm here tonight because Mr. Kaaiai asked me to arrange a meeting. I had no idea it was going to turn into a circus sideshow." She smiled up at Janx, her heart leaping with a sudden awareness of the size of the men—human and otherwise—surrounding her. "Have I missed anything?"

"I believe you've touched on nearly everything of relevance." Janx's green eyes were hard, none of the humor in his voice reflected there. "Where, pray tell, is Kaaiai?"

"You could at least tell me the truth, Margrit." Tony's voice shook with emotion. "I don't know who you are anymore."

"She is precisely who she has always been." Eliseo Daisani came lately to the match, his overcoat snapping in the wind. "A young woman of unusual audacity and self-confidence who, when forced into a corner, lashes out with all the weapons she can lay hands on. You lied to me, Miss Knight. Very few people are capable of doing that." Censure in his voice was tempered by respect that made Janx twist his mouth in what looked like agreement.

Margrit muttered, "Trust me, I amaze even myself," and then, more clearly, added, "I didn't lie to anybody. I was just selective with my truth. Sorry. Tony, this is Eliseo Daisani. I think you know everyone else here."

Daisani offered a hand. "The young man who sat vigil over Margrit's bedside so diligently it was difficult for the rest of us to see her. I admire your dedication." Tony, too stunned to do otherwise, shook Daisani's hand, then looked pained.

"Margrit! Hey, Margrit!" Cam waved with cheerful abandon as she led the whip around rink's corner, innumerable skaters stretched behind her. As one, Margrit's group of conspirators turned to watch her skim by with Cole immediately behind her. Over the scrape of blades on ice, his watch beeped, marking the hour.

The woman behind him dropped his hand and grated to a stop ten inches from the guardrail. No one behind her stumbled or tripped, though Cole let out a startled yell as he and Cameron, no longer weighted by the whip, went flying off balance. The noise of their skidding tumble was drowned out by the scrape and crunch as each skater in the whip came to a flawless, sudden halt.

Not only they came to a stop. A ripple shuddered the length and breadth of the rink, figures overwhelming the bright clear surface of frozen water. Hundreds of people spread across the rink, so many that Margrit could hardly see how they'd managed to move without creating chaos.

And the wave continued, gathering mass and spreading beyond the rink, until it seemed that every visitor to the Center had come to a stop and turned, eyes downcast, to face Margrit's little group at the end of the ice rink.

Daisani murmured, "No," in astonished disbelief. As if his whisper triggered action, every downcast glance lifted. Dark eyes, pupils swallowed whole by black irises, were revealed as the weight of hundreds of selkie gazes fixed on Margrit and her companions.

Cara Delaney glided one step forward from where she'd abandoned Cole on the ice and lifted her voice, clear and pure over the silent rink.

"We are here to tell you that there is strength in numbers, and that a balance has changed."

Tightly controlled chaos erupted within Margrit's group. She all but felt Alban's muscles bunch, as if he might leave behind his limited human form and spring into the sky, too full of shock and excitement to hold himself still. She reached for his hand, staying him, and he knotted his fingers around hers, agreeing to closeness for the first time since he'd reentered her life. Hope shuddered through her, stealing her breath and leaving a foolish smile curving her mouth.

A wash of memory swept over her with Alban's touch, his vivid recollection of an aging selkie man disappearing into the sea, the last of his people. As though the memory triggered Janx into life, the dragon turned on Alban with a snarl.

"You said they were—"

"It was the best of our knowledge." Alban's deep voice rolled over Janx's without pity, quashing his protest before he said anything damning to the one uninformed human in the group. "It was the best I could do."

"So many," Daisani breathed. "So *many.* All here, all in one place. How? How is it possible? If so many can be here—"

Cara came from the ice rink, walking with improbable smoothness despite the blades on her feet. She held her chin high, shoulders back, confidence and pride in her every movement. "Eliseo." Margrit's mouth fell open at the contempt in the selkie girl's tone. "Janx. Alban." The last name was accompanied by a raking glance. "Do you speak for your people?"

"I have no right to do so." Alban kept his voice steady, though he tightened his hand on Margrit's, and she thought she heard a note of reluctance in his words.

Tony, bewildered, stared from one face to another. "What the hell is going on? Who are these people, Grit?"

"This is Cara," Margrit answered softly. "Cara Delaney. The girl who went missing from her apartment in January, the one I asked you to help me find. She'd gone to a friend. To a lot of friends, it looks like."

"Then your people will have no spokesman at our table." Cara ignored the humans and dismissed Alban, glancing beyond the group toward Malik. "And you?" Her voice rose to carry to him, though Margrit had no doubt he'd hear even a whisper.

"Alban, you have to go." Margrit looked up at the pale gargoyle. "Better you than nobody."

"Margrit, *what*—"

"I have no right, Margrit."

"Tony—"

Everyone spoke at once, Tony's frustrated tones the loudest, and Margrit's useless attempt to find words to reassure him drowned out beneath Alban's certainty.

"Right is what you make of it." Malik used human locomotion to move to Cara's side, but for all the attention Margrit paid, he might have simply dissipated and reappeared. "I'll sit for my people." The glance he darted at Janx was laden with ambition, though avarice was wiped away again within an instant.

Her attention drawn to the dragonlord, Margrit saw the slow curl of a smile that revealed too-long, sharp eyeteeth well after Malik had looked away again.

"Much as I hate to say it, Malik's right, Alban." She turned from the gargoyle, releasing his hand to face Tony. She caught a glimpse of Cameron and Cole standing with human awkwardness amidst a throng of beings able to do something as mundane as *wait* with grace and patience. "Tony, I've got to go with these people."

"Excuse me?" Janx asked, amusement clear in his voice.

Margrit looked toward him, brazen confidence worn down by sudden tiredness. "One of each, don't you think?"

"Oh, I insist." Daisani broke off from his fascinated study of the selkies with panache, as if the conversation had only just become interesting enough to bother with. "Margrit's gotten us into this fine mess. I wouldn't let her go now for any price."

"Nor would we," Cara said. There was a formality to her voice Margrit had never heard before, as if she was taking part in a ritual translated to English for Margrit's benefit. "You three, then, to speak for your own." She nodded at Janx, Daisani and Malik. "The fifth will go unspoken for."

"If there's a little time," Janx offered, with a sideways smile at Alban, "I could call Biali to the table."

"That would—"

"No." Alban's voice rumbled over Janx's with a heavy note of finality. "I'll take our place at the quorum."

"For Margrit's sake or your own?" Janx turned from Alban, to watch dark confusion and anger crease Tony's face. "My dear detective, I'm afraid you're no longer needed here. It's been a pleasure."

"There's no way I'm—"

"Tony." Margrit broke free from the little group, as if a few steps constituted privacy. "Tony, I promise I'll explain all of this later, but right now I need to go with them. I know I'm asking too much, okay? But I'm asking it anyway. I need you to trust me and to let this go. I need you to tell Cam and Cole I'm all right and that I don't know when I'll be home, but not to worry."

"I can't do that, Margrit."

"You have to. You have to, Tony. I've never needed anything from you as much as I need this right now. Please. For me, this one time. I'll explain when I can."

"No." Tony shook his head, resignation mixed with bitter unhappiness. "No, you won't. Forget it, Margrit. I've heard that promise too many times. You're not gonna explain, and I'm tired of waiting."

"Tony." She reached for his hand. He pulled back, and prickles of embarrassment swept over her. "Tony, I will. I swear."

"You mean it now, but something's gonna change. It keeps happening. I'm sorry, Grit. I can't do this anymore." He took another step back, jaw clenched with resolution. "I love you, but this isn't working, and I don't see how it's ever going to. You go on. Do what you have to do." He hesitated a moment, then shrugged helplessly. "Goodbye."

She shut her eyes in defeat as he walked away. Warmth stirred the air a moment later, and she looked up to find that the members of the Old Races had closed ranks around her. "All of you," she said with a thin note of bitterness. "All of you with your different shapes and your amazing skills, and you can't even do something like alter somebody's memory a little so this kind of mess doesn't happen? What the hell good is being stuck in a fairy tale if you can't even magic away some of the trouble you cause in mortal lives?"

Malik offered a sharp smile. "Fairies rarely made life easy for those in their tales. And you've just told him the truth about all of us. You know the consequences."

"Oh, don't threaten me," Margrit said in disgust. She was glad for the emotion, letting it bury hurt and sorrow. "I'm happy to play Dorothy to your Wicked Witch, so just lay off."

"What were you thinking, Ms. Knight?" Janx hissed. "Telling him the truth?"

"It's not like he could possibly believe it. You're angry." Margrit laughed with more dismay than humor. "You haven't called me 'Ms.' in ages. I was thinking—"

"It doesn't matter." Defense came from an unexpected source, Daisani interrupting the bickering with controlled calm. "He neither could nor did believe her, and we have an enclave to call to order. Miss Delaney." He turned his attention to the selkie girl, who met his gaze without a hint of the shyness Margrit was accustomed to seeing from her. "If you could escort us to whatever quarters Kaimana has arranged for this meeting, we would all be deeply appreciative."

EIGHTEEN

CARA LED THEM into a Rockefeller Center conference room, then slipped out again, leaving one of every sentient race there. Kaimana was waiting for them, his black eyes very large and drinking in the low light greedily.

Daisani took the lead, easily confident. "Strength in numbers. What a very human sentiment, Kaimana."

"It is." The selkie got to his feet as his five guests fanned out to take seats at a round conference table. Janx and Daisani chose the chairs closest to Kaimana without argument from the others; even at a table without a head there were positions of power. Margrit sat on Janx's right, across from Daisani, whose mouth quirked curiously at her selection.

A surge of satisfaction burst through her at the vampire's faint change of expression. She upset the expected balances and alliances at the table by claiming that seat. Alban sat beside her, though *beside* was misleading. Margrit could stretch her arms out fully without touching either of the men she sat between.

Malik, mouth held tight with displeasure, took the final chair, allied neither with his employer nor managing to sit directly across from Kaimana as the effective second head of the circular table. Alban held that spot, his mass great enough even in human form that Malik seemed reluctant to make an issue of the fact.

"And we have a human to thank for it." Kaimana bowed toward Margrit, whose mouth curved wryly. Four other pairs of eyes turned to her, the knowledge of what she was and was not legible in their gazes. Human. A woman. A lawyer. A pawn. The only one of any of those things in that room, though she had no doubt both dragon and vampire would cheerfully assure her that everyone was a pawn.

"We've respected the laws of the Old Races for centuries." Kaaiai's Pacific lilt made his words into music, but inexorability lay beneath them. "Even slipped into exile, into nonexistence, when the only way to retain our numbers was to cross a forbidden barrier and interbreed with the human race."

Margrit, beneath her breath, asked, "Do you all sound like this in your native languages, or is this just courtroom talk?"

Alban chuckled and Kaaiai broke off, frowning. "I'm sorry?"

"Nothing." Margrit put a brainless smile into place and shook her head at the selkie. "Sorry. Go ahead."

He frowned a moment longer, while Janx and Daisani exchanged amused glances, then began again with the same pomposity. "We are tired of living in shadows, unacknowledged among the only peoples who might know us for who we truly are."

"And what are you?" That came from Janx, his voice unusually measured. "Half-breeds? Quadroons? Octoroons?" He took his gaze from Kaimana long enough to wink at Margrit, whose hands flexed against the tabletop of their own will. Janx looked pleased with himself as he returned his attention to Kaaiai. "How far does the blood dilute and remain true, selkie lord?"

"Half-blooded children are full selkie," Kaimana answered. "Born to either skin, able to change when and where they will. Quarter-blood breeds true half the time, with a stronger propensity for it among women. We don't know why. The chances of being a skin-changer fall off dramatically after that. We've kept very careful breeding records for centuries. Most of my people are close to full-blooded."

"And how many are you?" Daisani steepled his fingers in front of his mouth, lips pursed with curiosity. "I tasted five hundred heartbeats this evening alone." He unlaced his fingers, gesturing dismissively. "I have no dispute regarding your worthiness to call yourselves one of the Old Races. Your grace, your eyes, the scent of your blood…the vampires name you purebloods."

Malik inhaled, a sharp soft sound, and even Alban stirred with surprise. Triumph, quickly tamped, flashed in Kaimana's dark eyes as he inclined his head toward Daisani, whose expression remained pleasantly neutral as he awaited the answer to his question. Margrit wet her lips, breath caught in anticipation as she realized what he'd done. Whatever numbers the selkies laid claim to, Daisani's recognition of their legitimacy played him into the position of their first supporter, a political move that would not, could not, go unremarked. Only Janx seemed unimpressed by Daisani's preemptive move, his jade gaze slipping from vampire to selkie and back again.

"Thank you. Tonight's showing is perhaps a single percent of our strength. Perhaps not so much as that."

"Fifty thousand...?" Margrit didn't realize she'd asked the question until all eyes turned her way. "How's that even possible? I thought you'd been decimated."

Humor sparkled across Kaaiai's face. "Reports of our demise were greatly exaggerated." His amusement faded and he turned his attention to the other curious members of the quorum. "We lived at the edges of the sea, at river deltas and lake sides. Our natural habitat was the most appealing land for humans to settle. We had time to see and appreciate the changes that humanity could force on us, all unknowing. We began retreating long before our numbers fell as far as the histories were led to believe."

"You lied." The two words were almost a question. Incredulous, Alban shifted forward in his seat. "You lied to the memory-keepers?"

"We permitted you to believe the obvious and inevitable had happened," Kaimana allowed, then lifted a broad shoulder in a shrug. "We lied.

"Our numbers did fall. Further than we even imagined they might, far enough that we saw no other recourse than to mix with the coastal humans in order to save ourselves. We kept apart, living in small villages, struggling to retain our old ways of life. Human blood gave us our numbers, but our hearts belonged to the Old Races. We abided by those traditions, living in exile from both humanity and you."

"Until?" Janx spoke again, evidently more to take the table than any need to prompt Kaimana.

"Until Margrit Knight named herself our cousin, and gave us heart by telling us there was strength in numbers."

Margrit snorted loudly enough to gain the group's attention again. "What? That never occurred to you before? There's fifty thousand of you, and you didn't think, gee, we could strong-arm our way back into soci… You didn't," she said in amazement at Kaimana's faint, rueful smile. "You really didn't? What's wrong with you? That's not—" she shot a quick, bemused glance at the heavens "—human."

Reversing her gaze, she looked around the table at the five representatives of different races. "How do you do it? How do you live beside us, breed with us, and still retain this alien innocence that thinks so differently than we do?" She gestured at Alban, then at Kaimana. "Gargoyles don't lie, selkies don't think of strength in numbers, God knows what dragons and vampires and djinn, oh my, don't do. None of you make *war?* None of you think in terms of anything but isolated survival? How've you lived this long?"

"You're quick to judge, Margrit." Alban's voice was edged with hurt recrimination.

She rose to her feet, exasperation driving her to motion. "This isn't judgment, it's bewilderment. I honestly don't understand how you can live beside humans and not learn from them, unless you're deliberately keeping your heads in the sand. God forbid I should hold them up as shining examples, but look at those two." She snapped her fingers toward Janx and Daisani. "Like it or not, they *live* in the human world. They manipulate and power-play and hoard and make the best of their situations, and they're successful at it. The rest of you, what are you doing? Pretending the nasty humans will go away and leave you to your ancient rituals and pastoral ways of life if you only hide your eyes and pretend you can't see them for long enough? That's like hoping all the wars will stop if you don't read the news about them. It's *possible,* but it's also possible a million dollars will rain down on my head tomorrow. It's just not very damn likely. Don't," she added, noting an impish gleam in Daisani's eyes, "get any ideas."

He actually thrust his lower lip out in a laughing pout. "Oh, very well. If you insist." Margrit sank back into her seat, explosion over, as Daisani continued. "Miss Knight is right, of course. We as a group of peoples do not participate in the human world, nor announce ourselves with such firmness as you have, Kaaiai." He turned his palms up in invitation. "What do you intend to accomplish here by doing so?"

"Legitimacy amongst the Old Races. Allies, if necessary." The air in the room seemed to tighten, Janx, Malik and Daisani each hearing what they wanted to in Kaimana's words. Only Alban remained unaffected, watching the selkie leader with a calm expression. "A reconsidering of our traditional way of life," Kaaiai stated more quietly. "A new look at the exiling offenses and whether they are…relevant concerns in the modern world."

Another wave of anticipation washed through the room. Janx and Daisani meeting eyes and holding some wordless consultation within the space of a moment. Margrit watched them curiously, wondering at the weight of unspoken communication there. Janx's expression changed minutely, a flicker of eyelashes, no more, before Daisani turned his attention back to Kaaiai as if nothing had passed between dragon and vampire.

To her right, at the same time, Alban's chin lifted, faint motion that spoke volumes from a creature born to stone. Beyond him, Malik stiffened, the one reaction out of four that struck Margrit as actively negative.

"Are we five to make this decision?" Alban asked. "Without regard for what the rest of our people might say?"

"I wouldn't complain, Stoneheart," Janx said. "This is to your advantage. I think your lawyer would advise you to accept responsibility here and now, and deal with the consequences later." He arched an eyebrow at Margrit, who sighed.

"Of course that's what I'd advise. I don't think he'll do it, though. Self-promotion isn't exactly his strong suit. How many gargoyles are nearby? I know Biali."

"There's an enclave in Boston," Janx said, after Alban's silence stretched out. "Half a dozen or more. One or two in Philadelphia. Several in Chicago, in D.C. A few in Atlanta. One in Baltimore, heaven knows why. There are others, but those are the closest. The oldest is in Chicago."

"Remind me to ask you, not him, if I ever need to know where dragons are," Margrit said to Daisani, then turned her attention back to Janx, who smiled toothily at her. "Oldest as in older than Alban, or oldest of the others available?"

"Both. Biali's older than Korund, for that matter."

"Biali," Alban growled, "chooses passion over intelligence. He should not be trusted at a quorum."

"Speaks the gargoyle who left Europe over a broken heart," Janx said. Alban curled a fist and Margrit stretched to put her hand on it, wondering too late if the gesture would be welcome. His fingers tensed, then relaxed, and she withdrew her hand again, hoping his response was a positive sign. "Find a suitable replacement or carry the onus of deciding yourself, Stoneheart. Malik seems to have no qualms about thrusting himself into a position of power."

"Malik is not exiled among his own people."

"That was a lot more diplomatic than I would've been," Margrit said beneath her breath. Malik, silent throughout the proceedings, bared his teeth at her as if he were a dragon or a vampire, not a djinn at all.

"Three days hence," Daisani said with finality. "It's enough time for Malik and Alban to establish themselves or find other proxies before we gather and decide the fate of the selkies. Margrit, you'll be our moderator." Delight warmed his thin face, making him almost handsome. "Our token human." His smile faded and he rose to his feet. "Now. If you have a moment, Margrit, I'd like to speak with you."

At her side, Alban exhaled as though defeated, and when she looked at him he was moving away, the others following suit. She clenched her teeth and waited for the room to clear before falling in step with Daisani, who remained silent until they left the building. "You lied to me, Margrit."

Margrit locked her knees against collapse and nodded, wishing Daisani had chosen a stretch of ground nearer the ice rink to confront her. She didn't trust her legs to hold her, and the chance to lean against the railing would have been welcome. Alban walked several feet ahead of them, less a pillar of support than she might wish. "Only a little." Her voice was scratchy and she cleared her throat, managing a smile. "I was sort of impressed with myself."

Daisani's expression wiped her smile away. "How much of this were you aware of?"

"Kaimana wouldn't tell me what he was planning. He wanted to talk to you and Janx, but I didn't know he was going to have an army of loyal followers show up. He thought if I knew what was going to happen, you'd consider it a betrayal." She laughed. "And that that would be bad for me."

"He's right. How do I know you're telling me the truth now? You've successfully lied to me once already."

"I really didn't. I just didn't tell you everything, and you weren't expecting that. I wouldn't dare try again. Scout's honor." She held up three fingers, then folded them down again, hand trembling. "You were still fastest off the mark. Accepting their legitimacy. Offering yourself as an ally." Her voice steadied as she spoke, the edge of hysteria fading from it. "Or a leader."

"Not at all." Daisani shook his head once, then abruptly turned and walked away. Margrit cast one wild glance at Alban, then ran a few steps to catch up with the vampire. "Our peoples don't accept leaders from other groups. At best I might be a power behind the throne."

"I'd think that would suit you just fine. Either way, the economic potential is—"

"Staggering." Daisani's typical front of good cheer reemerged. "Oh, not within the context of human society, perhaps, not really. But as a position of power within the Old Races, for accomplishing anything I might want done…"

"Like what?" Margrit demanded, boldness overruling wisdom. "What do you want, Mr. Daisani?"

He stopped and peered the scant distance down at her. "Even if I were inclined to answer that, my dear Miss Knight, I wouldn't do so with your gargoyle lover hanging about. I trust we're not going to have a repetition of today's fatuous behavior in the future, are we?"

Margrit swallowed down a panic-induced apology, hoping understatement would prove more effective—and dignified—than gibbering promises. "No."

"Very well." He nodded as if satisfied, then gave her a brief smile. "Do pass on my regards to your housemates, Margrit. Lovely girl, that Cameron Dugan. Strong and vital." He strode across the plaza, covering distance rapidly for a man his size, and didn't look back.

Margrit stared after him, alone for a handful of seconds before Alban joined her, lines etched deep around his mouth. She transferred her gaze to him, then jerked it back to Daisani. "Did he just threaten to eat Cameron?"

"I doubt he'd put it that way," Alban said, but grimaced when Margrit shot an accusing glare at him. "Yes."

"How do you kill a vampire?"

"What?" Alban lost his usual aplomb and gaped at her.

"How do you kill a vampire?" Her voice came out high and thready, but full of anger. "Is it really holy water and wooden stakes? Garlic? Silver crosses?"

"Margrit, can you think of anything that wouldn't die if you thrust a stake through its heart?" A hint of humor colored the question, but faded quickly. "Wood isn't the important part. I don't know if you've seen how fast he can move."

"I have. So it's managing a kill shot that's important, rather than the specific tool used?" Margrit set her jaw, watching Daisani, little more than a silhouette in the distance, climb into his chauffeured Town Car. "That's good to know."

"Margrit, you're not going to—"

"Like I could. I'm not kidding myself. Still, I'd rather know he's got a vulnerability than be completely unarmed if I need the information." She folded her arms around her ribs, scowling at the gargoyle. "So you're talking to me now."

His expression grew wary. "Janx told me how you'd solved your dilemma with Malik. Margrit, I'd intended—"

"It doesn't matter." She pressed her lips together until they hurt. "It doesn't make any difference, Alban. I did what I had to."

"What you thought you had to."

She shrugged. "There's no difference."

He caught his breath and held it a moment, then exhaled deeply. "Perhaps not. And you're now more embroiled with our people than ever before."

"I've been telling you all along that there was no way out. I wasn't even looking for a way out. That was all you. It'd be easier if I'd never met you, but I did, and now I know the things I do, and there's no going back." Margrit thinned her mouth again. "Like I said, you guys aren't much of a fairy tale. You can't undo me knowing about you."

"But the life you had… I am saying this poorly." Alban's voice deepened. "Perhaps I made mistakes in trying to protect you the way I did. But I found there was hope in me, when Janx told me of your decision. I…do not want you to leave my life."

A sharp combination of relief and annoyance danced through her. "Fine way you have of showing it." She knotted her arms around herself more thoroughly, staring up at the gargoyle as guilt and apology appeared on his features. Her acid faded and she stepped forward to put her arms around him instead of herself.

The cool scent of stone enveloped her as he closed his arms around her shoulders, carefully. His heartbeat, slow and steady, sounded like the pulse of the world, never-ending and reassuring. The tightness of tears congregated in Margrit's chest, making it hard to breathe. It was easy to remember sensuality when she thought of Alban's touch, but his solid presence brought safety, as well. For a few moments she felt as though she was shut away from the world, left in a warm dark cocoon where exhausted emotion could rest a while. Alban, it seemed, could stand there forever, holding her safe against all comers, and she had never been so glad for refuge.

"Tell me." His low voice tickled her ear where it was pressed against his chest. "Tell me what's happened that I've missed, Margrit. Tell me why…" He hesitated, then murmured, "Tell me why your detective has left you."

Margrit muffled a rough sound against Alban's suit jacket. "My boss is dead. Russell Lomax. He was murdered yesterday morning, and Janx probably had it done, because Russell used to put Janx's men away on Daisani's say-so." The words, once started, flowed freely, her speech almost too quick with misery for even Margrit to follow. "And there's no obvious connection between Janx and Daisani except the tiny, tiny detail that they're Old Races and ancient rivals, which I can't exactly tell Tony. So he's furious with me, and I can't blame him. Even if I could, how the hell do you put people like them in jail? Not only is it probably physically impossible, they're not human. Applying our justice system to them is facetious."

Alban set her back a few inches, his hands on her shoulders as he studied her. "Even when they commit crimes in the human world?"

"I don't have a good answer for that. There ought to be some kind of balance, some kind of price, but knowing what I know, I can't see throwing them in one of our prisons and tossing out the key. It'd be like slapping handcuffs on a shark for eating a surfer."

"Sharks aren't rational, thinking creatures capable of making moral decisions."

Margrit gave another sharp laugh. "Haven't you been trying to impress on me that your people have different sets of morals from humans? That you don't actually think like we do?"

"And haven't you been trying to convince me that the only way for us to survive is to become more like you?"

Margrit dropped her head forward, thumping it against his chest. "I think if you want to survive as a people you're going to have to do something as drastic as the selkies have done. I don't know if that means *becoming* us. It shouldn't. They seem to have kept their sense of selves and their way of thinking. There's got to be a point in between. A place where…" Her shoulders dropped with defeat. "A place where it's not impossible for you and I to try being together."

"It's not impossible." Alban lowered his voice further and touched Margrit's chin, lifting her gaze to his. "If you can forgive my foolishness, Margrit…"

"Alban." Janx's voice cut across the distance. "I do hate to disturb your little lovers' chat, but my liegeman has disappeared again, and I'd like you to find him."

NINETEEN

AN UNACCUSTOMED PULSE of tension throbbed through Alban's temple. It took a moment before he trusted himself to move; a moment of examining unfamiliar irritation welling within himself. Two centuries of solitude had not prepared him to rejoin the world. Memory seemed briefly faulty, unable to tell him whether small daily annoyances had once pricked his temper as easily as they did now. He thought not; it went against everything he imagined himself to be.

Biali's shattered visage shot through his mind's eye, a painful reminder that at least once, he'd been moved to violence. More than once, he recalled, as Ausra's delicate amber features replaced Biali's rougher face in Alban's memory. What he was, and what he thought he was, lay further apart than he could have once imagined.

When he did move, it was to step back from Margrit, letting his hands fall from her shoulders. Denied hope slid across her face and she glanced away, making frustration leap anew in Alban's chest. The space between them was hardly an insurmountable obstacle for a creature born to flight, and yet he'd insisted on furthering it. He was abruptly uncertain whether it was Margrit he'd tried to protect by doing so, or himself. His hand made a fist of its own accord and he turned toward Janx with a scowl.

"Temper, temper, Stoneheart." Janx clucked his tongue, eyes merry with scolding. Beneath the veneer of good humor, though, lay a note of strain that almost no one would recognize. Daisani would see it, and Alban, and perhaps a handful of others not in this city. A surprising flash of sympathy scored Alban's heart. He, too, was learning what it was to lose control, and liked it no better than Janx did.

The dragonlord shook his head, mocking solemnity in the motion. "You were always so steady, old friend. Time's left a deeper mark than you'd like to think."

"On all of us," he growled. Janx would be no more pleased with a show of compassion than Alban would be offering it. He had always thought of Janx and Daisani as alike, and himself the outside third to their complicated friendship. In many ways it was true—the dragon and vampire's relationship stretched back centuries before Alban's birth. But for the first time in decades he recalled—*let* himself recall—that they had once, the three of them, shared a friendship that had set him on a path none of his brethren had ever taken. He most often let himself remember that with a kind of blame assigned to the others, but in truth, no one forced a gargoyle to a road he didn't want to walk. Time had left its marks, indeed.

Alban wrenched his thoughts away from the past, bringing his attention back to the too-tense dragonlord. "Would you have me chasing Malik across half the city like a frantic parent watching a fledgling spread its wings?"

Janx pursed his lips, eyes wide as he considered the

question, then spread his hands and smiled beatifically. "Yes."

Another growl erupted deep in Alban's throat, precursor to argument. Janx's smile grew broader and more pointed, his love of bartering washing away some of his stress. "I can set Margrit to it, if you like."

"Go ahead." Margrit's voice broke into the conversation with cool strength. "You're wasting everybody's time keeping Alban on him anyway. Anyone who goes after Malik is going to have you *and* Eliseo to deal with. Somebody that dumb deserves what he gets." Sotto voce but clearly aware she'd be overheard, she added, "I should know."

"Out of the wide variety of adjectives I'd use to describe you, my dear, 'dumb' is not one of them. Rash. Impetuous. Bold. Foolish. Dauntless. Audaci—"

"You can stop now." Margrit's glare earned a full laugh from Janx that sent a sizzle of envy through Alban. It was worsened as she struggled to maintain her glower, then lost the battle, her own mouth twitching with humor. They made each other laugh easily, and while nothing logical suggested Margrit—a lawyer and a principled woman—would find romancing a crimelord appealing, logic failed in the face of her amusement.

And if that unlikely love affair should come to pass, Alban would have no one to blame but himself. He gathered himself, searching for shadows where he could transform and leave behind the complications of the world for the silence of the sky. Margrit stalked past him as if he wasn't there and folded her arms as she drew breath to argue with Janx.

"He gave his word." Janx dismissed her argument before she spoke. Frustration rumbled in Alban's chest, but the dragonlord had the right of it. "Even if Eliseo's been so good as to offer his protection, our dear Stoneheart's word is—well." He widened his eyes, as though surprised at his own turn of phrase: "Solid as rock. Once given, there's no going back."

"Well, release him," Margrit said. "You can't expect his word to bind him indefinitely, especially when the source of danger as you defined it has been removed."

Janx smiled over her head at Alban. "Don't you love it when she talks that way?" He transferred his attention back to the petite mortal woman, who rolled her head in exasperation. "I can," he said more softly. "I've made bargains with gargoyles before, Margrit Knight. They are binding."

"They can't be that binding. He walked away from keeping an eye on me."

"Did he ever promise you in so many words that he would watch over you?"

Alban heard only the catch of Margrit's breath in reply, as long strides took him to the shadows. Janx's voice, cheerful and pitched to carry, followed him into the sky: "Do you think it was something we said?"

He never *had* promised her he would watch over her. The promise had been to himself, and that was hard enough to break, even with more than one warning that he would leave her to run alone at night. Then again, in accepting Malik as his responsibility, Alban protected Margrit in a different way.

Perhaps if he told himself that often enough, he would begin to believe it. Stone didn't take to deception easily. It had to be worn down through long exposure, the way he'd come to let himself lay blame for his own choices as Janx's and Daisani's feet. There was no such time to be had with Margrit; her brief span of years would end before Alban could teach himself to believe he guarded her life by watching over Malik's.

A familiar flash of brightness soared beneath him: Biali on the wing. Alban could feel Malik's presence—or that of the stone he carried—ahead of him, moving the same direction Biali did. There was time enough to pursue curiosity, and Alban tucked his wings to fall into a slow dive, watching Biali cut through the city canyons.

They rarely saw one another in the skies, but with such a grouping of Old Races as there'd been tonight, it wasn't a surprise to find Biali in the air. The other gargoyle, though, had clearly not known of the hastily met quorum. As both the elder and the one who was in good graces with their people, he would have rightfully demanded to take Alban's place. That Janx hadn't insisted on calling him was a gift of sorts to Alban, though it would no doubt carry a price.

So long as that price wasn't Margrit. Alban's wings flared, catching a draft as he followed Biali across Madison Square Park. Ahead of them both, color twisted in the air, a cyclone of light that had nothing to do with the amber lamps or office windows around it. It gusted upward, riding wind as surely as either gargoyle did, then coalesced atop the Flatiron Building. Malik stepped forward, a figurehead on the building's enormous prow.

Biali back-winged, falling into a crouch a dozen feet from the djinn. The reverberations of his landing rattled, and Alban climbed higher in the sky, head cocked to catch what words the wind could bring him. Malik, throttling the neck of his cane, stepped down from the rooftop ledge and faced Biali. They both worked for Janx; choosing to meet on a downtown building top seemed curiously secretive.

"Am I to be beleaguered by gargoyles?" Malik snapped. "What do you want? Korund couldn't do the job and Janx sent you to nursemaid me?"

Biali's exasperated rumble cut through the air, as if he shared Alban's sentiment about watching the djinn. "I'm not doing him any favors, al-Massrī." He shoved out of his crouch, massive and almost clumsy as he moved. "I've got nothing to gain by Korund's success. Nothing to lose by his failure, either."

Alban turned on an updraft, mild amusement replacing curiosity. Neither of the men below seemed pleased about meeting the other; the secretiveness of it all was in his own mind. He circled again, aware he wouldn't long go unnoticed, but more inclined to listen than interrupt. He could follow Malik from here, whether the djinn wanted him to or not.

"Do you *threaten* me?" Malik asked incredulously.

Biali stopped his pacing a step or two away from the djinn, appearing squat and ugly in comparison to Malik's delicate form. "If I were threatening you, I wouldn't do it with words."

As easily as that, he swung his arm, catching Malik's cheek with a backhand blow that knocked the djinn off his feet. Shock snapped Alban's wings wide, holding him frozen above the building for a few long seconds. Infighting was rare enough. To see one of the Old Races so blatantly attack another fell outside Alban's realm of experience, and astonishment held him motionless for a moment.

Then outrage surged that his ward, no matter how unwilling that station was on either part, had been assaulted. He snapped his wings shut and dove.

Biali turned as though he knew Alban was there, arms and wings spread wide in invitation. Alban slammed into him from above, bowling him over. They bounced across the rooftop in a snarling mass of claw and tooth, wings clamped against their bodies. For a few seconds chaos ruled, all of Alban's intellect swept away by the instinctive need to protect that which he had promised to. Biali caught him by the jaw as they rolled to a stop, lifting his head and cracking it back against the concrete.

Pain reverberated through his skull, shaking loose the control that held memory safe and intact within him. He felt Biali's glee as if it were his own, a spike of delight as he dived through the cracks of Alban's mind. Alban roared, using the sound as both distraction and focus, and slammed his hands into Biali's chest. The massive surge of power sent the other gargoyle tumbling. Alban sprang forward and pounced, Malik forgotten in his desire to know what memories Biali had tried to steal.

Biali had no time to regain his feet, but kicked upward as Alban jumped him, catching him in the belly and throwing him toward the roof's edge. Alban's wings snapped open, carrying him in a sharp-cornered glide back to the rooftop. Malik had risen, fury contorting his features, but he hadn't fled. Nor had he moved to attack Biali: Alban was far better-suited for that than he. It astonished Alban that Biali had so much as landed a blow, and if *he* were astonished, the insulted djinn would be livid.

Alban reminded himself that it was neither Malik's injured pride, nor his own angry curiosity at what memories Biali wanted that he fought for, but rather for the djinn's safety. He crashed into Biali a second time, tumbling across the roof in another hissing, spitting struggle for dominance. They landed on their feet, locked together in a titanic brace. Alban's height was matched by Biali's thick bulk: neither had the advantage as they strained and shoved against one another. A shudder tore through Alban as his taloned feet gripped the concrete beneath him, beginning to tear grooves in it. Biali locked gazes with him, and suddenly the battle shifted ground.

Memory mountains shattered the space around them, growing tall toward a clear night sky. Alban didn't need to look to recognize them. They had the feel of home: his own memories; Hajnal's. And Biali's, as intimate in their way as the ones Alban had spent a lifetime building with his mate. He and Biali were bound together in more ways than he liked to acknowledge, centuries of rivalry and love creating unbreakable bonds between them. The weight of years bore down, mountains crushing his will beneath Biali's as the other gargoyle sought answers for unspoken questions.

Alban stood fast, as caught by memory as he was by his rival in the physical world. Biali tore at his mind, and Alban strengthened his resolve. He had not endured centuries of solitude, had not earned the appellation the Breach amongst his own people, to fall beneath Biali's demands so easily. For an instant he felt Biali's will falter.

Victory sang through Alban's blood and he pushed harder, seeking not just to protect his own memories, but to mine Biali's. *Something* drove the other gargoyle, some need to possess memories that only Alban held, and of those, only one had the power to set Alban apart from all his people for all his years. He buried thoughts of promises made eighteen score years and more ago, and drove forward into stony memory, searching for Biali's motivations. Why attack Malik, why raid Alban's personal histories, why—

An answer broke, flaring bright and sharp on the surface of Biali's thoughts. No more reason to attack Malik than to draw Alban into battle, though below that lay a stony lack of care as to what happened to the djinn. His life was irrelevant, a trinket to use, as if Biali had learned lessons at Janx's feet all too well. Alban faltered, shocked, and his rival surged forward again, regaining lost ground.

A new peak shattered up from the earth, bolstering Biali's confidence, comfortable and uninvited all at once. It lay too close to their memories—to Biali's, to Hajnal's, to Alban's own—to be so unknown, and too far away to be welcomed within the stretch of range that was their own. But its roots went as deep as any other, making it belong whether Alban recognized it or not. Curiosity and caution drove him to reach for it, seeking knowledge of its maker to learn whose memory lay so close to theirs. To learn from whose memory Biali could draw such strength, and to see if it was a source from which his own reserves could be fortified.

Familiarity swept over him once more. The new memories tasted of Hajnal and Biali; and most of all, bitter hate born from insanity.

"Ausra." Alban heard himself speak the name in a scraping voice, and on the physical battlefield saw

Biali's eyes flash with angry triumph. Alban thrust memories of the girl who might have been his daughter away too late; for a bare instant all that he knew of her was laid out before Biali's silent inquisition. The tragedy of her birth, the madness of her life.

The method of her death.

Biali capitulated so quickly that Alban stumbled forward, off balance. He expected, but didn't see, the blow that caught him between the wings, and bellowed with pain. Biali skipped to one side with a harsh, derisive bark, not pressing his advantage. Alban scrambled out of reach, then faced his opponent warily.

"Breach." Biali spat the word, then simply turned away, scarred face wrinkled in disgust. As Alban watched, astonished, he opened his wings and caught a gust of wind, letting it carry him away from the Flatiron Building.

Malik, as if riding the same drafts, appeared at Alban's side, a thin smile beneath a bruise purpling on his cheek. "You've done yourself no favors by playing my champion."

Alban straightened, voice heavy in reply. "It's not a part to play. And no." He turned his focus on the djinn, ignoring the nastiness of Malik's smile. "I haven't. Why aren't you afraid?"

"Of *him?*" Malik's lip curled with derision. "What can a gargoyle do to a djinn?"

"That blow could have broken your neck. Djinn are hard to hit, not impossible." His gaze fell to Malik's cane. "Which it seems you should already know. And if not of Biali in particular, then of whomever it is who's hunting Janx's men in general. Djinn are only hard to hit," he repeated thoughtfully.

"Biali won't land another blow," Malik said through his teeth. "As for the others, they were only human. Humans are my prey, not my predators."

"Humans like Russell Lomax?" The question was born from Margrit's suspicions, rather than any detail stolen from Biali's memories, and Alban had no way to force a response. The best he might do was find an answer in Malik's reaction, and share with Margrit what he learned from that.

Disdain washed over Malik's face. "You'd like to run back to your human lawyer with all the answers, wouldn't you? Play her hero, having failed as mine." He began to disappear into an oily black shadow. "Try. You'll fail again, with no way to stop it. I'll visit her and hers in the morning. Sleep on that, Stoneheart."

TWENTY

MARGRIT STOOD AT her own front door, key in hand, oddly reluctant to use it. Beyond that threshold lay her ordinary life, not made up of Old Races' quorums or gargoyle lovers.

Beyond it lay explanations she didn't know how to make. She took a breath, then stepped back, abandoning her plan to go home in favor of somewhere—anywhere—else. Chelsea's, maybe, or even Daisani's office. Kaimana's hotel suite. Anywhere that wasn't home, facing friends who lay on the far side of a divide that seemed to grow deeper by the moment.

"Coward." She whispered that aloud, bringing the heat of another blush to her cheeks. Running was the coward's way out, an action that belonged to someone else. Finding the heart-pounding desire to escape within herself was an embarrassment. Even in the chaotic first days, when Alban had first come to her for help, she hadn't *run.* She'd *refused,* but it hadn't been a childish fear of confrontation that had driven her to do so. She thrust her jaw forward now and reached for the doorknob.

It turned under her hand and Cole pulled the door open. He had his coat and shoes on, relief spilling over his features as he stepped back to let her in. "There you are. We were worried. I was about to go look for you."

Margrit squeaked and put her hand over her heart, dragging in a deep breath. "I told you I was going to disappear. Sorry." She came in and toed her shoes off as Cole closed the door behind her.

Cameron appeared from the kitchen to hug her. "Yeah, but I thought you'd introduce us to Mr. Daisani first. Where'd you go?"

"For what it's worth, he noticed you." Margrit winced at the admission, wishing Daisani hadn't seen her tall blond friend amongst the selkies, and having no idea how it might've been avoided. "He said you were lovely. I had to…work."

Cameron's smile wobbled. "Tell him thanks. You okay, Grit?"

"No. Not really. It's been a horrible few days. Tony broke up with me." The last words came out randomly, surprising her. Margrit stared down the hallway, afraid to look at either of her housemates as she tried to sort out her emotions. She felt numb, primarily, as if someone could bounce coins off her skin and she'd only detect a distant thud of impact. Buried beneath the safety of that anesthesia lay an ugly worm of relief, and she didn't want to face that yet.

"Oh. Oh, no, honey, I'm so sorry." Cam walked her down to the kitchen and put her hands on Margrit's shoulders, slouching to get a look at her expression. "Are you okay?"

"I'm…" Margrit shook her head, trying to clear her thoughts. "I'm okay. I'm fine. This's been coming since January. I just… Do we have any ice cream?"

"I can send Cole out for some." Cameron's voice was already rising as she spoke.

"No. No, it's okay. I'm okay, really. I'm just…I don't know." She looked back at the front door. "We've been off and on for so many years, I think now that it's real I don't know how to…" Words failed her again and she ducked beneath Cameron's arm to pull open the freezer door. "How can I be out of ice cream?"

"Maybe because you eat it a pint at a time?" Cam asked. Margrit looked over her shoulder to find a gentle smile on her friend's face, and closed the fridge door again.

"Yeah. Yeah, okay, I guess that might be why. I should buy stock in Häagen-Dazs."

"You mean you don't own controlling interest by now?" Cameron crossed the kitchen to hug her. "What happened tonight?" she asked more quietly.

Margrit put her forehead against Cam's shoulder for a moment, hanging on. "It was a business meeting. I didn't know Alban would be there. I didn't know *Tony* would be there."

"Would it have changed anything if you had?"

Margrit looked away, caught. "I don't know. It might be better this way."

"Are you sure? I don't want to make this even more complicated, Grit, but you're talking about a guy who was wanted on murder charges a couple months ago, right?"

"For murders he didn't commit." Margrit set her front teeth together at the blasé application of truth in that claim, but left it alone, unable to explain further. "If Alban had never come into my life at all, Tony and I might be planning a wedding by now, and we might've even managed to live happily ever after. A good solid ordinary life. And I'd never know what I was missing."

"What are you missing?" Cole spoke from the kitchen door.

Margrit, hopelessly, said, "The chance to fly," and lowered her eyes so she didn't have to see the uncomprehending look her housemates shared. "I'm going to go get ice cream. Want any?"

"You want company?" Cameron asked.

Margrit shook her head. "I think I might go for a run first. I feel kind of sick. It'd make me feel better."

"It's eleven at night, Grit," Cole said doggedly. "Working for Daisani's got to come with a gym membership. If you're going to run, be safe, will you? Go use a treadmill."

"I hate treadmills, Cole. You don't go anywhere. I'll—*ugh.* All right, all *right,*" she said to twin disapproving glares. "I'll just go to the corner store. Shit," she added with feeling, as Cam scooped up her own coat from a dining room chair and gestured imperiously toward the door. Margrit sighed. "What, you don't trust me? I'm wearing heels. Not even I go running in heels."

"Extenuating circumstances. You've just been dumped. It may cause drastic behavior changes. Besides." Cameron herded her toward the door. "You always get me that chocolate banana stuff and I need a new favorite before I turn into a monkey. If we're not back in twenty minutes," she said over her shoulder to Cole, "we've gone out to drown Margrit's sorrows in Long Island iced teas, and won't be home until the bars close."

"Hey. You said ice cream, not a night of boozing it up. Wait for me."

* * *

"Cab," Margrit said firmly. It was the only word she could remember having spoken since the bartender had announced last call. She'd lounged on a bar stool until Cameron poured her off it, and in the interminable thirty-foot walk from the bar to the street, the only thing Margrit had been certain of was the need to take a taxi home.

"It's only four blocks, Grit," Cole said. "You can run four blocks in thirty seconds."

"Nope. Cab." A surge of giddy pride at inserting a second word into her protests knocked her off balance, and she stopped walking. The world wobbled precariously around her and she breathed slowly, keeping herself drawn up straight and tall.

"Grit, you only had one drink. You're faking it."

Margrit made a slow, ponderous turn to face her housemate. "I had one Long Island iced tea, Cole. That's seven shots." Smug delight bloomed at enunciating "seven shots" clearly. Buoyed by it, she put her hand out and worked her way toward the nearest wall, finally slumping with drunken exhaustion. "I'm just going to take a nap here. Let me know when we get a taxi." With her eyes closed, she felt less obliged to produce a facade of sobriety. "You want meet him?"

The urge to slap her hand over her mouth and take back the question was overridden by the lack of coördination to do so. Even prying her eyes open to find Cameron and Cole glancing at each other took more effort than seemed worth it. Margrit tilted her head against the building. "You can say no."

"Why don't you tell us a little about him first?" Cole's voice was guarded.

"What do you want to know?"

"How about, why didn't he go to the cops in January?"

Margrit drew in a deep breath, just sober enough to realize she shouldn't have opened herself up for questions when she'd been drinking. The influx of oxygen produced a feeling of nausea in a stomach awash with alcohol. "He's got a condition," she said very carefully. "He can't be out in daylight, at all, and there was no way to be sure he'd be in and out before dawn."

"What, like a sun allergy?" Cameron's voice drifted down the street. Margrit squinted, finding her standing on the curb searching the street for a cab. "I've never heard of a sun allergy that bad. What about hats and sunblock?"

"Sunblock and hats don't work. He can't be in the sunlight at all. Like dating Lestat. Only without the whining."

"Cops would've worked with a medical condition, Margrit." Cole's voice remained stiff.

Margrit sighed. "Maybe. But he felt like he couldn't go to them." She closed her mouth on further explanations, painfully aware that they, too, would fall short.

Cole eyed her a moment, then let it go. "So what's he do for a living, if he can't go out during the day?"

"He's got, what do you call it? Means. Not rich, but he doesn't work." Margrit rolled her head against the wall, trying to shake off a little of the alcohol. "He does soup kitchen volunteering and stuff. He's a decent guy."

"How does he know Eliseo Daisani? Hey! Hey, taxi!" Cameron's whistle ripped along the street, shocking Margrit into wakefulness. A cab down the block flipped its turn signal off and came toward them as Margrit took careful, precise steps toward the curb.

"They belonged to the same exclusive club when they were younger. Guess they still do. They're not friends. They just know each other. I don't know if anybody's friends with Daisani." Margrit bit her tongue to keep from babbling as Cole opened the cab door for her with a gallant flourish.

"So how come you took the job, anyway, Grit?" His question followed her into the taxi a moment before he did.

"It was better to have him over a barrel than be over one myself," she answered with forthright honesty, then made duck lips at him. "You're asking me questions because I'm too drunk to think before answering, aren't you?"

"Absolutely. Why'd you break up with me in college?"

Margrit threw her head back and laughed out loud, as Cole looked pleased with himself. Even Cameron laughed, too, giving the driver their address before saying, "Even I know that one. Everybody says you had all the chemistry of wet flour. Too bad. You're very pretty together."

The cab pulled up in front of their apartment building and Margrit paid, then put her hands out toward her housemates. "Help, please." They drew her from the taxi, trying not to laugh openly as she staggered to keep her feet. "You're horrible friends," she told them. "Laughing at my misfortune. I get dumped and drunk and never did get any ice cream and you're laughing at me." She shook their hands off, drawing herself up to her full three inches over five feet in height. "I'm going to get ice cream."

"Wired on sugar and buzzed on alcohol," Cole said to Cam. "I think we should go with her and watch this."

"Good. You can buy me ice cream. I just spent all my money on the cab." Margrit reeled around and marched off to the convenience store.

TWENTY-ONE

"MARGRIT." ALBAN STEPPED out of an alley, realizing his error when Margrit shrieked and stumbled away. He knew the pair she was with from glimpses through doors and a few seconds of watching them at the ice rink. The slender blond woman with the broad shoulders was Cameron, and she yelped as well, clutching Margrit's arm. Their escort was Cole, black haired, shorter than Cameron and instinctively protective as he stepped in front of the women. Alban opened his mouth and shut it again, startled at his own loss for words. "Forgive me," he said after a few seconds. "I didn't intend to alarm anyone."

Cole's belligerent growl died in his throat, stance relaxing a little as he half recognized Alban, though he cast a glance at Margrit for a cue as to how to behave. She said, *"Alban,"* in relieved exasperation as she edged past Cole. "What are you doing here?"

"No one was home at your apartment." He made a small gesture, more to the sky than the buildings. "I waited, and when I heard your voice, I…" Words failed him again, this time because the truth seemed peculiarly ludicrous in the presence of Margrit's housemates. It was easy to say "I came down from the rooftops" to

Margrit, but not when Cole and Cameron stared curiously at him. "Forgive me," he said again, and drew himself up. "I'm Alban Korund. We've never quite met." He offered a hand to Cole, wondering if the human male would take it.

Margrit muttered a curse and said, "Sorry," more clearly. "Sorry, sorry. Cole, Cameron, this is…this is Alban. These are my housemates, Cole Grierson and Cameron Dugan. Shit. Sorry. I've had too much to drink."

Cole scowled between Margrit to Alban before Cameron inserted herself in front of him. "Hi. I'm Cam. I'm glad we're finally getting a chance to meet you." She shook Alban's hand with an unexpectedly firm grip and offered a warm smile. "We're on our way to get some ice cream, just to make sure Margrit's really hungover in the morning. Want to come along?"

"Oh," Alban said. "I—"

"Might as well." Cole, clearly outplayed by Cameron, set his jaw, then shook Alban's hand without making a contest of it. "Sorry about the last time we met." There was little apology in his voice, but Alban inclined his head, in recognition of the form, if not Cole's sincerity.

"You had cause to be suspicious. It's good that Margrit's friends care enough to protect her."

"That's ancient history now," Cameron said firmly. "Come on. Grit's out of money, so we have to buy her her drug of choice. Triple-chocolate fudge ripple with brownie chunks."

Margrit smiled tentatively. "That sounds good. Except…what's going on, Alban?" Her smile faded. "It's pushing three in the morning. What're you doing here? I thought you were watching…"

"I was." Alban's voice dropped to a rumble. "He gave me cause to seek you out."

Margrit drew in a slow breath, nostrils flaring. Her gaze cleared, as though however much she'd had to drink only needed a firm chastisement to leave her system. A single sip of a vampire's blood offered health, but whether that chased away the ravages of alcohol, Alban didn't know. From Margrit's sudden steadiness, it seemed that it might. She said, "Shit," without the earlier enthusiasm. "Guys, can you—"

"Come on, Grit." Cole's voice had an edge. "You're not going to go running off again, are you? We can get some ice cream and chips and beer and stay up all night getting to know each other. Won't that be fun?"

Cameron elbowed him, then slid her arm through his and tugged. "Sure, Grit. Catch up to us, will you?"

"Cam."

"Cole."

"It can wait," Alban said abruptly. Margrit caught her breath and he offered her a cautious smile. "A little while. Long enough for ice cream, certainly. I can't stay all night," he added, returning his attention to Cole. "I have to leave before dawn."

"All right." Cameron pushed the store door open and squinted at the brightness within. "Everybody break for the freezer section. I'll get the chips and meet you at the cash register. Go, go, go!" She and Cole went opposite directions, leaving Margrit and Alban at the door.

Margrit offered a brief smile. "I've been eyeball deep in your world. Welcome to mine."

Gladness surged through him at the welcome, surprising him with its strength. A smile that felt foolish worked its way into place. "Thank you. I want to be here." That, too, had a more powerful ring of truth to it than he expected, and for a moment he was relieved that stone wasn't given to blushing. "Margrit, I am sorry for these complications. For my choices that have made things more difficult for you. For—" He broke off.

"Alban, why are you here? What'd Malik do?" Margrit's eyes and stance had cleared considerably in the time they'd been together, though the scent of alcohol still hung about her. He refrained from asking after her condition, suspecting she was unaware of her own recovery.

Alban cast a glance over her head toward the convenience store. "Nothing yet, and he won't as long as I'm with you. Explaining can wait until after the ice cream."

"Oh, so you're back on my watch, are you?" Margrit's tone was more laced with rue than acid.

Alban lowered his gaze. "I am, if you'll have me back."

Margrit sighed. "It's not as much fun running in the park when I don't trust you're there to watch my back. Just try not to do the strong silent hero thing again, Alban. I want a partner, not a protector. Can you do that?"

"I can try." Alban looked up to find Cole watching them from the freezer section, arms folded across his chest. "I think the rest of it should wait a while. Your friend won't like it if I don't..."

"Play along?" There was a note of pain in Margrit's voice and Alban frowned, guessing at its source.

"I would have said 'participate.' This is your life, Margrit, not a game."

"But you can play at being human. I can't even pretend to be one of you." Margrit finally stepped through the door and followed Cole to the ice cream.

* * *

Not until she saw Alban standing among her friends had it really struck Margrit how badly he might fit into her world. Awkward as it was, she fit into his better. At least the Old Races knew what she was. There was no pretense, no playing a role to make herself part of a society she hadn't been born to. No matter what Alban did in the human world, he was faced with either a lie or a truth so overwhelming it was almost inconceivable.

"Earth to Margrit. Hello, Grit? Are you that drunk?"

"What?" Margrit looked up with a blink, her thoughts interrupted by Cameron's good-natured teasing. "That sleepy, maybe. What'd I miss?" They'd retired to the apartment after buying four individual pints of ice cream, then partitioned the different flavors into bowls and handed them around. Alban had eaten his with the incredulous expression of a child who'd never tasted the sweet stuff before, while Cameron kept an easy conversation going despite Cole's taciturn responses and Margrit's tendency to fall silent as she watched the human-form gargoyle.

"An argument over whether pralines or chocolate made the superior ice cream. It's the kind of thing I'd think you'd have an opinion on."

"Job training permits me to have an opinion on everything." Margrit put her empty bowl aside and rubbed her hands over her face, the chill waking her up. "Pralines in chocolate with a caramel swirl would be most superior of all. Does anybody make that?"

"I do," Cole said from the couch. He hadn't moved since finishing his ice cream, except to drape an elbow over his eyes as he sprawled in the cushions. "Or I could. For a price."

"A place on Park Avenue?"

"I'm not greedy. I'd settle for…" He yawned, then flapped his hand. "Something less showy."

Cameron laughed. "Alban's the only one awake anymore. I guess night shift has its advantages. You're really that allergic to sunlight? What about cloudy days? It must suck, never hanging out on a beach at noon."

"I wouldn't know," Alban said so solemnly it made Margrit smile. "I don't miss what I've never had. And…yes," he added carefully. "My reaction to sunlight is fairly extraordinary. Clouds, unfortunately, don't block the reaction."

"Probably caused by UV rays." Cole waved a hand as if trying to encompass information with it. "I thought there were medical treatments for that kind of problem these days. Take a pill, solve all your problems."

Margrit met Alban's gaze, both of them bemused at the idea. "Imagine if it were that simple," he said.

Margrit huffed. "I can't. That would be too weird. Like vampires surviving on iron supplements." She eyed Alban, who shook his head, then set his empty bowl aside.

"Speaking of morning, I should go."

"I'll walk you out." Margrit got to her feet as Alban did. Cole remained on the couch, yawning until his jaw cracked, but Cameron stood, as well.

"It was nice to meet you, Alban. Maybe sometime we can get Margrit's new boss to send a car with really tinted windows around for you, and you can come to dinner."

"We'll have to make it a European sort of meal," Alban said apologetically. "Beginning late and ending even later. I simply don't go out in the daytime."

"We could come in," Cam volunteered, then caught Margrit's expression and subsided. "Well, I'm glad we met you, anyway, and that you're not a murderer."

Margrit put a hand over her face as Cole roused himself enough to stare at Cameron. "Even I've been more tactful than that, Cam."

"Not much," she muttered, then smiled brightly. "G'night, Alban. G'night, Grit. You can stay up all night," she said to Cole. "I'm going to bed."

"I already stayed up all night. It's way past all night and seriously into all morning." He dragged himself off the couch to follow Cameron out of the living room.

Margrit swayed in the abrupt silence, as if Cam's chatter had kept her grounded. Alban murmured, "That went better than I feared."

"Yeah. Yeah, I guess it did." She held out her hand. "Come on, let's get you out of here. Even if sunrise isn't for another two hours."

"Agreed." He slipped his hand around hers, enveloping her fingers, and she led him from the apartment, automatically choosing to climb rather than descend the stairs. Only on the rooftop did she release his hand and step back, wrapping her arms around herself as she searched for the right words to say.

Alban took away the need, shifting to his gargoyle form as he spoke. "Malik threatened you in daylight hours, Margrit. It's a gargoyle's weakness, that we can't defend what we—" He caught his breath and an anticipatory chill shot through Margrit, thoroughly wakening her. "What we care for," he said after a moment, much more softly. "Everything we hold dear is vulnerable during the day."

Disappointment at what he hadn't said cut through

her. Margrit dropped her gaze to the rooftop beneath her feet, swallowing against a tight throat. "Well, I can arm myself against him, but why go after me now?"

"The selkies have named you as the instigator of their revolution, and djinn and selkie are ancient enemies. You've upset our whole world, our balance. That's reason enough, even if he didn't already dislike you."

"The feeling's mutual," Margrit said beneath her breath. "I don't want to put on airs, but if Malik goes after me now that I'm working for Eliseo, isn't that just slow suicide? He's still furious over Vanessa's death. If I wind up dead, too…"

"It's not a risk I would take," Alban admitted. "Our laws may demand exile for killing each other, but if Eliseo were to lose two assistants to Janx's people within half a year, he may not care about the rules."

Cold sharper than the spring night shivered through Margrit. "You don't think this is all Janx's idea, do you?"

"No." The immediacy of Alban's response did more to reassure her than she'd thought possible. "Janx would consider killing you to be shortsighted. Murdering Vanessa was a blow in an eternal game, but you're still too finely balanced between the two of them."

"Am I? Even if I'm working for Eliseo?"

"You are." Alban's voice softened. "If for no other reason than you've involved me in their standoff, whether you intended to or not, and that's something they've both wanted for a long time. Without you, they have no control over me."

"That sounds like a good reason for you to stay away."

"It is, but my intentions to do so are thwarted at every turn. Perhaps it's past time I learned from that."

"It is," Margrit echoed firmly. "Alban, hear me out, okay? My life has seemed like a washed-out watercolor for the last three months. I didn't even notice it until you fell out of the sky again a few nights ago. It all looks fine until somebody throws a splash of real color onto the page, and then everything else looks pale and dull."

"I thought that was what sent you running through the park at night. I thought that was where you drew your colors from." Alban sounded bemused and sad, any flattery taken from Margrit's comment lost beneath deeper emotion.

She stepped back, gazing up at the gargoyle in astonishment. It took effort to whisper, "Nobody understands that," through a throat gone tight with longing.

Alban's heavy eyebrows drew down. "Isn't it self-evident? It's a dangerous behavior. Why would you do it if not to throw paint on the canvas, to use your words? It's why I began watching you all those years ago, before any of this." He made a brief circle with one hand, encompassing the two of them. "Before I knew anything about your life, I knew that you ran in the park at night to challenge the order of the world you lived in."

A fluting laugh escaped Margrit. "You should have said hello years ago. Nobody gets it, Alban. Not my parents, not my housemates, certainly not Tony. They just see me being stupid. I can't explain that I need to—" Her voice broke and she fluttered her hands, tiny gestures of desire as much for the right word as a burgeoning impulse to catch Alban and his understanding and never let them go. "To fly," she finally finished, feeling the explanation was wholly inadequate.

His strength enveloped her, solid as stone, yet filling

her with warmth and confidence. A surge of power sent them upward. Alban's wings snapped open, their apparent delicacy belied by the authority with which they swept down and drove them higher into the air. Margrit gasped laughter into Alban's shoulder, hardly knowing when she'd wound her arms around his neck. "I thought gargoyles weren't impulsive."

"Occasionally," Alban growled, good nature in the deep sound, "even stone is inspired to enthusiasm. I told you once you could fly now."

Margrit twisted, looking over her shoulder at the receding city. Hair blew in her face, stinging her eyes as much as the cold wind did. She felt tears slip through her lashes and streak her temples. "You did." The accusation that he'd then left her for months hung unspoken between them, until Margrit dared unwind an arm and wipe tears from her face. "I should get aviator goggles. And warm pants."

She shivered, drawing close to the gargoyle again. He rumbled, tightening his arms around her until she felt his heartbeat, slower and steadier by far than her own. She counted those heartbeats, both his and hers, until they became nothing more than a tangle of shared life, similarities played up instead of differences. Engines and horns honking in the city cut through the sound of wind rushing in her ears, a distant reminder of the world below them. *Her* world, the one she moved through every day, and at the same time separate from her in a way made clear not just by the gargoyle in whose arms she flew, but by the extraordinary men she'd encountered in the past day.

"Alban." She whispered his name against his skin, nose pressed into his neck so she could inhale his clean earthy scent. He curved his head over hers, listening, and she smiled at the temptation to brush her lips against his throat. His ears tapered to narrow, delicate points just in her line of sight, making an intriguing target. The temptation to discover if gargoyle ears were as sensitive to nibbling as human ones teased her. Alban's inhumanity seemed less of a barrier than it once had, time helping her to adjust and distance replacing caution with inquisitiveness. In his arms, the possibility of freedom from the ordinary seemed so close that she ached from the burden of wanting it. Margrit turned her face against Alban's shoulder once more, clinging a few long seconds before forcing practicality and the matters at hand to the forefront. "Where are we going?"

"To see Eliseo before the sun rises."

"He's going to have guard dogs. Or security. Or both. We can't just show up on his doorstep. He's Eliseo Daisani, for God's sake, and it's four in the morning." Margrit's protests were weak even to her own ears.

Alban dipped his head with a reassuring chuckle. "There's no guard dog in the world that could endanger me. And he may be Eliseo Daisani, but he's also a vampire, and he'll certainly see us. I doubt he'll bother his security. They're nothing more than showpieces."

"Shouldn't we at least call ahead?" It was too late by the time she asked, the Upper East Side building Daisani lived in already in view. "Why Daisani?"

"Because he has a deep interest in you, and he can move about in the daytime." Alban came to a landing at the edge of a helicopter pad, avoiding the ungainly white machine's tail. Without the wind from the flight, the air felt suddenly warm. Margrit shivered as Alban set her on her feet. Arms wrapped around herself, she stared at the helicopter and muttered, “My life has gotten so strange.”

“I beg your pardon?”

“Nothing. I’ve just never actually seen a helicopter from this close before.”

“Gargoyles and vampires abound, and yet a helicopter impresses you. I will never understand humans, Margrit Knight.”

“That’s all right. They’ll probably never understand you.” She set off for the rooftop door, which appeared to be half a mile away. “It’s going to be locked. How’re we supposed to get Eliseo’s attention?”

“Oh,” Daisani said out of nowhere, drolly, “you have it.”

TWENTY-TWO

MARGRIT SHRIEKED LIKE a little girl for the second time that evening, whipping around to locate the vampire. He leaned against the helicopter's running board, arms across his chest, and offered a wink when she located him.

Across the rooftop, the door banged shut, making Margrit look toward it again. "I didn't even see it open," she muttered. "I wish you people would stop doing that."

"Which part?" Daisani asked pleasantly.

Caught between laughter and a scowl, she said, "Stepping out of shadows and scaring the hell out of me, but zipping around faster than I can see, too, now that you mention it. How'd you know we were here?"

"Rooftop security is under my jurisdiction. Alban," he said with mock dismay, "this was one of your less wise decisions. Other people live here. What if I didn't control the security? The tapes are being wiped, but I'd think you knew better than to arrive quite so blatantly."

"I've known you for a long time," Alban said dryly. "There's no chance you wouldn't control the security where you live. Eliseo, we have a problem."

"We," Daisani echoed in fascination. "When was the last time we had a problem?"

"You know as well as I do." Alban's voice darkened. Margrit straightened, looking from one man to the other with curiosity bordering on alarm. After a few seconds, Daisani bowed his head in an acquiescence Margrit had never seen in him before. Alban rumbled in wordless acknowledgment, and as if he'd been released from an agreement, Daisani straightened and gestured toward the door.

"I'm sure whatever it is can be discussed inside where it's warm. Margrit's turning blue."

"Blue's a good color on me." Margrit started for the door again. Daisani held it open before she'd taken more than two steps, and she slowed, looking over her shoulder to gauge the distance he'd crossed so swiftly. "You just like doing that, don't you," she said when she was close enough to not have to lift her voice. "You don't get to show off in front of people very often, so you take whatever chance you can get."

"People?" Daisani's eyebrows arched in challenge.

Margrit blew an undignified raspberry. "Humans."

"Guilty as charged. The novelty does eventually wear off."

"Does it? Or do you just start reining yourself in so you don't forget and make a mistake in front of the wrong person?"

"I assure you, Miss Knight." Daisani's voice went soft with bitterness. "None of us ever forget."

Cold lifted goose bumps on Margrit's arms and she stopped just inside the door, waiting for Alban and Daisani to follow her into the echoing stairwell. "I was thinking, earlier."

"Congratulations." Daisani spoke lightly, as if wiping away the sour note he'd struck a moment before.

Margrit brushed off his teasing, putting together slowly the words she wanted to say. "Your secrets would get you killed. But I remember pictures of my great-grandmother." She looked up to find both Daisani and Alban studying her with uncomprehending curiosity. "We're pretty sure her family had been working in big houses for a few generations. Great-Grandma probably could've passed, except if she'd gotten caught they would've hanged her. Things changed," Margrit said softly, too aware that she spoke from hope rather than conviction. "Maybe a hundred years from now you won't have to hide."

"The difference," Daisani said after a moment, "is that no one has been championing our cause for two centuries."

Margrit let her breath out in a rush. "I'm working on it." She leaned over the stair railing, looking down the spiral, and heard Alban move behind her, as if he'd keep her from a fall she had no intention of taking. "I don't have a hundred years," she said. "You'll have to take my grandchildren out someday, and show them what pikers the four-minute-milers are."

"I would like that." Daisani's tone changed again, a host of regrets audible in it. Margrit pushed away from the railing to find both men studying her with much the same expression, as though she were a rare breed of animal neither had expected to come upon.

Uncomfortable with their gazes, she glanced away. "You're going to have to get me through Malik first, though. That's why we came."

Daisani's eyebrows lifted. "Malik's got enough native cunning to realize targeting you would bring my wrath down on him. And if he doesn't, Janx isn't that stupid. Not twice. Not like this. I doubt you're in any danger, Margrit."

"Ordinarily I would agree, but Malik made a direct threat against her, to me. 'I'll visit her and hers in the morning,'" Alban quoted. "In the morning, so I would know, but be unable to protect her."

"Her and hers," Daisani echoed. "Were those his exact words?"

"Yes." The faintest note of insult laced Alban's voice. Margrit ducked her head, hiding a sudden bright grin. She imagined gargoyles were unaccustomed to having their memories questioned in any fashion. If her people were meant to bear the burden of preserving racial histories, she suspected she'd also find a cross-examination perturbing.

"If I were Janx," Daisani murmured, "I would not dare threaten Margrit. Not after Vanessa. Not after…" He glanced at Alban, who lowered his eyes in a concession Margrit didn't understand. Daisani nodded, then said, "Malik is a fool," more abruptly. "He's a fool, but he's Janx's fool, so for all his threats I think he would not victimize Margrit."

"Even with the selkies?" she asked with what struck her as unlikely calm. Malik frightened her, and she had no doubt he would move against her, given the chance. Discussing the possibility should give rise to terror, not to a courtroom composure that didn't allow for so much as a tremor in hand or voice. "Alban said they're the djinns' ancient enemy. If they perceive the selkies' arrival on the scene in so many numbers as my fault, is he really going to hold off because Janx will cluck his tongue and wag a finger in admonishment?"

"Four-thirty in the morning and she can use words

like *admonishment.* I must remember not to exchange barbs with you when you're in top form, Miss Knight." Daisani smiled, then put away quips to answer her question. "I believe he would. I believe there are better targets. Safer, equally effective choices. He said 'you and yours.' If I were in Malik's position, in Janx's, I wouldn't hunt you, Margrit.

"I would hunt your mother."

The fear Margrit hadn't felt for herself rose up in an overwhelming wave of sickness. Daisani offered an elbow in support, but let it fall again as she felt Alban's hands at her waist and his reassuring presence beside her. A tremor flowed through her and she closed her fingers over Alban's, leeching warmth. "My mother?" Her voice scratched and broke. She let go of Alban to press a fist against her stomach, trying to make horror leave her. "Mom?"

Daisani spoke with such cool candor it took her long moments to realize it disguised a wealth of fury. "It would be a well-executed blow. Russell first, though he's a far more obvious mark, if you're privy to my relationship with Janx. Rebecca, though. Rebecca would make a subtle and splendid choice. It's been so long since I've spoken to her, and there are so many people who work for me, that I might not have even considered it myself. But look at the depth of symmetry. She's one of the scant handful of humans I've revealed myself to, so my trust is there. She's your mother, so your love is there. She is an admirable target. I'm tempted to applaud him."

To her own dismay, Margrit could see his argument so clearly her revulsion to it seemed overblown. Her mother was a nearly perfect piece in the game Janx and Daisani played, worth capturing for the damage it would do. She swallowed, trying to loosen her throat. "You won't let him hurt her."

"He will not," Alban said in a deep, certain voice.

Daisani looked sharply at the gargoyle. Margrit felt Alban shift beside her, and glanced up to see an unfamiliar challenge in his expression.

"No," Daisani said after a long moment. "I will not. Dramatics are unnecessary, Alban. Had I anticipated Russell's death, I would have moved to protect him, and I assure you." He flashed a smile, teeth unnervingly flat and terribly white. "I assure you, I will not permit Margrit's mother to be sacrificed to this game. I have lost my queen already this year. I will not lose a knight."

"A knight." Margrit laughed unhappily. "I wouldn't think she'd be that important. I thought we were all pawns."

"You do yourself an injustice, Margrit. If you knew how few people I have shown myself to in the past five centuries..." Daisani shot a quelling glare at Alban, who shifted at Margrit's side, but subsided without speaking. "I'll do whatever is necessary to keep your parents from harm."

"How? Malik's intangible. How do you stop somebody who can just materialize inside your house?" Fear was fading into its more exhausted brother, fatalism. Margrit put the heel of one hand against her eye as if she could push away despair. "I'm losing my ability to cope," she mumbled. "I just hit a wall. I don't know what to do anymore."

"If I may be presumptuous, you might consider

sleeping. A gift of health doesn't negate the human requirement for rest."

Margrit shifted her head enough to look at Daisani from the corner of her eye. "An immortal lunatic's probably going to try to kill my mother, and you think I should sleep? You think I *could* sleep?"

"I think that in sixteen hours' time, you'll be attending a masquerade ball peopled with not only New York's elite, but every member of the Old Races in this city. I think you'll want to be at your best for that."

"Oh, God." Margrit slumped and Alban tightened his arm around her, shoring her up, shoring up the blessed feeling of not being alone. "I forgot about that. Masquerade? You didn't say anything about a masquerade. I don't have anything to wear."

Daisani smiled. "If you'd permit me, I'd be glad to lend you my tailor. You could even invite your mother along. That would put her under my eye for the afternoon, at the very least, and I think I can manage a few hours' surveillance in the morning without anyone noticing me. Take her home, Alban." He glanced down the stairs. "And I'll make my way to Flushing, to play the part of a gargoyle for the day."

Margrit balked, shaking her head as Alban tried to draw her toward the door. "Mom won't want to come. She doesn't like you." No sooner were the words spoken than Margrit frowned, uncertain of their truth. Rebecca was extremely cautious with regards to Eliseo Daisani, but that didn't necessarily constitute dislike.

A flash of something unreadable crossed Daisani's face. "Perhaps, but if her daughter, who has suffered an emotional blow in the last few days, invites her, I doubt she'll turn you down. And she may want to give me that steely glare of hers, when she hears you're coming to work for me. Or have you told her already?"

Margrit stared at him a moment, then shook her head. "I don't remember. I honestly can't remember. I must not have. I'd remember her flipping out."

"Then I look forward to the battle meeting." Daisani moved toward the stairs. "Really, next time you should come in through the front door, Alban. We might have had this conversation in the comfort of my living room instead of a concrete-and-steel stairwell."

Alban huffed as Margrit glanced down the spiral of stairs again. "I seem to be having a lot of conversations in stairwells these days. Must be the company I'm keeping." She looked up again with a brief smile. "Can I invite my housemates to the ball? Cam'll never forgive me if I get all dolled up without her."

"You can even bring her to the fitting party," Daisani said. "I'm sure Henri would thoroughly enjoy having such a model to work with."

"Henri?"

"My tailor."

"Your tailor is named Henri? Is he really French? That," Margrit said, at Daisani's nod, "is the most surreal thing I've encountered all day. Normal people don't have French tailors named Henri. Lifestyles of the rich and famous, here I come."

"I think you'd better take her home," Daisani said to Alban. "Sleep well, and don't worry. I'll watch out for your mother. I'll watch out for them all."

"You've been very quiet. Are you going to tell me this was another bad idea?" Margrit nestled against

Alban's chest, his heartbeat a slow counterpoint to Daisani's quick footsteps on the stairs.

Alban curled his arm around her shoulders, lowering his mouth against her hair. A rush of warmth swept her, the safety of his arms offering more comfort than she wanted to admit to. "If it was, it was my bad idea. No, in this case, I…trust Eliseo to do as he says he will."

Margrit tipped her head up, eyes half-closed as she studied the line of Alban's jaw. "Why? There was all this subtext going on there that I couldn't read. Not after Vanessa, not after what?"

A throb of memory caught her off guard, as startling for its familiarity as its presence. For an instant she saw a woman with long brown hair, wearing a gown so functional and plain it could have come from almost any era in the last five centuries. Her gaze was solemn and straightforward, almost challenging, and a pang of regret cut through Margrit's breast. Alban's regret, not her own, though there was little telling them apart when she rode his memory as she did now.

The woman stood with two men, both smaller than Margrit and Alban in height and breadth. One wore his red hair loose, falling over a gaudy crimson-and-green cloak. The other, more dapper, wore a dark ponytail and a half-coat in somber colors. Margrit felt herself—felt Alban—committing them to memory, as though they were old friends he wouldn't see again, and then he turned away, leaving them alone in the moonlight.

She caught her breath as she shook the memories off, then frowned at Alban. "Who is she?"

Unfiltered surprise darkened his eyes. "Who?"

"The woman. That's the second time I've seen her. The first time was when you went into the memories to see if Hajnal was still alive. I saw this woman, and I saw Janx and Daisani and you, all in completely different clothes. I just saw it all again. Who is she?"

Alban went quiet, surprise still evident in his features, but shaded by more complex emotions. "Her name was Sarah Hopkins," he finally replied. "That's all I can tell you, Margrit. Hers isn't my story to tell."

"Is it Janx and Eliseo's?"

"It is, but I would be cautious in asking them. Neither would like to hear that you catch fragments of my memories. I have been outside my people for centuries to avoid just that."

A memory of the woman came to her again, this time from Margrit's own mind—a recollection of the gesture she'd seen Sarah use the first time she'd caught a glimpse of her inside Alban's memories. "Oh. *Oh.* Oh, shit, Alban. You—"

He put a fingertip against her lips, then replaced it with the pad of his thumb, brushing so lightly it tickled and made her smile. "Don't say anything else," he asked. "Don't tell me what you've guessed, and don't ask me to confirm. Will you do that for me, Margrit?"

Margrit pressed her lips together beneath his touch, then nodded. When he took his hand away, she said, "You know this is going to kill me, right? Not asking."

A quick smile that had little to do with humor creased Alban's mouth. "It may eat at you, but it won't kill you. The answers you're looking for, though, might."

Nerves churned in Margrit's belly. "Right. Yeah, okay. Dammit, I wish it was just melodrama when you say things like that." She made fists, then released them. "I think Eliseo's right. It might be good for me to get some sleep. Could you take me home?"

"I will," Alban murmured. "And I'll watch over you until dawn breaks. Come." He offered his hand and led her outside. Margrit held on tight as they sprang into the air, willing herself not to look back.

Willing herself to hold her tongue, and not ask whose child Sarah Hopkins had borne: Janx's, or Daisani's.

TWENTY-THREE

ONCE OR TWICE, from a great distance, the *William Tell Overture* had played. It had sent images of footraces and concert halls through Margrit's dreams, incomprehensible but enjoyable. Only when her bed shifted with someone's weight and a woman's voice said, "Margrit. Margrit? I called, but you didn't answer," did a hint of consciousness seep through to tell her the music had been her phone's ring tone.

"Whutimesit?"

"Nearly one o'clock."

Head still buried in the pillows, Margrit struggled to turn that information into something meaningful, finally deducing that she'd had almost eight hours of sleep. Alban had left her on the rooftop minutes before five, and she'd staggered downstairs to collapse into bed. Eight hours was enough sleep. She tried to convince herself of that, then tried to count the number of hours she'd slept in the last week. It took only a few seconds to give up and bury herself farther into the covers.

"Margrit, would you like to tell me why Eliseo Daisani called our house at daybreak and invited your father and me to a ball?"

A giggle erupted into Margrit's pillow, so unexpected that at first she didn't realize it was her own laughter. It awakened her enough to ask, "Daybreak? Really?" much more clearly.

"At seven thirty-four," her mother said with asperity. "On a Saturday, Margrit."

Margrit giggled again, knowing it would draw lines of irritation around Rebecca's mouth, but unable to stop herself. "I'm sorry. Have you been calling since then?"

"I waited until nine. When you refused to answer—"

"I was sleeping!" Margrit rose from the blankets and shook her hair out of her face, giving her mother a wounded look.

"As some of us might have liked to have been. I took the train in to see if you were all right. Why didn't your housemates answer the phone?"

"'Cause they were at work?" No, it was Saturday. Cole, at least, didn't have to work. Margrit flopped back down and pulled the pillow over her head, knowing it wouldn't block out Rebecca's voice. She ought not to have given her mother a key to the apartment. She would still be sleeping blissfully if she hadn't made that mistake. "Maybe they went to breakfast." Or maybe, like Margrit herself, they'd simply slept through the ringing phone. She'd gone to bed later than them, but not by much. "Is Daddy here?"

"In the kitchen. You really should replace that refrigerator, Margrit, even if this isn't your apartment. It's contributing to global warming all on its own."

"I *like* our fridge." Margrit sat up and scrubbed her hands over her face. "Okay, go steal some of Cole's leftovers for lunch while I shower, and then I'll talk to you about the ball."

"So it does have something to do with you."

"Mom! Go! Go!" Margrit flapped her hands at Rebecca, who pursed her lips, then got up and left the room. Margrit groaned and fell back over, fumbling for her phone.

Eliseo Daisani picked up on the first ring, sounding amused. "Yes?"

"Did you have to call her before eight o'clock? What'd you *say?*" Margrit lifted a finger, as if he could see her. "And are you lurking outside my apartment playing superhero?"

"I did, and I am. I think Alban is better suited to it. I find myself hoping something dreadful will happen so I have something interesting to do. Do you suppose that's how the Avengers feel?"

"I can't even believe you know who the Avengers are. And no. Superheroes aren't supposed to go looking for trouble. They should be happier out of a job. What'd you *tell* her?"

She could all but hear Daisani shrug. "I told her you and your friends had agreed to come to my little party tonight, and that given the events of the last few days I thought you might be happier if you had family around, as well."

"You obviously don't know much about my relationship with my parents," Margrit muttered. "I mean, I love them dearly, but Mother is a busybody and I try not to give her too many details to involve herself in. But you didn't tell her about the job."

"I did not." Daisani sounded pleased with himself. "I'll keep them safe until sunset, but I'll leave running that particular gauntlet to you."

"Who's going to keep *me* safe?" Margrit demanded, but he had already hung up. She called Cameron's cell phone and put an only half-mocking note of alarm in her voice as she left a message. "Come home as fast as you can. My parents are here and I have to survive telling them I'm going to work for Daisani. And we all have to go get fitted for dresses for his party tonight." Trusting that would bring Cam home the instant she heard it, Margrit dropped the phone on the bed and went to take a fortifying shower before facing her parents.

The smell of hot food nearly knocked her off her feet when she emerged. Checking her phone showed a text message from Cam proclaiming, On our way! and voices from the kitchen suggested they'd arrived. Relieved, Margrit dressed and went down the hall, towel-drying her hair, to find both her housemates chatting with her parents. Cole was frying ham and Cameron was perched on the counter, Rebecca and Derek Knight less casual, but still comfortable in the kitchen space. Her father grinned and swept her into a hug that Margrit returned before nervously examining her mother's expression.

It suggested she'd gotten the general story from Cole and Cameron. Margrit twisted the towel in her hands. "I hadn't decided when I talked to you yesterday, Mom, I really hadn't."

"You hadn't mentioned the possibility, either. Really, Margrit, how much of that conversation was about Russell and how much of it was about Eliseo? Why didn't you tell me?"

Cameron and Cole exchanged wary glances, but Margrit shook her head at them. "Might as well stay. This is a huge change and you all deserve to know why I'm making it."

Rebecca's expression altered, as if her daughter had said something unexpected. "Well, you do," Margrit said, half-offended. "It's a hell of a thing to spring on everyone, and I'm sorry for that. I really was there to talk about Russell yesterday, which is why I didn't tell you then." That only began to touch on the truth, and she struggled to find an explanation that was honest without being impossible to believe.

"I didn't think I was going to take the job. Then when I went over to Daisani's offices after talking to you, I ended up sitting in on a meeting and handling some contract work, and I enjoyed it, Mom. I really did. I wished you were there, because what I don't know about financial securities would fill libraries, but it was fun. And then there's..." Margrit searched for words again. "I chose Legal Aid because I wanted to make a difference. I knew it meant defending bad guys, but the positive side was being able to help people who didn't have anywhere else to go. People like Luka. But Russell was killed for doing just that, and that's scary. It probably wouldn't be enough to drive me away on my own." She gave Cole a faint smile. "Because I'm the world's most stereotypical Taurus, right?"

"Well, you are." He made bull horns with his fingers and mocked charging her. Margrit's smile grew wider before she turned her attention back to her mother, as if Rebecca were judge and jury.

"But working for Daisani, I'll be able to help direct where his company's charitable contributions go, and oversee how that money's used by those charities. I'll be able to do pro bono work on my own." Neither of those details had been discussed, but Margrit was confident Daisani would agree. He wanted her working for him badly enough to pull out extraordinary stops among the Old Races. By comparison, what she'd outlined to her family was trivial. "It's a different kind of making a difference, but I think I can do a good job." She sighed. "And I guess an Upper East Side apartment wouldn't be awful, either."

"Well," Rebecca said after a long, startled silence. "I suppose Tony will be glad you're not working for Legal Aid anymore. You two fight about that all the time."

"Yeah." Margrit jutted her chin out and looked toward the ceiling, hoping she might find escape there. Not in daylight hours, though; Alban couldn't rescue her until nightfall. "Tony and I broke up yesterday. For good."

Later, Margrit had the impression her mother had caught her by the ear and dragged her outside to talk. She hadn't; Rebecca would never stoop to such crass behavior. Regardless, there'd been an astounded silence that Cole had abruptly filled with banging pans and popping grease on the stove, and then Margrit had found herself on the street with her mother and no clear idea of how they'd gotten there. "Mom?"

Rebecca marched toward the cathedral, heels clicking on the sidewalk. Margrit ran to catch up. "Mom?"

She didn't stop until she reached the corner. Then she took a breath and faced Margrit with a calm that utterly belied her swift departure from the apartment. "All right, Margrit. This isn't a topic I care to discuss, and I won't in front of your father, but I feel I have to ask. Does your breakup have anything to do with Eliseo Daisani?"

"With— What, like am I dating him? Mom! God,

you're as bad as Cole! I'm going to work for him, that's all. Tony and I have nothing to do with that." On the surface it was true. For one sharp, aching moment Margrit searched for a way to tell her more. But what little Rebecca knew about Daisani went nowhere near allowing Margrit to explain the circumstances that had driven Tony to break up with her. Miserable, she said, "Tony and I just didn't trust each other enough in the end, Mom. It wasn't going to work."

Nothing was going to work without trust. Exhausting loneliness rose up in Margrit and she swallowed against the desire to share all of Daisani's secrets, just so she wouldn't be alone. Heat burned her cheeks and tears stung her eyes as she gazed at the sky, wishing again that the one person she *could* talk to wasn't out of reach during daylight.

Rebecca touched her arm. When Margrit looked back at her, her expression was gentle. "I'm sorry, sweetheart. It's been a very hard week for you."

"You can say that again."

A hint of a smile played around Rebecca's eyes. "I'm sorry, sweetheart. It's been a very hard week for you."

Margrit snorted a soft laugh and stepped closer to hug her. "Thanks, Mom. I really am sorry I didn't talk to you earlier about going to work for Daisani. I honestly didn't think it was going to be an issue."

"I believe you." Rebecca's assurance sounded like a deliberate choice more than inherent confidence. "And I suppose if we're celebrating, your father and I will attend the gala tonight. If you really want us to."

Surprise lit Margrit's smile. "I really do. You'll look amazing. Really?" She hugged her again impulsively, and caught her hand. "Come on, let's have breakfast, then go see what kind of costumes he's got lined up for us."

"Oh my God. We are so far out of our league." Cameron clutched Cole's arm, whispering her assessment. Margrit, fingertips on a silver-lined glass railing, could only nod in silent agreement.

"Don't be silly." Rebecca Knight sounded amused, her voice entirely at odds with the elegant linen-and-gold costume she wore. Margrit thought Egyptian queens would envy her mother, and that pharaohs would find themselves lacking next to her broad-shouldered father, whose skin gleamed with gold dust. "No one here is the least bit superior to you."

"Maybe not superior, but they're all a lot richer! I mean, just *look* down there!" Cameron gestured, laughing at both the excess and her own awe of it.

The Daisani ballroom spread out below them, a broad oval between two sweeping staircases. Their little group stood on a landing, with glitter and crystalline light bouncing all around them. Beyond the dance floor itself lay secondary rooms, walls peeled back to make one enormous functional area lined with buffet tables, bars and scattered seating. Between shards of crystal-born rainbows the lighting was golden, radiating from globes whose brightness mimicked the sun without hurting the eyes. Marble dance floors were covered with hundreds of guests, most in formal wear and wearing simple masks, but with a weighty contingent in costume, or bearing masks of delicate and exquisite creation.

"I can't believe who's here," Cole admitted. "I see these people in tabloids."

"I see them in entertainment magazines." Cam nodded toward a young Marie Antoinette whose powdered wig added two feet to her height. "I think that's actually one of the costumes from the movie she starred in. Come on, let's go down."

"Go on, all of you," Margrit said. "I want to watch you make your entrance. You all look incredible."

"So do you, sweetheart." Rebecca kissed her cheek, then went down the stairs, arm in arm with her husband.

Cameron beamed at Margrit. "You're going to have to introduce us to Mr. Daisani, so we can thank him."

"I will." Margrit smiled and waved her friends off, watching them with pride and pleasure. They made a desperately striking couple on the stairs. Cameron, taller than Cole in any case, wore heels that put her several inches above him in height, which seemed to bother him not at all. Her blond hair fell in thick, styled waves over a crimson satin gown, folds of fabric creating a low scoop neck and falling beyond the dimple of her back. The skirt's train was long enough to require carrying on the steps, and had a delicate loop fashioned into it for just such occasions. Long gloves played up the strong lean muscles in her arms as she clung to Cole's elbow. He wore a charcoal-gray zoot suit, pinstripes and shirt the same scarlet as Cameron's dress. Their masks were painted on, an idea Cole had objected to until he'd seen the effect beneath the long-feathered fedora the tailor had set on his head, and then he'd acquiesced so quickly Cameron had teased him.

"They're quite extraordinary." Daisani spoke from Margrit's side before she realized he'd joined her. She turned and he took her in with a glance, putting a hand over his heart before he bowed. "As are you, my dear.

Would you care to join me on the dance floor?" He offered an arm, but Margrit hesitated, still looking over his outfit.

"I expected you to come as the Phantom," she confessed. "This is better. You look like Professor Moriarty."

Outrageous delight sparkled behind the monocle Daisani sported, its presence his only nod toward a mask. He wore a top hat and a fingertip-length black cloak lined in red silk that lent bulk to his slight form. Beneath it was a suit cut in a fashion over a century old. Margrit saw clearly that the finely cared-for fabric was aged, worn to a lighter shade of black at the seams, and that it looked soft with wear.

"The Phantom." His eyebrows rose, shifting his monocle so it caught the light and glittered. "Why did you think that?"

"I don't know." She found herself smiling. "Because what better costume to make it clear that this is your party, and that you're in control?"

Daisani turned to the ballroom below, his cape swishing with the motion. A ripple ran across the dance floor, voices stilling and bodies pivoting toward him, heads tilted upward. He turned back to Margrit almost instantly, and the flicker of attention faded, leaving no doubt that he'd commanded it. "Do you really think I need the Phantom's extravagance to dominate this dance hall, Miss Knight?"

"Evidently not." His smile stayed in place, though sorrow crept through her as she studied the vampire. On impulse she asked, "You wore this the night you met Vanessa, didn't you?"

Daisani canted his head in surprise before he gave her

a brief, acknowledging bow. He offered his elbow again in an elegant gesture, and Margrit tucked her hand into it. "I would be honored to accept your escort."

Surprise filtered through his expression again, and this time it was he who hesitated. "Are you afraid of nothing, Margrit?"

A genuine smile blossomed. "I'm afraid of lots of things, Eliseo, but not you. Not tonight."

"An unexpected gift." Daisani tucked her fingers into the crook of his elbow and escorted her down the stairs. People made space and offered greetings as he spun her onto the floor. Skirts swirling, laughter on her lips, Margrit put care and politics aside, and gave herself up to the joy of dancing.

He had only seen her dance once before.

That time had been in a club, the raucous music there nothing like the strains of a string quartet, one of three groups spelling one another in Daisani's ballroom. She had worn less formal clothing then, and had ridden the pulse of music like it was lifeblood, lingering in his arms without a care for her own safety. Taking freedom where the world offered it, just as she demanded it from her nighttime forays into the park.

She wore gold, a color he'd never seen on her. The sheath shimmered with her movements, following her hourglass curves. Thin straps tied at her nape, their length helping to create an illusion of height. A handful of loose curls trickled around her shoulders, highlights of copper playing up the color of her gown. She wore no mask, only a glittering makeup that brought an exotic touch to her coffee skin tones. Everything about her was warm and full of life, a direct contrast to his own cool silvers and whites.

Tony Pulcella, maskless and clad in a simple black tuxedo, moved through the dancers, disturbing their enjoyment with his purposeful strides. Margrit had yet to notice him, but she was clearly his quarry. Alban fell back a step from the balcony railing, unexpected envy making fists of his hands.

"You can't back out now, Stoneheart." Janx's voice came from behind him, dry sibilance. "You're here and you've been seen, but more important, I'm sure she's expecting you."

Alban scowled over his shoulder. In the ballroom lighting Janx's costume was even more impressive than it had been at the House of Cards, red and gold patterned to subtle scales that gleamed and shimmered like a living thing. The cut was traditional Chinese, though his knee-length coat was built of fluttering layers instead of being fitted and stiff. Even the pants were loose enough to flow, and the turned-up toes of his shoes were bedecked with fanciful claws that matched long, painted nails on his fingertips. His mask was a wisp of dragon whiskers—thin ribbons of blue and silver that floated and tangled in the shock of red hair that fell over his jade eyes. The end effect was subtle and elegant, except to one of the Old Races. To Alban's eyes, Janx's costume was a statement of intent to dominate, such a blatant challenge that even he was inclined to rise to it.

Instead, he shook his head and turned his attention back to the dance floor, quelling jealousy that had no place in his heart as he watched the crowd below.

Tony stalked past Margrit and Daisani, jaw set, with no greeting for either of them. She slowed her movements and Daisani released her hand, an easy action hinting of long rehearsal. Dancers stirred and parted ahead of the detective, then closed ranks again to continue their revelry. Only Margrit and Daisani remained still among the swirl of people, Margrit watching Tony as he disappeared beneath the balcony, and Daisani's gaze on Margrit. A brief patter of applause rippled out across the floor as dancers turned toward the balcony, their attention directed forward, not up.

An arrowhead contingent wedged its way through them, led by Kaimana Kaaiai. His thick dark hair, cropped short, seemed to capture rainbows from the crystal chandeliers, but his masquerade costume was indefinable from above. Tony flanked him on the left, body language stiff as they strode forward. Others followed behind, a stream of selkies and humans. Cara Delaney walked among them, her pale shoulders left bare by a velvet gown as deep and soft a brown as a seal's fur.

The formation broke as Kaimana stopped to greet Daisani. His escort washed around them, moving forward, smiling, nodding hellos, promising dances. For a few seconds the order on the floor became elegant chaos, dancers no longer making patterns dictated by the music. Once more, the core remained still: Margrit and Daisani, the latter clasping hands with Kaimana as they exchanged pleasantries. Daisani ought to have been overwhelmed by Kaimana's bulk, but the slight vampire exuded confidence that belied his size and let him stand easily with giants.

Margrit watched Tony, vitality drained from her expression and quiet regret left in its place. The detective barely acknowledged her, his gaze skimming the room, so intent on not seeing the woman before him that she, out of all the partygoers, could most easily present danger to the selkie lord.

Kaimana clapped a hand on Daisani's shoulder, chuckling at something, then turned to Margrit, who pulled her attention from Tony to offer a tense smile that blossomed as Kaimana bowed over her hand. Alban, attuned to her voice, heard amusement in it as it broke through the general buzz of revelry: "You're all very good at making a girl feel like she's on a pedestal. It's nice to see you again, Mr. Kaaiai."

Kaimana replied, his deeper tone more difficult to pick out, and Margrit laughed.

Then Daisani, his voice lighter and, like Margrit's, more easily distinguishable, murmured, "I believe we've all arrived now."

Even Tony turned to see where Daisani's gaze had gone to. Alban stepped forward again, even knowing that doing so was foolish. More than foolish: he stood first among the three races on the balcony, taking the position Kaaiai had held among his people. Taking the position that Janx would most naturally fall into, but instead the dragonlord came up on Alban's right, and Malik on his left. Gargoyles did not put themselves into positions of dominance, and yet. And yet.

Tony's expression tightened and turned to displeasure, the glance he cast at Margrit holding betrayal. Alban kept his hands loose on the railing, unable or unwilling to fall back and concede a place of command while the human detective watched.

Janx, at his elbow, murmured, "My, my, my, what have we here," as open an acknowledgment of Alban's stance as might be had. Interest glittered in Daisani's gaze as he took in the trio on the balcony, and

Kaimana's eyes lingered curiously on Malik a few long seconds before turning to the gargoyle.

But it was Margrit who moved forward a few inches, Margrit who smiled up at him, Margrit whose attention was drawn away from Tony and fixed on Alban. Stepping forward had been rash behavior, *human* behavior, but it felt startlingly good, reflected in Margrit's smile and the surprise of those surrounding them.

"My, my, my," Janx murmured again, this time with a note of curiosity. Then light humor filled his voice, playful and mocking as usual. "Come, my friends. It seems we have a party to attend."

TWENTY-FOUR

IT WAS EASY to see, because she knew to look for it. Janx wore red: dragon colors, with whiskers of blue silk dancing around his face. Malik, on Alban's other side, wore colors of the desert: shimmering soft gold that moved so lightly it seemed like sunlight on sand, and hard pale blue that did incredible things to his long-lashed eyes. He'd set aside his cane, carrying a staff carved from ivory instead. *Beautiful* was an easy word to describe Alban or Janx, but Malik's nastiness had barred Margrit from using it for him. For a moment, though, removed from his poisonous air, she saw it in the loose-fitting desert clothes and his easy stance, and could admire the costuming that marked him as djinn by those who knew.

Alban, out of all of them, wasn't in costume. There was no pretense or subterfuge to the tuxedo he wore, except it was shot through with silver, catching and reflecting light until even the slightest of his movements looked like liquid metal in motion. He had no mask, only his long hair left loose as he never wore it in his human form. White strands fell forward to frame his face, highlighting the chiseled lines of his features, the cool stoniness of his expression. Standing between Janx and Malik, he seemed as alien and inhuman as they, no more a part of Margrit's world than a fish belonged in a bird's.

Then he smiled and the illusion of remoteness was shattered. He put his weight on one hand against the balcony rail, and with casual disregard for a fifteen-foot drop, vaulted it. The tails of his coat flew upward, a blur of silver that whispered of wings, and an instant later he landed among the crowd. Only then did Margrit recognize the sheer number of selkies around her: without looking up, the dancers spun away to leave a space just large enough for Alban to land in. That space rippled toward her, bodies swirling to make a path, so when Alban lifted his gaze, it was to meet Margrit's eyes. Incredulous laughter bubbled up inside her, and satisfaction washed through his expression when she smiled.

He stood, a silver figure towering above the small, dark-haired selkies. The path they'd made closed behind him as he approached Margrit, one hand folded behind his back, the other extended in invitation.

"I seem to have been outdone," Daisani said from her elbow. Margrit startled and he gave a low laugh. "Entirely outdone. I don't know if I should offer congratulations or take insult, Alban. It's not often someone can be made to forget my presence completely. Margrit, do leave me one more space on your dance card tonight."

"I will." She put her hand into Alban's as Daisani faded away. "Look at you," she said. "You look wonderful."

"As do you." Alban curled his fingers under Margrit's chin, smiling. "You're unmasked."

"So are you. Good thing. We might not have recognized each other, otherwise. Especially with you jumping off balconies. That's not your usual style."

"On the contrary." Alban slipped his hand around her waist, drawing her near. "The very first time we danced I spent a good portion of the night leaping off stairs and onto rafters."

Margrit laughed. "That's right, you did. Are you going to do this every time we go out dancing? Someone's going to notice." She glanced around the floor as Alban led her across it in a waltz. "I don't know why they didn't this time."

"Because no one reacted. It's not unlike a child falling. If his parents make a fuss, he thinks he's hurt and cries. If no one notices or reacts, he thinks all is well, and gets up again to play."

"You're saying a ballroom full of humans is like a ballroom full of toddlers?"

Delight sparkled in Alban's glance. "I would never say such a thing. Now that you've mentioned, it, however…" Margrit lifted her hand from his shoulder to threaten him idly, earning a chuckle. "Truthfully, I only dared because so many selkies had come in to greet Kaimana. I wouldn't risk it now." He gestured, indicating the greater blend of humans among the dancers.

"You dared at the Blue Room." Margrit moved forward, hips swaying toward Alban's, playful reminder of the dance they'd shared at a nightclub weeks earlier. His gaze darkened and he pulled her closer, one hand large and certain on her waist.

"The lighting," he murmured, "was far poorer there. What happened to the others?"

Margrit breathed a laugh. "I turn on my best vamp and you want to know where the bad guys went." She tilted her chin up, looking toward the balcony. "They split forces after Janx got his eyebrows down from his hairline. He went left, Malik went right. I thought Malik was his bodyguard."

"Malik is the one being guarded, of late. I would think here, amongst all of us, he would be safe."

"The things you learn." Margrit put her cheek against Alban's chest, feeling as though she flew in his arms. The music changed more than once, both in style and in instruments, songs ending and beginning anew as they danced.

"Margrit." Alban's rumbling voice was lower than usual. She tilted her head up, eyebrows quirked. "May I ask something that's perhaps none of my affair?"

"You may. I may not answer," she warned.

His mouth curved, acknowledging humor without participating in it himself.

"I saw Tony here tonight."

"Ah." Margrit glanced across the room, though she didn't know where the detective had gone. "He's not here for me. He's working security for Kaimana Kaaiai, part of a special detail. That's why he was at the ice rink last night. Kaimana had sent him on my behalf. He thought I might be more comfortable with him around." She sighed, looking back at Alban. "We've broken up."

"I am…sorry." The words seemed to come with difficulty.

Margrit nodded, her emotions torn. "Thank you. Me, too, but I think maybe it's better if it's over. We've done that dance, and it kept ending badly. I don't want to do it anymore."

"Perhaps you'd be willing to do another one." The query came from behind Alban, so unexpected as to stop Margrit in her tracks. Alban swung back from her like a door opening, revealing Malik. He bowed insolently, his gaze on Margrit as he spoke to Alban. "May I cut in?"

The crowd around them surged closer, a few dancers almost brushing Margrit's skin. Cara Delaney spun by, a smile in place though her eyes were serious and calm as she scattered her attention to the figures around them. Margrit followed that look, relaxing as she saw the reassurance Cara offered.

Dozens of nearby dancers met her eye with dark liquid gazes: selkie eyes. Selkies and djinns were natural enemies, creatures of salt water anathema to the desert dwellers. A peculiar note of respect for Malik rose up in Margrit, carrying curiosity with it. She put her hand on Alban's arm. "It's okay. I'll see you in a bit."

It took another instant to steady her nerves and offer that same hand to Malik. He'd abandoned his staff, the one weapon he might have carried, and a slight limp marred his step forward. They stood uncomfortably still on the dance floor, hands barely touching, until Alban, glowering, took himself away through the crowd. Margrit heard herself say, "I wouldn't have taken you for a dancer," in a high, light voice, and a smirk came into Malik's blue eyes.

"Who do you think inspired the Eastern sword and belly dancers?" His grip on her fingers became more certain as the music changed again.

Margrit laughed in protest, shaking her head as a tango beat slid over the floor. "No. Oh, no." Even as she objected, Malik pulled her closer and she responded, heartbeat quickening in anticipation. Better—or worse—than running in the park was the challenge inherent in the dance. Sensuality, sexuality, sheer abandonment: Margrit's skirt whipped out in a twirl and wrapped around her legs as Malik brought her back in again, a firm certain hand on her waist keeping her from toppling with the momentum. Under cover of the music, in that abrupt moment of stillness, Margrit demanded, "What do you want, Malik?"

"Support." He snapped the word out as quickly as he spun her into another turn, keeping his eyes on her. Margrit felt she couldn't afford the luxury of a lifted eyebrow or a startled laugh, concentrating instead on keeping her feet. The djinn was by far the superior dancer, and only the absolute certainty of his lead allowed her to keep up with him.

"And you're asking *me?* Why the hell would you do that? Are you out of your mind?" Her questions came breathlessly, tangling with her hair as it loosened from its pins, curls lashing around her face.

Malik pulled her close again, lowering her in a slow dip, and for all the fluidity of his motions, she suddenly saw tension in him, knotted in the muscle of his jaw and making a sharp line of his shoulders. The alien idea that the djinn was *afraid* struck her, and then they were in motion again, music pulling them along.

Margrit's thoughts sparked with chaos, ungraspable in the heat of the dance. Laughter burned through her, intellect drowned beneath the pure joy of outrageous behavior. Even Alban, who understood her need to run through the park, was too reserved to dance with her so aggressively.

The Old Races, it came to her in a burst of clarity, together, as a whole, the Old Races offered her the world she desperately wanted to live in. It wasn't bound by human conventions, though it went through those paces. Margrit waited for the sting of shame that she, a lawyer by trade and by choice, wanted to play the part of the king above the law, but caught in the tempo of the dance, there was only room for ruthless acknowledgment of that fact. Shame, if it came at all, would come later.

The music slowed, leaving breath for speech. Malik curled a sneer, clearly displeased with what he intended to say, just as clearly determined to say it. "Sands are shifting faster than we can see, and it's thanks to you." He drew her back, three quick steps and one to the side, and Margrit followed his lead like water through the easiest channel.

No. Like wind through hollowed stone. Margrit half smiled and Malik took it as encouragement. "Daisani acts on your behalf. Korund, who has been his own master for centuries, now bends to your whim. Janx makes bargains with you, and the selkies call you friend. I would not have thought you could be a dangerous enemy, but when all of our races parlay with you there's no gain in loathing you." The tension was back, singing like a bow line. The thought that Malik feared *her* struck Margrit and nearly made her laugh. The only thing that stopped her was a suspicion that the djinn would drop her on the dance floor if she dared.

Something in her expression must have warned him of her thoughts, because for an instant Margrit felt him slip away into mist, stealing her air. Then he was back, a solid form again, and she used her next indrawn breath to ask, "What about Russell?"

Malik's face contorted with irritation. "You and Korund. Didn't your pet gargoyle tell you? If I'd been going to take a life that night it would have been your own."

Disbelief surged in Margrit as the music stepped up in tempo and volume. "You mean Janx didn't send you after him?"

"Do you think I'm fool enough to take his breath when I'd done the same to you hours earlier? Janx did not send me after Russell Lomax, and if he had, I'd have chosen another method."

Surprise stiffened Margrit's body as Malik pulled her up again, both of them ignoring the music as they stood nose to nose. Unexpectedly, she believed him, more because he seemed more likely to claim credit for things he hadn't done than disavow things he had. "Then who…?"

Malik shrugged, making it part of the dance as he moved again with the beat. "It's not my concern, and not what I want of you. Whatever comes of the quorum, you'll be part of it. Support me as the winds change, and I will give you whatever I can of the Old Races."

There was no more subtlety in his negotiation or offer than in the dance itself. The blatant self-interest provided its own sort of appeal, but before Margrit could speak the music ended, abrupt and shocking. Her weight leaned into Malik's, bodies pressed together less erotically than challengingly, and their noses so close that even she expected, for a brief and unsettling moment, the kiss that the pose demanded.

Then applause broke out around them and she pulled her gaze from Malik's to discover a circle had opened up, giving them space to dance, and the room's attention was entirely on them. The selkies ringing them still provided protection, but beyond them delighted humans clapped and cheered.

At the edges of the ballroom, two or three steps

higher than the dance floor itself, stood the scattered leaders and representatives of the Old Races. Tony, his expression sour, stood just behind Kaaiai, whose placid, pleasant face was filled with curious amusement that only played up Tony's distaste all the more. Janx and Daisani stood near one another, far enough apart to be separate, but close enough to offer solidarity. Both watched Margrit with a vulture's eyes, gauging the dance and what it meant.

Margrit shifted her weight to her own feet, helped by Malik, and finally found Alban, far across the room, but watchful. Out of all of them, his gaze asked the least of her, though after a moment a wry smile curled his mouth and he lifted a glass in acknowledgment of her seeking him out.

Margrit brought her gaze back to Malik's, his eyes so close that focusing was hard. "Thank you," she breathed. "But I have everything I want of the Old Races."

Malik's face went white, sensuality draining from his body to leave only the threats that she'd known from him before. A warning stirred through the gathered selkies, and he smiled thinly, taking Margrit's hand to turn and bow to the watchers. Seconds later he stalked off the floor, grace marred by the limp that had been nowhere in evidence as they'd danced. Margrit exhaled heavily and worked her own way off the floor, smiling away invitations to dance.

Only after downing two glasses of water did she dare taste the champagne that a server offered, holding the flute as if it were her last link with the ordinary world. Alban was out of sight, and Janx and Daisani had separated, the latter now speaking with

Kaaiai. Cole whisked Cameron by, both of them waving frantically between the beats of a polka that looked equal parts ridiculous and fun. A slight, familiar female slipped through the crowd gathered beneath the balcony, and Margrit started forward with pleasure.

"Hello, lawyer."

Margrit tightened her fingers around her champagne flute, distracted from her intention to seek out Chelsea Huo. Steadying her breathing, she turned to find Biali a few feet away. A mocking smile carved the ruin of his face, no mask hiding the shattered socket and scarred left eye. He wore white as unrelieved as his hair, the harsh color and cut of his tuxedo making him look even broader and huskier than he normally did. His champagne flute seemed in danger of shattering in his hand, though he turned to set it aside on a passing waiter's tray with the consummate grace of all the Old Races. "We're putting our best foot forward tonight, aren't we? Making like civilized human beings, right down to hiding our faces from the world."

"Not all of us." A thread of admiration cut through the contraction in her belly as Margrit made a small gesture toward his scars. "I didn't expect you to be here."

"And if you had, you'd figure on me wearing a mask." Biali stepped forward to dangle his fingertips above the lip of Margrit's glass, his voice dropping so low as to hover on threatening. "Gargoyles don't wear masks." An instant later his voice returned to its normal depth and volume as he asked abruptly, "Dance with me, lawyer?"

Margrit huffed with startled laughter. "For any reason other than to upset Alban?"

"Stoneheart," the other gargoyle said. "Nothing upsets him."

"We both know better than that."

"Then because you had the stomach to fly with me," Biali said. "Because you're probably the only mortal to have flown with two of us in a century. Dance with me," he said one more time, and then in a concession, added, "Knight."

Margrit tilted her head, enough agreement for Biali to finally take her drink, handing it off as easily as he had his own.

There was nothing of Alban's ease or Malik's confidence in the way he danced with her, no comfort in being on the floor, certainly no camaraderie. They danced without speaking, and he released her as the music ended, his mouth a tight line of bitterness.

"Biali." Margrit caught his elbow, waiting for him to turn his sighted eye to her. "Why did you ask me to dance?"

A semifamiliar jolt caught her off guard, a wash of images that belonged to someone else. Biali's memories, blue with twilight, provided a backdrop for a woman much younger than Margrit's own memories, taken from Alban, remembered her as being. "Hajnal." She spoke the name in Biali's voice, his memories answering Margrit's question.

Hajnal was petite for a gargoyle, a loamy creaminess to her skin. Obsidian ringlets spilled down her back over wings folded in contentment. In her natural form and among her own people, she wore no clothing, her body all clean curves and angles of sculpted stone. She stirred desire in Margrit's loins, unexpected enough to evoke a blush, but lust was only part of a love as certain and strong as the bedrock of the earth. The smile she offered made Margrit catch her breath, and brought with it understanding.

Biali's offer to dance hadn't been to anger Alban, or even challenge him. Not to threaten Margrit, or claim her, but to reclaim for himself a piece of memory, lost when a dark-haired female gargoyle had chosen the heir to the Korund clan over him. Only to remember, as he had, briefly and painfully, when he'd carried Margrit above the cityscape, that there were other paths he might have taken. Might still take.

The world shifted and plummeted in Margrit's vision, as if she fell through mountain ranges toward a narrow canyon. Biali steadied her, his good eye bleak and without remorse. "You're all right, for what you are."

"You're not bad yourself."

He held her arm an instant longer, making sure of her balance, then inhaled before curling his lip against an evident impulse to speak. Margrit stepped back cautiously, still uncertain on her feet, and Biali's expression shifted a second time as he followed the impulse, after all: "When do they meet?"

"Who?"

He gave her a look that said she was smarter than that, and made a short gesture, encompassing the ballroom and, most specifically, Malik, who stood at Kaimana Kaaiai's side. "Janx, Daisani, all of 'em, they've been rotating by the selkie lord since he arrived. Everyone but Korund, and he's a fool. The quorum, lawyer. When does it meet?"

"How do you—?"

She earned another flat look from the blunt gargoyle.

"There's not a memory of all of us being in the same place at the same time in five hundred years, lawyer. There's always a quorum when we all come together, no matter what the reasons or what's to be discussed. When does it meet?"

"Monday, I think. Three days from agreeing on holding one. I don't know where."

Biali turned away, apparently satisfied, then looked back, his eyebrows drawn down in a scowl. "Watch yourself, lawyer. Our kind will tear yours apart with the best of intentions."

TWENTY-FIVE

BIALI LEFT HER, a bolt of white pushing the crowd aside without effort. Margrit stood where she was, watching him go, and was unsurprised when Alban's voice sounded beside her. "What was that?"

"I don't know. Maybe an overture of friendship."

"Friendship is not something Biali has any talent at extending."

"Maybe not, but he's been almost as isolated as you've been, hasn't he? Janx said you were the only two in New York." Margrit looked over the ballroom, searching for snowy-haired men and women. Those she found had neither a gargoyle's breadth of shoulder nor the ease of movement that marked the Old Races.

"We are. Our people have never congregated widely in the New World."

"So maybe he's finally forgiven you."

"Or perhaps you compel us all to actions we barely comprehend."

Margrit glanced back at him with an unladylike snort. "I'm one person, Alban. One person doesn't change the world."

"Tell that to Mahatma Gandhi."

Margrit put her teeth together, closing off an argument, and stared at the gargoyle. "Interesting choice."

"Would you prefer I'd said Osama bin Laden?"

"Not really."

Alban almost smiled. "One person *can* change the world. You've become a catalyst in ours whether you intended to or not."

"You started it." Margrit pulled a face at her own childishness, and Alban's near-smile became a full one.

"I did. Perhaps it's I who've changed our world. But it's you who's exotic to us, and therefore to be—"

"Blamed?"

Alban fell silent for long seconds. "That wasn't the word I intended, but now that you've said it, I'm hard-pressed to find another."

"Oh, thanks a lot." Margrit wrinkled her nose and looked away. Halfway across the ballroom, Malik still stood with Kaimana, observing the dancers. Tony, taller than either man but less broad than Kaimana, stood a grim watch over them, clearly unhappy with Malik's presence. "Biali's right. They've been rotating by Kaaiai all evening. Even when he's meeting with us, one of them has been close enough to overhear."

"Us? We haven't—"

Margrit flicked her fingers at herself. "As opposed to you." Another dart of her hand encompassed members of the Old Races. "You're the only one who hasn't paid court, Alban."

"No. You haven't, either. Come, Margrit," he said, when she elevated an eyebrow. "There were representatives of six races there last night. You, as much as I, are expected to have a certain stake in the final arrangement of power, but you haven't danced attendance on Kaaiai, either."

Margrit wet her lips, wishing for the champagne Biali had so handily rid her of. "I think it might be bad for my health to be more associated with your power balance than I already am. Kaimana and I have already discussed what we have in common."

"Secret meetings?" There was a heaviness to the teasing that made Margrit look sharply at her companion.

"De facto, yes, but not by deliberation. Not from you, at least. I'll tell you after the party, if you want."

"That had the distinct sound of dismissal to it."

Margrit put her hand on Alban's chest, smiling. "It was. We all know you're a lousy negotiator, but I think you should go loom next to Kaimana for a little while and make small talk. It'll make the rest of them feel like you're playing along. It might even worry some of them. Alban Korund, with an agenda? Surely it's a sign of the apocalypse."

"You're a bad woman, Margrit Knight."

"But a very good lawyer," she said cheerfully. "Go on. I have to dance with Janx, so he doesn't feel left out."

"Are you trying to infuriate me?"

"You're not that easy to infuriate." Margrit's gaze darted across the room to find Tony again. Alban followed it, then looked back at her.

"Are you trying to infuriate him?" His voice was low.

"No, but it will. I'm not trying to play jealousy games. It's just the situation." Margrit passed a hand over her eyes without touching them, for fear of smearing her makeup. "We were together for a long time, Alban. I can't help thinking of him. Having you and Janx and Malik—mostly you and Janx—here tonight couldn't be more of an in-your-face snub to Tony. I don't want that, but there wasn't any way to avoid it."

"We could leave."

Margrit laughed. "That's twice in one evening you've been impetuous, Alban. I think the world is coming to an end."

"Does that mean you don't want to?"

She looked over the room, then rose on her toes to curl her hands against Alban's shoulders and steal a kiss. "It means it's a fantastic idea. Talk with Kaimana. Let me dance with Janx. I'll meet you on the rooftop when we're done."

"I thought I would have to seek you out." Janx accepted Margrit's offer of a dance with a flourish and bow, and swept her onto the floor in a waltz, disregarding the four-four time of the music being played. She clung to the dragonlord, trusting his lead over her own feet.

"You've been hovering around Kaaiai so much I didn't think you were going to seek anyone out. Unless you were planning to ask Tony to dance."

Janx looked toward the police-detective-cum-security-agent and shook his head. "Ah, no. I have somewhat more respect for the location of my teeth than that. I don't like him being here," he added less blithely. "Your friend Anthony is a thorn in my side, Margrit Knight, and the more time I spend in his presence, in Eliseo's, in yours, the closer he comes to finding threads to bind us all together."

"Threads like Russell? Or my mother?" Margrit's voice sharpened more than she thought possible, bringing Janx's gaze back to her, surprise lightening the jade of his eyes. They slowed on the dance floor, in part because the music ended, but more because Janx was absorbing what she'd said.

"Russell Lomax. Rebecca Knight." He breathed the names with admiration. "Oh. Oh, Eliseo. Oh, Margrit. Oh, my dears. For Vanessa? For my men? Is this the story you've concocted? It's *very* good," he whispered. "So good I wish it were mine to tell." New music started up, this time an actual waltz. Janx moved with it automatically, still watching Margrit with respect and regret. "I am outplayed on every side."

Something new came into his eyes, a constrained uncertainty. "Stoneheart believing I arranged the mugging in the park to draw you back into our world. This game of tit for tat played in lives that touch all of ours. *You,* my dear girl. Cutting the wind from under my wings in the matter of Malik's safety, and ensconcing yourself in Eliseo's camp. I have not been so well stymied in three centuries and a half." His hands, usually cool, had warmed, and color stained dark shadows along his cheekbones. "I should like very much to be as conniving as you think me to be, but this one time, I fear I fall far short of your expectations. I had not yet thought out my retaliation for Patrick and the others."

His lip curled suddenly, revealing a too-pointed canine. "I've lost five men, and Malik not among them, no thanks to Alban. He was attacked a little while before dawn this morning."

Margrit stumbled over her own feet. "*Malik* was?"

"By someone who knew how to fight djinn. Three

humans. Unfortunately, his enthusiasm for revenge outweighed his common sense. They're all dead, and among our other failings, we fairy tales cannot speak with the dead."

"He didn't tell me that." Margrit's ears, heartbeat drowned out music and voices alike. Malik's tension, his approach, his offer, made abrupt sense. Made sense, except in no way could she imagine why he might think she would protect him. The disconcerting thought that he imagined her responsible for his assault, and therefore capable of calling it off, passed through her mind and left her shaky with confusion. "Not that I know why he would."

"Aside from the two of you having quite the little interlude on the dance floor?" Janx asked. Margrit nodded, though the dance hardly constituted grounds for exchanging intimacies with the djinn. "And Alban couldn't tell you," Janx went on, voice growing colder, "because he'd abandoned his duty."

"Because Malik had threatened me. My family." Margrit shook herself, upsetting her steps in the dance. Janx steadied her, his expression still cold. "Are you sure Malik didn't just kill some poor sons of bitches, and invent a story to make Alban look bad and himself look beleaguered?"

Janx smirked. "You give him too much credit."

"Maybe." Margrit glanced across the dance floor, seeking, but not expecting to find, the djinn. "If you didn't send him after Russell, why'd he threaten my family?"

"At a guess? Two of us will vote against the selkie in our quorum." Janx shrugged, then assumed a superior expression and measured, lecturing tones when Margrit wrinkled her forehead. "The gargoyles won't shatter tradition, especially not with Stoneheart holding the vote. Even if they've changed enough to accept half-breeds, he's been apart too long to know it. Kaimana himself can't vote. There will be a tie."

"So?"

"So then we must turn to the sixth in our quorum." Mischief replaced the solemnity of his words. "You hold the decisive vote, Margrit Knight."

"That's absurd." Margrit had no strength to put behind the objection. "I'm human."

"As are they. It gives your opinion power. Either way you choose, the weight is significant, my dear. Either way, you change a people's history forever."

"It's everybody's history," Margrit breathed. "All of the remaining Old Races', even humanity's. Even if most of us never know it. If I say they're Old Races, then the injunction against breeding with humans is shattered." Her heartbeat picked up speed, warmth spreading through her body. "That allows you all to go forth and be fruitful."

"God was *angry* when he said that," Janx said unexpectedly. The heat building in Margrit's cheeks broke with her laughter.

"Yes, he was." She laughed again, then ducked her head in thought. "Oh. Oh, so if I'm not there, if my boss has been murdered, or my family's been hurt, or even if I'm just afraid something might happen, and stay away…"

"Then the tie holds and the selkies are rejected. There must be a majority." All of Janx's humor drained away as well, leaving him as solemn as she'd ever seen him. "I'm afraid I wouldn't be above the plot you've accused me of, but this once, my dear, I ask that you believe me."

"Is that your third favor, dragonlord?"

Something in Janx's gaze became shuttered, as if Margrit's light question had struck deeper and more painfully than she'd imagined it could. "Must I make it so?"

The question hung between them for a few heartbeats before she groaned. "I'm going to regret this, but no."

"Thank you." Gratitude larger than the answer warranted infused Janx's response.

"There's something I don't understand."

"Only one thing?" His voice regained to its usual teasing charm. Margrit wanted to elbow him, but her hands and arms were caught by the frame of the waltz. She rolled her eyes instead. Janx's smile sparkled.

"There are more djinn than any of the rest of you, right? So maybe I can understand why they wouldn't want to take the path the selkies have. But why preemptively condemn everyone else? I know it's tradition, but you're dealing with an ancient law whose reversal could save your people. All of you."

"It might, if we chose to intermingle the bloodlines."

Astonishment widened her eyes. "Why wouldn't you?"

Janx shrugged as he spun her in a wide circle. "Look at your own people's racial divides. You shouldn't have to ask."

"But the Old Races don't have the luxury of numbers. Most of even our smallest ethnic groups have at least hundreds of potential mates to choose from. Those kinds of numbers can obviously be wiped out, but there's a fighting chance of survival within the group. When you're talking about mere dozens…"

"Then you may be talking about desperate pride that would prefer to die its slow death than contaminate its few survivors with alien blood."

"What would *you* do?"

Janx smiled. "I would choose to survive, Margrit. I would choose to live. And I know you, my dear lady Knight. You won't condemn my people to death. Not when you find such joy in discovering magic in the world." His smile turned serpentine and deadly. "Not when you share the nighttime sky with a gargoyle lover. You'll give us the keys to the kingdom and change all our people forever."

More than anything else, it was Tony Pulcella who stopped Alban from addressing Kaaiai. The human male watched over the selkie lord as though ferocity of expression might keep danger away. Despite recognizing its absurdity, Alban respected the detective. Being involved with the Old Races wasn't easy, especially when their bewildering lives went unexplained. Bad enough for Margrit, whom he'd given no choice, and who had grown to understand and accept what she'd become entangled in. Far worse for someone like Tony, whose nature was as protective as Alban's own, but who was purposefully excluded from comprehension. Approaching Kaimana seemed too much like flaunting the breach between where Tony stood and where Alban had brought Margrit. Too much like flaunting the woman he'd unintentionally won, for all that she wasn't now at his side.

As if Alban's thought brought Margrit to Tony's

mind, the detective looked beyond him, to where she danced with Janx. Alban glanced that way, then drew his attention back to Tony, watching difficult emotions change the other man's expression. Uncertainty, anger, envy; at least two of those were familiar to Alban when it came to dealing with Margrit Knight, most particularly when she flirted with Janx. Worse for the human male, though, for Janx was a criminal in his world, and for Tony to watch his newly lost lover amuse herself in Janx's arms no doubt cut deeper than Alban's own foolish fears. For a moment an ironic camaraderie seemed to join them.

With that sour thought in mind, Alban slipped through the crowd to approach the selkie lord and his human security agent. Tony's jaw set, though he deliberately looked beyond Alban, his focus roving over the gathering.

"Korund." Kaimana offered his hand, his voice jovial in greeting. "That was quite a show you put on earlier. Not like the man I've heard stories of."

"It appears none of us are quite what we seem anymore. Margrit tells me I should come pay court to you and make the others wonder what my agenda is." Alban hesitated over the last words, uncomfortable with them.

Kaimana chuckled and folded his hands behind his back in a relaxed, broad stance. "And what is your agenda?"

Alban fell silent, chiding himself for not anticipating the question, then lifted a shoulder and let it fall in a heavy shrug. "To find out what secrets you and Margrit have shared behind closed doors, I suppose. To wonder how those secrets affect the rest of us." He spoke carefully, too aware of Detective Pulcella within easy earshot, though he did nothing to indicate he was listening in.

Kaimana pushed his lips into a thick purse. "You know we're looking for legitimacy. She supports us."

"She would." Humor tinged Alban's answer. "She's drawn to those who need a champion."

"Just as well for you, I understand."

He nodded without speaking. Kaaiai waited a moment, then went on. "And what about you? You've needed a champion. Are you willing to be one now?"

"Alban is more of a watchdog, I should think." Daisani came through the crowd, taking up a position in front of them. Alban glanced over his shoulder to gauge Tony's reaction, unsurprised to find the detective had subtly tensed. "Safeguarding the old ways from new-fangled corruption."

Alban murmured, "Someone must," and Kaaiai stiffened as slightly as Tony had. Ruefulness almost sent Alban back a step or two. Negotiating was not, as Margrit gladly pointed out, a gift of his, and it was easier to draw lines in stone than he meant for it to be.

Amusement flashed over Daisani's face and he turned to examine the ballroom. "We're all here," he said. "Alban, have you decided to stand for your…family?"

Alban opened his hand and closed it again in a wordless agreement. Daisani nodded and drew himself up, full of purposeful, commanding attention despite his slight form. Halfway across the room, Janx glanced toward them, then stepped gracefully off the dance floor, Margrit's hand captured in his own. She lifted an eyebrow curiously, looking where he had, then fell into step as though they'd walked together a thousand times.

Alban's shoulders tightened and he refused to allow himself another glance toward Tony. Neither of them had a rival in Janx, but Alban doubted the detective could make himself fully believe that any more than he could himself.

Malik brushed past Tony and stepped up between Kaimana and Alban, their heights making the djinn seem petite. "What's happening?"

At the sound of his voice, Daisani relaxed marginally, letting go the commanding air that had drawn Old Races eyes to him. When Margrit and Janx joined them he said, "We are all here, with no plans to replace anyone. Why wait three days, when we can have this game done with tonight?" His focus sharpened on Janx, whose expression changed to a snarl and relaxed again so quickly Alban was half-unsure he'd seen it happen.

"To whose end?" Janx hissed. Margrit, to Alban's shock, put a hand on the dragonlord's arm, as if staying him. Daisani saw it as well, his eyebrows shooting up.

"To all of ours, I should think. Chaos surrounds us at every side. We would all be better pleased with order restored. Am I wrong?" The last words were cut from ice, falling amongst the gathered group in frozen shards. Tony Pulcella shifted forward, hands knotted into fists. Alban caught a glimpse of agonized sympathy on Margrit's face as she saw him move.

"Whether we have it done or not, this isn't the place to discuss it." Her voice was inexpressibly soft, drawing the attention of six men, all but one of whom understood her point. "Gentlemen, I believe we should retire upstairs. We can come back to the party when this is settled." She made a small gesture toward the ballroom stairs, and to Alban's astonishment, the motley quorum moved at her command.

So did Tony Pulcella. Margrit touched his arm, drawing him aside, and seeking out Alban's gaze as she did. Alban paused, and she gave the tiniest shake of her head and an even briefer smile that sent reassurance burning through him. He nodded, then turned to follow the other representatives of the Old Races to the balcony above. Without, this time, showing off; like the others, he took the stairs, and found a faint thrill of amusement that he even considered doing anything else.

"It was Daisani, wasn't it." Tony turned on Margrit and spoke through his teeth. "Your link between Russell Lomax and Janx was Daisani. Lomax was in his pocket. What're they doing together here? Why'd you lie to me, Grit? What the hell's going on? Why didn't you call me?"

"You have no idea how much I wish I could tell you." Margrit felt as though the fight had drained out of her. "It's business. I did think Daisani was the link, yeah. That's why I didn't want to tell you. I didn't call because it didn't pan out. Janx said he didn't have anything to do with Russell's death, and I believe him."

"I don't. I don't know what the hell's going on with you, Grit, but whatever it is, you need to get out of it fast. Those guys are dangerous. Janx, Malik—shit, Daisani, too, for that matter. People with that kind of money just fuck you over, and I don't want to see you go down for whatever they're mixed up with." Concern warred with anger in Tony's voice and face. "Whatever's going on, you can't go up there with them."

"I have to. What I'm dealing with isn't illegal, Tony,

and that's all I can tell you." Her quiet resolve sounded implacable to her own ears. "But I do need to deal with it, and it's something you can't help with."

"This is the same shit that's been going on since January, isn't it?"

Margrit pressed her lips together, then nodded. "Yeah. Yeah, it is. And you have no idea how sorry I am it means I've been cutting you out of my life."

"You're not." Concern faded, leaving anger and hurt. "You're not sorry, Margrit. Whatever the hell it is, it's more exciting to you than we are. More interesting. I'd love to be wrong, but I'm not. I'll tell you this, though. Whatever it is, I'm gonna find out, and if it's as dirty as I think it is, and you're tangled up in it, you're going down with them. You understand me? Whatever's happening, I'm not protecting you."

Margrit took a deep breath, an ache crawling through her entire body. "I know." She barely whispered the response, and with the whisper, stepped backward, toward the stairs the others had taken. "I know, Tony, and I don't blame you. I really am sorry it's happening this way, but I have to go." She hesitated, then, helplessly, said, "Goodbye."

Angry color flooded Tony's cheeks and he turned on his heel as abruptly as she'd ever seen him move. Margrit bit her lip, then climbed the ballroom stairs, stopping at the top to look back one last time.

The party carried on, the revelers all but unmindful of the handful of men and the solitary woman who slipped away. Only one face lifted to the balcony, unerringly seeking Margrit's gaze out of hundreds. An expression so subtle she couldn't read it crossed his face: pleasure, perhaps, or anticipation. Margrit shivered and turned away, wondering why his name lingered so heavily in her mind.

Biali.

TWENTY-SIX

KAIMANA HAD ALREADY left the gathering when she joined them on the balcony. The others waited on Margrit, holding back until she took the lead, as though it was agreed among them that the least important should go first, and take some of the problem of ranking away.

Bemused at the idea, Margrit led them from the balcony to the elevator banks that lay above and beyond the ballroom. For all that there was more than enough room for the five of them, the air in the elevator bristled, making it crowded with expectation. Margrit felt more than her own weight bearing down on her feet. The temptation to catch Alban's hand and hold on tight had passed as she'd realized that walking alone would carry greater impact than coming with the gargoyle. To walk with him displayed her loyalties too clearly, not that she—or anyone else—doubted where they lay. It was more a show of independence, of humans coming to the Old Races' counsel meeting as equals, than anything else. Janx and Daisani would find it laughable, but she did it to shore up her own courage, not cater to them.

The boardroom table in Daisani's conference room had been replaced. Margrit nearly laughed, swallowing the sound only through awareness of the occasion's importance. But Daisani had clearly intended to call the quorum together that night, rather than wait two more days. The table Kaimana sat at was round, and while he'd chosen the space farthest from the door, so he could watch people enter, it had no absolute head. He waited with an equanimity that gave lie to his peoples' fate resting on the evening's proceedings, and nodded in greeting as Margrit passed through the door. Unwilling to break the silence, she echoed his gesture.

Malik walked in a few steps behind her, making her uncomfortable. She'd known he was there, but discovering him so close to her made her want to run, as if she'd somehow become his unsuspecting prey.

Margrit watched him judge the five empty seats, his gaze lingering on those on either side of Kaimana. Another brief glance took Margrit in and dismissed her; her choice of seating was evidently irrelevant to the sour-faced desert creature. Piqued and amused, she took a seat, deliberately leaving one space between herself and Kaimana. Malik, half a step from the seat that would put him directly opposite the selkie lord, froze then snarled almost imperceptibly. The barest change of direction took him one seat farther away, leaving an empty chair between Margrit and himself.

Kaimana met Margrit's eyes without the slightest change of expression, but laughter seemed to sparkle between them. She felt a smirking triumph. Her presence unbalanced the table, and the situation, as much as it literally balanced it, three and three.

Pebbles sat on the table in front of her, a pair of equal size, one black and one white. Kaimana had none in front of him, and Malik palmed the two at his chair as he sat. Margrit felt as though she was making another irrevocable move as she took the stones and folded them in her hands, white in the right, black in the left.

Daisani and Janx came through the double doors together, as if they'd rehearsed. Margrit felt laughter slide around in search of release again, but kept it trapped. It was easy to imagine them staring each other down in the hall and finally choosing to enter shoulder to shoulder, neither willing to walk behind the other. They took the same places they had at the first meeting, Daisani to Kaimana's right and Janx to his left. Only a seat between Margrit and Malik remained, putting them all in the positions they'd held the night before.

Alban entered the silent room a half beat behind Janx and Daisani. Like the others, he glanced around and sat without preamble, the assembly quiet, as if waiting on some cue Margrit didn't know to anticipate.

"Who stands for the gargoyles?" The question snapped out from four mouths at once, startling Margrit so badly she squeaked, then winced, unable to cover either reaction. Alban, calm at her side, caught his breath to respond.

From the other side of the room, at the doorway, Biali's rough low voice broke in. "I do."

Not one of the Old Races—not even Alban—flinched at the other gargoyle's interruption. Margrit's hands spasmed against the table, but she kept herself quiet through force of will. Alban, to her shock, rose and stepped away from the table, as Daisani turned to Biali without so much as missing a beat.

"And who are you?" Daisani spoke alone, the others deferring to him for no reason Margrit could see.

"I'm Biali, born of the clan Kameh, cursed to work for a mangy dragon and watch over Alban Korund, called the Breach. I claim this position through right of age and right of acceptance among my people." He stumped across the room and Alban fell back, expressionless as he gave up his chair and his position to Biali. Margrit's heart throbbed against her ribs, making her dizzy with uncertainty. She could trust Alban to support her in the things she wanted from the quorum, but Biali was a wild card. She clenched her stomach muscles to prevent herself from leaping up and dragging Alban back, and knew the glance she cast at him was full of betrayal.

A hint of apology darted across his face, but then he was gone, closing the door behind himself gently, and leaving Margrit very much alone in a roomful of immortals.

Biali sat down with an intentional crash, scooping up the pebbles Alban had left behind. Every formal note the quorum had entered on was shattered, then made worse by his growled addition: "Bet you thought having Korund stand in meant this stayed out of the memories. You're fools. Breach or not, not even he would keep a quorum out of the histories, and neither will I."

A shared glance went around the table, unreadable to Margrit and garnering a dismissive snort from Biali. Then, again on a cue she didn't catch, voices lifted again to ask, "Who stands for the dragons?" Biali remained aggressively silent, though he turned his attention to Janx, as the others did.

The dragonlord bowed from the waist, making an elegant flourish despite the fact that he was sitting down. "I do."

"And who are you?" There was a lavish amount of humor in Daisani's voice as he asked, though his expression remained as grave as before.

"I am Janx." The sibilant hiss of his own name carried a soft challenge that sent another stir around the table. This time Daisani allowed himself a smile and returned Janx's half bow, evidently accepting the abrupt answer as sufficient.

"Who stands for the vampires?" Margrit still missed whatever subtle prompt allowed the Old Races to speak with one voice so easily, though Janx joined Biali in silence now that he'd been recognized.

"I do," Daisani murmured, then waited a delicious moment to see if anyone had the audacity to voice the question that was clearly his to ask. Malik shifted in his seat but held his tongue, and after a moment Daisani smiled again. "I am Daisani, called Eliseo, and I am the master of my kind."

A thrill shot up Margrit's spine and her hands went cold, though none of the others looked surprised by Daisani's statement. He saw her stiffen and cast an amused wink toward her, enough to throw her off as Kaimana asked, "Who stands for the djinn?" She joined in only on the last few words, her higher voice startling against his.

Malik's lip curled again, his gaze sliding to hers, but he restrained himself to an, "I do," before his focus became intent on Daisani and his question. "I am Ebul Alima Malik al-Shareef din Nazmi al-Massrī of the desert wind and I claim this place by rite of passage."

Surprise and admiration washed through Janx's expression, and he caught his breath as though he'd speak. He held his tongue, though, and a sudden warning flashed through Margrit. Kaimana was the only one left of the Old Races still unrecognized, all of the others having fallen silent after their introductions were made. There was no one left to demand she identify herself, her presence a disruption to what smacked of ages-old ritual. Before she could think, before anyone could speak, she lifted her voice, pleased with its strength and clarity. "I stand for the humans."

To her astonishment, approval flashed in Daisani's eyes as he asked, without hesitation, "And who are you?" Buoyed by his acceptance, and ignoring both a hard stare of offended disbelief from Malik and Biali's contemptuous snort, she lifted her chin. "I am Margrit Elizabeth Knight, advocate for the Old Races."

Janx looked delighted, and a surge of glee danced through Margrit. They'd invited her to their party, and she had no intention of going unnoticed. She turned her attention to Kaimana, and with everyone else, asked, "Who stands for the selkies?" Her own soprano contrasting with the thundering chorus lifted hairs on her arms and stirred the men, though none of them quite broke form to look at her instead of Kaimana.

He came to his feet with ponderous grace. "I do." He turned to Daisani, waiting out the question of identification before replying, "I am Kaimana Kaaiai, immortal selkie lord and leader of a changing race. I am your brother and tonight I am your supplicant, speaking for my people and their place in the Old Races." All the easy islander patois was gone from his speech, leaving it as formal and intense as any of his contemporaries as he brought his gaze to each of them in turn.

"We have broken a covenant. This I do not deny. We have survived by it. This, I put to you as a needful thing.

We hold true to our old bloodlines—not one among us is called selkie if he cannot change his skin. Our children are no less than half-blooded—more than this and we lose the core of what we are. Many of us are more than that, bred back and kept close. You hold our fate in your hands." He took one easy, deep breath, then turned his palms up as he sat. "I ask you to vote now."

"By age," Janx said to Daisani, and for once respect threaded the dragon's tenor voice. Daisani, to Margrit's surprise, seemed to accept that respect with uncharacteristic humility, bowing his head to the dragonlord before bringing his attention to the vote. He echoed Kaimana's gesture, turning a palm up to reveal a white stone. Janx, still more respectful and subdued than Margrit was accustomed to, echoed the gesture a third time, white stone held in his fingertips as he'd once held a priceless sapphire to tease Margrit with. Then both elders turned to Malik, expectation written on their faces.

Malik gave Kaimana a hard look of dislike. Kaimana's gaze remained neutral, but he nodded, an action so slight Margrit thought it could simply have been the strain of holding too still. Malik held out a moment longer, then slapped his palm on the table, a violent act of rejection.

Janx glossed a smile at Margrit, pleased with himself, and nervousness swept her. Advocate or not, she found the idea of holding an entire race's fate in her hands alarming. She looked back at Malik as he peeled his hand away to reveal his cast lot, then brought her attention to Biali. Thought caught up with vision an instant later and she jerked her eyes back to Malik.

A white stone lay before him on the table.

Janx inhaled, soft and sharp. Kaimana bowed toward Malik, a small gesture of thanks, and Biali grunted with surprise. Margrit's heart fluttered, warning her that she needed to draw breath. Tense pleasure stretched Malik's mouth, and for a long few seconds the quorum remained silent and still, absorbing the implications of his vote.

Biali scowled at the gathering, his gaze lingering most darkly on Margrit. Kaimana watched without change of stance or expression, but Margrit's hands went cold with the certainty that while the selkie lord had known how Malik would vote, the gargoyle's choice was unknown to him.

"No point in standing on shifting earth." Biali opened his hand with none of Malik's dramatics, the white pebble pale against even his skin.

Margrit breathed a laugh, knowing she should keep the silent solemnity of the moment, but unable to resist looking at Janx as she unfolded her own fingers, stone gleaming white against her palm. "I wasn't critical after all." The admission was a relief and a disappointment all at once, though relief won out as a shiver of portents swept her.

Janx ignored her, looking hard at Malik. "I wonder what the cost of that stone was."

"A peace accord," Kaimana answered. "That his people and mine will not stand in each other's way. There's room enough for all of us."

Biali growled, far more emotion than Alban would have allowed himself, and Janx leaned back in his seat, fingers templed in front of his mouth. Margrit dragged in a breath, her eyes drawn back to Malik. Only Daisani gave no outward sign of his reaction as he looked from djinn to selkie lord.

"That's it, then." Biali broke the new silence, glowering around the table. "Exile's lifted and time moves on. This quorum is—"

"Wait." Margrit's voice quavered, but she stood, making herself as large as she could in the presence of so many inhumans. "There are other issues to be addressed."

Mouths pursed and eyebrows lifted as curious attention was turned her way. Even Malik looked toward her without overwhelming antagonism. "Unless you've stolen children like changelings," Margrit said to Kaimana, "there's the issue of telling humans you exist."

She looked to the other four at the table, her confidence rising as she offered her argument. "This is a harder question, in its way, than whether to accept the selkies. Choosing to tell humans about yourselves is dangerous. A wrong choice could easily have disastrous consequences. But holding exile over someone's head is too much, if you're accepting the possibility of interbreeding. No one should make that kind of decision without their partner knowing the truth about them."

"Perhaps we should defer to those with experience in such situations," Daisani suggested, his tone all politeness that belied a mocking glint in his eyes.

Kaimana shrugged big shoulders. "Our tradition has been to try to choose mates from those who had already discovered us. Our seaside villages were easy to observe, and more times than we liked, seafarers and explorers came upon us. But when we've chosen to tell outsiders, we've only offered our secrets to those we hoped to build lives with."

"And when those explorers moved to capture or imprison you, to make you their pets or trophies? When chosen mates couldn't accept your nature?" Daisani spoke again, deference from the others due, Margrit now thought, to his greater age.

Kaimana turned his gaze to her, keeping it steady as his voice. "When necessary we dealt with them as strongly as required. We are far less plagued by unexpected discovery now, but when we choose to tell humans—which happens less often with our numbers so replenished—we're very careful. Most can accept us, and of those who do not, the larger percentage find it in themselves to guard our secrets." He kept to the formal phrases and vocal tones, as if doing so hid the nature of what he admitted to.

"And those who don't?" Margrit had no more need than anyone else at the table to have it detailed for her, but put the question forth regardless, challenging Kaimana to answer it.

He met her gaze for a long, quiet moment before replying, "There are accidents."

Even knowing what he would say, the answer buckled Margrit's knees. She locked them, unwilling to lose face in the quorum by sitting abruptly, but her hands clenched at her sides. Intellectual awareness that murder was done—even a grim understanding and a deep, sickening fear that she herself could be moved to such action to protect a whole race of people—made hearing it, effectively condoning it, no easier.

"I think we all agree it's better not to need accidents," Daisani said blithely, as if unaware of the real meaning of that word. "Perhaps a modification of our laws. We might tell those with whom we wish to mate of our true natures, but beyond that, to reveal us is still—must still be—an offense of significant proportions. I think exile is not unreasonable."

"And if you're discovered accidentally by someone who can't handle the truth?" Margrit asked.

Daisani turned an unrelenting look on her. "Accidents," he said, "happen." He let the statement hang a moment, then turned to the others. "Are we agreed? Shall we make a vote of it?"

The formal process went more quickly the second time, the identifications already made. Margrit offered her voting stones to Kaimana, respecting that he hadn't voted when it had been his own motion on the table. Only one of the five voted against her: Malik, and no one, not even Margrit, was surprised by that. White pebbles gleamed around the table, her own vote tacit and, she was all too aware, approving the murder of humans. She closed her eyes a moment, absorbing that, then spoke before the sounds of action around her could turn to the quorum's end. "Wait."

She opened her eyes to find surprise and irritation sweeping around her. "There's one more law I want to address."

It was Janx who answered, his tone deceptively mild. "We have only one other law common to us, Margrit. You wouldn't have us do away with order altogether, would you?"

"Your third exiling offense," Margrit said with determination. A chill sliced through her but she kept her voice steady, as she did in a courtroom. With Alban at her side she'd been confident of the vote. He would support her. With Biali in his place, she doubted the outcome, but it had been five hundred years or more since the last quorum. She would literally never have another chance. "Exile's a much more civilized response to murder than our system has, but if we're looking at your laws, that one needs changing, too. Even *our* laws allow for self-defense and acting to protect someone else."

Kaimana suddenly relaxed, becoming the casual islander he'd seemed when Margrit had first met him. "I hear that 'he needed killing' is still a viable defense in Texas."

Margrit flashed a smile. "I've never looked it up to see if that was true. I'd be too disappointed if it weren't." Humor faded, leaving her looking from each member of the Old Races to the next. "What happens if one of you challenges another? I know Alban's been in a fight like that. What if he'd shown no mercy?"

"Then he would have been exiled for it." Malik's reply was implacable.

Margrit gave up all pretense of formality and rolled her eyes. "Thereby removing two people from your already limited gene pool instead of one. What if one of you loses her mind and does something to endanger you all? What if the only way to stop someone like that is by killing her? Would you exile the one who moved to save all your people? You've got no compunction against killing humans to protect your secrets. Does the same law apply to your own, or are humans now just dumb breeding material, not worth thinking of as living, intelligent beings?"

"None of our people would be so reckless," Kaimana said with certainty.

Margrit took a deep breath. "Ask Biali about that."

The gargoyle straightened, as much a display of shock as she'd ever seen from his kind, and gave her a wary look that sharpened into anger.

Janx, his voice still mild, said, “My dear Margrit, have you some proof that Biali has been murdering our kind, or has otherwise lost his mind?”

Margrit muttered, “I’m not sure any of you are all that stable,” before lifting her voice to say, “No, but he might be able to provide some interesting insights about the changing nature of the Old Races.”

“Biali?” Daisani’s voice carried a note of command that the gargoyle responded to blandly.

“The lawyer’s not a fool, even if she’s human. All of us know about doing things we would never have dreamed of a few centuries ago. Who’s to say human madness can’t creep in along with human behavior?”

As Biali spoke, Janx turned a sudden look on Margrit, his lips pursed and his jade eyes bright. Her heart lurched, a telltale sound to ears like Janx’s, and the thoughtful curiosity in his eyes blazed into private delight. “Let us vote,” he said abruptly. “Margrit’s point is made, if not at the length she might wish, but we are not a people prone to debate. By age,” he proposed again, and Daisani, without preamble, opened his hand to reveal a black stone.

Disappointment surged in Margrit’s belly as Janx and Kaimana locked eyes, the former making his from-the-waist bow a second time that evening. “I defer,” he said politely. “I shall vote at the last.”

Giving himself the balance to tip, if it came to that, Margrit thought. Kaimana nodded and followed Daisani’s lead, not waiting for the formal question to be put to him before he, too, opened his hand to show a black stone.

Dismay surged through Margrit again, though Kaimana’s claim against the potential folly of people belonging to the Old Races tempered her surprise. Malik, too, turned up a black stone, though that, at least, came as expected. Alban would have voted her way, but with Biali at the table… She'd tried, she told herself. She'd tried, and at least Janx was likely to vote her way. It wouldn't be an utter rout, and perhaps it would signify a move toward getting the changes in law that she hoped for.

Biali turned his attention to Margrit, his scarred face dark with consideration. She met his gaze with as much forthright openness as she could, though her chest hurt with the possibility of defeat. Though he'd shown tiny bursts of crass emotion during the meeting, she could no longer read anything in his eye. It left her with a sense of being judged, and found wanting.

He put his hands on the table with slow deliberation, still watching her, and then suddenly his ugly smile shaped his features as he opened his fingers.

The same hand he'd opened twice before. Margrit's breath caught, sending another painful lurch through her chest.

A white stone sat in Biali's palm.

TWENTY-SEVEN

A RUSH OF NOISE filled Margrit's ears, heat rushing through her entire body as she stared at Biali's vote in disbelief. He dropped the stone on the table and leaned back, thick arms folded across his broad chest. Only Janx's flourish to Margrit's left took her attention away from the gargoyle's vote. She looked toward the dragon with a sense of curious unreality.

Janx rolled his stone in his palm, bringing it up to display between his thumb and forefinger before he laid it on the table with a soft click of finality. It gleamed white, a final show of support for Margrit's cause.

"Three and three. The law stands. Biali?" Daisani looked toward the history-taker with expectation.

The gargoyle shoved back from the table and stood, a block of flesh solid as a wall. "It'll go in the memories, and anyone looking to see how it came to pass just has to ask. Any more surprises, lawyer?"

"No." Margrit's voice cracked and she pulled her eyes from the white stone Biali had abandoned on the table. "No, I think that pretty much took care of it. I don't know about any other laws that need rewriting."

"Then we're done." Biali stumped out of the boardroom with no more ceremony than that. Malik followed him, leaving Margrit alone with three elders of the Old Races.

Janx stepped up to her side, eyes bright green with interest. "I believe you and I have some things to discuss. Perhaps I could escort you home. If you'll have me, of course."

"There's a question you may hear regularly, Miss Knight." Daisani, full of teasing formality, appeared beside Janx. "An attractive, intelligent woman already conversant with the Old Races, when we've just agreed to change our laws of survival. All sorts of propositions may come your way."

Margrit blurted, "I need to talk to Biali," and Daisani clucked his tongue in overweening dismay.

"I'm shocked. Had I guessed who our young Knight might choose as her squire, it would certainly not have been Biali. Generations of children who might have been weep in despair. Margrit, if you're returning to the ball, I'd be delighted to claim another dance."

"Sure." She nodded as Daisani left the room, then turned toward Janx. Kaimana, still on the other side of the table, offered a very brief smile that sent an unexpected chill over Margrit's skin. She believed the choices she'd pushed the Old Races to were the right ones, but the arrogance of that belief came back to her as she saw self-satisfaction in Kaaiai's expression. He, like Biali, seemed to have nothing more to say, and left her standing alone with Janx.

The red-haired crimelord offered his elbow, all graceful politeness, and looked pleased when Margrit took it. "I remember a time when you wouldn't let me touch you, much less take your arm or share a dance," he murmured. "Have you softened toward the hardened criminal, Margrit?"

Remembered irritation rose up at the casual, dismissive way Janx had captured a lock of her hair in his fingers the first time they'd met. Margrit banished the memory with effort, trying to distance herself from the emotion. "It wasn't your occupation that made me angry. It was the arrogant possessiveness. You don't go around handling people like objects just because you think you can."

"On the contrary." Janx pulled the door open, amused, and escorted Margrit toward the elevators.

She huffed, trying not to share his laughter. "You shouldn't. And you certainly shouldn't do it to me."

"Or you'll very nearly bite my hand, as I recall. I've learned caution. I'd like you to tell me about a name I once gave you, Margrit." The elevator doors chimed closed behind them and Janx leaned on one reflective brass wall, full of falsely casual interest. "Tell me about Ausra."

A new wave of surprise washed through her, part of an endless ebb and flow. Margrit was unexpectedly grateful for the sleep she'd gotten that morning. Without it, the ceaseless exchange of high emotion would overwhelm her. As it was, she felt like staggering under its weight, and wished Alban were at hand so she could lean on his strength. She needed to talk to Biali, but she *wanted* to talk to Alban, to find out why he'd given up his place in the quorum so readily. To ask why he'd abandoned her, though an itching conviction told her choosing that word was unfair. "Is that why you voted on my behalf?"

Janx gave a liquid shrug. "I voted with you because

I enjoy upsetting the balance, though I'll confess surprise at how badly it was upset tonight. But I'm reminded that I gave you a name—and a priceless stone—and I've heard nothing of either since."

"I gave the sapphire to Alban," Margrit said flatly. The egg-shaped stone had held a star within it, translucent blue and milky white making up the bulk of its color, though a fragile spot of lilac had marked one end. It had been a gift from Alban to Hajnal hundreds of years earlier, and had ended up in Janx's hands through Ausra and a corrupt policeman. "Take it up with him."

"Why, Margrit." Janx's tones were injured. "You promised you'd return it."

"Actually, I think you promised I'd return it. I never said I would. And even if I did…" Margrit smiled. "I lied."

"It's wonderful," Janx muttered, "that you feel confident in telling me that. I must be losing my touch. Ausra, my dear," he said more clearly. "Tell me about Ausra."

"She blamed Alban for something he hadn't done," Margrit said bluntly. "She was killing people and trying to frame him for it, no matter what happened to the rest of the Old Races. She almost killed me."

"Ah. Nereida Holmes, your attacker this winter. I see." Interest glittered in Janx's eyes. "She had a daytime life, Margrit. A job, family, friends."

"She was Hajnal's daughter, not Alban's. Her father was human, a man who'd captured Hajnal."

"And you fought her off. An attacker with easily two or three times your strength."

"What's the penalty for one of us killing one of you, Janx?" Margrit asked.

Janx slid a sour jade glance at her. "Ask Saint George. Ask Beowulf or Ulysses. Look to your legends, Margrit, and answer that yourself."

"Immortality?" Margrit breathed the question, less humor in it than she'd intended. "That's not what I meant, Janx, and you know it. What do your people do to us?"

"We retaliate when we can. If we know the guilty party. If he doesn't have a reputation for destroying seven of us in a single blow."

"So I'm better off keeping my mouth shut over what happened with Ausra. Let's just work under the principle that it's not unreasonable to hope that if the Old Races' strictures are loosened for you, they might be bent for me."

"You have bent us so far we struggle not to break, Margrit." Janx spoke lightly, but steel lined his words. "Change doesn't come easily to our people, and we've upset the balance greatly tonight."

"How is it that five of you can make these kinds of decisions for your entire people? We'd have gone through public hearings and arguments, and the whole process would've taken years."

"Malik can't," Janx admitted freely. "Unless he's faced the rite of passage. Succeeding would give him the voice he needs among the djinn to have his arguments heard."

"The rite of passage. You both mentioned that earlier. What is it?"

"A challenge, usually within the tribe. He'll have chosen a leader he thinks can be defeated and try to bring him down, thereby gaining that position. I wonder who he defeated. I wouldn't have thought he had it in him."

A knot tied in Margrit's stomach. "Within the tribe or the race?"

Janx looked askance at her and she swallowed. "What if he's far enough removed from the djinn to think of other people as his own? What if you're the leader he wants to take down? Does he have to have already done it to stand for his people?"

"Perhaps not if they're *very* confident of his success, but I think not, Margrit. Not with this morning's attempt on his own life. He's badly shaken, or he'd have never approached you." Janx pursed his lips in thought, then smiled brilliantly. "And I think that if I were him and intended on challenging me, I would have voted to overturn our third law. It would be ill-advised to strike at me without killing."

Margrit sighed. "Yeah, that's true enough. God, what have I gotten myself into?"

Janx turned an unexpectedly sympathetic look on her. "It isn't often that a human finds herself so thoroughly ensconced in our world. I wish I could be reassuring and promise that all will be well, but historically, it hasn't worked that way. Our good, true Stoneheart may yet come to regret speaking to you that night."

Margrit managed a weak smile. "Somehow I get the impression that I wouldn't necessarily be around in this scenario to share his regrets."

"Ours isn't an especially kind world, Margrit, not even to those of us born to it. I would warn you toward caution, but—"

"It'd be crying over spilled milk. Thank you, Janx," Margrit said dryly. "I think, now that I'm feeling so reassured, that I'll find Alban and have him drop me off on a nice high mountaintop until you've all settled this new way of—You didn't tell me." She broke off accusingly. "You didn't tell me why you could make this decision for your whole race."

"No." Janx smiled merrily and stepped back with an extravagant bow. "I didn't. Good evening, Margrit Knight." He turned on his heel and strode back toward the ballroom, leaving her with a helpless laugh on her lips.

A peculiar ripple went through the ballroom as Margrit entered a few minutes later. Dark-eyed faces turned toward her briefly, beginning with those nearest the balcony and washing out to the edges, like a stadium wave effect. She saw one or two who were familiar: Cara Delaney, whose enigmatic smile made her seem much older than she had only a month or two earlier. Kaimana Kaaiai, who acknowledged her as solemnly as he had in the boardroom. His personal assistant, Marese, didn't smile, but something in her expression suggested approval.

And in the rest of the faces she saw thanks, admiration, delight, excitement. Selkie faces, all of them, dotted among the oblivious humans at the party. It would have been a formidable source with only mortals as attendees; with the selkie ranks swelling the guest list, there were over a thousand people swirling through Daisani's ballrooms.

"No point standing on shifting earth." Biali's voice rumbled near Margrit's ear, startling her. He barely paused as he passed by, though he cut a glance from her to the gathered selkies and back again. "No point standing against the tide."

Then he was among them once more, white-haired

and broad-shouldered as he moved unceremoniously through the crowd of dark-haired selkies. They let him pass without comment, though Margrit saw from some faces that they knew how he'd voted in the quorum, and were pleased with him for it. Kaimana stepped aside for him, then turned back to Margrit and lifted a hand in question. She smiled and came down the stairs, fingertips light on the railing, to work her way to the selkie lord and fall into the steps of an elegant, formal dance with him. "I thought maybe you didn't dance."

Kaimana gave her a broad, bright grin with no artifice to it. "I wasn't sure I had reason to, earlier."

"What will you do now?"

"Party like it's 1999," Kaimana said drolly, then glanced around the ballroom. "As Eliseo would have it, it seems. I assume this extravaganza is his way of showing us the advantages of building an alliance with him."

"Is it working?"

Kaimana brought Margrit around in a slow, stately turn, offering her the chance to watch the fluid motions of the dancers around her. A sense of confidence imbued them, not that her dealings with the any of the Old Races had suggested they were less than confident. But it was more than that: a sense of belonging; of joy. "I guess I'd be pretty thrilled to be handed the keys to the—" She broke off, realizing she'd stolen Janx's phrase. "But you have money," she said after a moment's uncomfortable silence. "This isn't new to you."

"Dancing with the elite isn't," Kaimana agreed. "But dancing with my own people so freely? With all of us welcomed as what we are by the rest of our kind? I think we could do worse than ally ourselves with Eliseo Daisani."

Margrit nodded, unwilling to voice her own reservations. Alban had warned her about just such an alliance too many times—and fruitlessly—but she was human. Kaimana held more cards than that, and had moved with assurance from the moment she'd met him, all toward the end game he'd achieved during the quorum.

He spun her again, and she caught a glimpse of Tony, his jaw tense with strain. The sensation of dancing on a knife's edge suddenly blossomed within her. Kaimana had, from all appearances, moved *before* she'd met him, putting Tony into a position where the selkie lord could get to Margrit through him. Abrupt anger at her precarious position made her steps clumsy. It seemed that there had not been an unorchestrated moment in her life since Alban had greeted her in the park on a frozen January night.

Kaimana steadied her, his forehead wrinkled with concern. Margrit shook her head and put on a meaningless smile, trying not to feel as though she was baring her teeth. "It's been a long week. I guess I'm more tired than I thought."

The selkie lord looked rueful. "I think you've done your duty by us tonight. You've even danced with everyone. I know you support Alban, Ms. Knight. I'm honored that you've chosen to throw your lot in with my people, as well. And I think the fact that you've chosen Daisani as your benefactor speaks highly of him as a man worth having on our side."

"As opposed to Janx?"

"Janx runs a much darker empire than Eliseo does. There's something to be said for a life lived in sunlight, don't you think?"

Nothing in his expression changed, no hint of a threat

appeared in his pleasant gaze, but Margrit stumbled again, heart lurching. Kaimana came to a halt, his hands steady on her waist and his eyebrows drawn down, still with nothing more than genial concern and friendship in his eyes. "Margrit?"

"I'm sorry." She stepped back. "I just need to sit down for a little while and catch my breath."

She gathered herself and fled the dance floor in search of the man she would never build a life in the sunlight with.

TWENTY-EIGHT

MOONLIGHT SOFTENED THE city's shadows, turning concrete and steel to faded lilac and blue. A handful of stars glittered above, defying both city lights and the moon. Music and soft light rose from below, open windows carrying the sounds of Daisani's party up to the rooftop. Wind played in Margrit's hair, threatening to finish what the tango earlier had started and emphasizing bursts of chatter with its ebb and fall.

Alban alighted behind her with a soft thud and a rustle of wings. Margrit glanced back at him, smiling. His silver-shot tuxedo was gone, abandoned in favor of the jeans he typically wore in his gargoyle form. Typically, or rather, for her benefit: her first glimpse of his natural shape had been staggering, and he'd donned clothing he didn't normally bother with so she might be able to meet his eyes. Bare-chested and pale in the moonlight, he looked like a dream come to life, warm and comforting and not at all human.

"When I said meet on the roof, it didn't occur to me until too late that you didn't have an elevator key for rooftop access."

"It occurred to me that you didn't have wings." Alban sounded amused. "I assumed you had some method of getting yourself here, but it seemed like a curious place to meet."

"I wanted to see the view. Eliseo's office faces west. I wanted to see…" Margrit gestured to the south. "I wanted this one."

Alban stepped up behind her, gently resting a hand on her shoulder. "No, you didn't."

"What?" She frowned.

"This isn't the view you wanted. You're looking for something that isn't there." He offered a cautious smile as Margrit turned more fully to gaze at him. "I know a thing or two about searching skylines for memories, Margrit."

She looked back at the city. "I guess we all do now." Alban opened a wing and folded it around her, garnering a quiet sigh of contentment as warmth drove sorrow away. "We have the whole night to ourselves," she said after a moment. "I don't think there's a single member of the Old Races in town who's not at the party downstairs. What do you want to do?"

"With that introduction, I feel I ought to propose my insidious plan to take over the city."

Her voice brightened. "Do you have one?"

"I'm afraid not." Alban's tone went dry. "If you're looking for someone to conquer New York with, you might want to invite Janx up here instead."

"Not at all." Margrit turned against his chest, winding her arms around his waist and closing her eyes. "Why did you leave?"

"Because Biali was right." Alban's heartbeat counted long seconds beneath Margrit's ear before he spoke again. "Perhaps because I didn't want to bear responsibility. But mostly, because he was right. I haven't been part of my people's world for centuries, Margrit. I didn't have the right to answer the question the quorum asked tonight."

"Questions," Margrit corrected, and pulled a crooked smile when Alban leaned back to look down at her. "Kaaiai wasn't the only one with an agenda. I asked them to overturn the other two rules, as well."

Alban went so still beside her that Margrit glanced up to see if stone had swept over him. "On telling humans about us?"

"And exile for killing another of the Old Races. I was sure I'd lost that one, when Biali took your place."

"Margrit." Alban's voice sounded strangled, and he stepped back from her. "You thought I would *support* changing that law?"

Surprised offense pinked Margrit's cheeks. "Why wouldn't you? It's your neck I was trying to save."

"Margrit, we have those laws—that law—for a reason. We aren't so many that we can afford to lose each other to personal battles. Tell me it was overruled."

"What? I was trying to help you, Alban!"

"I understand that." The gargoyle's voice dropped low, edged with dismay. "But I would not have voted with you. Margrit, how did the quorum decide?"

"It was a hung jury." Margrit moved away, folding her arms around her ribs. "Janx and Biali voted with me. Daisani, Kaaiai and Malik voted against."

"Biali—" Alban made another strangled sound. "That Biali voted with you should tell you everything you need to know as to why we cannot allow that law to be undone, Margrit. Even if it's my neck, as you put it."

"But…" Embarrassed chagrin filled her. Margrit's chest ached with disbelief.

"No. Margrit." Alban came forward again, enormous hands curled to brush knuckles against her cheeks. "It is a gift that you tried," he whispered. "A gift I wouldn't have asked for. Wouldn't have thought to ask for. I understand that in the human world it makes sense. That there are circumstances when a despicable action is the only recourse, and when turning to it may save more lives than it takes.

"But we *must* hold a threat over our own heads to ensure our own safety. Banishment from our communities is a difficult thing to contemplate. We have so little besides each other. We can't let that go. If we do we may lose ourselves forever. I understand your reasoning, but I beg you, never try this again. Please, Margrit. If you would grant me a gift, grant me this. Do not try to undo this law, even to save me."

Tears pricked at Margrit's eyes. "You should've been a lawyer." Her voice cracked and she swallowed hard, averting her gaze. "I was trying to help you."

"Yes. As a human would, in the human world. But I don't belong to that world, Margrit. I glide on its edges. I know it's not easy, but you can't think of me as one of you. You're reluctant to imprison Janx or Daisani," he whispered. "Turn that reluctance to me. The laws that govern me are not the same as those that govern you."

"I should know that by now." Her throat remained tight, constricting her answer. "I thought—" She'd thought like a human. "Okay." A tiny, harsh nod accompanied the word. "Okay. I get your point. I shouldn't have tried. I should've talked to you first. I just—"

"You saw an injustice and were determined to make it right." Alban smiled cautiously, as if afraid the expression would earn her ire. "It is a gift, Margrit, but not one I can accept. One I'm relieved to hear has not been granted." He drew in a deep breath and dropped his hands, stepping back again. "Perhaps I should leave you."

Margrit reached for his arm. "Don't you dare." She consciously echoed him, taking a deep breath of her own and feeling it shudder in her lungs. "Don't you dare. We're finally talking. We're finally together. Even if we're talking about my colossal mistake," she added beneath her breath. "I'm not letting you go now."

"Not a mistake, Margrit. You meant well."

"I meant well, but I didn't think. I didn't think like one of you," she amended, and Alban chuckled.

"Perhaps because you're not one of us. All right." He drew her close again, Margrit sighing into his warmth. "What now?"

"Take me flying."

"You'll be cold, in that gown."

"Alban." Exasperated humor colored Margrit's response. "You'll just have to think of some way to warm me up."

"Humans," he murmured under his breath, but lifted Margrit with both hands, letting her bury her arms under his warm hair and snuggle against the expanse of his chest. She clung to him, nose against his shoulder to hide a grin, then squealed with excitement and laughter when he crouched and surged upward, broad wings snapping out to catch the air.

"You're better at that than Biali," she shouted into the wind, once they were airborne.

Alban turned his head, wrinkling his nose as strands of her hair came loose and whipped across his face. "You flew with Biali?" His low growl made Margrit hug him in reassurance.

"When he brought me to see Janx the other night. Wouldn't sully himself with the subway. It was like riding a roller coaster, all surges and stops. You flow." Margrit nuzzled his neck, putting her lips against his skin before she spoke again. "Don't be jealous. It doesn't suit you."

"It's more of a dragon's trait," Alban rumbled, "but we're not immune to it. Your ability to conquer the men around you is somewhat distressing, Margrit, you must admit."

"Oh, so now you're men." The wind stung her, bringing with it burgeoning desire as her nipples tightened against the cold, satin caressing them like a lover's tongue. She spoke to distract herself, a halfhearted attempt at taking her mind from the heat of Alban's body pressed against hers. "I haven't conquered anybody, Alban. Janx flirts like he breathes, without thinking about it. Daisani plays at being charming, but I'm just a tool to him. Don't fool yourself. Don't let them fool you. This house of cards you Old Races have is fragile enough without introducing trouble where it doesn't exist."

"And that tango?" The grumble left Alban's voice, leaving ruefulness behind. Margrit tucked herself closer, her nose in his hair as she breathed in the scent of cold stone and wind. He shifted a hand beneath her bottom, pulling her closer, and she slid her thigh over his hip, fighting slippery fabric to hold it there.

"If I'd had any idea it would be a tango…"

Alban chuckled. "Malik is the least of my fears, so far as your attention is concerned."

"Implying there's another reason to be concerned." Margrit tilted back, her eyes closed and her hair flattening as the wind pressed it against her cheeks and shoulders. Alban's grip tightened as she loosened one arm from around his neck, then the other, bringing them up straight above her head, as if she was diving through the air.

"I don't want to talk about Malik or the others anymore," she whispered, trusting the wind to bring the words to Alban's ears. Cold cut through her gown, heightening her awareness of its thinness. She'd felt the same erotic charge when flying with him before, arching in his arms in just such a way, but now her clothing hid nothing of her desire, the fabric fitted to her skin by wind as much as by design. "Do gargoyles make love in the sky, Alban?"

"Only if we've flown very high first." Alban's voice had gone deep. "We're not made for hovering."

"So you fall together." Dizzy laughter swept Margrit, blooming into body-weakening desire. "My God. I thought running in the park was a rush. I don't have wings." She drew her arms back down, folding them behind herself as if seeking them. Instead, she found the zipper of her dress and slid it open until Alban's arms, secure around her waist, stopped it. She pressed one hand to her breasts, keeping the dress in place, watching Alban's gaze darken. "Will I be able to catch you when you fall?"

"Far too late," he murmured. "I've long since fallen."

"Take me higher," Margrit whispered. "As high as we can go."

Alban said, "Look," very softly.

She tipped her head back and gasped. The city lay impossibly far below, glittering silently in the darkness. "How high are we?"

"High enough. You're not dressed to go higher."

"I'm not dressed to go this high!"

"But I've thought of a way to keep you warm." Alban drew her closer, creating more points of heated contact where their bodies met. He loosened an arm from her waist, confident in his own strength, and slipped his hand over her ribs, smoothing the fabric with his palm. Margrit caught her breath, slowly unfolding to allow Alban to draw the gown away from her breasts. She trilled laughter, half in dismay at the increased cold, half heady with excitement. Alban murmured something senseless and lowered his head, finding her nipple with his mouth and tasting her with absurd delicacy, given his size. Margrit wound her fingers into his hair, arching beneath his mouth, the gown's satin touch nothing compared to the exploring heat of his tongue.

His flight pattern changed, muscles no longer working to lift them higher into the sky. Instead his wings stretched wide, a faint cant coming into his gliding so they could sink in slow circles rather than in a dangerous plummet. Margrit made a soft dizzy sound expressing both relief and disappointment.

Alban lifted his head, pale eyes bright in the moonlight. "Forgive me. Was the fall the only rush you were looking for?"

Margrit shrieked in laughter and batted at the grinning gargoyle, tangling her fingers in his hair. "This will do. Stop talking. I need you close to keep warm." Giggles ran through her, boundless delight that increased with every sting of hair in her eyes and every shift of Alban's strong hands against her body. Loving was meant to be shared in laughter, but the outpouring of joy that flooded her went beyond that, a heart-pounding acknowledgment of danger and power, things outside ordinary human scope. Her cheeks ached from smiling, an expression so broad it seemed embarrassing.

Rather than try to trust words, she shifted downward until she could kiss him, her ardency rising as she learned the shape and softness of his mouth. Wide mouth, far wider than hers, but fitting better than any lover she could remember. He tasted of champagne and stone, a mix of ordinary and impossible ricocheting through Margrit's body like a call to battle, a delicious, irresistible challenge. He was so nearly human, so clearly not, as evidenced by the shifting moonlight above them, blocked and dimmed by Alban's wings, then bright again, even through the tangle of her closed lashes. That they soared so near the stars gave truth to both what he was and what he was not, a creature beyond her scope and yet possible within the compass of her arms. He was the dream she hadn't known she'd wanted, couldn't have imagined existed, until he came into her life in an erotic offering, fear superceded and drowned by excitement.

She could feel caution in his kisses—not a lack of passion, but borne out by gentleness, as if he knew how easily his size, his alien form, might overwhelm her. For all that they sailed amongst thin clouds and cool moonlight at Alban's whim, Margrit felt heart-pounding power, as if he offered her control by knowing how easy it would be to deny it.

She was sure her eyes stung from the cold wind, not a shocking rise of sentimentality and trust so profound she had to smile to avoid tears. Margrit slid one of Alban's hands to her lower back, finding the gown's half-fastened zipper and guiding it down, making the gesture as much his as hers. His chuckle, warm and low, came through the wind with a warning: "If I pull it any farther, someone will find a very expensive and beautiful dress strung over a flagpole or telephone wire tomorrow morning."

"You're only half-dressed." Margrit caught her lower lip in her teeth, smiling foolishly at Alban's intent expression. "Seems only fair I should be, too."

He stroked his thumb along her spine, creating a shiver that had nothing to do with gusting wind. "Are you certain?" His voice, like his touch, was gentle.

A pulse of desire ran through her, spiking in her groin and breasts, even making her hands ache with need. "I'm sure."

An instant later the gown slid down, tangling briefly in Margrit's shoes. She laughed, kicking at the fabric but unable to loosen the straps that held her shoes in place. For a moment the garment fluttered beside them, a living thing of twisting, pale gold in the blue light, before it began its descent to the city below. Margrit reached toward it, half envying its freedom to fall, but then brought herself back to Alban's warmth without regret. Only with him could she come close to having that very freedom, and the desire to do so grew within her, aching and demanding. She hitched her thigh over his hip again, pressing liquid heat against the waistband of his jeans and drawing a rumble from him. "You're considerably less than half-dressed now."

His fingers bumped over her hip, where the narrow line of a thong bikini was all that marred the skin. He tangled his hand in the elastic, turning his head to meet Margrit's gaze. She nodded, a tiny, breathless motion, and he snapped the band, easily, possessively. Margrit, half expecting it, still gasped with a thrill of pleasure as her heartbeat surged, a primal response to Alban's show of strength.

He murmured, "Hold on to me," and Margrit, as if she hadn't been, knotted her arms around his neck and sought his throat with her lips. His warmth against her was the comfort of heated stone, profound enough that even with wind rushing by, its chill seemed to pass over her unnoticed. Alban shifted her up his body again, moving her small mass rather than duck his head and endanger the pattern of their flight as he covered her nipples with his mouth. Margrit swallowed a cry, then let it go, amused at the idea that someone might be close enough to hear. Trusting Alban's grip on her, she loosened her hands from around his neck, but he made a sound of discouragement. "Hold on."

"But—"

"Later." Soft humor tinged the word. "There will be time for me later." He shifted his grip on her bottom, drawing her leg farther over his hip before he took advantage of the changed position and slipped a knuckled finger between her thighs from behind. Margrit went rigid, hands knotted in his hair as she keened, opening herself farther to his touch. His exploration was gentle, parting folds and seeking heat until she buried her face in his shoulder, trying to catch her breath. Alban murmured in delight, encouraging her response by finding her center of pleasure and covering it with a delicacy that belied the danger of taloned hands. The whimpered pleas that erupted from Margrit's throat were incoherent with need, earning a sound of pleasure from her lover. He folded a second knuckle inward, offering sweet teasing to a body aching to be touched, and then a whispered apology. "No more. These hands aren't made for a body as fragile as yours."

Frustrated heat swept Margrit's cheeks. "Other parts of you must be." She let her grip loosen, sliding down Alban's body a few inches, trusting him to hold her, and all but losing her grasp entirely when it was the hand between her thighs that caught her weight. Pleasure shot through her, whiting out the moonlight and briefly overriding any vestiges of cold she might have felt. Alban's breath hitched at the hard pulse against his fingers, then again as raging desire brought Margrit's hungry mouth to his chest, her tongue and teeth seeking out a nipple. She breathed, "Don't let me fall," against his skin, then flattened her hand against his belly and slid it beneath the waistband of his jeans.

Her own skin hadn't felt cold to her until she wrapped her fingers around the silken heat of Alban's length. He rumbled, a deep aching sound of desire, then suddenly surged upward, no longer content to glide in ever-sinking circles. Margrit gasped in shy delight as the very beat of his wings helped her find a rhythm to stroke him with, until impatience brought her hand free so she could tug open his jeans and explore him more fully. Alabaster skin, unmarred by curls, glowed in contrast to the denim, in contrast to the darkness of Margrit's skin in the moonlight. She blurted, "Look," in a high voice, garnering a rough laugh from the gargoyle.

"We may fall from the sky if I do. Your hands are…"

"Cold," Margrit offered. "Dark. Small."

"Extraordinary," Alban groaned. "Margrit, it has been…a very long time since anyone has touched me so." A shudder ran over him, extending to his wing tips, and he leveled out again, beginning the circling anew.

Possessiveness surged through Margrit, bearing hunger with it. She tightened her fingers around him, making a demand of the touch. "Good," she said irrationally. "That makes you mine." Her heart ached at the pronouncement, and unexpected gladness took her breath away. There was a world below that she'd moved away from, leaving little in the way of regret: things she might have done differently, perhaps, but no results she would change, not now, not sharing the sky with a gargoyle. "Your world," she whispered. "Your world is the one I want to belong to, Alban. Your world, with you. Can I be a part of it?" She drew herself up his body again, seeking his wide mouth, hoping he could taste the desire and hope in her kiss.

"You already are. Whether you choose to remain…" Loss sounded in his voice, sparking ferociousness in Margrit's resolve.

"I do." With her dark gaze fixed on Alban's, she shifted her weight, curling her legs around his waist.

"Margrit." Her name was a hoarse whisper. "Margrit." The same emotions she'd felt, hope and desire, conflicted in his voice. "Margrit, this form, your size—" It was her own once-voiced laughing objection that he tried to remind her of, but she stopped his objections with a kiss.

"I know." Her own voice was low, intense. "I know what I said. But tall men fit with small women all the time, and I want you. I want *you.* My Alban. My gargoyle." She nuzzled his throat, shivering, and whispered, "Don't let me fall."

"Never." Alban's reply was torn away by the wind, but his hands were certain, encompassing her waist as they guided one another in joining. Rough denim scraped Margrit's inner thighs, a delicious counterpart to the silken strength within her. Then there were only soft whispers of focused astonishment as Margrit clung to her lover in the night sky, circling, circling, always circling, toward the earth.

"Leave me on my balcony." Margrit pushed at Alban, moving him not an inch.

Gradual descent had taken them to rooftops, their bodies entwined in lovemaking until Alban lifted his head toward the east, his expression dismayed. Margrit had demanded his tuxedo jacket and shirt from his other form, and wore them now, hugging the oversize clothes to her body. The shirt fell halfway to her knees, almost a dress in itself, though she'd given her gold strapped shoes a rueful look for not matching Alban's silver-threaded suit. "Alban, dawn is coming. You need to go home."

"I don't want to leave you."

Margrit nudged him again. "You'll turn to stone with daylight whether you want to or not. I'd rather be home safe—because I am *not* walking through New York in this outfit—and I'd rather you didn't stay out so long you turned to stone in midflight. I'll still want you tonight," she promised more softly, then stepped closer to him, curling her fingers against the stony smoothness of his chest. "You could come to dinner. I could cook."

Teasing danced in Alban's pale gaze. "Is that incentive or reason to stay away?"

She laughed. "It's not too bad. Not as good as Cole cooking, but not too bad. A late dinner, maybe, around nine? That would give you plenty of time to get there."

"What about your housemates?"

"They'll be polite, at least. They were all right last night. Yesterday. Whenever that was."

"All right." Alban stole a kiss before murmuring, "Though I don't see what's wrong with your outfit." He chortled over Margrit's splutter of protest and scooped her up, springing skyward. Winging across the Manhattan skyline seemed to take no time at all, Margrit stepping out of Alban's arms onto her balcony only minutes later.

"Nine o'clock, okay?"

"I'll be here." Alban bowed his head to linger in a kiss. "Thank you, Margrit."

She crooked a smile, wanting to brush off his thanks, and at the same time feeling she understood the impulse that prompted it. "Good night, Alban."

He shared her smile, then turned and cast himself off the balcony into the lightening sky. Margrit watched him go, then tipped her head up, smiling at the few stars left in the night, before tugging on the balcony door.

It stuck, making her grimace in dismay. A second pull verified that it was locked. She spun around, knowing it was too late to call Alban back, hoping it might not be. Not even his shadow was visible in the burgeoning light. She smacked her palms against the balcony railing in a nonverbal curse. The street below was comparatively quiet, but climbing down the fire escape ladders in her current clothing… Margrit gnashed her teeth, seeing nothing to be done for it.

She'd stepped up to the railing, about to swing her leg over it, when the balcony door's lock clicked, resounding in the morning stillness. Margrit froze as the door slid open, then forced herself to turn her head and look back.

Cole stood framed in the doorway, his expression unreadable. He looked Margrit up and down, then, blandly, said, "Nice shoes."

TWENTY-NINE

SICKNESS CHURNED IN Margrit's stomach, bringing a cold sweat to her skin. Cole's expression was accusing as he moved out of the doorway. She hugged herself, trying not to touch her housemate as she brushed by. Cool air followed her in, then was shut away again with the sliding of the door. "Lock yourself out?"

Margrit took a breath to answer, realized the futility of trying and released it again unburdened by words. Cole's voice followed her to the kitchen door, stopping her. "'Course, you don't have your purse. And I was in the kitchen anyway, so you'd have had to come past me to get onto the balcony. Or, oh, did you come down the fire escape? In *that?*"

Margrit turned her head toward him, trying a second time to find words. Cole leaned against the counter, arms folded across his chest. Tension radiated across the room, making the air hard to breathe. "What was that thing, Margrit?"

Horror plummeted through Margrit like a dead weight, cutting strength from her legs. "Who—"

"Don't. Whatever you're going to tell me, whatever bullshit story you're about to make up, don't even fucking bother with it, Grit. I *saw* that thing. Alban?" he asked incredulously, unfolding one arm to gesture sharply at her borrowed clothes. "Is that what that thing was? I saw it land on the balcony with you. I saw you kiss it and I saw it fly away again. What the fuck is it?"

"*It* is a *he.*" Forcing the reply made Margrit's throat hurt, as much physical pain as the desperate, panicked beat of her heart. "That was Alban, yes. That was… Alban." The delight and wonder of the night she'd just shared with him seemed horribly fragile now, slipping away in the face of Cole's furious bewilderment.

"Then what the fuck is he?"

"He's a gargoyle." Margrit heard herself answer from a distance, no prevarication offering itself in lieu of the truth. "He belongs to another race. Where's Cameron?"

Cole made a strangled sound. "She's sleeping. What do you mean, another *race?* Like an alien?" Disbelief struggled with the evidence his own eyes had provided, the ability to dismiss Margrit's weary statement already corrupted.

"Yeah." She dropped her chin to her chest. "Not from another planet. Just…a leftover evolutionary tract, maybe. That's what they think. Like Neanderthals," she whispered. "But more incredible. That was why he couldn't go to the cops in January." She lifted her gaze again, staring down the hall. "He couldn't risk it." She dared a glance at her housemate and found his countenance bleak. "You can't tell anybody, Cole."

"Tell anybody?" His voice shot up a register. "Who the hell would I tell? The tabloids? Great front-page headlines. My roommate's fucking an alien."

Margrit flinched. "Don't." Her delivery of the word held more beseechment than his had. "Last night was the first time Alban and I were together. Don't make it ugly, Cole. He means more to me than that."

"How can he mean anything to you? He's—he's—"

"Not human." Margrit shifted her shoulders. "He's still a person, and I care about him."

"Are you out of your *mind?*" Cole shoved away from the counter and came to stand over her, a grasping hand suggesting he wanted to grab her and shake her. "What the hell do you think you're doing with that thing? Does this have something to do with your new job?"

Margrit stared up at him, some of her cold horror breaking away to reveal kindling anger. "My— Why would it?"

"Because it's one more thing that's not fitting. Daisani and that freak—"

"Cole!"

"What? He's a freak, Margrit! You just said he wasn't even human. Jesus Christ, like I'm supposed to know what to say, what to think? You think I should just be cool with this? I wouldn't even know how to start being cool. I sure as hell don't get how you can justify *screwing* something like that."

Anger bloomed, burning her sickness away. "You screwed me."

Cole's jaw dropped. "What the hell does that have to do with anything?"

"You ask ten people on the street and seven of them will tell you I'm a different race from you." Margrit thrust her hands toward Cole, cafe-latte skin pinked with anger. "Sure, we only went out a couple weeks, but hey, you still had sex with somebody from a different race. So Alban's a different race from me. It doesn't make him less of a person."

"Jesus, Margrit, we both belong to the human ra—"

"But they call it racism. Believe me, I've had this conversation with myself about a thousand times since January, and the only answer I can come up with is to keep it all secret." Margrit shoved out of the doorway, removing herself from Cole's space. "I keep thinking maybe I could tell somebody, but look at how humans treat each other. I have some idea of what would happen to him if we knew his people existed. We'd tear them apart. And you—you're proving my point for me. You're supposed to be well-educated and liberal, and you're freaking the fuck out. Not exactly a great start to outing a whole different race of people to the world."

"What the hell do you expect me to say?"

"I really don't know!" Margrit threw a frustrated punch at the air, the silver-shot sleeve of Alban's jacket reminding her painfully of the warmth and happiness she'd found in his arms. "Maybe, 'Gosh, it's great you met somebody, Margrit.' That'd be nice. Unfuckingrealistic, but nice."

"I can't believe you invited that thing into our *house.*"

"Jesus Christ, Cole! He's not a monster! Ted Bundy was a monster. I just wanted you to meet this guy I really like, this guy who understands why—" An angry laugh broke her voice. "Who understands why I run in the park at night. No, I wasn't going to tell you he wasn't human, because first you'd never believe me if you didn't see it for yourself, and if you saw it you'd do this!" She tore her hand through the air as if their fight had a physical presence. "What else could I do?"

"Get married to Tony!" Cole kept the shout between

his teeth, robbing it of volume but not passion. "Have babies, have a career, have an ordinary life!"

"I'm not in love with Tony!"

Cole stepped back as if the admission had been made to break his heart. Margrit's anger drained away, strength of emotion wiped out by the weight of confession. It had been barely a day since she'd voiced her love for the detective, but only now did she consider the quality of that love, and found truth in what she said next. "Tony's a great guy. But somewhere along the line I stopped being in love with him. Maybe we're too much the same, I don't know. Both of us too determined to fix the world our way to try to accept the other's. Maybe we were too much in the habit of each other to let it go. I care about him. But he wants me to be something I don't want to be."

"What?" Like hers, Cole's voice sounded drawn. Margrit turned her palms up, lacing her fingers together as if joining them would provide an answer.

"Tethered." The word hung between them heavily, as Margrit stared at her hands. "Tony's grounded. All the things I grew up working toward. Practical, sensible, earthbound. Working toward making concrete, possible changes in the world." She looked up again, feeling helpless. "Alban has wings."

"I thought that was what you wanted. You're so damned focused, Grit. You always were. Five-star high school, top-notch college, ambitious public servant career. It's what you've been after as long as I've known you. All you need to make the picture perfect is a husband and two point five kids. Instead you've decided you… I don't even know what. You want a *thing,* and a career as Eliseo Daisani's errand boy?"

"I want to make a difference." Margrit slumped

against the counter. "The school, the job, the whole point was getting to a position where I could leave the world a better place than I found it. Townsend…" She put a hand over her face. "You know this. Townsend High School makes a big deal about doing just that, with an oath about it and everything. I took it seriously, and I can make more difference to Alban and his world than I can possibly explain. This is what I want. It's just that the trappings aren't what I expected."

"What about a family, Grit? What about a real life? You can't have that with—*him*."

"We haven't gotten that far," she said quietly. "Come on, Cole. Tony and I broke up two days ago, for heaven's sake. I hadn't seen Alban for months, not until this week." She sighed, lifting her hands to her face. They were cold against her burning cheeks. "And it's not impossible. If that's what we decide we want."

"What's not? A family? A life? A *family,* Grit?" Cole's voice rose in dismay. "How could you—"

"Look at me, Cole." Margrit lowered her hands, spreading them and gesturing at her skin tones, then at the loose curls falling over her shoulders. "I come from two or three definable ethnic backgrounds. Bloodlines mingle. It's not impossible."

"But he's not even—"

"It's possible, Cole," Margrit said more firmly. "You're just going to have to trust me on that."

Fresh horror bloomed across Cole's face. "Trust y— You're not pregnant, are you?"

"What?" Margrit stared at him, then flung her hands up. "No! No, I'm not pregnant! *Jesus.* Forget it. *Forget* it, I'm not having this conversation anymore. Jesus, Cole!" She stalked out of the kitchen to her bedroom, narrowly remembering not to slam the door and risk wakening Cameron.

Only when the door was closed behind her did her knees give out. Margrit slid to the floor, hands shaking as she folded them over her abdomen. *Pregnant.* That sort of risk was beyond her scope; she'd been on the pill since college, with no mishaps. Still, they'd used no other sort of protection, and she had no idea whether human medicine could stand up to alien invasion. Fingers pressed against her belly, Margrit shook her head and whispered, "I'm not pregnant."

She woke up huddled on the floor beneath Alban's silver-shot jacket, unable to remember when wide-eyed fretting had turned to sleep. Cameron's voice slipped under the door, words indistinguishable. Margrit pushed up, wincing in anticipation of stiffness from sleeping on the floor.

Not a muscle complained. It startled her enough that she stopped trying to get to her feet and simply flexed and stretched, searching for soreness. "Daisani." She breathed the name, almost a laugh, and sat all the way up. It was the little things that his gift surprised her with.

"Grit?" Cameron tapped on the door. Margrit got to her feet, yawning as she pulled it open. Cam had the phone pressed to her shoulder. "Are you awake? It's Joyce Lomax."

"Awake enough." Margrit took the phone and knotted an arm around her ribs as she said, "Hello, Joyce. This is Margrit."

"Margrit." A shaky smile sounded in the older woman's voice. "I have a favor to ask."

"Anything."

"I wondered if you'd be willing to speak at Russell's service this evening." Joyce's voice cracked and Margrit bit her lower lip, trying to ward off sympathetic tears. "I know it's very short notice, but I think he would have liked it. Most of the other speakers are older, and I think he would have liked a colleague from your generation to say something."

Margrit pressed her fingers over her lips as tears stung her eyes sharply enough to hurt. Cameron put a hand on her shoulder, and Margrit tried to twist her crumpled features into a smile. "Of course I will." Her own voice sounded as strained as Joyce's. "I'm honored to be asked. Would you like me to come early and help with anything?"

Joyce sighed. "That would be wonderful. The children and some friends have been helping, but we're all exhausted. Keeping busy is better than doing nothing, but…"

"I'll be there at six," Margrit promised quietly. "Take care of yourself, Joyce." She hung up. Cameron stepped forward to wrap her in a hug.

"You doing okay?" her friend asked.

"I don't know what okay is anymore, to tell the truth."

Cam gave her a cautiously sly smile. "You sure about that?" She gestured to the tuxedo jacket and long shirt Margrit wore. "He's not here. What's the story with that? Don't tell me he's one of those guys who bails the second the alarm goes off."

"No, he dropped me off last night."

"In *that?*" Cameron squealed with delight. "Damn, sister! What happened to your dress?"

"Uh..." To Margrit's dismay, a blush erupted over her cheeks. "It got lost."

"Lost? Oh my God." Cameron seized her hands and pulled her toward the bed. Margrit stumbled along after her, laughing despite herself, and sat down as Cameron plunked onto the mattress. "I want all the details, and I want them now."

For a moment the impulse to blurt out *all* the details overrode everything else. Margrit bit the tip of her tongue to keep herself from speaking, and instead frowned uncertainly at her blue-eyed friend. "Do you remember the stained-glass windows in the speak-easy?"

Cameron's smile faltered with confusion. "Yeah...? They made a picture when you put them together. Dragons and mermaids and stuff. So? Oh my God." Her smile brightened again, her eyes widening. "Did he take you down there? That's so cool! Did you lose your dress because security chased you out? Man, I never get to have any crazy sexual hijinks!"

Reality trumped the desire to confess. Cameron wouldn't believe her without seeing what Cole had seen, and that had gone as badly as it possibly could have. Better to let it pass, and try to talk to Cole again later. Margrit dredged up humor, trying to keep a smile in place. "Something like that. I don't know, Cam. You could talk to Cole about the sexual hijinks thing, but really, sneaking home through New York City when you've lost your dress and your underwear isn't something I'd recommend."

"You only say that because you've had a chance to do it. I think it sounds like exactly the sort of thing everybody should experience once." Cameron squeezed

Margrit's hands, her expression growing a little more serious. "You like him, huh?"

"Yeah." Her voice dropped. "Yeah, and Cole and I had a fight about him this morning, and this…it's not going to be easy to make it work."

"It wasn't easy with Tony, either."

"And look how that turned out."

Cameron nudged her reassuringly. "Maybe it didn't work with Tony because it wasn't supposed to, Grit. What'd you and Cole fight about?"

This time Margrit didn't have to quell the impulse to tell the truth. She only shook her head. "Alban in general, my new job, everything. He doesn't like me dating the guy Tony suspected of murder a couple months ago. And he and Tony are friends, and…" And Alban was a gargoyle.

"We're all friends. Unless you're going to make us start choosing sides." Cameron eyed her. "This isn't going to be one of those breakups, is it?"

"I don't think so. Although Cole's angry enough to choose sides himself, maybe."

"I'll talk to him," Cameron promised.

Margrit winced. "Let me try again first, okay? He's got reason, I guess, and I don't want to put you between us."

"If you're sure."

"I am." Margrit leaned over on the bed, snaking a hand beneath the pillow. "Besides, I've got protection if I need it." She pulled out the small water gun Cameron'd had a few days earlier, and squirted her friend twice. Cam shrieked in dismay and jumped off the bed, hands making a useless shield.

"You're sleeping with water guns? That's a whole

new kind of kink. Isn't it leaking all over your mattress?"

Margrit waggled the gun threateningly, then tilted it, looking for leaks. "It hasn't been, actually. This is not your standard-fare ninety-nine cent plastic water gun here. This is a top-of-the-line polyurethane-sealed .38 Special with a fitted cork plug that swells to keep the ammunition in place."

Cameron squinted. "It is?"

"I have no idea, but it sounded good, didn't it?" Margrit put the gun on her nightstand and got up, smiling. "It's got a cork plug, anyway, and it doesn't leak. I thought I'd start carrying it instead of my pepper spray."

"It's neon-green, Grit. Nobody's going to believe it's real."

"Well, maybe I can fill it with pepper spray or mint oil."

"Minty fresh bad guys. I like it. Carry the pepper spray." Cameron glowered, good nature only half masking her seriousness.

"I'll become the most dangerous gun in Central Park. Mint oil in one hand, pepper spray in the other. *Raar.*" Margrit felt as if she was forcing levity, trying to ward off memories of the fight she'd had with Cole and the funeral service she had to face in a few hours.

Cameron's scowl gentled, as if she suddenly understood what Margrit was trying to do. "Well, all right. But I expect you to show me both gun and spray before you leave the house today, young lady." She hesitated, then added, "You want me and Cole to go with you to the service? You know we'd be glad to."

"Cole's pretty pissed at me. I don't know if he would be."

"He has his moments of being a jerk, but I don't think he'd be that much of one." Cam tilted her head toward Margrit's bathroom. "Go take a shower and get ready to face the day. And when you come out again, I want you armed and dangerous."

THIRTY

"I'M GOING TO tell her if you don't, Grit."

"She won't believe you." The water gun, its nozzle plugged with another cork, was actually tucked into Margrit's trousers at the small of her back, beneath her suit jacket. Cameron had laughed out loud when Margrit had shown it off, just before Cole drew her aside to speak with her through clenched teeth. The whim to drench him caught her, and Margrit folded her arms over her chest to stop herself. "You wouldn't have believed me if you hadn't literally seen him with your own eyes. And it's not my secret, or yours, to tell."

"I don't give a damn. I'm not keeping it from her—"

"You shouldn't have to." Margrit shook her head. "You shouldn't have to. It's too big and too weird to keep to yourself and you shouldn't have to exclude her. But will you please at least give me a chance to talk to Alban first? He's going to have to show himself to her to make her believe it."

Even through Cole's anger and dismay, Margrit could see the logic of her request hit home. He clenched his fists and fell back a step. "Will he?"

"Yes. He'd risk it because I trust you. I trust her. He trusts me. Cole..." She held her breath a moment, searching for the right thing to say. "Look, I'm sorry for some of the things I said this morning. I was—scared." The degree of understatement seemed ludicrous. "I did pretty much the same thing the first time I saw him. I threw a…a bowl, I think, at his head. And then I ran away. The night the car hit me. That was the night the car hit me. Alban saved me."

Cole made a choked sound of disbelief. "Tony would've seen him, Margrit. He would've said something."

"Would he?" Margrit sighed. "It happened so fast, and would you believe your eyes if you thought something big and pale and winged had swept down and snatched me up? Or would you think, no, you must've seen me go flying, nothing else would make sense?" She offered an unhappy smile. "And I can't ask him if he thinks he saw something impossible, because Alban's life depends on secrecy."

Frustration contorted Cole's features as he opened and closed his hands. "You're protecting him. You've been lying to all of us to protect that…*thing*."

Anger bubbled in Margrit's chest and she tightened her arms around herself, trying to keep it in. Letting Cole bait her only gave him control over the discussion. It did no one, least of all Alban, any good for her to rise to the fear and accusation in her housemate's words. Still, several seconds passed before she trusted herself enough to say, "Yes," in a neutral voice.

"I thought I knew you, Margrit." Distrust hollowed Cole's eyes. "I thought we were friends."

"You do. We are. You have no idea how much I would've liked to have told you about all of this from the beginning."

"You should have."

Margrit swallowed. "Should plantation owners who helped run the Underground Railroad have told their families what they were doing, Cole? Should Germans who sheltered Jews have announced it to the neighborhood?"

Real anger flashed in Cole's eyes, so sharp Margrit clenched her thighs to keep from stepping back. "That's not the same thing at all, Grit."

"Why not?" She kept her voice soft, knowing the argument Cole would make, but waiting to hear it said.

He didn't disappoint her, though at the same time, he did. "Because slaves and Jews are *human*."

Margrit nodded stiffly, her entire upper body swayed slightly with the motion. "Not if you asked most slave owners. Not if you checked Nazi doctrine." She had once read a facetious argument that claimed that once Hitler came into a conversation, any rational discussion was over. She felt as if she balanced on that line, trying hard not to stray into overblown rhetoric. "You see my point?"

"I see it." Cole bared his teeth. "I just don't accept it." He turned and walked away, leaving Margrit slumped by her bedroom door. She turned her wrist up, looking at her watch, and her shoulders sagged farther. It was hours until she had to be at the memorial service. She should've waited to shower and dress, and taken time to go for a run. Without consciously planning to, she pushed away from her door to find a pair of socks, then pulled her running shoes on.

"I'm going for a walk," she said quietly and slipped out the door to no response from her housemates.

It wasn't as good as running, but it was vastly better than being cooped up in the apartment with Cole's censure hanging over her. Margrit stalked along, hands in her pockets, letting her feet take her where they wanted while her thoughts hopped in exhaustive detail from one moment of the past week to another. More than once emotion threatened to overwhelm her, making her steps unsteady as she worked her way through the park. It would have been easier with Alban at her side, but sunset's refuge was still far away. She had to face daylight troubles alone, as long as she was with him.

Cole's anger and fear came back to her, and she sat on a bench, face buried in her hands. Any fantasy of sharing Alban and his world with her friends and family had shattered at his reaction. Worse, promising Cole that she would explain to Cameron created a new level of danger for them. Margrit herself had petitioned to lift the law forbidding humans to learn of the Old Races, and had done so with full understanding of what could happen to those who couldn't bear the weight of their secret. She hadn't thought that threat would strike so close to home, or so quickly.

She would have to make him understand the necessity of silence. Margrit pushed to her feet again, mouth set in a grim line. Of all the shocks and upheavals in the last week, she might at least be able to address that one before anything terrible came of it. One small victory would seem a candle against the dark, and she would take whatever light she found.

"What is it you've done, love?" The soft transatlantic accent came out of nowhere, startling Margrit into a stifled shriek. Grace O'Malley, catlike in her amusement, sauntered up the pathway and took the seat Margrit had just abandoned. She spread her arms along the bench's back, using all the space, and smiled at Margrit, though the expression didn't reach her brown eyes.

Margrit glowered at her as much from envy as embarrassment at being taken off guard. She'd never seen Grace in daylight before. In the sun, her pale vibrance was set off even more dramatically by a black trench coat. Some of her height came from the extra-thick soles on her heavy boots, but even without them she was taller than Margrit. Sprawling across the bench showed her long limbs to their best advantage. Her platinum-blond hair, cropped short, had much darker roots, a nod toward humanity that Margrit imagined would be bleached away again in a day or two.

Not that the leather-clad vigilante was inhuman, according to Alban. She was merely leggy, gorgeous and looked good with the pale gargoyle, which was offensive enough. Margrit's glare faltered into rueful humor. She approved of what little she knew about Grace, and if Alban found her attractive, it seemed evident he found Margrit more so. "What do you mean, what have I done?"

"I've been watching." Grace pulled herself together, taking up less room on the bench, and Margrit sat down again. "The ice rink. The ball. You've got them all dancing to your tune."

Margrit laughed in disbelief. "I wish I had your confidence about that. You've been watching? Why?"

"What goes on with you and yours affects me and mine. Don't pretend you're not the fulcrum, love. Change swirls around you like a maelstrom, and you stand steady at its center."

"You've got a funny idea of steady. I'm barely keeping my head above water." Margrit shifted, uncomfortably aware that, protests aside, Grace had a point. "I didn't mean for all of this to happen. Everything has just snowballed, from the night I met Alban. What was I supposed to do, dig a hole and put my head in the sand? Snowball and sand," she muttered. "I'm mixing my metaphors."

"Might have been better. Grace likes a steady boat, and you're running like a mad thing, trying to overturn it."

"Like I overturned the demolition of your building in Harlem?" It hadn't been Grace's building at all; it had been one of Eliseo Daisani's properties. But beneath it lay one of the major hubs for Grace's complex under-city existence. Daisani had deliberately moved against her, in retaliation for Grace exposing his subway speakeasy to the world. "How did he even know that building's subbasement was one of your centers, anyway?"

Grace's voice sharpened. "He's Eliseo Daisani. What doesn't he know, if he wants to? I didn't think anyone used it," she said more lightly, though it sounded as if doing so cost her. "That chess set down there with the selkies and the djinn, well, I recognized that, didn't I? But the place was sealed off tight as a tomb, not even any dust to come filtering down. If I'd known the Old Races still used it, I'd never have shown it to the city, good press or no." She brought her focus back to Margrit, a crinkle appearing between her eyebrows. "But aye, even that, like overturning the demolition of that building. It would have wreaked hell with our network, but vengeance would've been a done deal and all of us let alone after that. Now?" She opened her hands, a fluid gesture that reminded Margrit of Janx's grace. "Now we're still riding the troughs and peaks of the storm you're stirring up."

"Not stirring," Margrit said, sitting, suddenly lightheaded with clarity. "Stirred. I think we're moving toward reaping the whirlwind now." Her laugh turned to a shudder, and she leaned forward, elbows on her knees and fingers laced behind her neck. "I mean, I've got a funeral to go to in a couple hours, for someone who's dead pretty much because I agreed to help Alban clear his name. A few tens of thousands of selkies declared themselves because I made an offhand comment about strength in numbers. My housemate's angry and scared out of his mind because he got a glimpse of Alban's real form. I'm past stirring. I'm standing in the storm."

"Back off." A note of pleading tinged Grace's voice. Margrit lifted her gaze to find her expression grim with hope. "Back off, love. Let them fall back into the patterns they know. They're too old to change their habits without someone forcing them along. I like stability. It's all that keeps my kids safe."

"They asked for my help." Margrit's voice dropped. "Alban. The selkies. What was I supposed to do, say no? The selkies have come out, and that changes the Old Races even if I never talk to another one of them in my life. I don't think they're going to quietly slink back into the ocean."

"Then do what you can to keep the ripples from affecting my kids. My world must look like madness to you." Grace turned her attention toward the park, refusing to meet Margrit's eyes. "All of us skulking around underground, on the run from coppers half the time, not for anything we've done, but for the idea of what we are. Living where we do, how we do, on the edges of society, it makes folk nervous. But my kids take care of each other. There's no drugs, there's no fights. You remember Miriah." Grace looked at Margrit, who smiled with happy recollection.

"She made the best chili I've ever had, the night Alban and I were down there. How is she?"

"She's going to college in the fall." Grace sounded justifiably pleased. "She'd lost a brother to a gang fight and was on the road to leading a pack of her own when she came to me. She's still a leader, but now it's in setting an example for other kids to follow, teaching them to cook, to take care of themselves. Maybe it's the wrong place to change the world from, starting at the bottom, but Grace's got nowhere else to go."

"You're not part of their world, though," Margrit said softly. "The Old Races. There's the building, and Alban's staying with you during the day, but he could find a new place to live. There's nothing else, is there?"

"Janx knows I'm down there, and he tolerates me and mine because we don't steal his business. We're not so far removed from their world as it seems. Will you do what you can?"

"I don't know what I can do, but yeah. I'll try. I don't want you to lose what you've got down there."

Grace nodded and rose to her feet. Margrit followed suit, hesitating before saying, "Grace?"

"Yeah, love?"

"Why do you do it?"

"Looking for a new answer, love?" She went silent a moment, then shrugged easily. "Past sins, that's all. Making up for past sins." She took herself away with long, lithe strides. Margrit watched her disappear into dappled sunlight wondering what those sins might be. She didn't know enough about Grace to even imagine them but she was curious. Maybe someday Grace would tell her.

And maybe if pigs had wings they'd be pigeons. No one conversant with the Old Races on any level seemed especially prone to sharing their life details. Margrit struck off in the opposite direction, as if she was telling herself not to pry by doing so.

She arrived at Trinity Church even earlier than she'd promised Joyce Lomax. The afternoon whisked by in a blur of activity and high emotion, Margrit fielding phone calls when Russell's exhausted family looked as though they could take no more. It felt good to be useful to ordinary people, doing mundane things like giving directions to the memorial service or handling last-minute catering questions. Margrit only stepped back from being an all-purpose gofer as bells sounded the half hour and mourners began to arrive.

She knew many of them by name, more still by sight. People she didn't expect, though should have, were in attendance. Governor Stanton nodded gravely to her when he caught her eye after expressing his condolences to Mrs. Lomax. It seemed impossible that it had barely been a week since he'd escorted Margrit around the reception for Kaimana Kaaiai. The mayor and his wife were there, as well as judges and lawyers Margrit had worked with or under. A sizable portion of the city's legal and political elite were present, and Margrit wondered cynically how many of them were there simply to be seen, or if it mattered.

Light faded as the service began, the gold of sunset bringing life to stained-glass windows. Margrit watched the colors change as family, friends and colleagues stepped up to speak briefly about Russell Lomax. Then it was her turn, and she climbed the steps to face the podium and a hall full of faces.

Later she would be confident that her voice was steady and her words well-chosen, but blood rushed through her ears as she spoke, deafening her to her own speech. She focused instead on the people present, trusting a career's worth of training to not allow a wobble of surprise in her voice when she picked her mother's face out of the crowd. Like Cole and Cameron, Rebecca Knight was there for Margrit's sake; even at his death, she was unlikely to forgive Russell for his transgressions thirty years earlier. A shock of gratitude ran through Margrit, stirring up too much other emotion, and despite herself, her voice shook. It took a moment to gain control again, and in that instant she saw a scattering of others whose presence she'd never have predicted at the service.

Eliseo Daisani sat far enough toward the back as to go relatively unnoticed. His expression was solemn, the lack of animation somehow serving to cloak him. A sense of certainty arose in her that she wasn't meant to see him, but the slightest tilt of his head told her he knew he'd been spotted. Then, with unerring confidence, she looked toward a corner of the church and found Janx's fiery hair a bright point in the darkness. Humor tightened her lungs, but not her own; it felt as though Daisani had been caught out, and transferred the reaction to her. Her skin itched, as if her blood were trying to work its way free.

Margrit tore her eyes from Janx and drew a deep breath, steadying herself to continue speaking.

For a moment she could hear herself talking quietly

about what she'd learned from Russell Lomax, wryly admitting to the tricks that infuriated her even as she made use of them herself. Then her thoughts darted to places her voice and words didn't go: if Janx was there, then Malik would be.

The djinn was harder to see, a thing of shadows himself, but light finally caught his cane and drew Margrit's eyes to him. He stood farther from Janx than she might have expected, staking his own territory, making his own place. Whatever he'd done to earn the right to vote for his people had infused him with confidence. Cold bubbled up inside her. Malik had lacked neither confidence nor arrogance to begin with. She had no desire to learn what new heights he might reach for now that he reckoned himself a force, but was certain she'd find out.

Of all the Old Races attending, Kaimana Kaaiai sat front and forward, at the end of a pew near the governor. His presence was a political choice, a clear decision to be seen. Tony sat beside him, one of three bodyguards. As Margrit watched, Kaimana tilted his head toward the detective and murmured something.

Disapproval contorted Tony's face, but he nodded, and Kaaiai stood up quietly, padding toward the back of the church. His shoes made no sound on the stone floor, his exit distracting from her speech as little as possible. Very few people glanced at him as he left, though Margrit thought her own gaze on his shoulders would make everyone turn to see what she was looking at.

Instead they watched her, intent on words she once more couldn't hear herself saying. Gladness at having worked with Russell, sorrow at losing his wisdom and guidance. Sick humor shot through her with an impulse to add, carelessly, that she would be leaving Legal Aid in a few weeks, to go to work for Daisani. She squashed it, swallowing as she finished speaking. A brief, unhappy smile flitted over her face and she dropped her gaze, gathering herself to leave the podium.

When she looked up an instant later, Kaimana was gone, the door closing silently behind him. She took stock of the Old Races once more, knowing the attendance of each was dictated for each by another's presence: Daisani for Russell, but Janx for Daisani, and Malik for Janx. Only Kaimana stood outside that cascade of dependency, the only one able to leave without setting the others askew. As Margrit expected, Daisani remained where he was, half-cloaked by his own quietude. Janx watched the vampire rather than Margrit, as if aware of the steps to the dance they shared.

Margrit's shoulders dropped as she found a kind of relief in that. For all the changes that were coming, the structure she'd come to recognize among New York's Old Races seemed unscathed. That would be something to reassure Grace with. She worked her way back to her seat, glancing Malik's way only as an afterthought.

The corner where he'd waited was empty.

THIRTY-ONE

STONE SHUDDERED AND fell away, sunset's gift even when the sky lay many levels of tunnels and streets above him. Waking rarely brought such a sense of anticipation, and Alban pushed out of his crouch with a smile. There was enough time—just—to change from the silver-shot slacks from the night before and wing his way to Margrit's apartment. The chance to do that, to see her, to speak with her friends again, held the potential of a new life. It was something that a few months ago—a mere scattering of days, to a life as long as his—had been so inconceivable as to have never crossed his mind. His heart—*his* heart, usually so steady—betrayed him with rapid beats, anathema to a gargoyle's stolid nature. Laughing at himself was surprisingly easy, another trait unfamiliar to his people. The rueful idea that Margrit was right about too much isolation curled his mouth again, and it was with near jauntiness that he left the tunnels. Grace, unusually, was nowhere to be seen. She often greeted him at sunset, giving him the sense that she'd sat watch over him as much as he watched over her and her ragtag band of children.

He was barely to street level when his phone rang. Expecting Grace's lilting accent, he answered with a smile, but it was Janx's sibilance on the phone, more soft-spoken than usual. "It seems I've misplaced Malik again. Find him."

"Something else requires my attendance, Janx. Malik's safe enough under Daisani's peace." Alban lingered in an alley, watching traffic in the street. "If you're worried, use Biali."

"How bold you've become, Stoneheart. Other plans, indeed. They must include our delightful Margrit, or you'd never shirk a duty you'd agreed to. She's with me. The sooner you bring Malik to attend me the sooner you'll see her."

"With you. Why?" Alban folded his hand around the cell phone as if to crush it, though it was Janx, not the phone, that sparked his ire.

"Ah, that would be telling, and it's much more fun to let you wonder what we all do during the long daylight hours."

Alban kept his voice deliberately low, refusing to rise to the dragonlord's bait. "Where are you?"

Janx made a delighted sound, as if he could tell by the steadiness of Alban's reply that he'd hit a mark. "Your old home, Stoneheart. We're at Trinity Church. Join us, when you've found Malik. Someone's hunting him, and I won't lose another man. I'll give your regards to Margrit," he added. "I'm sure she'll be very understanding."

Alban growled, "Do me no favors, Janx," and clipped the phone shut, again resisting the urge to crush it. Heedless of passersby, he crouched and sprang upward, shifting form midleap as he strove for the sky.

The djinn was in motion, his fogged form impossible to follow, even with the sapphire he carried. Alban cut broad sweeps through the sky above Trinity, waiting for Malik to settle so he could trace him. Until then, city lights winked below him, buildings blocking his view. Blocking the city's view of him, so he was never visible long enough for any witness to believe what they might have seen.

Margrit was down there, probably one of the dozens spilling out of the sandstone building. From this distance, Alban couldn't pick her out, but he'd find her soon enough. Malik first, so that duty could be put aside in favor of the dark-haired beauty whose life had changed his. And if duty couldn't be denied, perhaps Margrit would join him through the small hours of the night, watching over a djinn who wanted no such protection.

As he thought it, Malik's presence—the stone's presence—solidified. He turned on a wingtip to follow it, darting above rooftops near the church.

A blur of whiteness on the roofs caught his eye, bright enough to make him expect Biali. A moment later he realized it was Grace, her bleached hair making her a beacon, though the black leather she wore hid her well, otherwise. He dropped down beside her, already wearing his human form. "Grace?"

"Korund." She glanced sideways at him, knowing her name had been a question and obviously enjoying drawing out the answer.

A corner of Alban's mouth curled, despite himself. "What are you doing here, Grace?"

"Watching over your lawyer, as you asked. But then that bearded devil slipped out, and I thought that was more worth watching. And hello to you, too." She crept toward the building's edge, beckoning Alban forward.

He followed, suddenly amused. If any two people he knew were less suited for trying to go unnoticed in the darkness than he and Grace, it had to be himself and Biali. Only another gargoyle's hair rivaled his in glowing whiteness, but Grace's came close. He murmured, "We should have nightcaps," and Grace shot him a look laced with more flirtatiousness than censure.

"Sure and I'd be glad to share one with you, but I think Margrit might have a thing to say about that. A thing or even two. Now look." She snaked a hand toward the alley below.

Malik paced across its mouth, throttling his cane in one hand. Alban shook his head. "I'm astonished you could follow him. Tracking a djinn is nearly impossible."

"Grace has her tricks," she said absently.

As she spoke, another man, this one carrying a briefcase, stepped into view. Alban inched back with surprise, recognizing the broad-shouldered form. "Kaimana?"

"Malik came in with the briefcase Kaaiai's got now. I thought selkies and djinn didn't play nice. Makes me nervous, it does."

"I didn't think anything made you nervous." Alban offered a brief smile that earned a snort of laughter from the white-haired woman.

"That's what you're supposed to think, love. There he goes, then." She nodded toward Malik, who dissipated in the alley below.

"He's done his job." Alban leaned thoughtfully on the rooftop's half wall. "He'll return to Janx to report."

"Go on, then." Grace straightened, a slim, curvaceous form in black leather. "Go find out how the world's changing, and tell me before dawn, if you can."

"You don't need to worry so much, Grace. I wouldn't let anything happen to you or the children."

"It's not a matter of 'let,' love. Try as you might, you can't stop the world from spinning. I know you'll try, and so will your little lawyer, but it's better for us if we have a hint of what's coming."

"When I came to stay in your tunnels, I didn't realize I'd become a spy for you." Alban pushed away from the wall, deliberately coming to his full height.

Uncowed, Grace shrugged. "You protect us in exchange for safety during daylight hours. Call it spying if you like. I call it doing your part. Protection doesn't just come in the form of stone and wings. And like every one of my kids, you know where the door is, if you want to use it."

A low chuckle rumbled through Alban's chest. "It's difficult to tell the difference between persuasion and bludgeoning with you, Grace."

She answered with a quick and wicked smile, stepping forward to walk fingers up his chest. "I can be very persuasive," she promised in a purr, then smirked when he closed his hand around hers and moved back. "There you are, then. If I bludgeon, it's only your own fault. Will you go?" she asked more quietly. "Will you watch and learn, and tell me what you know?"

"As long as I'm able." Alban made a half bow, suddenly aware that he'd borrowed the action from Janx. It seemed unlikely he'd influenced the dragonlord similarly. Perhaps someday he would ask. "I'll see you before sunrise."

At Grace's nod, Alban took to the skies as if he'd been released from a cage, returning to the pursuit of his duty.

Returning to Margrit.

* * *

She'd spoken almost at the last, only the erratically bearded Episcopalian clergyman she'd met once before following her. People began filtering out, escaping the church and its oppressive sorrow in favor of the clear April night. The mood remained restrained, everyone cautious of their behavior, but it was easier to breathe outdoors. As Margrit searched for Janx, she saw Cole and Cam departing, and smiled her thanks. She found Rebecca Knight, relief sweeping away all thoughts of the Old Races as she hugged her mother. "Thanks for coming. Is Daddy here?"

"He was called into surgery," Rebecca said reluctantly. "He's sorry, sweetheart. We both wanted to be here for you. We didn't get a chance to say goodbye last night."

"It's okay. I hope it goes well." Margrit held on a moment longer, then broke the hug to take Rebecca's hand. "I'm glad you came. It's a long trip for…"

A brief, wry smile curled Rebecca's mouth as she, too, opted not to finish the sentence the way it was meant to end: *for someone you didn't like.* "But you did," Rebecca said instead. "Despite his flaws."

"Not all of us are lucky enough to be as perfect as you," Margrit said ruefully.

Her mother laughed. "I suppose someone has to be." She squeezed Margrit's hand, growing more serious. "Will you be all right, sweetheart? I can stay in the city overnight, if you'd like."

"I'll be okay. You don't have to—"

"Margrit." Janx, voice full of outrageous charm, cut through the dispersing crowd to stop at her elbow and smile at Rebecca. "Don't tell me you were going to allow this extraordinary woman to leave without making my acquaintance." He offered a hand, and when Rebecca elevated an eyebrow and took it, he bowed extravagantly. Margrit, caught between dismay and amusement, wished he had a hat to flourish.

"You must be Margrit's mother, which I say only because I suspect the flattery of suggesting you're her sister would only set you against me. Instead I'll say I offered to kidnap you a few days ago in order to provide an excuse for Margrit to talk to me. Now that I've met you, I'll admit that if I were to stoop to such nasty activities, I'd be doing it for my own benefit. My name is Janx. I'm sure Margrit's gone on about me to no end." He straightened again, no longer holding Rebecca's fingers, but resting them over the edge of his own. To Margrit's fresh bemusement, her mother didn't retreat.

"To no end at all." Rebecca's eyes sparkled and Margrit's heart sank with helpless laughter. Bad enough that Janx could charm *her* against all good sense. If even Rebecca was susceptible to his shameless blarney, it seemed unlikely there was anyone who could withstand him. "Rebecca Knight. It's a pleasure, Mr. Janx, and you're quite right. False flattery only annoys me."

"Your daughter is more like you than she suspects."

Rebecca shot a look toward Margrit, who turned her palms up, unsure if she was ceding control of the conversation to Janx, or simply unable to take it back.

"I try not to point that out to her," her mother murmured. "She's doing a fine job of realizing it on her own."

Janx turned from Rebecca to Margrit, offering another bow, this time mockingly apologetic. "Do forgive me, my dear. I should hate to be a bump in the road on your path to self-actualization."

"Did you really just say 'self-actualization'?"

"I did." Janx sounded inordinately pleased with himself. Rebecca caught her eye and Margrit clenched her jaw, trying not to let a laugh escape.

"I think while you're trying to recover from the horror, I'll do my best to whisk your mother away for an illicit affair."

"You certainly will not." Rebecca sniffed at the redheaded man. "I'm sure being kidnapped wouldn't agree with me at all."

Janx snapped theatrically, about to speak again when a fourth voice joined the discussion.

"You're quite the vortex tonight, aren't you, Margrit? Rebecca." Eliseo Daisani nodded toward the older Knight woman, looking all the more dignified in comparison to Janx's dramatics. Margrit's shoulder blades pinched together in anticipation of disaster, though she had no idea what form it might take. Janx, though, only twisted his mouth in teasing disappointment, and Rebecca inclined her head, murmuring Daisani's name in turn. Then all three of them turned their attention to Margrit, as though she was responsible for calling them there.

In a way, she supposed she was. "I seem to be developing a knack for that," she admitted beneath her breath. "I'm surprised you're here tonight."

"Should auld acquaintance be forgot?" Daisani infused the line with genuine compassion, no hint of music or mockery to his voice. "Where else would I be?" He glanced around, elevating one eyebrow. "But where are the rest of us?"

Margrit kept herself from saying, *That's what I wanted to ask Janx.* She could think of no reason

Kaimana and Malik might slip away, one after the other, except to keep some arrangement made by the dragonlord. But she felt oddly reticent to ask in front of Daisani, as if her loyalties were torn between the two ancient rivals.

Janx followed Daisani's gaze and expanded on it, turning to search the church grounds with an air of concern. "I set Stoneheart searching for Malik a few minutes ago. I hadn't realized, until these proceedings sent him skittering for the shadows, how accustomed I was to his sour countenance haunting me. I've seen less of my so-called bodyguard in the past week than in the past five years, I think." A moment passed before he shook off heaviness and looked back to Rebecca. "Do forgive me. I don't mean to be such a bore as to bring business into a social occasion."

Her eyebrows flickered upward. "Is that what this is?"

"Not a merry one, and perhaps also an obligation, but also an occasion. The one hardly precludes the other."

"They left together. I thought—" Margrit broke off, staring at Janx.

He tilted his head, mouth quirked with a lack of comprehension. He was a consummate actor; he had to be, and yet his jade eyes held none of their usual taunting mirth. "Who did, my dear?"

Margrit's heart rate leaped. No doubt she shouldn't believe what she read in Janx's gaze; no doubt she shouldn't trust the all-too-human impulse that told her to. But human or not, emotion rode all of them, and Margrit blurted, "I thought you knew. I thought— You didn't send Malik after Kaimana?"

"Margrit," Janx said, full of gentle sarcasm, "if you

had a golden slipper with which to tempt the prince, would you send a lackey in your place to do so? We all know how fairy tales go. It is the servant girl bearing the gift who catches the hero's eye. Her cruel mistress is banished to the forest, and she is lifted to the throne to be good and generous and wise for all of her days. If I was putting on a ball, I would not send Malik with the invitations."

"Then what—"

"Margrit." Rebecca's voice was thready and washed out, utterly drained of the vibrancy she'd had only moments earlier. Mist danced behind her, as she put a hand over her chest, her eyes clouded with confusion. "I think there's something wrong with me, Margrit. Something wrong with my..."

A sleek black-haired man Margrit had never before seen coalesced behind her mother, one hand thrust out. Thrust *in*to Rebecca, from behind, his arm turned up to suggest he held something in the palm of his hand. His smile was sharper than Malik's, more deadly, and he finished Rebecca's sentence for her with one soft word: "Heart."

THIRTY-TWO

MIST AND SHADOWS. Malik had become mist and shadows, and had failed to return to Janx's side. He'd gone north instead, the corundum head of his cane quietly pulling Alban's attention. The gargoyle circled the island reluctantly, staying closer to its southern end than he ought to have, as though he could draw Malik back that way through willpower alone.

Amusement flashed through him. It was of little enough use to ferret out bits and pieces of sapphire, except as a way to earn money now and then. If he could draw those who wore or carried the stone to him, now *that* would be a talent. One he'd never confess to: the idea of what Janx would do, knowing Alban could command those who were enamored by sparkling stone, didn't bear considering. The dragonlord would find himself an enclave of gargoyles, each tuned to the stone of their family name, and wreak havoc with his influence. With that skill, a thousand years past, when Aztec priests sacrificed their subjects to the gods with obsidian knives, a gargoyle of Hajnal's line might have made herself an immortal queen to an eager people.

Oh, but Margrit was a bad influence. The *world* was a bad influence; Alban had never, in all his long years, entertained such thoughts, much less found entertainment in them. Bad company, as he'd told Janx, but he couldn't find it in himself to regret it.

Malik had settled wherever he was; a low thrum of contentment was coming from the stone. Even long accustomed to being moved, it seemed more comfortable, somehow, when at rest—or perhaps that was Alban bending his own perceptions to suit an object. No matter; the point was Malik could be found easily enough, and watched over whether he liked it or not.

It would take a little time for Alban to wing his way there, but the church was only moments away. A few seconds to glimpse Margrit from above would mean nothing in matters of Malik's safety.

It might compromise Alban's own, though. Enough people were still gathered at the church that he sailed away and found an alley, transforming as he landed. Humans might not look up as a matter of habit, but soaring above an open space would be taking an unnecessary risk.

Leaving the alley behind, Alban hesitated at Trinity's gates, his pale hand curled around wrought iron as he looked beyond it at what had been his home for so many decades. The hidden door was still there, less of a secret now, but it would take no time at all to slip through it and visit the room he'd abandoned hastily and never since returned to. Yet there was no reason to do so. He had his belongings, and the deep vault was no longer a safe haven.

All unconsciously he was moving, intent bringing him where wisdom would avoid. He knew the dark graveyard intimately, had no need to watch his feet as he whispered greetings to those whose tombs he'd slept beneath. A few more steps would have him hidden below them again.

"Alban?" The unfamiliar voice was curious and friendly. Alban went still for the briefest instant, resisting the urge to allow stone to sweep him and hide him from prying inquiries. But that would be suicide, where facing his questioner would be nothing more than a brief delay. He turned, wondering who knew his name when he didn't recognize the voice.

A priest with an untamed white beard stood a few yards away, his solemn expression and dark cassock suggesting he'd just left the mourners who were dispersing from the church's front walkways. "It is Alban, isn't it? I must have startled you. I'm sorry. I've never had the opportunity to say hello before."

"Before?" Even to his own ears, the word grated dangerously, though less from threat than surprise.

The priest's beard shifted with a wry, hopeful smile. "You're a subtle creature, for all your size. This has been my parish for years. I've…caught a glimpse of you, now and then." He nodded toward the hidden door, and Alban looked that way as well, half expecting it to stand open, as if it had somehow betrayed him. "From the days when you slept beneath our church. My name is Ramsey. I spoke with Margrit Knight about you once. She promised me that I was right to believe you were one of God's creations."

A chuckle rumbled from Alban's chest before he could stop it. "And not from your imagination born?"

Ramsey's eyebrows wobbled up. "Or anywhere more dire. I've been watching for you, since January. I hoped to tell you that you still have a home here. Maybe not as discreet as that hidden room, but the church is a sanctuary, and you're welcome to use it whenever you need."

Surprise struck Alban silent, too many questions coming to mind for any of them to be spoken. "I would love to hear your story," Ramsey said a bit wistfully. "Miss Knight made it clear it wasn't hers to tell, but perhaps someday you might want to share it with an old man who loves this church and its secrets. Not tonight," he added more briskly. "You look like a stoned ox just now. I imagine you're not used to being noticed."

"Or accepted." Alban rumbled, and Ramsey dipped his head in acknowledgment.

"God is much more creative than I am. Why should I refuse what he's seen fit to give life to? Someday," he repeated. "Perhaps someday… I should get back to my parishioners. Good night, Alban." He strode away as though the conversation had invigorated him, for all that most of it had been on his side. Alban remained where he was for long moments, staring after him in pleased astonishment before reminding himself of his purpose.

The time to dally had been eaten away. He turned from the hidden doorway reluctantly, searching the scattering crowd for a glimpse of Margrit. He found her embracing an older woman, and when he might have taken a step toward her for a brief greeting, Janx arrived at their sides, his outrageous flirtation visible across the distance.

Rueful annoyance pulled Alban's mouth out of shape. Janx would be most displeased to find him there, and Alban didn't relish a confrontation with the dragonlord. There would be time later, he promised himself; they would have time later. Sufficiently convinced of it, he slipped back around the gates, casting one last regretful glance toward his onetime retreat.

Tony Pulcella emerged from the hidden door, a briefcase in hand.

An unexpected breeze in the evening air chilled Margrit's skin, and with it her throat constricted. Panic bloomed within her, adrenaline spurting through her system. She wanted to run, to fling herself at the djinn, knock him away from her mother—*anything,* so long as it was action. But she had only one weapon on hand, and terror wouldn't leave her mind clear enough to remember whether its use might save or condemn Rebecca. Tremors were all Margrit could allow herself, a tiny outlet for outrage and fear. "Let her go."

"Or you'll attack?" The djinn moved subtly, closer to Rebecca. "I think not."

Her mother gasped, a tiny cry of dread and pain. Margrit recognized the sound too well, though it'd been her throat, not her heart, that a djinn had sought. Tears had scalded Malik's hand, making him pull away, but Margrit could not recall whether he'd released her before salt water had stung him. There was no way to act, nothing more to offer than a shaky promise: "It'll be okay, Mom."

Daisani shifted at Margrit's side, touching the curve of her back in reassurance. Margrit swallowed hard, trying to keep herself in place, and caught a hard glance shared between vampire and dragonlord. Janx shook his head, a jerking of motion that, had it not been so graceless, she might have imagined it. Daisani's answering nod was equally short and harsh, an acceptance that Janx disavowed responsibility. *God help him,*

Margrit thought with icy clarity. God help the charming dragon if he lied.

With no further communication, Daisani and Janx moved in tandem, casually placing themselves so that passersby couldn't easily see the impossible: that the djinn stood with his arm half folded into Rebecca's back. Daisani broke the silence, his voice so low Margrit strained to hear it from only a step or two away. "Release her and you may yet survive the night."

Sneering laughter curled the djinn's mouth. "Had the glassmaker made that threat I might heed it." He threw the jibe at Janx, who tensed and relaxed again so faintly that Margrit looked twice at him. There was nothing in him to read, but certainty made her cool: they were acquainted, the djinn and the dragon. But the djinn didn't pursue it, turning his attention back to Daisani. "You voted to stay your hand within our peoples."

"So did Malik." Margrit's voice broke on the accusation and brought the djinn's gaze to her. His eyes, like Malik's, were crystalline: amber, the color of sand. Malik's were aquamarine, both startling, Margrit thought, in a people born of the desert. A heartbeat later she understood; they were the colors of their world, sky and sand. Maybe a few djinn had jewel-green eyes, the color of an oasis.

"Malik." The djinn drew out the name as if it tasted of mud. "Malik was wise in voting conservatively, but his choices did not necessarily reflect the will of our people. He does not, as yet, hold the rank to speak for us."

"Margrit." Rebecca's voice faded with pained exhaustion. "Margrit, I love you, sweetheart."

"Mom—" Margrit jolted forward, but Daisani lifted a hand to stop her, such confidence in the gesture that she froze.

"I will be fascinated to hear the details of that admission," Daisani breathed. "But now you have a choice. Let Rebecca Knight go, and survive, or die with her within the circle."

"Circle?" Disdain broke over the djinn's face. "I see no salt water to make a cage with."

Daisani whispered, "Look down."

A thin river of blood glistened around the djinn's feet, around Rebecca, a wet ring on the stones. The scent of copper rose up and made Margrit gag, now that she knew to breathe for it. She wiped her hand across her mouth convulsively, her gaze jerking to Daisani.

He lifted his right hand to tidily fold a torn coat, a torn sleeve, to reveal a still-weeping crimson gash down the length of his arm. It closed bit by bit, visibly healing even in the brief moment Margrit took to understand.

The djinn grasped its portent before Margrit did. He howled in pure outrage and lashed his free hand toward Daisani. Scarlet flashed in the air, a surge of power that for an instant turned the djinn to mist.

Another breeze stirred Margrit's hair, and then Rebecca was outside the circle, free of the djinn, caught in Daisani's arms. For a few bewildering seconds, Margrit felt as though she'd come upon two lovers who were otherwise hidden from sight.

They might have been gargoyles caught by sunlight, so sculpted and motionless did they seem. Rebecca was slightly taller, but Daisani held her weight, her hands on his chest as she leaned into him. Margrit could see the pulse in her mother's throat, and how near to Daisani's mouth that fluttering beat was. His attention, though, was on Rebecca's eyes, and all Margrit could read in their locked gazes was an intensity that embarrassed and enthralled her. She strained for a memory she didn't have, as though trying hard enough could call up Alban's recollections of Hajnal, or perhaps of Sarah Hopkins. As though her own regal mother, standing so close to Eliseo Daisani, had somehow taken on a leading role in a tragedy played out over centuries. Margrit's throat and heart tightened, fear of losing her mother tangling with a weightier loss of years, so heavy she could barely comprehend it.

Daisani drew breath to speak, breaking the stillness. Rebecca put a fingertip against his lips, a sharp, smooth movement. Daisani froze again, the pair standing together for another impossibly long moment with an intimacy that made Margrit look away in discomfort.

Her gaze found Janx, who watched Rebecca and Daisani with avarice, unfathomable calculations visible in his jade eyes. His expression was harder to look upon than theirs were. Margrit dragged her attention back to her mother, as much to escape Janx's solitude as from morbid curiosity.

It was Rebecca who disengaged from Daisani's grasp, gently, as if she suspected the man who held her might somehow shatter if treated shabbily. Tears stung Margrit's eyes, and she choked on a breath when her mother turned to her.

Rebecca drew herself up and faced her with eyes still

bright from anguish. A constricted squeak broke from Margrit's throat and she stumbled forward to pull her into a hug. Rebecca drew in careful breaths, as if assessing her ability to do so. Margrit wanted to cry out with sympathy, but words caught in her throat. Even shared experience left a barrier between them, one that she couldn't break.

Rebecca stroked her hair, strength returning to her breathing and her touch. "It's all right, sweetheart. Everything's all right now." Then she put her hands on Margrit's shoulders and smiled. "I'm glad to have seen you tonight, Margrit. I'll tell your father you acquitted yourself well at the service, and I hope you'll come out to see us next weekend as we'd planned." She kissed her cheek, then walked away with quick, precise steps, leaving Margrit and the Old Races behind.

Margrit made a protest, her voice nothing more than a croak as her mother hurried away. It seemed impossible that she could do so, impossible that she wouldn't stand and face Daisani, or even Margrit herself. Loneliness rose up again. Every hope of sharing the incredible world she'd discovered seemed to be swept away with her mother's departure.

"Forgive me." Daisani spoke from beside her, his approach too quick or too quiet for her to have noticed. "Forgive me, Margrit. I said I would protect her. I'd hoped danger wouldn't come so close. Forgive me for my carelessness."

"Why?" Margrit clenched her fists, turning miserable eyes on Daisani. Janx stood a few feet behind him, his own hands knotted loosely and his head turned to the side, gaze cast downward. Only the djinn, who'd fallen silent after his first shout of protest, looked pleased.

"Why does she do that? Why does she leave without answers? Why—?"

Profound regret slid across Daisani's thin face. "Because she prefers not to know them, my dear. You are very like your mother, but not in this regard. I like to imagine she refuses answers because she prefers the world to have mystery in it."

"Not my mom. Not—"

"Shh." Daisani echoed the gesture Rebecca had used with him, fingertips not quite touching Margrit's lips. "Be so kind as to leave me my illusions, Margrit. Let me imagine that mysteries are sweeter unsolved, rather than know that I'm too fearsome to be investigated."

Margrit swallowed, trying to make room for words in her throat. "So we do matter," she said hoarsely. "I mean, I knew Vanessa did—of course she mattered. But the rest of us. We're here and then gone again so quickly. I wondered if you even noticed, if you made friends, or mourned us when we're gone. Do you have to decide who's worth it and who isn't in the space of an instant, because taking time to decide will waste all the years of our lives?" Her heart beat slowly and tears stung at the backs of her eyes, high emotion brought by the audacity of her questions and the weight of their answers. Humans wanted to live forever. Only in asking did she realize that immortality was a dangerously lonely business.

Daisani met her gaze evenly a long time, then lowered his eyes a moment before lifting them again with all the grace of age. Behind him, Janx looked toward her even more steadily. Unable to bear the answers in their silence, Margrit nodded jerkily and turned toward the djinn, making a rough, human gesture intended to bring the men back to the topic at hand.

The djinn spat as their attention turned back to him. "You can do nothing to me. I have no answers for you."

"Perhaps not." Alban's voice cut across the nearly empty courtyard, stony with assurance. "But I think I do."

THIRTY-THREE

"ALBAN!" MARGRIT RAN across the courtyard to him, aware as she crashed against him that his embrace was gentle, whereas hers used all the fragile strength she had to command. He coiled his arms around her and buried his nose in her hair, murmuring a sound of reassurance. After a few trembling seconds she loosened her grip enough to look up at him. "What're you doing here?"

"Indeed," Janx said, far more dryly. "What *are* you doing here, Korund? I set you a task."

"Malik is settled," Alban replied without rancor. "What did you give him, Janx, to give to Kaimana?"

The dragonlord's eyebrows drew into a dark line and he sent Margrit a glance that hovered between knowing and accusing. "Nothing. There's no profit to me in sending a lackey to negotiate."

"Then what," Alban asked, "has Malik delivered to him that you would not want Kaimana, in turn, to give to Tony Pulcella?"

Margrit drew in a sharp, quiet breath. "Tony? Oh God." She turned toward Janx in time to catch a snarl ripple over his face. "They took Al Capone down for tax evasion, Janx."

"Don't be concerned, glassmaker." The djinn spat. "By the time the police arrive there'll be nothing of yours left to claim. The selkies will have helped us take it all."

"The *selkies?*" The astonishment in her own voice would have embarrassed Margrit had it not been echoed so wholeheartedly by the other three who stood outside the bloody circle. Then she found herself speaking, putting pieces together aloud.

"There are more of you than anybody else. More djinn, more selkies. But you're enemies. Kaimana didn't risk it all on the quorum, did he. He came to you first. He offered you something you wanted in exchange for your support. He offered you…" Her gaze flickered to Daisani and Janx, then back again, as she guessed, "Economic power, outside of your deserts? He told you there was strength in numbers and offered you— Oh, the smooth son of a bitch." She turned away from the djinn, from all the Old Races, and pressed the heels of her hands against her forehead as she paced and spoke.

"He offered you a chance to get back at us, didn't he. Us. Humans. For destroying your habitats, your peoples, for not knowing you were there. God, has he got Biali on his side, too?" She swung back around to face the djinn, suddenly moving with a predator's confidence. A churchyard was nothing, and everything, like a courtroom, and she was fearless there, even as she turned guesswork into statements.

"And the best way to get back at us, in a really violent way, is through Janx's organization. He's already the underbelly. Daisani's up there at the top, and besides, Kaimana's already got money. If he wants to he can take Daisani on in the boardrooms. But somebody's got to run the seedy underside, and I bet he sleeps better if it's not him. So he offered it to you, didn't he. Because nobody'd expect it, and your people have the greatest numbers after his. God, it's a great idea. He'd hand Janx's world over to you if you'd support his people within the Old Races."

"And Malik's place in this?" Janx hissed the question, sending hair-raised alarm over Margrit's arms.

The djinn smiled, sharp and vicious, the kind of expression Margrit expected from Daisani, but rarely saw. "Remains to be seen. He declared rite of passage to stand at the quorum, claimed a challenge that has not yet been fulfilled."

"Against Janx," Margrit whispered.

The djinn folded his hands together, index fingers extended, to point first at Janx, then Daisani. "Blood-taker to glassmaker, old rivals, ready to fight. So easy to manipulate, so easy to sow dissent. A few of the glassmaker's men, a few of the *algul*'s people, destabilizing and setting you at odds. Should one be defeated the other always moves along soon after. Yes." His gaze, brown with irritation, landed on Margrit again. "Against the glassmaker. Should Malik win, his place in this is an investigator, a visionary. Should he lose, he will walk alone amonst the sands for a lifetime. It is, as you say, all or nothing."

"Everything is with you." Margrit's voice stayed low. "But someone went after him yesterday morning. Who?"

The djinn shrugged, fluid and airy despite his prison. "It was necessary. Including him as a target removed any hint of his complicity with our plans, and had he not survived, we would have known he was unworthy to be one of our leaders. As it is, he refused in the matter of your mother. Feared the *algul* who haunted her steps too much to make the attempt."

"That," Daisani murmured, "was wise."

Coldness rose in Margrit like a tide. "So you thought you'd cap off the week by murdering her yourself? In front of us all?"

Anger flashed through his eyes as he glanced down. "We didn't know an *algul's* blood made cages."

Margrit laughed, a crack of anger. "Wouldn't have risked it if you'd known, would you?"

The djinn snarled again, but Daisani brushed off his anger with a gesture. "The blood is drying."

Margrit's gaze, like everyone's, went to the smeared circle around the djinn's feet. Daisani continued, his voice soft and deliberate. "If you're still within the circle when the last drop has dried, you'll be trapped. A djinn in a bottle, bound to my desire. Does it constrict? Do you feel the blood eating up the air, binding you bit by bit to human form? Jailing you in that shape, freed only at my command?"

The djinn exploded into a storm of sand, of air, all caught within the confines of the blood circle. An instant later he coalesced, panting with rage, amber gaze locked on Daisani.

"Let him go." Margrit's voice scraped. "Let him go, Eliseo."

"I made you a promise, Margrit." A light, unnerving note came into Daisani's voice, a hint of dangerous intent. "I promised your mother's safety. And now I hold it in the palm of my hand."

"You don't." Margrit wet her lips. "You've got one djinn, and there are hundreds. Thousands. Putting one in chains doesn't alleviate the risk, and it's morally repugnant. I'm not going to have the cost of Mom's life be someone else's freedom."

"So sentimental of you. Would you have said the same thing if he still stood with his hand wrapped around Rebecca's heart?"

"I don't know." Her answer was charged with uncertainty. "It doesn't matter. We're not talking about Mom now. We're talking about slavery. I'll deal with the consequences later, but I won't have anybody turned into a belonging on my watch. Let him go, or every deal we've made is void."

The vampire locked eyes with her for a long, drawn-out silence. "You're very bold, Miss Knight."

"You've gone to one hell of a lot of trouble to keep me on your team, Mr. Daisani. Be a shame to blow it all now, wouldn't it?" To her own surprise, she felt no fear. Whether she'd moved beyond it or whether she trusted Daisani more than she liked to think, Margrit found herself able to meet his eyes without flinching, without her heartbeat racing. "Your choice."

Daisani's lip curled, and then a handful of dirt broke the blood circle, absorbing liquid, smearing it across flagstones. Margrit drew in a sharp breath, searching for Daisani, but nothing was left of him but a fading breeze. The djinn remained frozen within the broken ring for a few long seconds, his expression blank with disbelief before he said, "You're a fool."

"Leave my family alone and I can live with that."

"You should have made that bargain before you set me free."

"It wouldn't have meant anything if I'd coerced you."

"It might have meant your mother's life." Then, like Daisani, the djinn was gone in a gust of wind, leaving

Margrit to sag against Alban and stare at the ruined circle at her feet.

"I thought you said the gargoyles were the only Old Race to have ever been enslaved." Her voice came from a far distance, as if disbelief or weariness had made an unbreachable wall around her.

"I didn't know." Alban slipped his arms about her, offering strength and support. Margrit groaned and turned against him, feeling distance melt away into comfort. "Perhaps it's somewhere in the memories, buried in mountain roots. I've never studied the djinn histories that closely."

"Maybe you should. Maybe it's all a lot more complex than we think." Margrit let the slow steady beat of Alban's heart drown out the world for a moment. Then she lifted her head, a sense of unease sliding through her. "Alban…"

"Yes?"

"Where's Janx?"

As if her question triggered it, her phone rang, the *William Tell Overture* out of place in the churchyard. Margrit swore and dug it out of her pocket, muttering, "I can't believe I didn't turn that off before the service. God. Yeah, hello?"

"Margrit, why didn't you tell me you were going after Janx?"

Margrit stepped away from Alban, trying to control the surprise that popped through her. "Tony?"

"All of this makes more sense now," Tony went on. "Even the job for Daisani. Is that real, or are you looking for a connection between the two of them? They obviously know each other. I saw them at the ice rink. Why couldn't you tell me? I might've been able to help, Grit."

"You—what? Tony?" Margrit pressed fingertips to her hairline, as if doing so would help her order her thoughts.

"Kaaiai gave me the documents half an hour ago, Grit. You could've told me."

Margrit let out a slow breath. "I couldn't have. It's…" She'd done so well earlier, putting together Kaimana's association with the djinn. Following Tony's logic shouldn't befuddle her now. "I couldn't have," she repeated. "How do you—why do you think it's me?"

"Oh, come on. The way you've been acting, and the way you've been working those two? Why else would somebody like Kaaiai get Janx's tax records? You really think you can get Daisani, too?"

Margrit laughed unhappily. For a moment, as she grasped Tony's interpretation of events, she wished he was *right,* that the twists and turns of her life over the last months had been part of a sting intended to bring down one of New York's crimelords, and maybe even one of its business moguls. He was right twice: in that light, her behavior had a certain logic to it. It looked like a pursuit of justice above all else.

Agreeing to the fallacy made her stomach churn with distress, but the truth was even more difficult to explain. Dizziness wrapped her as she pushed herself to lies of omission. "Probably not. Daisani's too big a target, unless Janx comes in willing to talk, which doesn't seem likely. I didn't mean to be in a position where I knew both of them, Tony. It just happened."

"Because of me." He made the accusation she refused to.

"Maybe, yeah. Because I met Janx because of you, maybe. Everything's happened fast, and I had no idea where it would end up." She laughed again, this time out of frustration at the magnitude of her understatement. "I didn't talk to you about it because..." Because there'd been no plan in place, but admitting that left her with nothing more than honesty, both unpalatable and improbable.

"Because we were having problems anyway." Tony filled in the silence again. Margrit knotted her hand in her coat pocket as the cop sighed. "I wish you'd told me, Grit. I might not've said some of the things I did."

"There's a lot of regret under the bridge. It's okay."

"I hated seeing you at that ball with him," Tony admitted.

Margrit turned to look at Alban, a little of the tension running out of her. He met her eyes without challenge or concern, nothing but trust and support in his gaze.

"I know," she said quietly. "But I'm seeing him now. Right now nothing you and I said or did would change that. The best I can do is be sorry that I've hurt you, but I've got to try this."

"And if it doesn't work?" Tony's voice was low.

"I can't think about that right now, either. You broke up with me. Not that you were wrong to, but don't stay up nights waiting for me, not after that. You earned the Janx sting. That's not about me, or you and me. It's you."

"First a black-tie job with Kaimana, now a takedown that any cop in the city would envy. What are you, Grit? My good luck charm with a catch?"

"He giveth and He taketh away." Margrit gave a lopsided smile, looking at Alban again. "I'm glad to talk to you, Tony. I—"

"Don't. I'm not ready for that yet."

Margrit swallowed. "Ready for what?"

"I know you pretty well, Grit. That was about to turn into an 'I hope we can still be friends' speech, and I'm not up for that. Breaking up and then finding out you've been acting so weird because of this sting is bad enough, and knowing you're dating that guy is worse. So don't do the wouldn't-it-be-great thing. Not now and maybe not ever. Sorry." He said the word without meaning it; Margrit was all but able to hear the stiff shrug accompanying the apology. "I'm not that big a guy."

"I think you probably are." She took a deep breath, unable to hide the shakiness in it. "But okay. I won't. Just—well, I was going to say let me know how it goes, but I guess I'll read about it in the papers sometime in the next couple months."

"No." Tony's voice roughened. "With any luck you'll read about it in the papers tomorrow. We're going in tonight."

Alban caught Margrit in his arms, propelling her toward the shadows and then leaping skyward before she had time to protest. None of the usual sensuality filled the movement of his body against hers as he pumped his wings, climbing higher. Urgency, yes; she'd known that in his body before, but not with this sort of purpose, words and thought for once left behind in the name of action. The "*What?*" that burst from her lips was as much directed at the gargoyle as Tony.

"No choice, Grit. I know Janx owns people on the force. We gotta move in before he's tipped off. If we're lucky we'll nab him coming home from that service with no fuss. Look, I have to go. We're moving out."

"Okay. Be—be careful, Tony."

"Always." Rough amusement filled the word, and then he was gone, leaving Margrit clutching the phone and staring from it to Alban.

"I'm sorry," he rumbled as she hung up. "I could overhear your conversation."

"I figured. But where— No. *Why?*"

Alban didn't answer until the sharpness of his upward climb leveled off, his concentration solely on reaching the heights above the skyline. "Not for Janx. Not even for you," he admitted in his deep voice. "He'll destroy them, Margrit. He'll kill your friend Tony and anyone with him."

Margrit made an abortive move to dial her phone again. Calling would be useless; it wasn't as though Tony didn't know raiding a criminal's lair was dangerous work. He hadn't gone into policing for the safety or the extravagant benefits. Margrit put her face against Alban's shoulder, trying to will away fear.

For once, Tony's Italian good looks stood out clearly in her mind, dark hair and ruddy cheeks and easy white smile. He still seemed overblown and lush compared to Alban's stark paleness and chiseled features, but remembering his good humor and simple humanity, suddenly so fragile, made Margrit's heart hurt. Fear for his life made overlooking his flaws easier, though it abruptly seemed unfair to consider his worry for her a flaw. If she could have made him understand that she needed the nightly run in the park as much as he needed the excitement of his job…

Margrit tried to push regret away. The choices had

been made on both their parts. Still, the *what-if* loomed large in the face of *never again.*

"Are you all right?" Alban's voice, quiet with concern, cut through the rush of the wind. Margrit nodded against his shoulder, aware it was the first time she'd ever consciously lied to him.

"I'm fine. Just scared."

A hitch came into Alban's wingbeats. He drew her closer, gentleness and hesitation in the action. "Margrit, I don't know what I was thinking. I shouldn't have brought you."

She stiffened, glowering at his jaw. "Like hell you shouldn't have. I would've just taken myself if you hadn't."

"It's going to be dangerous. Your people are so fragile."

"You'll protect me." She spoke with simple confidence, glad to shuffle off even the smallest deception. "Look at it this way. At least you'll know where I am if I'm with you."

Alban chuckled, a sound without humor. "Given that I'm likely to be the only thing capable of standing between Janx and the utter destruction of your friends, I'm not sure that's the reassurance you intended it to be." He tucked her closer, though, and drove forward through the sky, threats to abandon her left behind in the wind.

THIRTY-FOUR

THEY HIT THE House of Cards' rooftop at a run, Alban shifting into human form between one step and the next. A startled guard barked a protest, and Alban hit him in the chest, knocking him against the wall effortlessly. Margrit squeaked, then put on a burst of speed to outpace the gargoyle as they took the stairs down toward Janx's alcove.

Alban caught her as she crashed through a second door, literally wrapping an arm around her middle and hugging her to a stop. Margrit pinwheeled as he whispered a warning into her hair.

Madness reigned below them. The casino was in an uproar, voices pitched so high in fear and anger Margrit was surprised she hadn't heard them earlier. Alban, though, must have. Margrit relaxed in his arms as she understood why he hadn't wanted her to charge in.

Most humans wouldn't have eyes to see it. Djinns and selkies moved with too-fluid purpose, rousting people toward the streets. Certainty seized Margrit: the Old Races below knew their window of safety had ended. Word had flown ahead of them, warning that Janx had learned of the coup attempt. Humans didn't belong in the burgeoning frey; they were customers and users, too valuable to waste in a fight between the Old Races.

Angry the mortals fought back, refusing to be assuaged or moved until the warehouse's front doors blew open. A blast of cooler air rode in, then burned away as Janx stalked into his casino, nearly blazing with fury. Margrit's breath seized, a too-familiar response to the dragonlord's presence. Alban's arms tightened around her reassuringly.

Humans scattered before Janx where they'd stood their ground against the other invaders. Desperate men scraped up poker chips and clutched them as they ran for the doors, only to be repelled by bouncers too savvy to let them escape, even amid chaos. Margrit caught a glimpse of Biali's thick form and brilliantly white hair among the darker heads below, and wondered which he fought for—his employer or vengeance.

"Malik is nearby." Alban's voice was low enough to cut through the noise.

Margrit twisted in his arms, looking around. "How can you tell?"

"His cane's made of corundum." Alban tipped his head as Margrit frowned at him. "Sapphire. My family is sensitive to it, and a piece that large is easy to track."

"That's a sapphire?" Sheer childish greed rose up in Margrit. "It's as big as my fist. Where'd he get a stone like that? I thought it was *glass*. My God. Did he get it from Janx? Does Janx really have a hoard? I want to see it." Below near-hysterical interest lay a bitter awareness that people fought for their lives only a few yards below them. Margrit clenched her teeth, trying to control herself, and hoping it was fear and adrenaline that drove her spate of words rather than a sudden loss of faculties. "Never mind the hoard." She scanned the space below with renewed concern. "Where'd he go? How did he *get* here so fast?"

Alban gave her a look that bordered on pity and brought confused heat to Margrit's cheeks. It said too clearly that mere humans could never hope to match the speeds even the slowest of the Old Races could achieve; that questions of locomotion were so basic as to be embarrassing. She remembered, uncomfortably, how Janx's way of moving often seemed to be a simple transference of attention, focus flowing from one place to another and drawing his body along with it nearly instantaneously. Lower lip in her teeth, she glanced away. "People are going to start dying down there."

"Then we'd better put a stop to it if we can." Alban finally released her, and Margrit broke into a run again, just as glad to have not encountered the mob unprepared. Alban strong-armed another pair of men, these ones scrambling to escape the fight.

Margrit found a certain reckless satisfaction in bursting into Janx's office unannounced a few seconds later. The door banged against the wall, steel on steel, and Janx flinched, whipping to face her with his hands clawed, ready for a fight. Margrit skidded on the floor and stopped herself with both hands planted on the cafeteria table he used for a desk. Malik was nowhere to be seen, so she put that aside to blurt, "Cops are coming."

"What?" The startled question was as human and unplanned as his angry flinch had been. "Margrit, I admire your alacrity in arriving, but police? Coming here? I own half the department, my dear. Don't you think someone might have mentioned an attempt as audacious as… Bother. I can't think of an alliterative way to end that sentence. Never mind." He fluttered his hand dismissively, with no hint of any emotion beyond his usual lightheartedness. "No one would dare."

"There hasn't been time for anybody to tell you. Forget the selkies. You're about to be arrested."

The dragonlord blanched, his skin nearly as white as Alban's and his fiery hair contrasting to make him look sickly. The green in his eyes was swallowed by rage, leaving nothing but blackness. He leaned forward, fingertips white against the table's surface. "And you know this how?"

"Tony tipped me off, because he never imagined I'd warn you!"

"The police. So quickly." Janx's answering whisper bordered between accusation and question. He wrapped his fingers around the edge of the table, as if controlling his anger. "You've brought this on me."

"Oh, give me a break. You're the one who never saw what Malik was up to. We can fight about it later, unless you want to do it from jail. You—"

He twisted his arms, a violent explosion of motion, and the cafeteria table flipped lengthwise, squealing as the metal legs scraped the floor. It slammed into the windows, shattering cracks in the glass before it bounced away again, a clattering counterpoint to Janx's roar, "You did this!"

He pounced, a lithe, quick movement transferring great size and weight from one focus point to another. Margrit shrieked, flinging her arms up in useless self-defense. But Alban was there between her and the infuriated dragonlord. Even in his human form, Alban had the breadth of shoulder and a stone-solid ease to his defensive crouch.

"Margrit is not your enemy, Janx." He spoke in a low, steady voice, as if trying to make reason more appealing than battle. "Margrit is not your enemy, and this is not the time or place to argue about it. You don't share my daylight weakness," the gargoyle admitted with a faint smile, "but I'd rather not see any of us locked away in human jails. Don't be a fool, dragonlord. Leave the fight for another time."

Janx curled his hands into talons, his mouth twisted in a snarl. He heaved one sharp breath, then dragged himself upright again, his countenance black with anger. "Not until I have dealt with Malik. You, I'll deal with later."

The air burned out of Margrit's lungs again as Janx locked his green gaze on her. "Janx, I'm not—"

"Malik!"

Margrit bolted for the door, responding more to the sound of authority than any impulse to find the djinn. Malik coalesced in front of her, smug triumph in his eyes as he focused on Janx. "You called?"

She exhaled and stepped back, putting herself where she could see both dragon and djinn without feeling in danger herself. Janx stood at the windows, his fingertips white against the cracks he'd caused. "Tell me, Malik." His voice was oil-smooth, once more full of light pleasure. "Who did you challenge in your rite of passage?"

The barest smirk shaped Malik's lips, answer enough. Margrit's stomach cramped and she took one more step back against the cracked windows. Janx turned his head, the slithering motion of a mongoose watching a snake.

Then he moved, a flowing of action larger than

Margrit could take in easily. Malik showed no surprise, simply dissipated where he stood, impossible for even Janx's quickness to catch. The dragonlord bellowed, too large a sound for a man his size, and whipped around, following Malik's movement without needing to see where he went. He surged forward again to the sound of the djinn's laughter, mocking and cold in the steel alcove.

"I can do this forever, Janx." Malik reappeared long enough to speak, his thin face dark with delight. Janx snarled and pounced at him again, Malik holding his ground and brandishing the sapphire-headed cane. Margrit closed her eyes at the sound of a faint click, half afraid Janx wouldn't stop himself in time. A hiss made her open her eyes again to watch Janx skitter back, silk shirt sliced open, though no trace of blood gleamed red on the blade within Malik's cane.

"Oh, Malik." Undiluted pleasure rushed through Janx's voice, and below it Alban rumbled, "Janx," in warning.

Janx slid his hand over the cut in his shirt, then rubbed his fingertips together, as if savoring the near miss. "Oh, Malik," he repeated. "My dear Malik. Are you so confident in yourself as to risk my death? You voted against clemency, djinn. You should not have pushed it so far," he whispered.

"Janx," Alban said again.

The dragon snapped his gaze away from Malik, a snarl contorting his features. "Keep out of it, Stoneheart. This is not your battle." He flowed forward again, transferring his weight, only to come up hard against Alban as the gargoyle put himself between dragon and djinn. Outrage flushed Janx's skin, and Alban put a hand on the other man's shoulder.

"You set me to be certain of Malik's welfare, Janx." Wry regret infused Alban's voice. "I'm afraid it *is* my battle."

"I didn't mean keep him safe from me!"

Margrit clapped a hand over her mouth, trying to silence laughter too late. For an instant the three men focused on her and she pressed herself against the window, wishing she'd kept silent. Then Alban returned his gaze to Janx. "You set a gargoyle to watch over someone's safety, dragonlord," he said quietly. "It is not a task to be altered at your whim. You knew that well enough when you put it to me the first time, and you know it now."

A ripple went through Janx's body, a shudder that seemed to begin in the marrow of his bones and work its way out. "Do not test me, Stoneheart."

Alban smiled, an expression unlike anything Margrit had ever seen from him. There was no cruelty in it, but rather anticipation full of sharp edges. "The police are coming. Your House is about to fall. Do you really wish to do this now?"

"Let him." Malik sneered, confident behind the barrier Alban's body made. "His time is over. The djinn are rising, and the dragons will fall."

Staggering defeat swept Janx's face, his shoulders dropping and the strength draining out of him. "Perhaps." Even his golden voice was dull, the fight gone from him. He looked up, ruin in his features, first to meet Alban's eyes, then to look beyond the gargoyle at Malik.

Nothing in his body language gave him away. No tension, no preparation, no coiling for attack. Margrit watched his broken gaze settle on Malik, and nearly laughed again at the outrageous falsity of it all. Everything about him, to Margrit's eyes, bespoke the skill of a consummate actor drawing in his audience, and she wanted to stand tall and applaud.

But Alban was relaxing, believing Janx's posture and words. Malik looked triumphant, as if he'd won a battle. The sheer humanity of Janx's act and the blatant inability of the others to read it took Margrit by surprise, leaving her unable to speak.

Janx exploded.

The concussive force of his transformation threw Margrit back, his size and shape so much greater than Alban's that the air around him shattered. Overhead lights exploded, leaving a whiff of burnt ozone and a glow of neon from the casino. Windows, already weakened, blew outward. Margrit was saved from a plummet by a steel bar catching her shoulders, she slid down the metal, barely hearing her own terrified scream, and came to her knees on the cold floor, staring at the elegantly defined chaos before her.

Alban had transformed as well, stony form lit with garish colors in the ruined alcove. Margrit couldn't put a size to Janx's dragon form, other than *big,* too big to be possible. Sinuous and slender, he twisted himself around Alban, scales gleaming through the darkest shades of red. Silver lined the undersides where Margrit could see them bending, making the length of him glitter and shine. Fine, delicate-looking wings ran two-thirds of his body length, each rapid clap breaking the air and making Margrit dizzy with force. His long, narrow muzzle streamed blue smoke as he squeezed Alban.

The gargoyle bellowed, a sound of irritation rather

than injury, and dug both hands around the edge of a scale, ripping back with all his force.

The scale tore free to Janx's shriek of pain, and his coils loosened enough for Alban to leap away. The gargoyle's wings flared, catching a draft of air, and he landed a few yards away, hands curled around the scale he'd pulled from Janx's hide. Blood spattered his arms, lurid in the neon light from the casino. Everything about him was alien, from the power surging through heavy, thick muscles to the battle lust rising in his eyes. All the familiarity Margrit had come to recognize, all the humanity, was drowned. He flung the scale away, sending it skittering toward Margrit's feet.

She picked it up, hands instantly sticky with Janx's blood, and dented her palms with even an ordinary grip against the scale's edge. Then, deliberately, she pushed her hand against its edge, feeling her skin slice open and blood flow. It hurt, but distantly, as if she'd seen the injury happen to someone else. Turning her palm up to watch the cut heal reminded her of the gift she, too, carried, but even its impossibility faded before the simple fact that Alban had been absolutely unharmed by the scale's deadly edges.

Fire tore through the room, searing the air. Margrit screamed again, shoving herself back toward the shattered windows, the scale falling from her hands. Janx's long neck whipped around, following Alban with another burst of flame. Alban dove through it, wings tucked close to his body, and came up on the other side with his pale skin unmarred by darkness, his fine white hair unsinged, though the denim jeans he wore were singed and smoking. Margrit's heart lurched and she cringed at the very idea of that fire.

Alban leaped over Janx, and the dragon followed his movement, spouting fire. Wings tucked to roll, Alban hit the wall feetfirst and sprang back toward Janx. The dragon ducked his head too late and Alban seized him around the throat. Stone squeezed forgiving flesh, scales cracking under pressure. Muscles bulged in Alban's arms, his face contorted with concentration. Nothing recognizable was left in his features, only bared teeth and a killing rage in his eyes.

Margrit fisted her hands against her mouth, holding back screams that she feared would draw the titanic combatants' attention to her. Alban had insisted to her that he was not a man. She'd argued for him being a person, if not a human, finding excitement in his exotic form and alien capabilities.

She'd thought she'd understood what it was to be a gargoyle. Now, cowering in the darkness as a battle raged around her, she knew she had understood nothing at all.

Of the remaining Old Races, dragons had most to be wary of from the gargoyles. Stone burned, but not easily or quickly at the temperatures they could sustain, and even a dragon's great size made no difference once a gargoyle's strength took hold of a vital body part. The wings were easiest, even clamped close to the body, but Alban ignored them, flinging himself toward Janx's throat for a crushing grip there. He had left one of his own kind crippled and blinded. Biali had spat on that mercy, and Alban would not offer the same opportunity again.

Janx drew his legs beneath himself, catlike, then slammed upward with all the violence he could muster.

Alban crashed into the steel ceiling, stunned. His grip loosened enough for Janx to claw him free and fling him away, sending him crashing against a wall. The dragon landed with a grunt, shaking himself and pulling in breath to spout flame again.

Alban dragged himself into a crouch, ready to face the oncoming flame directly. Only his low vantage point gave him eyes to see what he'd forgotten: Malik's reappearance, below Janx's wing, his sword-cane lifted to strike. A warning ripped from Alban's throat: *"Janx!"*

The dragon twisted too late, Malik driving his sword into the softened spot where Alban had ripped away Janx's scale. Janx howled, bucking in pain, and Malik dissolved again, taking the cane with him. A moment later he coalesced once more, this time slashing a deep and terrible cut through Janx's wing. Janx screamed again, spraying fire across the room, but it whisked through Malik harmlessly, the djinn re-forming as heat faded. Janx's next breath was shallow with pain, too weak to birth new flame. Triumph flashed in Malik's eyes as he lifted his cane-sword to strike a final time.

"Malik!"

Margrit's voice tore through the room, the high feminine sound a shocking contrast to the deep male roars and the crackling fire. Malik twisted as she rose up out of the darkness, a ludicrous lime-green gun in her hand.

Thin jets of water shot out from the weapon, splashing the djinn's face and shirt. Steam hissed and sizzled up, silvery burns appearing on Malik's skin. He howled, full of pain and outrage, and abandoned Janx to fling himself at Margrit.

She stood her ground, firing the water gun at him,

then turning it as though it had the weight of a real gun, holding its muzzle as if she might pistol-whip the djinn. He knocked her to the floor, both of them rolling with momentum. Her hand lifted, then fell again, gun brought to his temple.

Plastic shattered, emptying the remaining water over his face. Malik screamed once more, rearing back to claw at his eyes. Margrit scrambled away, feet dangerously bare on the glass-littered floor.

Pride rose up in Alban and mixed with an overwhelming feeling of loss. That Margrit could defend herself against one of the Old Races was to be celebrated; that humanity could find so many easy ways to defeat them was to be mourned. Malik reached for his cane and shoved to his feet, hair dripping and skin still silver with burns.

Janx had wound his way around the alcove in the brief moments the djinn had been distracted. Now pleasure filled his roar as he bore down on Malik, intent clear even if words were lost to him. Malik unsheathed his blade, lifting it as though he would dive straight down the dragon's throat, taking Janx's life even if the price was his own.

Time crystallized, until each moment of the fight seemed to last an eternity in which Alban could consider it with thoughts racing ahead. Neither combatant would survive Malik's suicidal attempt, and Janx, most particularly, could not be allowed to die like this, in the midst of human territory, with human police only minutes away.

Thought, it seemed, was too slow after all. He didn't remember the decision to leap forward, intent on knocking the dragon's head aside or shattering Malik's blade on his own stony hide. Weaponless, the djinn would be forced to dissipate or suffer Janx's fire, and a resolution could be visited off the battlefield.

Janx flicked his head to the side as Alban pounced, and instead of crashing into him, his gargoyle bulk smashed into Malik, driving them both against the burnished steel wall.

Bones shattered with sickening clarity above the sound of fire.

Alban staggered back in shock as Malik's body, as solid and mortal as any human, slithered to the floor, the cane bouncing free of his hand.

A new eternity was born, marked by the crackle of flame and a bewildering hiss of incomprehension inside Alban's mind. He stared down at the djinn's broken form, unmoving until Margrit's voice, small with horror, broke through the chaos to ask, "Is he…?"

Janx, panting, shuddered back to human form. A grunt of pain escaped his clenched teeth and he clamped a hand above his kidney, trying to stop a flow of blood that didn't lessen by his shift from one form to another. Even kneeling, even in pain, he dragged in a breath and inserted lightness in his voice as he looked at Malik's body. "Oh, yes, he certainly is. It's a shame your third proposal didn't pass, Margrit."

"How—" Alban's voice cracked.

Margrit, pale even in the shattered light, came forward with her hands clenched. "Salt water. I had salt water in the gun. I'd been keeping it under my pillow because I was afraid he'd come after me again. I…oh my God. I killed him."

"No." Despair laced Alban's voice. "No, Margrit. I did."

Janx laughed, a hoarse sound of pain that turned Alban back to him. "Oh, don't be so greedy, Stoneheart. I think we all deserve some credit for this. Margrit, why on earth did you not use that absurd weapon against Tarig?"

"Tarig?" Margrit's voice was high and shaking.

Irritation displaced pain on Janx's face for an instant, his teeth bared and his gaze dropping as though he chastised himself. "The djinn who held your mother."

Margrit lifted her eyes from Malik to stare at Janx for a few long seconds of befuddlement. "You knew him? And you didn't…" She stopped, clearly unable to think of what the dragon might have done, then put a hand over her face. "I couldn't remember if it solidified them right away or just made them unable to mist. I was afraid it would turn him solid with his hand in Mom's chest."

"It seems we now know." Janx glanced around the disaster of his alcove. "If I may make a humble suggestion, Margrit?" She nodded tightly and Janx's voice went dry. "Run. Get away from here. Be anywhere but here tonight, my dear."

Margrit dropped her hand to look first at Janx, then at Alban. Then she nodded, another jerky movement, and ran silently from the burning alcove. Alban made an abortive gesture to follow, then closed his hands into fists, uncertain of himself. Uncertain of anything, anymore. Empty horror coated his insides, an overwhelming numbness where true emotion should lie. Bad enough to fail to protect a charge. Actually causing his death… Cool disbelief wrapped him in safety, leaving him unable to process what had happened.

Janx exhaled painfully. "Good girl. Probably the only sensible thing that woman has done since meeting you." He reached for Malik's cane, teeth gritted as he twisted the sword back into its sheath, then used it to shove himself upward. "She's human, Stoneheart. We're not. Don't expect too much from her." He curled his hand around the cane head, dropping his voice. "I cannot fly, Alban. I cannot escape this place and the human police without your help."

Anger and sorrow knotted themselves in Alban's chest as he looked at Janx. "This will cost you, dragon-lord."

Thin, fluting laughter escaped Janx's lips and he lowered his head. "Yes. Yes, of course it will, my old friend. Come." Pain sharpened his voice, but not enough to make the word a demand. "Let us leave my fallen House and discuss the price of salvation."

THIRTY-FIVE

ONE BEWILDERINGLY CLEAR thought stood out: Janx's scale could not possibly be found by the police. Glass lay everywhere, shards glittering and dangerous as they reflected neon and firelight. Margrit hadn't thought there was enough wood in the place to burn, but Janx had done his work well, if not deliberately. Fire ate at the building's structure, heat sending lights into brilliant sparkling explosions as it leaped around, working its way from one vulnerable spot to another. It moved faster than she thought it could, gobbling up its resources and sending showers of sparks down to the casino floor. She searched through the arc of glass below the dragon's alcove, heartbeat hammering sickly.

There was almost no screaming anymore in the fire-ridden building, only men and women accustomed to desperation turning their focus on getting out before the walls came down. Most of those who were left moved with the uncanny grace of the Old Races, and they, having chased off the mortals, eyed one another. Treaties meant little in the face of ancient rivalries. Margrit ignored them, digging through glass and rubble more frantically.

Screams *did* come from the dance club directly

below Janx's alcove, a more youthful and enthusiastic crowd discovering the fire there. The fire, or police raids. Margrit turned her gaze up as a new burst of flame gouted from the alcove. Not the battle any longer; that was over. Just the effects of disaster laid down by monsters. Janx was right. Getting out, getting away from the Old Races, away from the world she'd immersed herself in, was the only way to stay alive and retain her own sanity. They were not what she'd thought they were.

Fury, fear and self-disgust rose at her own silent protests. Alban was precisely as he'd always claimed he was. Her refusal to see it, her inability, was her own flaw, but infuriatingly, she'd blamed him. Easier. Safer. She was not a woman who ran from things she feared or didn't understand.

Margrit closed her hands around the scale and, clutching it to her belly, ran.

Cops poured into the abandoned casino. Margrit came up against a wall of them and scrambled backward, running for the shadows, as if she had something to hide. An ancient sprinkler system finally kicked on, dribbling water over five stories of fire-blackened warehouse. She slipped in a sooty puddle, crashing to her knees. An officer grabbed her arm, twisting it up behind her, his commands to not resist all but lost in the roar of fire and shouts of police and Old Races alike. Pain from banged knees and a twisted arm, combined with the acrid scent of smoke, brought tears to Margrit's eyes, feeling thick as they trickled down her cheeks. She looked up, blinking through smoke and water and fire, uncertain she could trust her eyes.

No, Alban's broad pale form was unmistakable, even

in the fire-guttered conditions of the ruined casino. He took the steel stairs up to the rooftop three at a time, unburdened by the weight he carried in his arms. Janx.

A thrill of alarm tempered by confusion and fear shot through Margrit. She dropped her head, gasping out a sob, not knowing if it was relief or dismay that the two combatants had fled. Relief; she held on to that belief, heart aching with it. There would be police on the roof. Despite everything, Margrit hoped Alban would look for them before transforming, before making his escape into the night sky. She wanted to run, wanted freedom from the world she'd become embroiled in, but even so, the idea of losing the fantastic people she'd met to human science and curiosity horrified her.

The cop hauled her up, and she went without protest, stumbling over her own feet. Voices remained raised all around her, some young and frightened, others older and belligerent. A few people moved as she did, shoulders slumped and eyes downcast, only visible in glimpses as they moved past her. Many more walked with the smooth arrogance of the Old Races, and she wondered how long any of them would stay behind bars. Janx's scale lay against her stomach, inside her shirt, where she'd once hidden a selkie skin. So many things were hidden under the surface. She wondered if she would ever find clarity again.

As if in answer, she began to cough when clean air filled her lungs, coolness a salve to the smoke and bitterness of the burning casino. A hand on her head pushed her down into a cop car, and she leaned on the door when it was closed behind her, tears still trickling down her cheeks. Exhaustion more emotional than physical swept her, and for a while she was only distantly aware that bright flashes of red and blue assaulted her closed eyelids, or that people bumped against the vehicle, shaking it as they were removed from the House of Cards. Sirens howled, fire trucks announcing their arrival—all the sounds of city life compressed in a microcosm.

A sharp rap on the window startled her awake. She stared first through the windshield, the officer outside her window little more than a blur at the corner of her eye.

The House of Cards was in ruins, only the alleys between it and other warehouses keeping the whole block from bursting into flames. Smoke and steam rose up in equal parts, a few areas of heat still glowing through the wavering silver. Margrit half expected Janx to stalk out of the aftermath of destruction, eyes bright.

Instead, the knock came against the window again, and then the door was pulled open, Tony bracing his hands on the car's roof. "Grit, what the hell are you doing here?"

She turned her attention to him, sudden bleakness rising up. "I don't know."

"You look awful. What were you, inside? Jesus, Grit, you could've gotten killed. Come on, get—"

A voice rose in sharp protest and Tony waved it off, calling, "She's all right, she's the one who got us here," before finishing, "Get out of there." He offered her a hand and Margrit took it numbly, allowing him to help her out of the car. "You just can't stand not being part of the action, can you. You don't belong here, Margrit."

"I know." She knotted her hand around Tony's, looking back at the fire. "I'm sorry. I won't do this again."

He ducked his head and breathed a curse she was

sure she wasn't meant to hear, then looked up at her again. "You said that last time."

"No." Margrit flinched as something within the House collapsed, sending a boom into the air. "Last time I very carefully didn't say I wouldn't get involved in this kind of thing again. This time I'm saying it. Did you…get him?"

"There's a body upstairs in his office. We don't know who it is yet. Crushed, though. Doesn't take a genius to see it wasn't the fire that got him." Tony glanced at her. "I hate to ask, but you know anything about that?"

"You mean, did I come by here this evening to pulverize Janx before you got a chance to arrest him? I didn't." Margrit smiled faintly. "There was some kind of fight up there," she said a moment later, smile gone. "Just before you guys came in. The fire started there."

Tony sighed. "Maybe somebody tipped him off. There're people on the force working for him, I know that. Arson might've been his way out. Grit, you should go home, get some sleep. You're going to be all over the news tomorrow. We lost Janx, but we took down his operation, all because of you."

"Not because of me," Margrit said softly. Tony looked askance at her and she shook her head. "You've got no real link to me, Tony. Deep Throat gave you those files."

Tony scowled. "Why?"

Dizziness swept her and Margrit pressed the heel of her hand against her eye. "There's always Daisani." Another lie. Misery swirled around her and she shoved it away, unable to offer anything else to the detective. He frowned, then nodded slowly, and she managed to drag a smile into place. "Don't forget to take a shower before the press conference. Good luck."

He nodded stiffly, full of uncertainty, and Margrit waved herself off, leaving Tony behind in a halo of firelight.

"So this is what your promises come to." Grace O'Malley's voice came out of the darkness. Margrit jerked awake with an aborted scream clogging her throat, clutching covers like an ingenue. She flung them away, disgusted with herself, and shoved out of bed, squinting in the faint red light offered by her alarm clock.

"Grace? What're you— How'd you get into my house?"

"Grace has her ways." The black-clad vigilante stepped forward, light gleaming off her leathers, highlighting her curves. "You promised your war wouldn't come to my world."

"I don't know what you're talking about." Margrit reached for the bedside light, dismayed when clicking the switch did nothing. She rubbed her face and kicked a pile of laundry out of the way as she stalked to the wall switch. Light flooded the room and she squinted again, eyes watering. Grace turned to follow her path, one hand lifted and wrapped in gold links. "What is that?"

"Payment," Grace spat. "From Janx."

"A dragon gave you gold?" Margrit chuckled hoarsely. "He must really be trying to curry favor. What's going on?"

The blond woman tightened her fist, metal shifting with quiet clinks. "Your gargoyle brought him to me. Down to where my kids are. He's made my haven Janx's new center of operations." She opened her hand abruptly, flinging the gold links onto Margrit's bed. "You promised me!"

Margrit pulled her gaze from the snake of gold on her comforter. "You invited Alban into your world, Grace. This one's not on me. I'm sorry, but I never dreamed he might do something like that. Where is he? I need to see him." She'd come home without trying to find him, and closed herself in her room, unwilling or unable to face her housemates. She'd showered and then crawled into bed still clutching Janx's scale; it lay beneath her pillow now, where the water gun intended to keep her safe from Malik had once been.

Malik. She had been so careful not to let herself think of him, of the way his body had fallen, salt water preventing the transformation into mist that would have saved his life. Janx was right: they all shared the burden for that death, and the price would be higher for her than for Malik's Old Races brethren.

Dark light slid into Grace's eyes, nothing kind in her expression at all. "Yeah, love, and I want to taste the kiss of angels. We don't get what we want, do we. I can't have Janx down there, stealing my children and showing them the posh life crime can earn them. You promised me, Knight. I don't care what it takes. Get him out of my tunnels and out of my kids' lives, or angels help me, I will haunt you for the rest of your days."

"How would I get somebody like Janx out of your life?"

"You got him into it," Grace said implacably. "You'll figure it out, love." She turned away, hand on the doorknob before Margrit said, "Your necklace."

"Keep it. A prettier piece than Iscariot got, don't you think?" She closed the door behind her as Margrit surged forward to snatch up the links, then run for the bedroom door, to fling the necklace after Grace.

The hallway was empty, the front door closed and the chains on the locks in place. Margrit threw the necklace anyway, sending it clattering against the door, then sat down on the floor, her face in her hands. A creak announced Cole and Cameron's door opening. Margrit cursed into her palms, then looked up to find Cole frowning down at her. "I thought I heard voices."

"Just me talking to Casper."

"What time is it?"

"I don't know. Late. Probably about time for you to get up and go to work."

Cole sat down beside her, looping his arms over his knees and glancing at her through bangs growing too long. "Grit…"

"Whatever you're going to say, Cole, can it wait until later?" She could still smell smoke on her skin and hair, despite having showered. "I don't have anything left to fight with now. Can it just…wait? Please?"

He answered with a long silence, finally ending it with a sigh. "Are you okay, Margrit? I mean, really. Are you okay?"

"I don't know."

Cole sighed again and reached out to put his arm around her shoulders and tug her toward him. "Okay. For right now, okay."

"Thank you." Margrit turned her head against his arm, grateful for his silence, grateful for his simple humanity. They sat together a while before he pulled in a deep breath. "I'm not picking a fight. But do you smell like a bonfire?"

Rough laughter scraped Margrit's throat. "Yeah, I do. I—"

"Nope." Cole cut across the beginning of her explanation firmly. "I don't want to know. We're *not fighting* tonight," he said, stressing the words. "You can tell me later. We can fight about it then."

"Okay." Margrit unwound from his hug and scrubbed her face tiredly. "I should go back to bed. You should go back to bed. You have to be up in ten minutes."

"If I have to be up in ten minutes I should just take a shower." Cole crooked a smile. "You could make me an omelet for breakfast while I shower."

"I could make you scrambled eggs with stuff in them," Margrit countered wearily. "I never made a successful omelet in my life. I can't flip them."

"Lawyers, always negotiating. Scrambled eggs with stuff in them sounds like a great breakfast." Cole's smile improved a few degrees and he got to his feet, offering Margrit a hand. She let him pull her up and they parted ways, Cole into the hallway bathroom that was by default his and Cameron's, and Margrit to the kitchen.

A white shadow on the balcony, little more than a blur against the night, caught her eye. For a moment the impulse to pull the curtains and ignore the world outside swept her. Then she lifted her chin and opened the balcony door, uncertain if it was relief or dismay that made her stomach jump as Alban turned to face her.

"You're all right." He remained at the balcony's far side, and she in the doorway.

"I'm not dead, anyway." Margrit hesitated, then dropped her shoulders. "Janx?"

"Alive. Infuriating our hostess with his presence. I had to bring him to—"

"I know. She dropped by to let me know." Margrit looked over her shoulder to where she'd thrown Grace's necklace, reminding herself to pick it up before Cameron or Cole saw it. "The police have got Malik's body, Alban."

"No." He all but whispered the word. "Or, perhaps, but they won't by morning. Djinn were arrested tonight. They can't be held with iron bars and metal handcuffs. They'll take him away before any examination is done."

"Great. Accessory to murder and now responsible for missing bodies." Margrit pressed her lips together and looked away, though she glimpsed Alban shaking his head.

"Neither, Margrit. You acted in self-defense, and by human law, I acted to save another. Not that human law will judge me. We know how my people will rule."

A breath of laughter escaped her. "And I thought I was the lawyer here."

Alban returned her smile cautiously. "I may have learned a thing or two from you in the last week. Margrit—"

"No." She held up her hand, uncomfortably aware she was echoing Tony's sentiment from earlier. "Not right now, okay, Alban? No apologies, no explanations, no anything. I need a couple of days. I can't escape your world." She bit her lower lip, searching for the truth within her. "I can't, and I don't want to. But I need a little time to back off and breathe. This…has been a hard week. So give me some time, okay? I'll be fine. I just need space."

"Are you certain?"

"I'm very, very certain. And right now you have to go, because Cole's going to be out of the shower in a minute." She had never had the chance to tell Alban that Cole had seen him. The impulse to do so rose and faded in the same breath; it would not send the gargoyle from her balcony, and she needed him to go. There would be time later to deal with the ramifications of Cole's discovery. "Just give me a few days, Alban. It's been too much." Another wave of familiarity swept her; she'd pushed Tony away too often using that same argument. It was a mistake she didn't want to make again.

For the first time in what felt like days a genuine smile broke over her face. Margrit stepped out the kitchen door, crossing the step or two to Alban and winding her arms around his neck. "I'll come back to you, Stoneheart. Just give me a chance to catch up on my sleep, okay?"

Before he could speak, she stood on her toes and stole a kiss, heart hammering with joy that came from nowhere. Then, still smiling, she darted back into the apartment and turned to wave at the stunned gargoyle.

There was hope.

Alban watched Margrit slide the door closed, astonishment making him thick and slow. He had come in all expectation of finding refusals and goodbyes, and instead had been offered hope. Slow delight washed through him, and he turned to do as he was bade: give her space and time.

Seconds later he settled on the roof across the street, crouching where he could see her apartment windows.

She had not, after all, said how *much* space.

* * * * *